THE REAL

THE
REAL

For Bob Netterville

James Cole

JAMES COLE

NightTime Press

Copyright © 2010 by James Cole

All rights reserved

First Printing, August, 2010

ISBN: 978-1-936377-33-6

Published by NightTime Press, LLC

Printed in the United States of America

This book is a work of fiction. Names, characters, and places either are the product of the author's imagination or are used fictitiously. Any resemblance to actual persons, living or dead, is purely coincidental.

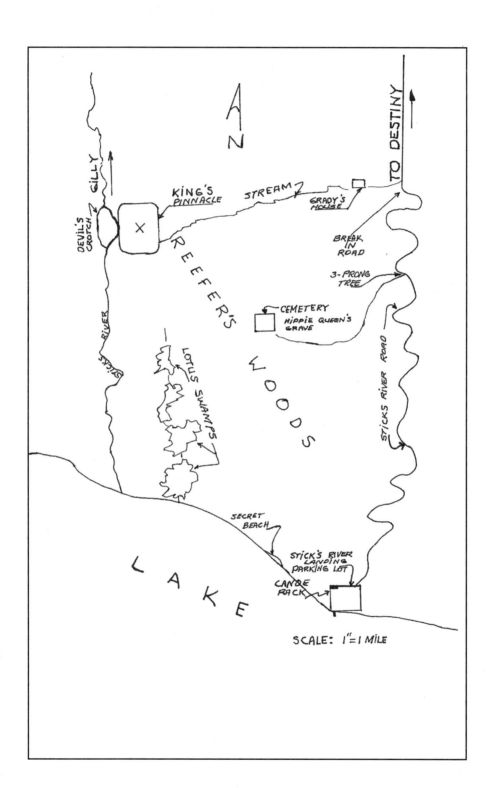

*Now, for the first time,
there burst upon me the idea
that there might be real marvels
all about us, that the visible world
might only be a curtain to conceal
huge realms…*

Clive Staples Lewis

Sunday, November 23

The Raven

It was Sunday, first light, the morning after the Destiny RockFest.

Grover's Field had seen better days. The park-like area, located in the heart of the University campus, was defined by ten acres of manicured grass, widely scattered picnic tables and old oak trees. Sadly, last night's festivities had transformed its pristine beauty into a picture of ugliness, a virtual garbage dump of empty bottles, cans and plastic food wrappings.

With squeaking suspensions, a caravan of navy blue trucks rolled over the curb to park single file on the grass. A young boy emerged, popping excitedly from the cab of the lead truck. One by one, the workers followed suit, though with a great deal less eagerness. They gathered their tools and in drudgery began to harvest the trash.

The boy set out to explore, surveying the scene with a pointed enthusiasm and freshness almost always reserved for young hearts. He marveled at the massive oaks and their long shadows, stretched by the low angle of the early morning sunlight. He kicked at crumpled beer cans and sniffed an empty pint bottle of Jim Beam when he thought no one was looking.

From nowhere, the cold wind gathered strength. Droves of dead leaves rained down from above and scurried about the boy's feet like hungry rats. With regret he noticed a charcoal stain on his snow-white high-tops. As he knelt to wipe away the dark mark, a curious sound registered; a siren song, beautiful and strange.

Kaugh! (Come!)

Lured by the sound, he followed, searching for the source. The calling originated from a raven that hopped around the perimeter of one of the dumpsters temporarily placed in Grover's Field.

Kaugh! Kaugh! (Come see!)

The raven stood by, its eyes ruthless and wild as it contemplated the one who dared encroach upon the fringes of its world. A new sound, a buzz, tickled in the boy's ears, drawing him closer still. Blowflies swarmed in and around the open lid of the dumpster. Something was there, something more than garbage.

With skinny, brown biceps, the boy hoisted himself up and peered over the rim, directly into dead eyes. Sprawled within this unholy coffin was a human corpse, her legs spread perversely in the stark immodesty of death. Etched into the flesh of her forehead was an intricately-designed symbol, the indentations of which were filled and outlined with crusty blood, like a new tattoo.

The guttural moan that erupted from deep within the boy evolved into a full-blown scream of terror. Letting go his grip on the dumpster rim, he fell, landing flat on his back with a breath-stealing thud. Panic reigned supreme as he bounced to his feet and ran helter-skelter across Grover's Field, gasping for air and wishing in vain for deliverance from the grisly images that would forever be burned into his mind.

Two hours later the phone rang at the apartment of Jeremy Spires. It was the police.

CHAPTER 1

Saturday, September 6

*J*EREMY took the roundabout way from his apartment to the Biotechnology Facility so as to approach from a less conspicuous direction. Typically he parked his motorcycle under the ginkgo trees at the northeast corner of the building and entered there. Tonight, however, he maneuvered the hyper-sport Hayabusa onto the sidewalk near the side door at the opposite corner of the building. He scanned the hedges for any suspicious movement but saw none.

So far, so good.

Using his key, Jeremy turned the lock as gingerly as he could, but the lock disengaged with a conspicuous *clack* anyway. He winced, hoping the noise wouldn't give him away. He opened the door just wide enough to squeeze through to the long, darkened hallway on the other side. Energy-saving timers installed in the newly-renovated Biotech Facility dimmed the lights in the common areas after ten p.m. The muted illumination, useful as it might be for energy conservation, only increased the advantage of his adversary.

He sneaked through the labyrinth of dimly-lit hallways until just one corner separated him from the elevator. He peeked around the corner at another empty hallway. At the end of the passage, past the elevator, was the front lobby where he was supposed to meet Tavalin. This was the most likely ambush area. He listened for two protracted minutes, unmoving and barely breathing. The longer he waited, the louder and more uncomfortable the silence became.

Jeremy checked his watch: Five past eleven. He drew a deep breath and ventured into the corridor, hugging the wall like a spider man.

Just as he drew even with the elevator door, the succinct *ding* of the elevator bell jabbed him like a hypodermic needle. As the door slid open, Jeremy slipped into the pitch-black classroom opposite the elevator. A stressed grin pressed itself onto his face as he peered through the crack of the inward-opening door. Much to his chagrin it was not Tavalin but Dr. Cecil Cain who exited the elevator. This was not the first time Jeremy had seen the executive director in the building late at night, nor was it the first time Jeremy had wondered why Dr. Cain kept such odd hours.

Jeremy watched as Dr. Cain walked expeditiously down the hallway and disappeared around the corner. Suddenly, a shriek shattered the stillness. Jeremy hustled to the lobby just in time to see the terrified look wilting across Tavalin's face and the rage blooming on Dr. Cain's.

"What in God's name are you doing?" exclaimed Dr. Cain.

"I'm sorry," Tavalin sniveled. "I thought you were him." Tavalin pointed an accusing finger at his friend.

The executive director whirled around to glare at Jeremy.

Jeremy, revealed, stepped out from behind the corner. Feigning innocence, he said cheerfully, "Hi, Dr. Cain. How are you?"

Dr. Cain directed his attention back at Tavalin. "Explain yourself, young man," he demanded sternly.

"I was just trying to get him back," whimpered Tavalin. "He scares me all the time."

"This is not the sort of behavior I expect from my graduate students," scolded Dr. Cain. "If you boys think you can act like this and work for me, you're dead wrong."

"Sorry, Dr. Cain," Jeremy said. "It was just a practical joke that got out of hand. You understand we certainly never meant to target you."

"I understand," Dr. Cain said as he eyed first one and then the other. "It's just that I disapprove."

As the director turned his back to leave, Jeremy and Tavalin exchanged wide-eyed looks but said nothing until he was out the door.

"Traitor," Jeremy said, though with an absence of any real hostility.

"What?" Tavalin asked.

"I can't believe you tried to lay the blame on me."

"It is your fault," said Tavalin. "You started all this."

Jeremy asked, "What's Dr. Cain doing in here so late anyway?"

"I have no idea."

"You gave him a pretty good scare, didn't you?"

"Oh, yeah." Tavalin grinned sheepishly. "I got him good."

"This is not necessarily a positive development for our graduate school careers." Jeremy's sense of humor ran toward the dry side.

Tavalin laughed. "Scaring the devil out of the executive director can't be a good thing, can it?"

"No, not really," Jeremy said, laughing. "I don't think Dr. Cain appreciates the subtle delights of our little game."

"Did you hear him holler?" asked Tavalin.

"Screamed like a little girl," Jeremy replied. "Or was that you?"

"Ha, ha, very funny," replied Tavalin sarcastically. "I'll get you next time, you'll see."

CHAPTER 2

Monday, September 8

JEREMY punched the accelerator, pedal to the metal, as he guzzled the last two or three swallows of his beer. The high-revving engine accelerated the two-seater with stomach-tingling authority down the straightaway.

Nervously, Tavalin asked, "How many beers have you had?"

Jeremy scrunched his forehead as if performing complicated mathematical calculations involving large numbers, all the while pretending to ignore the road ahead. After a moment, satisfied that he had further raised his friend's anxiety level, he truthfully answered, "Counting this one, one."

Tavalin leaned over to peer at the speedometer needle, then directed his attention to his safety harness and clamped himself in. Jeremy's seatbelt was not fastened.

"I don't know why I ever agree to go anywhere with you."

Tavalin Cassel was Jeremy's fellow graduate student and friend. Tavalin was lanky and tall with a concave chest, and he had recently accessorized his look by growing a wiry-haired soul patch under his bottom lip and by bleaching the tips of his spiky brown hair. Tavalin's too-small, yellow-orange, tie-dyed T-shirt sported the words *Chemically Altered*.

With the sunroof open and the windows down, their ever-increasing speed created a crescendo effect of rushing air, like the roar of some mythological beast's awakening.

"Could you *please* slow down?" Tavalin had to compete with the wind as well as the blaring music in order to be heard. "I'm really not in the mood to die today."

Jeremy flashed an exuberant smile. "Don't pretend you're not having fun," he said. "If you weren't here, you'd be stuck in the lab, wasting your time on some boring experiment."

"I might be wasting my time, but at least I'd still be alive."

Jeremy, his sandy blond hair blowing and his eyes burning with turquoise fire, shot back, "No, Tavalin, can't you see? We're as much alive this instant as we ever have been."

Jeremy was well aware of the possible repercussions of his actions. Driving fast was just Jeremy's way to thumb his nose at the grim reaper, who, he knew, would come calling one day anyway. Daring death gave the illusion of control over that which he knew was ultimately uncontrollable.

The dichotomy of the road from Destiny to Sticks River Landing was unmistakable. For the first seven miles the route ran straight and smooth through wide-open cotton fields. At the end of the straightaway, the landscape and the passage within abruptly transformed like the most cunning of chameleons. Marking the break in the road were two low posts on either side of the road. Still attached to the left-hand post was the chain that had presumably once draped across the road as a blockade. Now the chain lay rusted and broken on the pavement.

Stabbed into the dirt on the side of the road was a weathered sign. It read:

Keep Out
Area Closed

After the break, what had been wide smooth asphalt became a thin, convoluted ribbon of concrete, weaving its way up and down steep hills and around dangerous curves made blind by thick tangles of trees, bushes and vines. They had now entered government land, and the forest encroached close to the road's edges and over it in places, providing only a narrow, tunnel-like passage.

As Jeremy slowed to cruise mode, Tavalin relaxed noticeably. He unbuckled his seat belt and leaned out the passenger window, his gaunt face stretched into a clown-like grin. Without warning, he let loose a blood-curdling scream like the howl of a rabies-crazed wolf.

Jeremy had never known anyone quite like Tavalin. In spite of Tavalin's obvious intelligence, he had an uncanny knack for doing and saying the wrong thing. Even though his shenanigans grated on Jeremy's nerves at times, especially when in the company of more normal people, Tavalin was his friend. Whenever possible, Jeremy focused on Tavalin's redeeming qualities, not the least of which was his willingness to go anywhere or do anything at any time, day or night. Most missed it, but Tavalin could also be hilariously funny, often at his own expense.

After seven miles of twisting and turning through the deep woods, Sticks River Road plunged downward and ended in a clearing at the edge of the colossal waters of Sticks River Lake. It was obvious that there had been no maintenance or upkeep in the area for quite some time. Jeremy wasn't sure why the area had been closed but a sign on a leaning pole offered a clue. *Sticks River Landing*, it read. In actuality, Sticks River emptied into the lake several miles north of their present position. Years ago, the river had been dammed and this portion of the river valley replaced with Sticks River Lake. Jeremy guessed that the area was originally a recreational site on the river that had been abandoned after the lake was built, perhaps due to the long way in. Other, more accessible locations had been chosen at which to build new marinas and other lakeside developments.

This was, or once had been, a take-out point for one of the commercial canoe rental outfits located up-river. Presently, a single canoe was racked in a meager trailer that was chained to a tree in the back corner of the parking lot. Like everything else at Sticks River Landing, the boat and trailer had been dormant for a long time, as evidenced by the thick layer of leaves and twigs piled on the bottoms-up canoe.

They lugged the cooler down to the water's edge, took off their shirts and donned sunglasses. As they sipped their beers and soaked in the glorious late-summer sunshine, Jeremy remembered another positive aspect of his friendship with Tavalin. It was Tavalin who had introduced him to this particular place in the world, and for that Jeremy was deeply appreciative. Had it not been for Tavalin, Jeremy might never have known what lay beyond the *Keep Out* sign at the break in the road.

***

About halfway back to town they passed a pick-up truck parked on the side of the road. Someone, presumably the driver, had his head buried underneath the raised hood. Just as they whizzed past he looked up and caught Jeremy's eye.

"You think we ought to stop?" asked Jeremy. He watched as the broken-down truck grew smaller in the rear view mirror.

"What?" Tavalin had been dozing.

"Somebody's broken down on the side of the road back there."

"Sucks for him," Tavalin said callously.

"Maybe we should turn around and offer to help."

"No, not me," Tavalin promptly replied. "I've got stuff I need to do. Take me home."

"Yeah, okay," agreed Jeremy.

It would be easier to head on in. After playing hooky from school for most of the afternoon, Jeremy also had plenty of work he could tackle. They were almost to Tavalin's apartment when Jeremy heard a muffled rendition of a certain familiar rap song.

"Tavalin!" Jeremy poked his friend, who was asleep again. "Your pocket is ringing."

Tavalin returned a confused look before he understood and dug his phone from his front pants pocket.

"Hello?" Tavalin sat straight up in his seat and turned the radio all the way down.

"I know I should be working, it's just that...No ma'am...No ma'am...We're just riding around... Jeremy and me."

Jeremy, who could only hear Tavalin's side of the conversation, mouthed the words, "who is that?" to his friend. Without taking his ear from the phone, Tavalin spun his forefinger around his forehead in the universal sign for crazy.

"I'll call you back when I get home...Okay, bye." Tavalin flipped his phone closed.

Jeremy asked, "Who was that?"

"Just my mom," Tavalin replied sheepishly.

"She sounds a little overbearing."

"You don't know the half of it."

While Tavalin spoke to and of his mother on a regular basis, Jeremy could not recall Tavalin ever having mentioned his father.

"What about your dad?" asked Jeremy. "Is he still around?"

"No," replied Tavalin. "He went insane and killed himself in a car wreck." Tavalin's gaze remained focused through the front windshield. He declined to elaborate.

Ten minutes later Jeremy dropped Tavalin off at his apartment.

Before Tavalin got completely away, Jeremy rolled down the window and called after him, "You owe me for half the beer."

"We'll settle up later," replied Tavalin with a dastardly grin.

They both knew the chances of Tavalin ever repaying him fell somewhere between slim and none.

As Jeremy drove home, he thought again about the hapless driver broken down on the side of the road. Though there had been plenty of similar instances when he had passed by folks in need, he felt guilty as he passed by the turnoff to Sticks River Road.

Jeremy turned up the radio but could not drown out the nagging little voice. *What if that were me broken down on that lonely country road?*

***

Jeremy pulled up behind the truck and slammed his car door. A brown face, framed with graying hair, peeked from around the raised hood. An apprehensive expression pinched the man's features into a grimace. Jeremy hoped in this day and age that any concerns the fellow might have had nothing to do with the paleness of Jeremy's skin.

"You need some help?" Jeremy asked as clearly and expediently as possible. The left rear bumper of the truck protruded into the road and as he passed by, he checked for traffic from behind. The road was empty.

"It's looking more and more that way," replied the stranded motorist.

When Jeremy made his way around to the front of the truck he asked, "Any idea what's wrong with it?"

The man was again face down as he tinkered with the engine. He answered without looking up from the engine. "Might be the alternator."

"What's it going to take to fix it?" Jeremy asked.

The man straightened up and meticulously wiped his hands on a dirty old cloth. "Probably a new alternator," he replied with a straight face.

Satisfied that his hands were clean, the black man turned and peered unflinchingly, directly into Jeremy's eyes. What Jeremy saw rendered him speechless. It was his eyes – his striking, *pale-blue* eyes.

When Jeremy was finally able to speak, he asked, "You want me to call someone – maybe a tow truck? I've got my phone right here."

"No, I can fix it. I just need to get it home somehow. I live just down the road. I don't suppose you could give me a tow, could you?"

"I'm afraid my car is not suited for towing."

The man stepped out into the road to get a better look at Jeremy's little car.

"No, I reckon not." He rubbed his chin as he looked thoughtfully at the truck's engine.

"By the way, I'm Jeremy."

"Pleased to make your acquaintance. They call me Grady." After studying the situation a bit longer, Grady added, "If I had a fresh battery, I could get her home."

"I don't suppose you've got a fresh battery?" Jeremy asked before awkwardly adding, "I guess if you had a fresh battery you wouldn't still be sitting here on the side of the road."

Grady smiled. "I do have a battery charger at home."

"I can take you," Jeremy volunteered, "if you like."

"That'll work," the man said jovially as he proceeded to loosen the battery cables.

Grady rode with the battery between his legs on the floorboard. He had thoughtfully placed a newspaper on the mat to prevent any battery acid from leaking onto the floor mat.

Grady's house was only a few miles down, on the threshold of the break in the road and the *Keep Out* sign. Jeremy had never noticed the small house, as it was set back from the road and was barely visible from the pavement. At the end of the long dirt driveway Jeremy stopped the car and shifted to neutral but did not kill the engine.

"I could give you a ride back to your truck when the battery is done," offered Jeremy. He thought he could easily kill a couple more hours at the lake. This would be his second trip out there today but he meant to see his favor through to the end.

"I wouldn't want to put you out," Grady was saying.

"I think I might just ride out to the lake and swing back by in a couple of hours to pick you up."

"I wouldn't do that if I were you."

"What?" asked Jeremy, not catching the man's meaning.

"You don't want to go past the break in the road."

"Why not?" asked Jeremy.

"Those woods have a history of strange happenings, things that don't concern you." Grady's tone was more threatening than the weathered *Keep Out* sign had ever been. "Why don't you come inside and sit a spell instead?"

Jeremy was about to decline but reconsidered. What would it hurt? The blue-eyed black man probably didn't get too many visitors way out here.

***

Inside, Grady insisted on cooking a meal for his guest. "It's the least I can do," he said.

Jeremy sat at the table and watched his host scurry around the time-worn, but scrupulously clean, kitchen.

He prepared a traditional breakfast, despite the hour. "Come fill your plate," Grady instructed as he dumped homemade biscuits from a cast iron skillet onto a paper towel. "And have some juice – I squeezed it myself."

Jeremy loaded his plate and settled into his seat at the kitchen table.

Apart from complimenting his host on the good food, Jeremy found it difficult to keep the conversation going. Grady contributed nothing to their interaction other than a propensity to stare. At times his head bobbed in a subtle up and down motion as if he were grooving to the beat of pleasing music. As the latest period of silence stretched toward the extreme, Jeremy retreated into a defensive mode, directing his attention down at his plate and his thoughts toward an exit strategy.

Finally Grady broke the silence. "You've got potential," he announced.

Jeremy shook loose from his reverie. Grady's gaze was direct and unwavering, and those blue eyes of his were just about too freaky to regard.

Jeremy swallowed. How long had he been working that same bite of omelet? "Potential for what?" he asked.

"Potential for great good."

"Well, thank you, Grady." Jeremy replied in a tone he hoped was not patronizing. "I'm not sure how you arrived at that conclusion, but I appreciate the compliment."

Quickly, Grady added, "Don't let it go to your head because you've also got an equal potential for bad. Potential is a double-edged sword, and you could still go either way."

"Then I suppose I'll just have to make it a point to use my potential for good." Jeremy offered a wink and a smile in an attempt to counter the weightiness.

"See that you do." If Grady were kidding around it was with the driest of humor. "And, remember what I said before about the break in the road – don't ever cross that line."

"Why not?" Jeremy fought back the urge to tell Grady that it was none of his business where he did or didn't go. "I know the road is closed."

"There's danger on the other side."

"Danger?" asked Jeremy. "What danger?"

"Reefers Woods."

"I wouldn't know Reefers Woods from Old McDonald's Farm," quipped Jeremy.

"Just stay to this side of the break in the road and you'll be okay."

"Tell me why." Jeremy was adamant.

"Do you really think you want to know?" Grady's blue eyes were afire. "Before you answer, realize that with this knowledge comes great responsibility. By knowing more you must do more."

"Sure, why not?" replied Jeremy flippantly.

"Alright, then, if you insist. You see, a bunch of kids died out there a while back – burned to death by the woods witch. People will say she died along with them, but I know better. She still comes around, even after all this time. I know, cause I've seen her, and I'm telling you right now, she ain't someone you want to mess around with."

"Woods witch, huh?" Jeremy didn't remember ever hearing that particular term yet something about all this rang familiar.

"The witch burned her friends alive, and she's killed other folks who've ventured in. You spend much time in there, she'll get you too. Hers is an evil soul."

Jeremy racked his brain, trying to remember a previous reference to a fire, people burned alive... and hippies – something about hippies.

"Listen to me good, Jeremy," continued Grady. "Reefers Woods holds the source of certain objects of desire, both good and evil."

It took him a moment to dredge it up but Jeremy remembered having been told a ghost story soon after he moved to Destiny two years ago. "Hippie queen," he said out loud and laughed as it came to him. "You scoundrel. You really had me going there for a second."

Grady glared at him from his end of the table.

"Let me guess how it ends." Jeremy recounted the tail end of the ghost story as it had been told to him: "The hippie queen – that is, the woods witch – still haunts Reefers Woods to this very day, and sometimes, on dark, moonless nights, her flaming ghost appears, hoping to find victims to kill and souls to steal." Jeremy snickered. "Like that silly old ghost story is going to scare me off."

Without breaking eye contact, Grady very deliberately wiped his mouth with a napkin. "Fools rush in where angels fear to tread," he said. "You go in those woods and you could lose things you don't even know you have."

"On account of the woods witch?" asked Jeremy contemptuously. "I'm a scientist, Grady. I don't believe in witches."

"Then I suppose it wouldn't do no good if I told you about the nymphs and devil dogs either?"

Jeremy had had enough of this ridiculous conversation. He downed the rest of the odd-tasting fruit juice and pushed away from the table. "That really hit the spot," he said politely, "but I really should be going now."

Grady followed him out the door onto the old tongue-and-groove front porch. Just when Jeremy thought he might get away clean, Grady's voice rattled out from behind.

"I can see that you have a mind not to listen."

Jeremy stopped and turned around. "I'm listening," he mumbled impatiently.

After a brief stare-down, Grady asked, "If your eyes could be opened to truths and realities you never knew existed, would you want to see?"

As Jeremy fidgeted at the ambiguity and the implied assumptions of the question, he realized something: Grady's speech patterns were not consistent. Sometimes he spoke more like the country bumpkin Jeremy had at first assumed him to be, but at other times, including the words with which he posed the pending question, Grady communicated in a more elegant fashion.

"Uh, huh," Jeremy muttered affirmatively, hoping that this would somehow mollify his ranting host. He had passed the point of being able to pretend that this was a normal interaction between sane human beings.

"Well?" Grady asked expectantly.

By now Jeremy had backed down the steps, making for his car which was only a few paces away. "I'm not sure what you are asking," he replied.

Grady held his position on the porch. "Why do you think our paths crossed, Jeremy? Don't you know everything happens for a reason?"

Jeremy stopped when he reached his getaway car, turned, and forced himself to meet Grady's forbidding gaze. "Our paths crossed because we happened to be on the same road at the same time."

"But why did you stop?" asked Grady. "And why did my truck break down then and there?"

"I don't know. It just happened, that's all – a coincidence."

"You're wrong, Jeremy. Nobody else stopped to help."

"Whatever you say, Grady." It wasn't worth the effort to argue.

"Just remember, Jeremy – and this is very important – *there are no coincidences.*"

"Right, right – no coincidences." Jeremy no longer tried to conceal his patronizing tone.

"And don't tell anybody about our little talk," Grady warned, "or anything else about me either. And whatever you do, don't tell nobody about my blue eyes."

"All right," Jeremy mumbled as he swung his leg into the driver's side.

Before Jeremy closed the door, the ranting man squeezed in one last admonition: "Otherwise, people could get hurt."

As Jeremy turned the car around in the driveway, he could not peel his eyes from Grady, who stood motionless on the porch, his arms straight by his side as if wrapped in duct tape. Jeremy watched in the rear view mirror through the dust cloud kicked up by his hasty departure, waiting – indeed wishing, for Grady to break rank and move.

But he didn't. Grady did not wave, and he did not take a seat in the old-timey rocking chair on the porch. He didn't turn and go back inside to clear away the dishes from their meal and he didn't go about the business of getting his broken-down truck fixed. He didn't raise a hand to cover a giggle at the tall tales he had passed off as truth to an unsuspecting Good Samaritan. He just stood there in his apparent *rigor mortis* and watched Jeremy drive away.

People could get hurt. Grady's last words, obviously a threat, echoed ominously in Jeremy's head. On first impression, Grady seemed to be an uncomplicated man with simple thoughts. In one short hour he had dispelled that notion. It occurred to Jeremy that sometimes the more you know, the less you understand, especially when it comes to the inner workings of a human being, especially one who is delusional.

It wasn't until Jeremy came upon the broken-down truck that he remembered why he had agreed to kill time at Grady's house in the first place – he had promised to give him a ride back to his vehicle. It didn't matter, however. Jeremy had no intention of going back.

***

On the drive back to town, Jeremy managed to dredge up all his recollections related to the hippie queen ghost story. It had been two years ago in the autumn of 2006, soon after he first moved into the dormitory, when some of his hall-mates had informed him of a time-honored tradition at the University: the retelling of the hippie queen ghost story to first-time students.

Jeremy remembered how they gathered in a circle with beers cracked and candles lit. The ghost story mirrored Grady's version, beginning with hippies burned alive by their evil leader, the hippie queen, and ending with her flaming ghost still roaming the surrounding woods, waiting to devour anyone who dared venture in. The one part Jeremy recalled from the initial telling that Grady failed to mention concerned a monument, an angel sculpture that had been mysteriously placed over the hippie queen's grave soon after her burial.

With a smile, Jeremy remembered how he and his drinking buddies had piled into a car for an ill-advised ride, ostensibly to track down the reputed grave. The trip, however, had been cut short after one of his friends threw up in the rear seat of the car, and they never made it to any grave. At the time, he had assumed the story to be purely fictional, nothing more than a typical round-the-campfire ghost story. But, after hearing it twice now, Jeremy wondered if parts of it could be true. Grady certainly seemed to believe.

At home, Jeremy conducted an internet search, starting with *Reefers Woods* and *hippie queen* and *woods witch*, but no relevant links came up. After ten minutes of fruitless search, he stumbled across searchable archives from the local newspaper going back 50 years. He didn't know if this was common practice for newspapers in the internet age, but it certainly fit his current need. In no time he found several articles devoted to the 1969 fire that took the lives of seven young people. Although the word *commune* was never used, it did say that they had been living illegally in a *rudimentary structure deep in the heart of the Sticks River National Forest*. Another article revealed the names of the victims and their hometowns. One girl's body went unclaimed and was, it said, *laid to rest in a local cemetery*. Her name was Claire Wales and though the newspaper articles never referred to her as such, Jeremy knew that he had uncovered the identity of the elusive hippie queen.

Jeremy spent the better part of the next two hours canvassing the archives for information on the fire, Sticks River National Forest and Claire Wales. All relevant articles he printed out and saved in a folder. Though he could not find many particulars, he learned that Claire's main legacy – besides the ghost story inspired by her death – was her paintings, which were apparently of some artistic worth.

Using the newspaper archives as a primary source, Jeremy verified more of what Grady had told him. Grady was correct in saying that there had been others who had since lost their lives in Reefers Woods. One year after the commune fire, a man committed suicide by gunshot while sitting in his car at Sticks River Landing. Also, around the same time, a biologist from the University went missing in the same area and was never heard from again.

Jeremy had a curious streak, and all these details he uncovered about the hippie queen, the fire, and Reefers Woods were plenty to entice his inquisitiveness. He wanted to investigate further the details of the ghost story inspired by Claire, specifically, the part about the stone angels that supposedly guarded her grave. The first step in that process would be to visit the grave to verify the existence of the monument, but none of the articles revealed the location or the name of the cemetery where the hippie queen was buried.

Regardless of Grady's warnings and all his other mumbo-jumbo, wild horses couldn't keep Jeremy on this side of the *Keep Out* sign at the break in the road. In that vein, the seed of a plan germinated in his mind. Perhaps he could arrange some sort of overnight stay in Reefers Woods, just to prove Grady wrong – all witches, nymphs and devil dogs be damned.

Reefers Woods – July, 1969

(Thirty-nine years ago)

Lotosland

When Claire began her graduate school stint in the fall of 1967, never in her wildest dreams would she have guessed that two years later she would found a commune in the middle of the Sticks River National Forest.

Her introduction to the area had come while she was still a student. Claire would get up before dawn and drive out Sticks River Road until she reached the old cemetery road turnoff. Coaxing her old jalopy over the three-mile-long dirt strip was arduous under the best of conditions. The road, which was little more than a narrow pair of ruts to begin with, became two mud-filled trenches after a rain. On the days that she dared drive all the way in, she parked her car at the road's end in the shade of a grove of cypress trees at the edge of the cemetery. Typically, she would tromp through the woods all day, gathering plant samples for her research project, and hike back to her car before dark.

Claire rapidly tired of this exhausting routine and set up a camp site down by the river. Once she overcame her fear of spending nights alone in the woods, her love grew for the otherworldly serenity of the forest. When she discovered a long-abandoned homestead in another part of the woods, she moved her base camp next to it. After a few repairs, she was able to use the covered front porch as a storage area for her ever-increasing cache of supplies and as a shelter from the summertime thunderstorms. Soon she began fixing up other parts of the house. That marked the beginning of the commune that would come to be known as Lotosland in the stretch of woods that would come to be known as Reefers Woods.

Living in the woods, Claire tried to be as self-sufficient as possible, using natural products whenever she could. Today, she mixed a paint made from linseed oil and a pigment known as the King's Yellow. Claire discovered the pigment, which occurs naturally in a particular mineral, in a rocky area near the rapids of The Devil's Crotch. Curiously, the mineral is formed by thermal processes such as those in volcanoes and hot springs.

Because of its toxicity and its tendency to react with other pigments, the King's Yellow was not one Claire routinely used for her paintings, but it would work well for this particular project. While the river and the willow trees and the slanting sunbeams would surely make for a lovely scene on canvas, today she painted on a plank. She was making a sign to hang over the front door of the house.

She had never bothered to name the commune, but now it seemed imperative to do so. She thought of those early communes: Tolstoy Farm, Gorda Mountain, Drop City. Perhaps, everyone would one day know the name Lotosland. After all, she was the one who had found the key to living in harmony with her fellow hippies. She had discovered the all natural, perfect instrument of peace and love. Over the summer her aspirations grew from modest to grandiose.

This could change the world forever. Just think of how they will love me.

The only problem with Claire's little fantasy was the lotus. How could she supply the world when she wasn't even sure if the swamps would produce enough lotus blooms for the seven of them?

She had regretted not having been party to the Haight-Ashbury summer of love, now two years past. Instead, she had been here, the better part of a continent removed, sitting through botany classes at the University. Who could have predicted that, of all things, her schoolwork would lead to this? But one never knows where the road of one's life will lead, and now here she was, living her own grand summer. It was her summer of love and, perhaps more appropriately, the summer of the lotus.

When she was done, she hung the sign on the door and stepped back to read its proclamation, painted in the vivid King's Yellow:

LOTOSLAND
anno domini 1969

CHAPTER *3*

Tuesday, September 17

THE parking situation, a never-ending complaint of most campus commuters, was of no consequence to Jeremy Spires. Today, like almost every other day, he parked his motorcycle, a hyper-sport Hayabusa, in the shade of the ginkgo trees that lined the east side of the University Biotechnology Facility.

In the lobby, Jeremy picked up the daily--distributed University newspaper and bought a Coke from the machine. He could not help but eye the artificial plants where Tavalin had been lying in wait for him the other night, even though he knew he would not be hiding there now. As he rode the elevator, he chuckled out loud when he recalled how Tavalin had unwittingly scared Dr. Cain, the executive director of the Facility.

The entire fifth and sixth floors were reserved for the laboratories of Dr. Cain. Desks of the various lab workers, mostly graduate students, were scattered throughout the nooks and crannies of the various laboratories. Jeremy had been assigned the lone desk in one of the smaller labs, squirreled away from the much larger and busier labs located down the hall and on the floor above.

He stopped at the door to his lab and frisked his pockets for his keys. The janitor emerged from the lab three doors down. Jeremy watched as he fished through the contents of a small trash can with slow, measured movements. The janitor removed an empty soda can which he placed in a bucket on the back of his cart. The remaining trash he dumped into the main receptacle on the cart.

Jeremy's search for his lab keys continued. He emptied his pockets of their contents – cell phone, wallet and his personal key ring. His lab keys, which he kept on a separate key ring, were not there. With some irritation he pulled off his backpack and unzipped one outer pocket and then another. When he did not immediately locate the keys, he dropped the heavy backpack to the floor. When he first bought the bag, he assumed that having so many little pockets would be a convenience. After he searched in vain through most of them he began to rethink that assumption.

"Did you lock yourself out?"

The voice startled Jeremy and, when he turned in that direction, the proximity of the pushcart startled him again. The black of the janitor's wrap-around sunglasses matched the man's face.

When Jeremy recovered enough to speak, he said, "I seem to have misplaced my keys."

"Normally I'm not allowed to do this, but I can make an exception for you."

Jeremy studied the profile of the janitor's face as he unlocked the door. The fellow reminded Jeremy of someone, though Jeremy could not think who, especially considering the oversized sunglasses he wore.

"Thanks," said Jeremy as he hoisted his backpack.

"One good turn deserves another."

The janitor did not immediately step aside from the doorway. Rather, he stood toe-to-toe with Jeremy in a challenging pose and a deliberate look on his face.

"Do I know you?" asked Jeremy.

"Only rarely can a man assume to know another," he replied circuitously.

Only one person Jeremy had ever met spoke in such a manner. "It's Grady, right? From Sticks River Road?"

"Greetings, Master Jeremy."

"I didn't recognize you with those glasses on," Jeremy muttered as he tried to process this unexpected circumstance.

"Sometimes we see only what we expect to see and nothing more," replied Grady.

"I didn't know you worked here."

"Yes, it's true. I'm your trusty janitor."

Grady removed himself from the doorway and went about his business of removing the trash from Jeremy's lab.

"How long have you been employed by the University?" asked Jeremy.

"Three days, give or take," replied Grady without looking up from his chore.

"What's the deal with those sunglasses?"

Grady lowered the glasses to reveal his strange blue eyes and winked. "The glasses must stay on at all times, doctor's orders. Understand?"

"I guess."

Grady pushed the glasses back into place and ambled toward the back of Jeremy's lab. Jeremy watched with mild interest as the Johnny-come-lately janitor tried in vain to get through the silver-steel door to the cold room at the back of his lab. After tugging at the handle of the locked door and rummaging through the keys on his key chain, Grady said, "I don't appear to have a key to this door. Is there any trash in there I should take care of?"

Jeremy stood, reaching into his pocket before remembering that he would not be able to unlock the door, at least not today. "I'd let you in with my key to check, but since I seem to have temporarily misplaced my lab keys…"

Grady mumbled the words, "Right, right," and walked a few steps toward the door before stopping dead in his tracks. He had the look of someone who had just forgotten what it was he was about to do next. Finally, he turned to Jeremy and asked, "Do you dream dreams?"

"Of course," Jeremy said with a grin. "Just last night I dreamed I was giving a lecture in my underwear."

Ignoring Jeremy's attempt at a joke, Grady said, "Pay attention to your dreams, Jeremy. They just might be trying to tell you something." After glancing over his shoulder, presumably to verify that no one else was listening, Grady added in an ominous tone, "And don't forget what I said before about steering clear of Reefers Woods, you hear?"

All morning long Jeremy pondered the peculiar ways and words of Grady. Was it a coincidence that this man he met on Sticks River Road now worked at the Facility, or had Grady gotten the job just to harass him? And why was this odd man so hell-bent on keeping Jeremy out of Reefers Woods? Whatever Grady's motivations, Jeremy didn't take well to anyone telling him what he could and could not do. In fact, Grady's mysterious talk and admonitions to stay away made him want to spend more time in Reefers Woods, starting this very weekend. If there really were strange goings-on there, Jeremy wanted in on it, or so he thought.

Despite his defiant attitude, Jeremy was not at all enthralled at the prospect of working in the same building as that man. Having to share the hallways and other common areas of the building with him was bad enough, but even Jeremy's lab provided no refuge. With his master key, Crazy Grady could come and go anytime he wished.

Chapter 4

Friday, September 19

BEEP-BEEP-BEEP!

IN one continuous motion Jeremy turned over, switched off the alarm, and rolled easily out of bed. He had talked up the camping trip all week and, when the alarm went off at six a.m., he hit the floor running. It was nice to have a reason to want to get out of bed for a change.

Jinni Malone, his girlfriend, picked him up one hour later. On a typical Friday she could be found at the local hospital where she worked as a nurse, but not today, as she, like Jeremy, took the day off. Jinni arrived in her late model, four--wheel drive SUV, a vehicle well suited for road trips like this one that called for extra gear.

"I'll drive," he said after he had loaded his stuff in the back.

Jinni rolled her eyes but knew any resistance was futile. Jeremy always insisted on driving. Trying to be pre-emptive, she said, "There's no need to speed."

They set out for the podunk town of Gilly, about a one-hour drive north of the University. They arrived ahead of schedule and easily found the general store, an old one-story structure down by the river that, as far as they could tell, *was* the town. Jeremy parked next to an antique pulp wood truck, pale green with an overlay of rust. The cab had no doors. A hound dog, brown and white splotched, lay motionless on the old wooden porch. Jinni thought it might be dead. Jeremy suggested it might be a clever decoy, one prop among a thousand, placed in Gilly to give it the look and feel of Andy Griffith's Mayberry.

They entered the store through a screen door, the kind with a spring that pulls the door shut with that characteristic stretched-spring *squeak* and *slam*, which triggered a non-specific memory of Jeremy as a boy at his grandmother's house. Both the old country home and his Mammaw were only memories now.

The store, a *general* store in every sense of the word, was a one-stop shopper's dream: Here, one could buy firewood, split or not; ice, block or crushed; and groceries, including those sometimes hard-to-find pork delicacies such as chitter-lings, fatback, ham hocks, and pig's feet. There were guns, ammunition, fishing poles, and a bait shop in the back corner that lent a grating background noise of live crickets to the ambiance.

While Jinni went mulling about the store, Jeremy headed for the counter. The cash register was manned by a middle-aged, bearded hillbilly reading a newspaper. He wore what looked to be real-issue army pants and boots and a faded tee-shirt that read:

Women WANT me
Fish FEAR me

Jeremy had to clear his throat to get his attention. The clerk glared at Jeremy and asked in a gruff tone, "What can I do you for?"

"We'd like to rent a canoe."

Jeremy picked a map up from the counter and pointed to the lower section of Sticks River, the part that ran through Reefers Woods. Not surprisingly, the map did not indicate any reference to Reefers Woods.

"We'd like to do this part."

"From here to the lake?"

"That's right."

"I'd have to advise against that." The clerk used his pinky finger, its nail nicotine yellow, to indicate a different section of Sticks River on Jeremy's map. "Now your best canoeing would be here, in the middle section of the river, anywhere between Ratcliff Ferry and here, depending on how far you want to go."

"What's wrong with us doing the lower part?" Jeremy asked.

The man fiddled mindlessly with the hair on his chin. "Nothing's wrong with it, it's just that most folks avoid the lower part on account of this one set of rapids they call *The Devil's Crotch*."

Jeremy looked back with inquisitive eyebrows.

The man snickered from behind the unkempt mustache that originated from inside his nostrils. "I guess that's got your attention, huh?"

Jeremy stared at the map, wallowing in his indecision. He certainly didn't want to endanger Jinni, but the whole purpose of the canoe trip was to explore Reefers Woods from the river side.

Finally the clerk broke the silence. "One thing in your favor is that we ain't had much rain around here and the river's running on the low side. With the river like it is now, I would say the rapids are only a hard class three. So that takes it from darn-near impossible to just plain tough as all-get-out."

That was all the encouragement Jeremy needed. "We can handle *tough as all-get-out*," he said in as confident a tone as he could muster. Jeremy pulled out his credit card and slapped it on the counter. He wanted to settle the transaction before Jinni came over. "We'll need one canoe for two nights. Can you pick us up at the lake landing Sunday, say, around noon?" he asked.

The clerk was shaking his head. "That's the other thing; we don't do pickups way down there. We do have a rack at Sticks River Landing. I can give you the lock combination but y'all will have to get your own ride out."

"I think we can manage that."

"My question to you, son, is why are you so dead set on running that part of the river? There's a reason why hardly anybody goes down that way."

"We just want to enjoy some peace and quiet."

Over the years, Jeremy had been known to fixate on certain things, whether the sport of triathlon or some obscure rock band or the chicken pizza that he never tired of eating from the local hole-in-the-wall pizzeria. It was the same for the strange stories connected to Reefers Woods, but Jeremy wasn't about to try and explain himself to Hillbilly Joe behind the counter, nor to Jinni either. How could he when he himself didn't fully understand the reasons behind his infatuation with Reefers Woods and Claire Wales?

The clerk was still talking. "I wouldn't be surprised if you didn't see anybody else at all. And I reckon that's all fine and good as long as you don't get yourselves in a pickle and need some help. And don't think your cell phone is gonna work way out there either."

As the clerk filled out the paperwork, Jeremy looked across the way and caught Jinni's eye. She walked over with a small bottle of sunscreen and a giant bag of potato chips.

"Well hello, little lady," said the clerk.

Cheerily, Jinni replied, "Hello."

"I hope you know what your boyfriend here is getting you into."

"What...?" she asked with a perplexed look.

Jeremy quickly ran interference. The last thing he wanted to do was to spook Jinni. "I'll show you a map of where we're going in a minute," he said. "Right now, you just need to sign this waiver."

Jinni signed the line but not before throwing a mistrustful glance over her shoulder at Jeremy.

Once outside, Jeremy called Tavalin, explained his and Jinni's predicament, and persuaded his friend to pick them up on Sunday at Sticks River Landing.

"Don't forget us, Tavalin," urged Jeremy. "I know how you are."

***

The occasional bumping of paddles on the sides of the aluminum canoe resonated like thunder in the stillness of the Sticks River National Forest. At the moment, only Jeremy was paddling, though sporadically. There was no hurry. From his position in the back of the narrow craft, he had a wonderful view:

the natural beauty of the river, the trees, the sky, and Jinni, basking in the still-powerful rays of the September sun.

She leaned back, her face cocked towards heaven and her elbows propped by the large Coleman ice chest behind her seat. Her muscular legs, sculpted by several seasons of triathlon training, draped over either side of the canoe. An inverted "V" trailed from the point where her toes broke the water's surface. With blonde hair, eyes the color of the sky, and a fit body, Jinni had the physical attributes of a goddess. Jeremy wondered, not for the first time, what he had done to deserve her company.

Two hours before sunset, they set up camp on a stony outcrop that plateaued some forty feet above the level of the water. They wrapped potatoes in aluminum foil and cooked them in the hot coals of the campfire. Jeremy used a multi-pronged stick, like deer antlers, to roast an entire can of seven Vienna sausages at once. After supper, they lounged lazily on the still-warm rock slab, staring at the fire, mesmerized by its ever-changing form. Periodically, Jeremy got up to add more sticks from the pile they had collected earlier until he noticed with a start a pair of snakes lying mere feet from their spot by the fire.

"Bedtime," he declared, as he hoisted Jinni to her feet.

"Already?"

"Yes," he replied. "We've got a long way to go tomorrow."

As they headed for the safety of the tent he stole a glance back at the spot where he had seen the snakes, but strangely, they were gone. Had he imagined them?

Chapter 5

Saturday, September 20

IT was late afternoon on Saturday, the first full day of fall, and it had been a perfect day. Amazingly, they had seen no one else since they left the outfitters some 30 hours prior. Jeremy waited until after lunch to tell Jinni about the rapids. As much as possible, he downplayed what Hillbilly Joe told him back at the general store. Initially this worked, but only until he made the mistake of referring to the rapids by its proper name.

"The Devil's Crotch?" asked Jinni. "That sounds – well, wicked. Where is it?"

"Not exactly sure," Jeremy replied. "Somewhere between here and where Sticks River empties into the lake. That's all I know."

At first, the sound was barely discernable, like wind stirring high in the trees. A few minutes later, the current increased and the river banks grew into sheer rock walls that towered over both sides of the river but higher on the left side. They checked that their supplies were properly secured and strapped on the cheap orange life jackets. Never before had Jeremy thought a canoe so precarious a vessel, but it was all they had.

By now, the growling of The Devil's Crotch rapids was unmistakable. Jeremy knelt in the front of the canoe, the position best suited to the person able to deliver more powerful strokes. For maneuverability, the canoe must maintain forward momentum relative to the moving water. His directive was simple: paddle as hard and fast as possible. It would be mostly up to Jinni to steer from the rear using the rudder action of her paddle blade.

When he was situated, Jeremy turned to steal a look at Jinni. Her fearful countenance fed his rising anxiety. He wondered, not for the first time, if it had been a mistake for them to come alone. Jeremy felt ill-prepared. He should have gotten more information from the clerk. Instead, his effort had focused on convincing the store clerk that they could handle it and on trying to prevent Jinni from hearing the clerk's warning.

"Can we swing this?" Jinni's voice seemed to emanate from a point farther away than the back seat of the canoe.

"We have to."

Jeremy stretched his spine and his neck tall and in perfect perpendicularity to the plane of the water. He could see a definite drop-off dead ahead. He couldn't judge its magnitude, but it sounded *huge*. Jeremy clinched the paddle as if it were a medieval battle ax, as he prepared to engage his foe, The Devil's Crotch.

The first chute was straight and smooth, and the canoe slid through as slick as a puck on an air hockey table.

So far so good, Jeremy thought. A spontaneous *wheeee...* sounded from behind, but any glee was fleeting as the boat bumped down a rough section of whoop-dee-doos. Despite the fact that this was the roughest water they had experienced, the boat stayed straight and true, but its bucking was nerve-racking. The intensity meter swung to extreme at what came into view next. Up ahead, the river appeared to slam head-on into a rock wall. This was the source of the high-decibel roar. Jeremy's heart beat against his chest wall and in his head like a bass drum.

Frantically he tried to discern the nature of the beast. *Was it possible that the river somehow flowed under the rock wall? Would they be squashed against the rock like bugs on a windshield?*

A second later, the illusion melted. It was not a dead end but rather a house-sized rock squatting in the middle of the channel, splitting the river in two. The water funneled furiously to either side, narrowing and thus accelerating the flow even more. It was not obvious if one side were less treacherous than the other but they were headed straight for the rock and turn they must. Since Jeremy was already paddling on his stronger right side, which automatically inclined the boat to the left, he screamed, "Left! Left! Hard left!"

Jeremy could only hope that Jinni heard him over the water's roar as he dug his paddle into the froth, pulling with all his might. But the river had them in its cold steely grip and meant, it seemed, to crash them into the rock wall.

An even-keeled voice in his mind advised: *Paddle harder or you're not gonna make it.*

The rock wall loomed large, larger than life, or perhaps as large as death itself. The canoe did not turn.

Jeremy screamed, "Hard left! HARDLEFT!"

He had no way of knowing if Jinni heard him or not. He couldn't even be sure that she was still behind him. Jeremy's panicked thoughts overflowed from his mind and poured into his vocal cords in synch with the brutal strokes of his paddle:

NOT...GONNA...MAKE IT... NOT... GONNA... MAKE IT...

At the last possible second, even as Jeremy's body obtained maximum tension in anticipation of impact with the wall, the canoe turned. Jinni swung the rear of the canoe around like a pro. With a few more digs of the paddle, they passed by the left side of the rock but not without the canoe scraping an obnoxious squeal along the final 20 feet or so. They endured another drop and flopped awkwardly over another series of waves. A slight lull in the action gave Jeremy a few seconds to gather his thoughts and to look downstream. Smooth water beckoned in the not-too-far distance.

Take that Hillbilly Joe! We might just make it after all.

Out of nowhere a wall of water slammed into the right side of the boat. There was no way to recover. Jeremy had totally forgotten the other half of the river, the part that flowed around the right side of the rock island. The canoe capsized, catapulting its occupants over the side. From behind, Jinni's scream cut off abruptly as Jeremy hit the water head-first and was immediately sucked under. The weight of the water swept him down as his body rolled and somersaulted violently.

Up, up, which way is up?!

Jeremy tried to swim to the surface, flapping his arms like a panicked chicken, but he had no idea which way was up. He was blind, and there was no up and no down. The river had him and there was nothing he could do but hope that he was not stuck in a re-circulating current, hope that this washing machine would not hold him under until his air ran out and his instinct to inhale overrode the knowledge that breathing river water is fatal and he would be drowned.

And what of Jinni? Had he sealed her fate? Would she die right here in The Devil's Crotch on a Saturday in September? Was she breathing water even now? Had he in his arrogant stupidity murdered his soul mate, the love of his life?

Just when he thought his situation hopeless, the churning river beast released him to the surface. Free to breathe the air, Jeremy drifted up and down over the last throes of the rapids, a series of three or four standing waves. Once clear, Jeremy found himself alone, no canoe in sight.

And no Jinni either. At that moment, he remembered how Grady had warned him to steer clear of Reefers Woods, and for the first time, Jeremy admitted that it had been a mistake to come here.

He tried to call her name but he could only choke out river water.

When his voice worked again, he gargled out her name, "Jinni! Jinni!" but there was no reply.

Frantically, he scanned the water. There, in a lazy eddy thirty yards distant floated a shiny mass, something shimmering in the sunbeams.

Something blond.

Jeremy called out to her again but there was no answer. He swam furiously toward her and tried to be positive, but in his mind's eye he imagined an awful image of his beloved Jinni, floating face down, her body here but her soul departed.

When he got to her, he still could see only her long hair floating in the water.

"Oh no, Jinni. Oh no."

When Jeremy could reach her, he pulled her toward him, meaning to pull her face from the water, ready to give her mouth-to-mouth, his insides screaming for him to bring her back. But she was not floating face down, as he originally thought. Jinni's face had been there all along, hidden behind her thick locks. Gently he pushed back the hair to reveal her wide-open, blue eyes.

"Are you okay?" he asked. His feet felt the rocky bottom. It was shallow enough to stand here.

She nodded vigorously, the nodding of her head a complement to her chattering teeth. Jeremy had not noticed, but the water was very cold.

She's alive. Thank God, she's alive.

***

At the tail end of The Devil's Crotch, the river bank transitioned from sheer rock wall to low sloping bank. Jinni climbed out first with a little help from Jeremy. For once she didn't object to his hand on her ass.

"Are you okay?" Jeremy asked for about the fifth time.

Finally she was able to speak again, the shock of the cold water and the scare wearing off a bit.

"Our canoe is getting away."

Jeremy looked in the direction of Jinni's gaze to see the boat's dull silver bottom, floating like a dead fish in the water. It was in the middle of the river about 100 yards distant. Without hesitation, he dove back into the cold river and swam downriver. Luckily, the current was weak here, and he was able to overtake the capsized canoe and pull it to the bank where he tied it, still upside down, to a tree. He was untying the supplies from underneath and piling them on the bank when Jinni arrived.

"How about we camp here for the night," Jeremy suggested.

"Sounds good to me," Jinni replied. "I think we deserve a rest. Did we lose anything?"

"Don't think so," he replied. "Still got our paddles."

Jeremy allowed his smile and gaze to linger as he studied Jinni's appearance.

"What?" she asked as a little smile tiptoed across her lips.

"You look like a drowned rat," he said, and their smiles grew into laughter.

The way her wet clothes clung to her was comical but Jeremy also couldn't help but notice the way it revealed the curves of her body.

They pitched the tent on a suitable flat area on the river bank and hung up the wet contents of one of the bags that had leaked. They walked the short distance back toward The Devil's Crotch and ran into the sheer rock wall that bordered the east side of the rapids. Forced to turn inland, they continued walking alongside the border of the wall, hoping to discover a route to the top.

"If we find a way, I imagine it will be quite a view from way up there," Jeremy said.

"How high do you think it is?"

Jeremy tilted his neck skyward. "It's a good bit higher than the tree tops. I'd say it's at least 100 feet to the top, give or take."

After about ten more minutes of steady walking, the wall made a 90 degree turn to the left – still they found no way to climb its sheer face. Moving parallel to the river, they came upon a crystal clear stream that ran alongside the base of the stone wall. They stopped at the point where the water gurgled down a small hole.

"I wonder where it goes?" asked Jinni.

"Who knows?" replied Jeremy. "I suppose it must empty into the river some-where nearby."

They followed the perimeter of the monolith around another left-hand corner and walked until they reached the river.

"Can you hear it?" Jeremy cocked his head to listen, thinking he had seen dogs strike this same pose when trying to pinpoint the direction of some faraway sound. "It's The Devil's Crotch," he added with melodrama. "Now that we know what to expect, next time we should be able to make it all the way through without capsizing."

Jinni looked at him in all seriousness and said, "There will not be a next time, not if I can help it."

***

Back at camp, they spent the balance of the afternoon sunning on the boul-ders along the riverbank and swimming in the cold water.

"Are we going to build a fire?" Jinni asked, as the towering rocks and trees served up an early invitation to the dusk. "If so, we should probably gather some wood."

"I'm thinking not," replied Jeremy. "Not tonight."

Prior to his conversation of a few days ago with Grady, Jeremy considered himself a stanch unbeliever in the supernatural. How could one who fancied himself a rational scientist believe otherwise? However, he could not deny that a part of him wanted to accept that there could be something strange and unworldly here, something not readily explained. Wasn't that the real reason he was here?

But what exactly did Grady say about this place? Jeremy wished he had paid more attention during the meal at Grady's but he had been preoccupied with getting away. Primarily, Grady had said to stay away from Reefers Woods because of some unspecified danger, possibly the ghost of the hippie queen. He also mentioned something about *objects of desire* though Jeremy had no idea what that might mean. He did clearly remember one question Grady posed:

If your eyes could be opened to realities you never knew existed, would you want to see?

Apparently Jeremy's answer to that question was *yes*, even with the stipulation that responsibility came with this knowledge. That had been the clincher. Simply advising Jeremy to stay away made him want to check it out. Who wouldn't want to become cognizant of secret realms?

There were two reasons why Jeremy vetoed the campfire idea: to see, and to not be seen. A fire would provide illumination to the immediate campsite but would also give away their position to anybody (or anything) in the vicinity. Also, the light from the fire had a blinding effect that would prevent them from seeing anything lurking beyond its circle of light. It occurred to him that sometimes one must join the darkness in order to perceive that which is in the darkness.

The evening was uneventful. For a while they sat outside on a sleeping bag pad, but the moon had not yet risen and there wasn't much to look at. There were, however, plenty of sounds to entertain, but as Jinni pointed out, these could be experienced just as well from inside the tent. And, as a bonus, they could escape the pesky mosquitoes that whined in their faces despite repeated applications of bug spray.

***

At some point during the night Jeremy awoke. The diffused light that filtered in through the thin tent fabric seemed a little brighter than it should be.

Just the moonlight, he told himself. As he continued staring upward he thought he could make out a few pinpricks of light. *The stars and moon are so much brighter out here,* he told himself. He rolled onto his side and shut his eyes but a wayward thought nagged his mind: *Not moonlight, not stars: Something else.*

Open your eyes.

Jeremy didn't want to open his eyes. He wanted to sleep. His logical side, which tonight happened to agree with his sleepy side, insisted that there was nothing out of the ordinary going on. Not here, not anywhere. There are no devil dogs, no nymphs and no ghosts of dead hippies. There is only the natural. Supernatural is just another word for impossible. (*There is no supernatural.*)

But the other side of his psyche, the side that brought him out here in the first place, wanted to believe, indeed *needed* to believe that there was more to life than the mundane. (*I can hope for more, can't I?*) Could he dare to hope that maybe, just maybe, he might one day (*tonight?*) look past ordinary and find extraordinary? Could the natural be superseded by the supernatural and normal by paranormal? Might those unlikely stories about Reefers Woods hold some truth?

Sleep or wake?

Jeremy opened his eyes. As he watched, the pinpricks of light multiplied and brightened and shone through the tent with crystal-clear clarity. It was as if the tent fabric were melting away, receding, blackening; becoming the canopy of the sky on which the stars were strewn.

Jinni needs to see this, he thought, and tried to tell her but, strangely, he could not manage even a peep. It was as if his vocal cords were paralyzed or perhaps nonexistent. Things got even more interesting when he heard the sound of children's voices, like from a distant playground. Gradually, Jeremy became cognizant of an underlying, rhythmic quality to the clamor. Voices joined together, repeating words in unison, until their message could be discerned. The children were chanting, *"Red rover, red rover, send Jeremy right over…Red rover, red rover, send Jeremy right over…"*

As Jeremy listened to the words and watched the hypnotizing lights, a peculiar out-of-body sensation overtook him. Every other part of his surroundings – Jinni, the tent, the pillow under his head – faded from his awareness. The lights danced together and drew closer until his perspective changed and, as in a dream, he was flying. The chants became louder and the lights beckoned like unexpected runway beacons to a wayward pilot.

He landed like a bird on the rocky upper rim of the cliff that towered over the rapids of The Devils Crotch, the very place that he and Jinni had earlier tried in vain to reach. On the other side of that sheer rock wall, opposite the river, the landscape was molded into the shape of a crater, or, more accurately, a natural amphitheater. Metallic music wafted through the air. Gyrating below was a huge crowd, mashed so close together as to appear as one humongous organism composed solely of heads and uplifted arms. Held above the hoard was a flickering sea of flames, born of Zippos and Bics.

A slight movement on the rock shelf caught Jeremy's eye. With a jolt he realized that he was not alone. So still was she that he had not noticed the old woman crouched at the far side of the rock shelf, like a stone-statue gargoyle set upon the upper reaches of the edifice. For a breathless minute or more, he waited for her to acknowledge him, but it was as if he were invisible to her. She held her crouched posture and her gaze remained fixed on the abyss.

When Jeremy turned his attention back to the crowd, everything had changed. The crowd below had become a throng of luminescent creatures. The brilliant white light that emanated from within these winged beings lit up the rock walls of the amphitheater and the sky above. Jeremy watched, awestruck, as the glow grew larger and brighter until it became a giant ball of translucent white radiance. Beams of blindingly-bright light shot out in all directions, like from some supernatural disco ball. The intensity of the music rose in lockstep, thundering forth from the host in a song of such otherworldly beauty, power and grace, that he fell into utter love with it and the feelings it inspired in the depths of his soul. As he watched and listened with ecstatic awe, one of the beings broke free and flew up toward him. Closer and closer it came, floating as if suspended by invisible cables and glowing with the ubiquitous light.

Later, Jeremy would not recall any specific details of the creature's face. He only knew that, like the music, it was wonderful and strange. He would, however, never forget the words that passed between them.

"The forecast calls for rain," she said in an assured tone with a voice like that of a young child.

Jeremy hadn't known what to expect from the angelic creature, but a discussion of the weather wasn't it.

"What is all of this?" he asked.

"Open your mind and experience *the real*," she replied, and with a fluttering of her angel's wings, she flew up and away.

She ascended toward the lighted sphere in the sky, which was larger and more distant than Jeremy initially thought. In the instant that the ball of light enveloped her, thunder clapped and white torrents of snow – not rain – spewed forth from above. Gleefully, Jeremy spun around with arms outstretched and eyes fixated on the heavens, unconcerned with the precipice beside which he danced and oblivious to the old woman still crouched at the cliff's edge. Nothing existed, save the marvelous music, the thunder snow, and the supernatural disco ball pulsating in the sky.

Jeremy felt as he did as a child, alive in the moment; living in a dream.

I am alive!

***

When Jeremy awoke, he was back in the confines of the tent. He felt as if he might be glowing with white light but the darkness refuted that supposition. He put his hand on Jinni's shoulder, meaning to wake her, but thought better of it. There was no way he could put into words the feeling of the experience, which he would henceforth refer to as his *vision of the real*.

CHAPTER *6*

Sunday, September 21

O^N Sunday morning, Jinni and Jeremy slept in as late as the cacophony of
bird calls would allow. Leisurely, they packed up and made their way toward
the endpoint of their long weekend. The river's current slowed considerably as
they approached the lake, requiring more constant paddling. By noon, the banks
of the channel opened up to the unrestrained waters of the lake. They dug in for
the last five miles of their journey, working together in a concentrated synchron-
icity of exertion. In silence they toiled, the only sounds their rhythmic breathing
and the choppy lake waters lapping like dogs at the heel of their canoe.

The lake, like the river that fed it, was vacant except for a single speck of a
boat in the distance. After twenty minutes or so they passed between it and the
shoreline, close enough to identify it as a houseboat sitting still on the water.
Jeremy caught sight of a sunbather on the roof. As he watched, the shapely girl
sat up. Even at 500 yards Jeremy could she that she lacked any bikini top. And
why not? Hers was the only boat in sight.

"What'cha looking at, Jeremy?"

For a moment he had forgotten about his companion in the rear seat of the
canoe and the sound of her voice startled him. How long had he been staring?
Caught, Jeremy tried to gloss over it by asking, "Do you realize that she is the first
human we have seen since Friday?"

"And when's the last time you've seen a girl sunbathing topless?" Jinni asked
accusingly.

"Oh, is she? I hadn't noticed," he said, feigning innocence.

"Yeah, right," came Jinni's good-humored reply.

In not-so-good humor, Jeremy muttered, "Nobody in this canoe will show
me anything, that's for sure."

He didn't bother checking to see whether Jinni heard him or not, but it
didn't matter anyway. It wasn't the first time he had voiced similar complaints.

At half past two they reached Sticks River Landing. Tavalin was supposed to
meet them here at two o'clock but, predictably, he was nowhere in sight. They
unloaded their gear onto the old rickety pier and used their last bit of energy to

carry the canoe to the rack in the back of the parking lot. As instructed, Jeremy used the combination lock supplied by the outfitter to secure the canoe in the rack. Just when Jeremy was about to bad-mouth his unreliable friend, up pulled Tavalin's little yellow Honda, tooting its Herbie horn as it approached.

CHAPTER 7

Monday, September 22

*J*EREMY stared in disbelief at the digital display as he marched angrily toward the back of the lab. He opened the incubator door to find a great deal of work wasted.

"What a piece of junk!" he exclaimed, slamming the door shut.

"Problem?"

Jeremy whirled around in the direction of the voice. Filling the doorway was the plump frame of Dr. Skip Sloan, Jeremy's immediate supervisor. Dr. Sloan was not a tenured professor but rather a post-doctoral student whose job was to teach classes and to supervise a subset of graduate students that ultimately answered to Dr. Cain, the director. The grad students were supposed to refer to the post-doc supervisors formally, as in *Doctor* Sloan. While it was true that the post-docs had doctorate degrees, they generally only stayed for a couple of years until they accrued enough research publications with their names on them to land a real professorship. Like the grad students, the post-docs were low-paid, temporary workers that generally did not command much respect. Skip Sloan made matters worse by his sour disposition. Moody, sarcastic, and petty, his position of authority did not sit well with Jeremy, and that was putting it nicely. To his face, Jeremy honored protocol and called him "Dr. Sloan", but behind his back Jeremy used the more demeaning moniker of "Skippy."

"The thermostat on our incubator locked up again," replied Jeremy. "That's two weeks' work wasted."

"Remind me this afternoon after the group meeting and maybe I'll help you tweak a few wires." Dr. Sloan pinned a wooden smile on his face with his donkey teeth.

Yeah, right, Jeremy thought to himself. *Maybe you will and maybe you won't.*

Skippy had a habit of pretending to be helpful, but when it came time to do the work, he typically conjured up some excuse as to why he couldn't help.

"Meanwhile, why don't you look up the part number and order a new thermostat," Skippy continued.

"Will do," Jeremy said. "Did you say 'group meeting'? What group meeting?"

"I told everyone else Friday," Skippy replied in a biting tone. "You were nowhere to be found."

"I told you I would be out Friday," Jeremy countered.

"Not my fault," Skippy said. "And, by the way," he added, "you are slated to present your work to the group today."

"You're serious? Me? Today?"

"I didn't stutter, did I?"

"Couldn't we put it off until tomorrow?" Jeremy asked, lobbying for a reprieve. "That way I could prepare some tonight." It was tough for Jeremy to beg, but he tried anyway and offered what he hoped was a pitiful please-don't-make-me-do-it expression.

Skippy ignored Jeremy's objections. "Downstairs in the auditorium, two o'clock." He was almost out the door before mentioning in a tone that sounded almost gleeful, "Also, just to warn you, Dr. Cain is going to listen in."

Before Jeremy could ask why the chairman of the department would be attending their group meeting, Skippy was gone. Speaking to freshmen lab students didn't bother Jeremy as much as it once did, but he still got anxious in front of more knowledgeable audiences and the incident involving Dr. Cain in the lobby only increased Jeremy's apprehension.

The balance of the morning, Jeremy spent organizing his notes and worrying. At five till two Jeremy sat on the front row thumbing through his transparencies and trying desperately to recall the words that went with each one. At least with the visual aids he could direct attention to the screen and away from himself. Sustained eye contact with members of the audience, he had discovered, tended to disrupt his train of thought, as if they were not mere humans but rather evil, alien brain-snatchers.

Dr. Cain and a small entourage of grad students arrived a few minutes after the designated time. Even though Dr. Cain was technically Jeremy's research advisor, Jeremy was only one of approximately forty grad students working under him. Besides an initial brief interview, Jeremy had only the rare occasion to speak to the man and then usually only in passing. Only a few of the most gifted grad students were assigned to work personally with Dr. Cain, while the vast majority, including Jeremy, were left to toil in obscurity under post-docs like Dr. Sloan.

Dr. Sloan recognized their *distinguished guests* and gave a brief overview of his group's research goals. Jeremy waited impatiently, his stomach in knots and the Sahara in his mouth. Finally, with little ado, the floor was his. He stood and turned hesitantly toward his audience as if facing an execution squad.

Jeremy swallowed hard and began, "The major aim of my research is to produce a viral vector potentially useful in the exciting new field of gene replacement therapy."

Jeremy heard his voice quiver and saw the slight shake of the pointer shadow on the projection screen as he tried, in vain at times, to remember those same canned lines he had memorized for the departmental seminar earlier in the summer.

"The primary goal of my work is to genetically engineer a virus to insert a gene of our *choosing* into the host cell. There are currently more than four hundred diseases that are known to be caused by a defective gene. Viral vectors, such as the one I am attempting to assemble, are just beginning to be used as a cutting edge treatment for genetic disease. In short, the major goal of my research project is to produce a viral vector capable of adding a gene to the host DNA. Now I'll discuss some of the methodology we employ to transform a native virus into a tool for specific genetic transfer."

At the conclusion of the customary question-and-answer session at the end, Jeremy exhaled a breath of relief, a little too obviously, eliciting some good-natured laughter from his fellow students. He was afraid he invoked an awful, empathetic reaction in those trying to listen, dragging them laboriously with him to hell and back. Now, he supposed, they were back and everyone could be relieved, their tours of duty complete.

Everyone stood and Dr. Cain offered a smile and a handshake. Standing beside and slightly behind Dr. Cain was a young Asian student whom Jeremy knew to be one of the few students privileged to work as one of his personal research assistants.

"Jeremy, do you know June?" asked Dr. Cain.

"Yes, of course," replied Jeremy. "How are you, June?"

"Very well, thank you."

To say that they knew one another was a stretch. June Song's lab was just down the hallway from Jeremy's, but his only interactions with her had been brief in passing.

Preemptively, Jeremy apologized, "Sorry for the awkwardness of my presentation. These things make me very nervous."

"I must say it wasn't the most polished delivery but you've got plenty of time to work on that," Dr. Cain said. "I really have only one question for you."

"Yes sir?"

Dr. Cain had a suave, politician-like air about him and even Jeremy felt besieged by his deft charm, if not by his authoritative position.

"Do you think you could take the time to work with June and walk her through the virus cultivation procedure?"

This was strictly a perfunctory gesture since Dr. Cain was, after all, the big boss.

"Of course." At this point, Jeremy would have agreed to roll naked on a bed of hot coals, so relieved he was that his presentation was over.

Dr. Sloan, who had been itching to get into the conversation, tossed in his two cents worth: "Obviously, Jeremy," he began in his droning manner, "it will be necessary to verify whether we have successfully added a gene to our vector and since Dr. Cain is the undisputed expert on gene sequencing," he added, as he directed a brown-nosing wink in the director's direction, "we are very fortunate to be invited into a more direct collaboration with his group."

"I'd like for us to get started on this right away," Dr. Cain continued. "June will shadow you for as long as it takes for her to learn how you do what you do."

"Sounds like a plan." Jeremy turned to June who had been standing quietly by, and asked, "When would you like to start?"

Before June could answer, Skippy interrupted, eager to reassert his presence. "Why don't you two work out a compatible schedule, Jeremy, and I'll fill you in with more details later on."

Jeremy was happy to be dismissed from the company of the professors and extremely relieved that Dr. Cain did not mention the incident in the lobby.

Maybe, thought Jeremy with a hidden smile, *Dr. Cain is just embarrassed.* Jeremy could still hear the way Dr. Cain had shrieked – like a hysterical woman – when Tavalin jumped out.

Jeremy accompanied June upstairs to her desk, which was situated just inside the door to the main laboratory complex on the fifth floor of the Facility and just down the hallway from Jeremy's lab.

"How long have you been living in the States?" asked Jeremy. "Your English is very good."

"I've been here for two years," replied June.

"I can't imagine having to learn all this chemistry in a non-native language. I have trouble understanding the lectures as it is."

June laughed. "The chemistry I understand. Learning the nuances of the English language is a great deal more difficult."

June explained how she had added an "e" to the end of her given name, "Jun", so there would be no confusion as to the pronunciation of her name. Her stylish clothes and contemporary haircut were in sharp contrast to that of most of the other Chinese graduate students working in the Facility. June was an attractive young woman, but Jeremy thought that her most distinguishing characteristic was her intelligence, which seemed to radiate with a palpable energy from her coffee-brown eyes.

"Did my talk raise any questions in your mind?" asked Jeremy. "I'm pretty sure I left out some stuff."

June opened her notebook, and they discussed various aspects of his project. In less than an hour, Jeremy suspected that his new coworker had a better grasp of the material than he did.

"When would you like to start?" she asked.

"I guess as soon as we get our incubator running again," replied Jeremy. "The new thermostat should arrive in a few days."

"We have plenty of incubators here," said June. "We can start right away, if you like."

Jeremy could see that June was going to work him hard and groaned inwardly. "Before we get into all that, I was thinking about getting something to eat. I skipped lunch today. Would you care to join me?" he asked.

They shared a pleasant conversation over a mediocre meal, which they ate on the black wrought-iron tables outside the Student Union. It intrigued Jeremy to learn how life had been for June, growing up in Red China.

CHAPTER 8

Saturday, September 27

IF not for the dead space between the songs blaring in his headphones, Jeremy would not have heard the spotter's declaration: "One minute, forty-four seconds behind the leader, three miles to finish!" he shouted as Jeremy loped by.

Jeremy thought he must have misheard. He had always been a middle-of-the-pack racer, consistently finishing with respectable times but rarely coming close to placing in his age-group, much less in the overall.

Though crunching numbers in his oxygen-deprived state was difficult, he reviewed his progress, starting with the swim. As always, he swam as a man unto himself, ignoring the other swimmers except when they happened to get in his way or vice versa. His swim strategy consisted of nothing more than concentrating on his technique while aiming for the next buoy. Upon his exit from the water, Jeremy had no idea if there were six or sixty racers ahead of him. He assumed the latter. As for his swim time, it did seem faster than usual but that anomaly could easily be explained away: Triathlon swim courses were notorious for their imprecise measurement. Apparently, setting up a swim course of accurate length in the open waters of a lake or ocean isn't the simplest of tasks.

Jeremy had been a bit surprised that no one overtook him on the bike leg, his weakest of the three disciplines. During the ride, he had assumed his handlebar-mounted computer was on the blink. He had been training for triathlons for three summers and knew the average speed it indicated to be far beyond his historic capabilities. He couldn't understand how it could be so, but now, in light of his lofty standing in the race, Jeremy wondered if maybe it had been right all along.

Jeremy was close enough to the leader to recognize him as last year's winner of the *Fryin' Bacon Triathlon*. The wagging of his trademark ponytail gave him away. Amazingly and inexplicitly, Jeremy began to reel him in. Jeremy's first thought was that Ponytail must be injured or sick and lagging because of it. With two miles to go Jeremy timed the gap that separated them at 55 seconds. At the one-mile-to-go mark Jeremy had shaved another 25 seconds off his lead. At 200 yards Jeremy moved to within ten paces. It was now or never. Ignoring the pain, he forced his legs and cardiovascular system to full exertion. With each stroke, sweat slung from his arms like rain from a windmill. Ponytail acknowledged Jeremy's presence with a quick peek over his shoulder. Jeremy suppressed the urge to smile and instead put on his best game face. Ponytail picked up the pace slightly, but Jeremy could tell from his gait that he was already maxed out. Jeremy felt good but never better than when he pulled alongside and accelerated past, a mere 50 yards from the finish.

"Unbelievable!" Jeremy exclaimed as he crossed the finish line to the cheers and applause from the sparse but enthusiastic crowd.

After exchanging congratulations with the second-best man and helping himself to the complimentary refreshments table, Jeremy lollygagged back to the finish chute to wait for Jinni. He applauded politely for the other racers as one by one they filtered through but cheered wildly when Jinni appeared over the rise. As she sprinted in, she threw a broad smile Jeremy's way.

Jeremy caught up to her at the water coolers. "Good race," he said. "You beat last year's time, didn't you?"

"Yep – almost a minute faster." Jinni gulped water between gulps of air. "How'd you do?" she asked.

"I won," he deadpanned.

"Yeah, right," she replied sarcastically.

"I was the first one across the line," he said, trying to make her believe. "I beat last year's winner by a couple of steps and shaved 25 minutes off last year's time."

Jinni could see that he was serious but could not quite grasp this unlikely result. "You've hardly been training," she said.

"I've been training," maintained Jeremy. "If you don't believe I won, just ask him."

Jeremy motioned toward the approaching race official, easily recognized as such by his zebra-striped shirt. Jeremy thought he might be coming over to offer congratulations or instructions for the awards ceremony.

"Jeremy Spires?" he asked as he glanced down at Jeremy's race number.

"That's me," Jeremy replied proudly. "Could you please tell my girlfriend that I won the overall? She doesn't believe me."

"I'm afraid I have some bad news," said the referee. "You actually did not win due to an assessed two minute time penalty."

Jeremy stared at the man in disbelief. "What did I do? Did y'all get me for drafting?"

Like most of the regional races, the *Fryin' Bacon Triathlon* was a non-drafting event. Riding too close behind a competitor on the bike was a common and sometimes unavoidable infraction, especially in a crowded field.

"Actually, it's your headphones," replied the somber official. "Certainly you know music players are against the rules."

"You've got to be kidding."

"Sorry to be the bearer of bad news but it's my job to enforce the rules." The referee dismissed himself with a cliché: "Better luck next time."

Jeremy angrily pumped the keg while Jinni held the hose to the lips of the cheap plastic cups. They sat down under the same tree they had the year before and sipped their beers. Jinni tried to lift his spirits by calling attention to the significance of this particular spot in the world.

She asked, "Do you remember what it felt like sitting here the day we met?"

"I do," he replied with a distracted smile.

He should have reminisced with Jinni of that bright, sunny day, one year removed. He should have told her how sweet it had been, sitting under this tree getting to know his soul mate and the most beautiful girl in the world. He should have told Jinni how that moment marked a sea change in his life and how the ensuing year had been the best of times.

"It's not like the music gave me any advantage," he complained, not able to get past the time penalty. "It's just some stupid insurance requirement."

Jinni tried to console him. "It's really not fair, but you know," she said, "in reality, you won. Maybe not officially, but you finished the race ahead of everyone else."

He smiled tentatively. She was right. He shouldn't sweat the technicalities.

"I guess I did, didn't I?"

"I've just got one burning question," she said.

"What's that?"

"How'd you do it?"

"That's what's so strange," he replied. "I didn't really change the way I prepared for this race. If anything, I've been lax for the last two or three weeks."

"You must have done something differently," Jinni said. "Nobody improves that much without being intentional about it."

"I don't have an explanation."

"You haven't been doping, have you?" She cast a suspicious look his way.

"Oh, come on now," he said, bothered at the charge. "You know me better than that, Jinni."

"I just don't understand how you did it."

"Me, neither." Jeremy stood up and stretched. "You want another beer?" he asked.

"Maybe just one," she replied.

CHAPTER 9

Wednesday, October 1

ONE year ago Jinni persuaded him to undergo an endurance performance test at the University Human Fitness Lab. At the time, Jeremy had been training hard for about a year and a half, time enough to reach a high fitness level. He learned more than he cared to know about the various parameters of cardiovascular fitness. One such marker, known as the maximum oxygen uptake or VO2 max, is considered the ultimate indicator of one's overall cardiovascular fitness. His test results were just what one would expect, typical for a young male of average genetic endowment for endurance and above average conditioning.

Curious to uncover the reasons behind his surprising performance at the recent triathlon, Jeremy scheduled a return trip to the lab. He dreaded the test itself, a grueling ordeal on the treadmill in which the subject is pushed to exhaustion at ever-increasing work-loads. While the physical exertion was bad enough, Jeremy especially disliked the confining mask they placed over his mouth and nose to measure his oxygen exchange. The mask made him feel more than a little claustrophobic, but at least he knew what to expect this time.

It took 16 minutes to reach his breaking point, about five minutes longer than he had endured the first go-round. The lone technician, an aloof and seemingly disinterested co-ed who looked as if she had never exercised a day in her life, perked up about ten minutes into Jeremy's evaluation.

"Hey, Dr. Calhoun," she called out to an unseen coworker. "Come take a look at this."

An older man, obviously fit and dressed in all-white tennis attire, ambled over to peer over her shoulder at the monitor. After a bit, he asked the technician, "Are you sure you've got him hooked up right?"

Because of his labored breathing and the oxygen-uptake mask, Jeremy could not verbally respond to the next question posed by Dr. Calhoun, though the good doctor certainly had no difficulty in reading the why-do-you-ask expression pasted on Jeremy's face.

"By any chance, are you related to Lance Armstrong?"

Afterwards, as soon as Jeremy got outside, he punched in from easy memory Jinni's work number.

"Six-C," answered a hurried-sounding female voice.

"Is Jinni available please?" Jeremy asked.

"She's with a patient, can you hold?"

"Yes," he replied, and the earpiece filled with a strings version of Barry Manilow's *Mandy.*

Jeremy's mind drifted back to the day he met Jinni.

He was halfway through the run leg of last year's *Fryin' Bacon Triathlon.* Even though the race had begun early, there was no denying the brutality of the wet, mid-summer heat. Jeremy raced against himself, fighting the ever-strengthening urge to let up and coast to the finish. As he caved in to his lazy desires, he heard the *clump, clump* of soft footfalls behind him. He did not turn to look but listened, and in a bit he could hear her rhythmic breathing. One minute later she pulled even with him. She wore traditional female triathlete attire, basically a skin-tight sports bikini. Perspiration dripped from the tips of her blonde hair, and her fit body glowed in the early morning sunshine. He suddenly felt stronger and upped his pace to match hers.

"Hi," she said sweetly.

He asked, "How are you?"

"Hot," she panted.

"I'm Jeremy," he announced, seizing the opportunity of the moment.

"Jinni," she replied. Her smile lingered.

"C'mon!" she admonished, as she had begun to pull ahead. "Push it!"

Her encouragement induced a spurt of adrenaline and he caught back up. Jinni pushed the pace constantly, and even though it was tough keeping up, Jeremy's interest in her had been stoked. One half hour later they crossed the finish line together.

Afterwards, they sat in the grass under a shade tree drinking the complimentary beer and shooting the breeze. He remembered how knowledgeable Jinni had seemed. It was she who had, after their first date, encouraged him to set up his initial endurance test at the performance lab. He couldn't wait to give her the details of the test just completed.

The telephone on-hold music cut off abruptly.

"This is Jinni," she said in her official, at-work phone voice.

"Cut the crap," he said. "It's just me."

"Hey there," she said cheerfully. "What's up?"

"I just left the performance lab. You'll never believe what my VO2 max tested as."

"What was it before?" asked Jinni.

"54."

"And now? she asked.

"Guess."

"I don't know – 61?"

"Higher."

"You know I'm busy," she said impatiently. "Just tell me."

"89," he replied dramatically.

"Say again," she said, after a pause.

Carefully enunciating the words, he said, "Eighty-nine milliliters per minute per kilogram."

"That's impossible," she said. "Nobody has a VO2 max that high."

"Dr. Calhoun said mine is among the highest ever observed," he boasted, "my only company being a handful of world-class athletes, mostly professional bicyclists and cross-country skiers."

"But you are no world-class athlete," she said pointedly. "A person has to be born with that kind of engine. No amount of training can produce an increase like you've experienced. Something's not right."

"Actually," Jeremy confessed, "Dr. Calhoun, the lab director, requested that I come back for a second test, personally administered by him. Apparently, he did not believe the results either."

"You're going to do it, aren't you?" asked Jinni.

"I don't know," replied Jeremy. "Maybe I'll just sit back and watch my legend grow."

In actuality, a plan had already begun to ferment in Jeremy's mind and it didn't include Dr. Calhoun. Maybe Jeremy could investigate this anomaly himself.

After all, he thought, *I'm a scientist too. If there's something interesting to be discovered here, why let someone else get all the credit?*

CHAPTER *10*

Wednesday, October 8

*T*WO weeks had passed since Jeremy and June first met, and almost every day they spent at least some time together working. On several occasions, tonight included, their work had stretched toward midnight.

"At this rate I'll graduate at least a year ahead of schedule," Jeremy muttered.

"What do you mean?" asked June.

"Before I met you, I thought I worked pretty hard, but you, June, have shown me what true dedication is."

"Oh, look at the time," she said. "I'm sorry. If you need to go home, I can finish up here."

"Oh, I have no doubt that you could." With a smile he joked, "What, are you trying to get rid of me now?"

When they first began working together, June had been shy, but as she got to know Jeremy better, she loosened up considerably. In fact, they were quickly becoming good friends. He gleaned scientific knowledge from her while she queried him on details of the English language and American culture and customs. Jeremy always went the extra mile to explain his comments, especially his jokes.

"You know I'm just kidding, right?" he asked. "I don't really think you are trying to get rid of me."

"How little you know," she replied.

"Very funny, June. Thanks a lot."

Her eyes twinkled mightily.

"I guess I had that coming."

June was a quick study. Perhaps she didn't need for him to explain his jokes anymore.

With a slam of a door and the *clop, clop* of dress shoes, Jeremy was alerted to Dr. Cain's presence as he walked across the hall and into the main lab. Jeremy checked the clock on the wall. It was half past midnight.

"Hello June – Jeremy," he said and nodded to each in turn. "How's the virus prep coming along?"

Dr. Cain, his wiry physique emphasized by the stark whiteness of his full-length lab coat, stood a head taller than Jeremy. His facial features were similarly elongated and framed by his most physically striking feature, an unruly mop of bright red hair.

"Fine, Dr. Cain," June answered. "We should have viable viral stock in approximately two weeks."

"Wonderful," he replied with genuine enthusiasm. "And Jeremy, I trust June has been her usual cheerful self?"

"It's been a pleasure working with her," Jeremy replied and smiled at June and her ensuing, familiar blush. "I have come to realize, however, that she's quite the taskmaster – seems all I do these days – and nights – is work."

Dr. Cain cracked an officious smile, nodded and said, "Keep up the good work."

Jeremy watched with interest as Dr. Cain retrieved a stock buffer solution from the lab and walked out.

"Where is he going with that solution?" Jeremy asked in a baffled tone.

June laughed. "He has a small, private lab adjoining his office."

"None of the other professors have that, do they?"

"I suppose that's just one of the perks of being the executive director," June explained.

Jeremy scratched his head. "I'm surprised Dr. Cain still conducts experiments himself," he said. "Why wouldn't he simply ask one of his many underlings to do the work for him?"

"I don't know," replied June. "Maybe he likes getting his hands dirty now and then."

***

Almost all of Jeremy's and June's time together was spent at the Biotech center. Tonight, however, the routine deviated.

"I wouldn't mind getting out of this building for a while," Jeremy suggested. "I've been craving something sweet all night. Are you hungry?"

They finished off their fattening snacks in the car at the drive-in, Jeremy his chocolate milkshake, and June, a huge banana split. On a whim, Jeremy suggested they take a ride out to the lake.

"It's beautiful here. Look how the water shimmers," June remarked as they pulled up at Sticks River Landing. "How did I not know about this place?"

"Maybe it's because you haven't been hanging out with the right people," he replied.

"I really don't – how do you say – hang out with anyone. I am always so busy. But it is nice out here, Jeremy. Thank you for bringing me."

In the lab, Jeremy and June were only coworkers. Out here, unexpectedly, they became more: young members of the opposite sex, alone and in the dark.

Jeremy broke an uncomfortable silence with small talk. "What do you do for fun, June? Do you have hobbies?"

"Sometimes I think maybe I concentrate too much on work. I like to read American novels but even that is, in part, to practice my English," she replied sheepishly, as if her strong work ethic were a bad thing. "For exercise, I swim," she added.

Jeremy had one of those thoughts which can spontaneously reveal itself in one's brain, zipping at the speed of light up from unconscious recesses to acknowledgment: *And I would love to take you swimming, skinny-dipping in the cool black water of Sticks River Landing, right here, right now.* It was the voice of the devil's advocate.

Wanting, but not wanting, to wade into those black depths, he only said, "I didn't know that about you. Where do you swim?"

"On campus, at the Aquatics Center."

"Really? Me too. I usually go a couple of times a week – especially if I have a triathlon coming up. I'm surprised we've never bumped into each other."

"I always swim early in the mornings, before class," she explained.

"That's probably why," said Jeremy. "I never go early. I'm lucky if I can drag myself out of bed in time for class."

June giggled like a teased schoolgirl. Jeremy began to wonder if she might be attracted to him. *Was this June flirting?*

June further surprised him by asking, "Do you have a girlfriend?"

The battle lines within were drawn. Jeremy longed to answer *no* to her question and *yes* to his hormonal urges. A part of him wanted to lie and take advantage of the situation.

The devil's advocate sounded off again: *Just one kiss. What can it hurt?* Jeremy wavered, but in the end he could not do it. For Jinni's sake, as well as for June's, he would not.

"Yes," he replied. "I have a girlfriend. Her name is Jinni."

"How long have y'all been together?"

Jeremy felt the disappointment of a challenge unmet but hid it in a smile at June's mixture of Chinese accent and Southern colloquialisms. "We just celebrated our one year anniversary," he replied.

"I bet she's very beautiful," June said in her unique, polite way.

***

On the way back to town, the subject of his racing came up again. Jeremy told June of his unexpected results at the triathlon and also of the stunning improvement in his cardiovascular capacity as measured in the Human Fitness Lab.

"There's really no easy explanation for the new result. I had established a baseline of performance over three years. My times improved significantly over the course of the first year but leveled out after that – at least up until last Saturday," he rambled. "There is no justification for the sudden jump in performance."

"That is interesting," replied June. "Something must have changed."

"Something changed in me," Jeremy said finally, "something that I had nothing to do with."

The statement hung in the air like a strange odor. Jeremy needed to explore this enigma – he just didn't know exactly how. He had not intended to ask June tonight; indeed, he had not even settled in his mind that bringing her into this was the proper course of action. He wanted to pursue the project, but he needed expert help and June represented the logical choice. Her biochemical expertise complimented his, and she had access to the equipment essential for the in-depth study he envisioned. Additionally, Jeremy knew her to be dedicated, trustworthy and, unlike Tavalin, discreet. If they were going to do unauthorized research using materials and equipment that did not belong to them, it would have to be done in secret. Perhaps now, in the privacy of his car, he could feel her out.

"June," he began, "I have something I want to ask you."

"Yes?" she asked.

"But this has to stay between you and me." Jeremy hesitated as their eyes locked in the dim glow of the dashboard lights.

Why did this feel like such a big deal?

"What is it?" she prodded in the uncertainty of the moment.

Just ask her.

"Would you consider helping me research this question of my increased endurance?" he asked. "There's something odd going on there and I would very much like to find out what it is."

"If I may ask, why would you choose to involve me?"

"Because you are the smartest person I know and you are very nice and I know you can keep a secret," he replied earnestly.

"Thank you," she said, sounding embarrassed.

"Are you interested in exploring this with me?" he asked. "I don't want you to feel like you have to or anything…"

"I am, how do you say, flattened that you asked me," she said. "But I'd like to think it over first. Do you mind?"

"No, no, not at all. Please, take your time." Jeremy wondered if June meant to say *flattered* but did not correct her. Maybe she was *flattened*.

After not quite kissing June and then her not quite agreeing to help with the secret research, small-talk did little to dent the awkward silence that defined the long ride back to the Facility.

CHAPTER 11

Thursday, October 9

THE very next day, it was June who breeched the subject.

"Can you explain to me again why we must keep this a secret?" she asked. "Wouldn't it be more honest to ask Dr. Cain for permission to use his lab and equipment?"

"Yes, it would be more honest, but what if we asked and he said no? Or, if he thought this is worth investigating and we did discover something publishable, I'm afraid he might take credit as the primary investigator."

"What if he catches us?"

Jeremy felt as if he were corrupting June, but if she wanted to be a part of this, she would have to learn to be a little sneaky. "Just make up something if he asks you what you are working on," he suggested. "Otherwise, we can work on this mostly after hours when it is less likely to be noticed."

"Okay," she finally said. "I'll do it."

"That's great, June. I really appreciate this," gushed Jeremy. "And if at any time you want to quit or whatever, just tell me."

"I will," she said with a tenuous smile. "Have you ever had a muscle biopsy?"

"I see you've already given this some thought," remarked Jeremy.

"I couldn't sleep last night for thinking about it."

"No, I've never had a muscle biopsy." He could guess where this was leading but he asked, "Why?" anyway.

"Because we have to collect a sample of your skeletal muscle for the metabolism studies we'll be conducting."

"Couldn't you just take some blood?"

"I'm afraid not," she replied apologetically.

"You're going to take a plug of meat from where, my leg?" he asked.

"Or," June replied jokingly, "We could get it from one of the other mitochondria-rich tissues like the liver, brain or heart."

"Alright, the leg it is. How exactly does one conduct a muscle biopsy?"

"With a biopsy needle, of course."

With some concern, Jeremy watched as June opened and began to dig around in her desk drawer.

"You're not going to do it now, are you?" he asked.

June pulled a book from the drawer as she laughed at Jeremy's skittishness. "I checked out this book from the library this morning. We have to figure out how to do it first."

"Oh, that makes me feel a whole lot better," he said sarcastically.

Together they read over the procedure. Jeremy was loath to learn that he would have to endure not one, but several sticks of the rather large biopsy needle. Worse, they had no means of obtaining an anesthetizing agent to deaden the affected area.

"We would need a medical doctor to obtain the Novocain," June said. "I presume you don't want to involve a physician in all this?"

"No, I don't think we can do that," he said. "I guess I'll just have to suck it up and take it like a man."

From June's perplexed look, Jeremy could tell that she didn't understand the expression. "That's just another way of saying I'll have to be brave and tolerate the pain," he explained.

✳✳✳

On Monday, the needle arrived. On Monday night they locked themselves in Jeremy's lab. Jeremy switched his blue jeans for a pair of gym shorts in the privacy of the cold room located in the back of his lab. When he came out of the cold room, he did not know if his shivering was due to the cold or to his apprehension.

"You know this is going to hurt," June warned.

"I know," he replied. "I've seen the needle."

"I don't want to hurt you, Jeremy."

"All this was my idea," he said, trying to bolster her. "Let's just get it over with."

June, for her part, did fine, at least once she got over her initial squeamishness and after she figured out just how much force was required to bury the needle in Jeremy's leg.

After the first stick, it was all Jeremy could do to sit still for the subsequent jabs.

When at last she was finished, June asked, "Are you okay?"

"I'll live," he said as he held a wad of paper towels on his bleeding thigh. "At least we can move forward with the project now."

CHAPTER 12

Monday, October 27

TWO weeks later, while Jeremy was working in his lab, Tavalin sneaked up from behind and yelled *Boo!* so loud that it left Jeremy's left ear ringing.

"Alright, you got me," Jeremy conceded. "I'm gonna get an ulcer from this stupid game."

"Just remember, you're the one who started it," said Tavalin.

"I know. If you've told me once, you've told me a hundred times."

"What are you doing for Halloween?" Tavalin sounded excited.

"Jinni and I have a date," Jeremy replied. "I'm supposed to take her to Mario's for dinner. Why do you ask?"

"Because there is this band playing Friday that we *have* to go see."

"What band?" asked Jeremy.

"*Singe.*"

"Never heard of them."

"They're new to the scene but I hear they're awesome," insisted Tavalin.

"It sounds like fun, but I don't know if Jinni will go for it. She generally prefers quieter outings."

"So leave her at home," suggested Tavalin. "It might be better if she doesn't go anyway."

"I really can't break my date with Jinni."

"Aw, come on, man," implored Tavalin. "I can't go by myself."

"I'm not making any promises but I'll see what I can do." Jeremy didn't have the heart to shoot down Tavalin's plans, at least not right now.

As they were about to part ways, Tavalin asked, "Where did you say we were eating?"

"We?" asked Jeremy. "Jinni and I are eating at Mario's."

"Mario's sounds good," said Tavalin expectantly.

Jeremy had hoped that Tavalin's desire to go to see Singe would wane as the week wore on. It didn't. If anything, Tavalin's enthusiasm grew. Jeremy knew it would be next to impossible to get out of going to see the band play on Friday night.

CHAPTER 13

Friday, October 31

IT was Jeremy's idea that they meet at the Facility. Just over one week remained before the dreaded advanced organic chemistry exam, and he thought he might study some this afternoon. He meant well, but for some reason he felt compelled to clean out his desk drawers and straighten up the lab first. Only after he finished those low-priority tasks did Jeremy turn his attention to the high-priority task of studying. He had read a grand total of nine pages when Jinni called a little before six p.m.

"I'm almost ready," she said. "I'll be there in 20 minutes."

"I'll meet you out front."

Even though Jeremy could have used those 20 minutes to read a few more pages, he immediately closed the book and vacated his lab.

Jinni had not been especially pleased to learn that Tavalin had inserted himself into tonight's agenda. Jeremy rang Tavalin on his cell phone and proceeded to make one last ditch effort to nudge his friend away from their date at the restaurant.

"You know," said Jeremy, "if it were up to me, I'd say we just grab a burger somewhere, but Jinni insists we eat at Mario's. I would understand if you don't want to spend your money on such an overpriced establishment – you may want to wait and meet us at the Singe show later."

"Don't be ridiculous," said Tavalin. "I'm looking forward to some fine dining for a change."

Jinni, as promised, arrived a few minutes later. She parked her SUV in the street and sat beside Jeremy on the front steps of the Facility. As they waited for Tavalin to arrive, Jeremy glimpsed Grady as he exited the building from one of the six front doors. Jeremy didn't know what time Grady normally left work, but six p.m. seemed later than usual for him to be wandering about.

Jeremy and Jinni sat off to one side of the broad steps, well out of the direct path of anyone leaving the building. Thinking, or at least hoping, that the strange janitor and his albino-like eyes would pass them by, Jeremy focused his full attention toward Jinni. It wasn't until Grady spoke that Jeremy looked up.

"Aren't you going to introduce me to your beautiful friend?" asked Grady. As usual, his eyes were hidden behind the dark sunglasses.

Jeremy stood up and, as politely as he could muster, introduced Jinni as his girlfriend.

"Hi," said Jinni hesitantly.

"What does Jeremy say about me?" Grady asked, immediately putting Jinni on the spot.

Jeremy had described to Jinni his dealings with Grady, including his penchant for off-the-wall – or even threatening – comments.

"Not that much, really," she replied. Fidgeting under Grady's direct gaze, Jinni added, "I know he gave you a ride home, or something."

"That's right," Grady said. "Someday, God willing, I'll pay him back. Did he also tell you about Reefers Woods?"

Jinni's uneasy eyes shifted first toward Jeremy, then to the ground and back to Grady. "I don't think so," she replied hesitantly.

Fibbing did not come naturally to Jinni. Jeremy wondered if it were as obvious to Grady as it was to him.

"Good," said Grady. "You're going to have to be the one to keep Jeremy on the straight and narrow. I don't think he can do it on his own."

Jinni nodded but otherwise did not respond.

To Jeremy, Grady added, "Don't let this one get away. She's one of the good ones."

"You don't have to worry about that," replied Jeremy. "Jinni is the best thing that ever happened to me."

With Jinni looking curiously on, Grady leaned in close to Jeremy and whispered, "Remember, the harlot always sets herself up in opposition to the bride."

Jeremy drew back, made uncomfortable by the janitor's forced proximity. Grady, however, was not finished. He placed a hand on Jeremy's shoulder, as if to hold him still, and added, "Beware the point of no return."

Grady turned his attention to Jinni, who was still sitting on the steps beneath Jeremy. Putting his hand on her cheek, he asked, "Wouldn't she make a beautiful bride?"

Bristling with anger, Jeremy could not answer. It was one thing for Grady to intrude upon his personal space but quite another to violate Jinni's. At least Jeremy knew to whom *the bride* comment referred. Perhaps sensing Jeremy's antagonism, Grady quickly stepped back, adding, "Nice to meet you Jinni. Don't forget to keep Jeremy out of trouble."

As Grady walked away, Jeremy put a protective arm around Jinni. "I'm sorry about that," he said. "I should not have let him get so close to you like that."

"Why?" she asked innocently.

"He's not right in the head."

"He seems harmless enough," she said. "What did he whisper to you?"

"Just a bunch of *Grady-speak*."

"Grady-speak?" asked Jinni.

"That's the term I coined for all the incomprehensible things the man says."

"I guess he is a little strange," agreed Jinni. After a thoughtful pause, she added, "but, for some reason, I like him."

"He sure seemed to take a shine to you," muttered Jeremy, "so I guess the feeling must be mutual."

"Can you blame him?"

For comic effect, Jinni batted her eyes in a most exaggerated fashion.

***

Jinni squealed and Jeremy jumped in response to the unexpected *POP!* and they watched with shocked amusement as the purple grape girl let loose a vicious string of obscenities. Someone in the considerable line behind her had popped one of the balloon-grapes that comprised her costume, and she was mad. Tavalin, too, got a piece of her anger, a fierce go-to-hell glare as he doubled over in a spasm of nerve-grating, hyena-laughter. Jinni, embarrassed, rolled her eyes at Jeremy and took a giant step up in line, away from Tavalin and his antics.

A few other patrons, in addition to the purple grape girl, wore Halloween costumes, but just as many did not.

"I'm here as a drunken graduate student," Jeremy said with an exaggerated (but simulated) slur and authentic beer breath, "and look," he whispered in Jinni's ear, "Tavalin is dressed as the town idiot."

"It's a very convincing costume, for both of you." Jinni laughed heartily at her own joke.

A burly bouncer, ridiculously dressed as a French maid, took up their tickets at the door. The place was packed, and Jeremy volunteered to buy the first round. He stood in line while Jinni and Tavalin pushed through the crowd toward the stage to claim a good spot.

After inching forward for a good five minutes, Jeremy stood only one person back from the bar and a cold beverage. He turned in response to a gentle *tap, tap* on his shoulder and found himself face-to-face with an angel, wings and all. She was the most beautiful creature he had ever seen, with long, dark hair and eyes as black as night.

"I don't mean to be forward, but could you do me a big favor and buy me a drink?" she asked. "The band is about to start and this line is so long. I'll pay you back, promise."

For a second Jeremy couldn't speak or break eye contact.

"Yeah, okay. What?"

Angels, he discovered, even those of the costumed variety, had a way of shrinking his vocabulary to simple words, four letters or less.

"How about a White Russian?"

"Just one?" Jeremy wouldn't have been surprised if he had just agreed to buy drinks for two, her and her date.

"What, do I look like a lush or what?" she asked with a cunning grin. "Yes, one will do just fine. I'll wait for you over there," she said, motioning toward a less crowded spot behind the lines of people.

She swished seductively away in her delicate, black-lace angel wings, matching gartered stockings, a skin-tight black spandex top and a skimpy black miniskirt. She looked like a lingerie model, and Jeremy couldn't help but ogle her for the few seconds while her back was to him. He noticed that he wasn't the only one checking out the girl with the raven hair and angel's wings.

A few minutes later Jeremy squeezed away from the bar, precariously cradling the four drinks. She stood alone, near the steps that overlooked the pit area where Jinni and Tavalin waited. As he approached, her mouth smiled a little smile, but those black eyes smoldered with a faraway, unfathomable expression.

She spoke, shaking Jeremy from his reverie. "Listen, I really appreciate this. Here's some money."

"No problem, just glad to help a damsel in distress."

The girl picked her drink from the four with one outstretched hand and extended a folded bill toward him with the other. Even her hands were beautiful, smooth and delicate with long, slender fingers. A ricochet of reflected light focused Jeremy's gaze on a silver ring, intricately designed, which she wore between the second and third knuckle of her left forefinger.

Jeremy almost, but not quite, refused the money. After all, wasn't this just another example of a girl using her looks to get favors from gullible guys like him? But he was wrong, or so it seemed, as evidenced by what happened next.

"So are you here with someone?" she asked.

"Yes, I'm here with my date." Jeremy noticed with a curious detachment that he hadn't said *girlfriend*.

"That's too bad," she said, and asked, "Have you ever been to Bar Nowhere?"

"No, is that the place to be?" he asked, even as he cringed inside at the stupid remark.

"You should check it out sometime," she suggested. "I'm there most Saturday nights."

In a quick and totally unexpected maneuver, the dark angel kissed him, square on the mouth, her warm moist lips parted, her mysterious eyes locked on his. And then, without another word, she turned away and was gone, swallowed by the crowd.

For a moment Jeremy's senses turned inwardly; he could no longer hear, see or smell the bar and its humanity. He was alone in the crowd, his heart and brain racing dragsters, burning rubber down a hot pavement strip.

Like a movie fade-in, the external world slowly came back into focus. Guiltily he scanned the mob for Jinni and Tavalin. When he finally picked them out, thankfully, neither appeared to be looking his way.

"What took you so long?" Tavalin asked as Jeremy fought his way over to where they stood.

"Too many drunks, too few bartenders," Jeremy replied distractedly, feigning great interest in the stagehands' last-second checking of instruments and microphones.

Jinni didn't say much, just *thanks* for the beer. She gave no indication that she had seen anything. This was good, except that in his guilt, Jeremy began to worry that she had seen the kiss and was waiting to see if he would confess. Before he had a chance to fully gauge her mood, the band members took their places on the stage and began to play.

As Tavalin's taste in music did not always match Jeremy's musical palate, Jeremy came tonight not knowing what to expect. For once, Tavalin's inclination was correct; the band was awesome, not withstanding its members' strange appearances.

On one side of the stage a skinny platinum blond played bass guitar, her bra worn outside her shirt instead of underneath. On the opposite side stood the guitarist, a cross-dressed male with Asian features and blank, cadaver-like eyes. Between the two towered the vocalist, a tall long-haired character with searing eyes and crooked teeth who commanded the astute attention of the crowd that groped and grabbed at him as if he were Jesus himself.

The arrangements performed by Singe were of a unique passive-aggressive style which oscillated between two extremes, often in the same song. Soft and melodic sweetness would suddenly transform into intense driving metallic rock where riffs rolled from screaming electric guitars and the never-ending beat of drums pounded with the intensity of some great natural force. It was as if the music were a living, breathing organism, bound to experience the same highs and lows, exuberance and despair, beauty and repugnance, that exists in all of God's creatures.

After the band began, any communication was accomplished only with difficulty. Simple hand signals worked best, like pointing in the direction of the restrooms or bar before going to empty one's bladder or to fill it up again, respectively, or the occasional thumbs-up in appreciation of the band members' talent. Only Tavalin, unable to disable the direct line between brain and mouth, attempted to be heard over the auditory onslaught, unaware, Jeremy supposed, that most of what he said was no more interpretable than monkey grunts.

Through a fleeting peephole in the boisterous crowd, Jeremy caught one brief glimpse of *her*, the girl with the raven hair and angel's wings, as she head-banged to the beat, seemingly oblivious to everything and everyone, save the music. Again, he felt her soft warm kiss, and again, he worried that Jinni had witnessed it. His guilt did not, however, prevent him from looking for her during subsequent trips to the bar and the restroom, but she was nowhere to be found, hidden from his sight.

Maybe she really was an angel.

***

After the show, Jeremy pulled up in front of the Facility to drop Tavalin and Jinni off at their cars. Tavalin got out first.

Jeremy glanced up at June's lab. The lights were on. "I think June is still working," he said, thinking aloud. "I wish I were half as committed as she is."

Jinni said, "Don't sell yourself short. I know you've been spending a lot of time up in June's lab lately – especially late night."

For some reason, perhaps because he had nothing to hide, Jeremy had told Jinni of the night he and June drove out to the lake together. At the time, Jinni didn't say anything to indicate that she was bothered by it, but, based on a smattering of comments she had made since then, he wondered if she were becoming suspicious of his relationship with June.

Changing the subject, Jeremy asked, "Do you want to come over to my place?"

"No, thanks," replied Jinni predictably.

Jinni paid him a goodnight kiss before she exited his car. Jeremy waited until she got safely inside her SUV and drove off before he pulled away from the curb. He waved to Tavalin, who was sitting inside his own car, having not yet left. However, instead of going home, Jeremy circled around to the small parking lot behind the Facility, the one that was supposed to be reserved for faculty. Like Jinni, Tavalin had taken note of how much time Jeremy was spending in June's lab, and Jeremy didn't want Tavalin to see him go inside.

Jeremy had not told anyone, not Jinni and certainly not Tavalin, about the metabolism studies he and June had been feverishly pursuing over the last three weeks. While Jeremy simply did not trust Tavalin to keep a secret, it was for a different reason that he chose not to inform Jinni. If he asked Jinni not to tell, Jeremy trusted that she wouldn't. In fact, it was largely because of her squeaky-clean persona that he didn't mention the clandestine project to her. Compared to him, Jinni was an angel and he generally made it a point not to call attention to the difference between them. He could tell her later, if and when something came of the research.

"Boo," Jeremy said in a conversational tone as he entered June's lab. He didn't want to scare June but rather alert her that he was there so he wouldn't startle her.

"Hey, Jeremy," she said.

"You sure are working late," he said. "I was driving by and saw the light on and thought I would come bug you."

"I'm glad," replied June. "I've got some results I think you might be interested in."

"Oh yeah?"

"It's your mitochondria," she said.

"What about my mitochondria?" For some reason, probably because of the beer, the sound of his question sounded comical in Jeremy's ears. He suppressed a smile.

"They're not normal," she said.

"How so?" he asked.

"We've already determined that your metabolism runs very fast at the cellular level. That, in and of itself, is not unusual in well-trained athletes who have a high density of mitochondria. More mitochondria are naturally expected to produce more energy. Yet, with you, there seems to be an additional energy component – this is what I've been stuck on. Finally, I figured out that this extra energy component must be due to more energy output per *single* mitochondrion."

"In laymen's terms?" he asked.

Early on, Jeremy made every attempt to understand all the implications of the various experiments but swiftly came to realize that June's knowledge and understanding far surpassed his own.

"Mitochondria are the engines of the cell," she explained. "Trained athletes extract more energy from their cells by growing, if you will, extra engines. In your case, you not only have extra cellular engines but each of your engines has more horsepower."

"And that would translate into faster race times?" asked Jeremy.

"It is definitely one component of performance," she said, "There are other factors that come into play. The delivery of oxygen to the muscles is equally important but that is not what we are looking at here."

"Any idea what's causing this?" asked Jeremy.

"No, I don't know what's causing this effect and I don't know how we might remediate it."

"Remediate it?" Jeremy asked, puzzled. "Why? This is a good thing, is it not?"

"Good, yes, but maybe some bad too," she said.

Before June could expound, Tavalin appeared unexpectedly at the doorway.

"Hi, guys," he said jovially.

"I thought you'd be home in bed by now," said Jeremy. "What are you doing here?"

"I was just about to ask you the same thing," replied Tavalin.

"June and I were just going over some results."

"Can I see?" asked Tavalin as he approached them.

"We're trying to wrap it up here so we can go home," replied Jeremy as he closed the notebook.

Tavalin returned a puzzled look and then asked, "So did you have fun tonight?"

"I did. You were right about the band," replied Jeremy. "They're really good."

"Yeah, but did you have a *good* time?"

Tavalin's tone made Jeremy wonder if his friend had witnessed the kiss he shared with the angel.

"Yes, I had fun," replied Jeremy in a neutral tone.

"Where's Jinni?" asked Tavalin.

"She went home."

"Does she know you're here?"

"I don't know." Jeremy did not try to hide his irritation. He wanted to finish his conversation with June. "I suppose not. Why does it matter?"

"I was just wondering."

"Alright then," Jeremy said leadingly. "We're trying to get out of here so I guess I'll see you Monday in class."

"Yeah, whatever," said Tavalin grudgingly as he headed for the door.

After giving his friend ample time to extricate himself from hearing range, Jeremy said, "I think Tavalin suspects we are up to something."

"We can't let him find out because I'm sure his big mouth would never be able to keep quiet."

Jeremy laughed at June's out-of-character remark. He said, "Tavalin does have a big mouth, doesn't he?"

June opened up the notebook with the results but, before she could speak, Jeremy raised his hand and whispered, "Wait." He walked to the door and looked up and down the empty hallway. "I want to make sure Tavalin isn't still hanging around."

June took advantage of the delay to scribble something on a piece of scratch paper. "What is this word?" she asked.

Written on the paper was the 7-letter word, "helluva".

"I came across this word in a novel yesterday night and it was not listed in the dictionary."

Yesterday night was June's unique jargon for *last night*.

Jeremy smiled. "That's just a casual spelling of this phrase," and he wrote the words "hell of a" on the same piece of paper. "It's a mild explicative."

"Oh," she said, embarrassed.

He smiled affectionately at her and she responded in kind.

"You are alright, June," Jeremy remarked impulsively, "and I'm so glad I got the opportunity to get to know you. I hope it's alright for me to say that I think of you as my good friend."

"It's okay," she said, blushing. "I think of you as my friend, too."

The touching moment bordered on the awkward, and Jeremy relieved the pressure by turning the conversation back to their research. He asked, "You were saying there could be drawbacks to my accelerated metabolism?"

"Yes, maybe," June replied. "A by-product of metabolism is the production of free radicals. Free radicals, because of their highly reactive nature, cause injury to the cell in general, and specifically, to the mitochondria within the cell and also to the DNA in the mitochondria. DNA acts as the blueprint for the production of the next generation of mitochondria, and so, when the blueprint becomes error-ridden, the new mitochondria are less efficient and produce even more free radicals as byproducts. This cycle repeats itself causing each successive generation of mitochondria to produce less energy and more free radicals."

"In laymen's terms?" Jeremy asked again.

"It's as if your cellular engines are over-revving, generating extra energy but potentially causing extra damage to themselves in the process," she explained in simpler terms. "Free radicals damage the mitochondria, including the DNA blueprint. The net result of a damaged DNA blueprint is that the next generation of mitochondria produces even more free radicals. It is a self-perpetuating cycle where the damage is multiplied over time."

"That doesn't sound good, does it?" he mused. "What impact might this have on my overall health?"

"Maybe none," replied June. "One must remember that this process of damage by free radical production is common to us all – everyone's mitochondrial DNA accumulate errors over time. The worry for you is that the process might be occurring at a faster-than-normal rate, but I'm not sure about that yet. I need to do some more reading."

Though Jeremy chose not to pursue it, he thought that perhaps June was holding out on him and that the negative health repercussions might be worse than she let on.

He said, "I would offer to stay and help but I gotta tell you, I'm beat."

"You look beat."

Jeremy laughed as he turned to leave and replied, "Thanks a lot, June."

She smiled. "Goodnight, Jeremy."

"Goodnight."

***

Back at his apartment, Jeremy readied for bed. On emptying his jean pockets of their contents, he discovered a stray five dollar bill. He unfolded it and, as he was about to stuff it into his wallet, something caught his eye. Written in red ink along all four edges of the bill, on both the front and back sides, were the repeated words *burn baby burn baby burn…*

Jeremy might not have given it a second thought had the bill not been the one passed to him as payment for a certain White Russian. He wondered if a certain girl with raven hair and black-lace angel wings might have penned the curious message, and if so, what in the world she meant by it.

CHAPTER 14

Wednesday, November 5

DESPITE untold hours spent thinking about Claire and the ghost story, Jeremy had no accurate mental picture of the hippie queen. Though the quality was not all that great, one of the old newspaper articles included photographs of five of the seven hippies killed in the fire. It gave no explanation for the two omitted photos, but Claire's was one of those missing. All five were posed shots of the typical head-and-shoulders style. Though this was not the first time Jeremy had seen the pictures, it was the first time that he realized their likely origin. Most, if not all, of the commune members had likely been students at the University. These were their yearbook photos.

Claire, he recalled, had also attended the University. Exactly when or for how long he did not know, but for a time she was a graduate student in the biology department. He did know she died in 1969. In the library he easily found copies of the four years prior to and including the 1969 edition of the University yearbook. While he found it interesting to see how people dressed and wore their hair 40 years ago, he found not one photo of anyone by the name of Claire Wales.

Though a long shot, Jeremy decided that a visit to the biology department should be his next move. They might have an old photo of Claire floating around somewhere. Jeremy ran across only one person, a secretary, who even had an inkling who Claire Wales was. The talkative secretary, an old maid who went by the name Ms Lang, had been working in the biology department for 30 years. Even so, Ms Lang knew few details of Claire except that she was the one who died in the fire.

Ms Lang did, however, direct Jeremy to a bank of filing cabinets in a musty-smelling storage room.

"We switched to electronic files for students 20 years ago, but this is where all our old student records ended up," she said. "I'm not sure how far they go back or how complete they are."

"And it's okay that I look through these?" asked Jeremy.

"There's probably some law against it somewhere, but I think it's okay if we make an exception in your case," replied Ms Lang.

For two hours Jeremy rummaged through the files. Most of the records contained only sketchy personal information, primarily local addresses and phone numbers of the students. Included in most were their University transcripts, which included the courses taken, grades received and the date, if applicable, of graduation.

Jeremy's job might have been easier if the files of the graduate students had not been mixed in with those of the much more numerous undergrads. It also would have helped if the files had been in a more ordered state. Two hours passed before he found the skinny folder labeled WALES, CLAIRE.

Upon reading its contents, Jeremy learned that Claire had been enrolled for three semesters, starting in the fall of 1967. During her final semester at the University in the fall of 1968, she received a research fellowship under the direction of Dr. Ray Nevins. Included in her file was her research proposal abstract, which very vaguely outlined how she planned to study the *local flora*. The last detail Jeremy gleaned from Claire's folder was that she apparently quit before receiving any degree.

The only lead Jeremy thought might be worth following up on was her research advisor, Dr. Nevins. Jeremy took the folder and tracked down Ms Lang, who was in the small break room drinking coffee from a large Styrofoam cup.

"Are you still here?" she asked in a tone too playful for her advanced years.

"Have you ever heard of a Dr. Ray Nevins?" asked Jeremy. "Apparently he worked in the biology department as a professor in 1968."

"The name doesn't ring a bell so I know he wasn't here when I started..."

"When did you begin working here?" asked Jeremy.

"That would have been on the bicentennial year of our great nation, 1976. I started what I like to call my *sentence* in June of that year."

When Ms Lang finished her coffee, she was nice enough to look up Dr. Ray Nevins. Old faculty records, unlike those of the students, had been preserved and were easily accessible. Approximately 35 years had elapsed since Dr. Nevins, a botanist, retired from the department at the age of 65. Though Jeremy would certainly like to talk to him about Claire, it seemed unlikely that the man could still be alive after all this time.

"Anything else I can do, just let me know," offered the perky old secretary.

"I will," replied Jeremy, "and thank you for all your help."

Though Jeremy had been very excited to find Claire's folder, he was disappointed at the scant information it held. There had been no photograph of Claire and no indication as to where she might have lived before moving to Destiny.

***

"There's no way I'm going to be ready for this test."

Jeremy was talking to Tavalin on the phone.

"You do know it's not required that we take it, don't you?" asked Tavalin.
"What?"
"Only the final exam is required."
"I did not know that…"
"Of course you realize the risk," warned Tavalin. "If you skip a test, then the final exam must necessarily constitute a larger proportion of your final grade."
"I won't decide until I see how the studying goes this week," replied Jeremy, though the seed of procrastination had been sown.

Jeremy hung up the phone and promptly turned his thoughts to his afternoon visit to the biology department and to the hippie queen's research advisor, Dr. Ray Nevins. A quick search revealed no reference to the man on the general pages of the internet, nothing about him on the University site, and no obituary. Jeremy wasn't sure how information on the professor would help him learn more about Claire anyway, though it might be interesting to learn more about the nature of Claire's research project.

In a flash Jeremy knew where to look next. If Dr. Nevins ever had the occasion to publish any of his research, or even shared in a publication, all Jeremy had to do was search the library's scientific publications resource site. After navigating to the appropriate page, Jeremy typed the name *Nevins, Ray* into the search field. When the reference listing popped up on his computer screen, Jeremy's eyes immediately locked onto the third-listed author.

Raymond C. Nevins, A. Maurice Anthony and Claire Wales
The phylogeny and a newly-discovered variant of the purple lotus of the Nymphaeaceae family (American Journal of Botanical Studies. 1971;66:55-62.)

The full article could be viewed online in exchange for a hefty charge. Though Jeremy could have read it free of charge at the library, he opted for expedience over economy.

The first few pages of the paper were concerned with the very boring subject of classification and nomenclature of the family of plants called *Nymphaeaceae*. After that, the subject matter became more interesting. Just as the title of the paper indicated, Dr. Nevins and his group discovered a new variant of *Nymphaeaceae*, but that wasn't the noteworthy part. What caught Jeremy's eye was that this plant – a lotus, whatever that was – had been discovered growing in the wetlands of Sticks River National Forest.

Claire's name was listed as one of the authors because, as the article revealed, it was she who conducted all the field work. She was the one who discovered the purple lotus of Reefers Woods. Though interesting, this information did little to advance Jeremy's understanding of Claire's role as the hippie queen. However, it seemed reasonable that it was the field work that brought her to Sticks River National Forest in the first place. That, Jeremy theorized, began the cascade of events that led to the founding of the commune and culminated in the deaths of Claire and her friends by burning.

CHAPTER 15

Saturday, November 8

O N almost any other Saturday night Jeremy would be with Jinni, but tonight she was out of town, having gone to attend a friend's wedding in Atlanta.

Over the past several weeks, he and June burned the midnight oil as they tried to better understand Jeremy's *condition*. They were sure his mitochondria were producing more energy than would be expected, and they succeeded in isolating a sample of his mitochondrial DNA, the blueprint for his mitochondria. Strangely, the initial result indicated his mitochondrial DNA to be nearly four times larger than is normal. June wanted to repeat the assay to verify or to refute that unlikely result. Knowing June, she would probably be finished with the task, come Monday.

The excitement of that project had kept him occupied all week, but now the time had come to pay the piper. He had to study. Grudgingly, Jeremy drove to the library, shuffled inside to a secluded spot in the stacks and laid out his notes. He stared vacantly at the first of a long list of reactions to memorize, but he could not concentrate. His mind was a blank.

Forbidden thoughts – thoughts of the angel and her kiss – seeped into the void. All week Jeremy had done his best to push the strange and stirring incident at the bar from his mind. But now, with Jinni conveniently out of town, temptation beckoned. Well Jeremy remembered the dark angel's mention of a certain establishment she frequented.

Most Saturday nights you can find me there, she had said, in what could only be an invitation for him to do just that.

Maybe tonight would be a good time to check out this Bar Nowhere.

Jeremy faced up to his dilemma. On one hand there was the intrigue of the angel's kiss, her mysterious vibe and the exquisite excitement of the chase. On the other hand there was Jinni. He hated to sneak around behind her back, but what could one tiny excursion hurt? Odds were he wouldn't cross paths with the angel again anyway, and even if he did, what could possibly come of it? Girls like her didn't date guys like him. She was too cutting-edge, too much of a wild child to go for him. In all probability, if she were at the club and if he garnered enough courage to approach her, he would quickly discover that she wasn't interested in him after all. At the very least, he might learn what possessed her to kiss him, a complete stranger, like she did.

He left the library without a plan except to check out this place, this girl, and to talk to her if she were there. If his memory served him right, Bar Nowhere had only been in operation a few months. It was located downtown in the old warehouse district. Jeremy chose to walk from his apartment, in part because it was a nice night, but primarily so his car could not give away his presence at the night club. This was a clandestine affair. He approached from the north, passing the old boarded-up church and its dark steeple that poked defiantly at the night sky. The muffled beat of the music summoned him on a primal level, like a savage to some ancient, midnight ritual.

The first doorman checked Jeremy's license and grudgingly gave the okay, all the while mumbling how young Jeremy looked for his age. A second doorman took his money for the cover charge and rolled a rubber stamp across the back of his hand. Jeremy glanced down to see a little cartoon gargoyle in heavy black ink grinning up at him. He followed a group of tittering girls down a narrow, wooden stairwell, by necessity, in single file. The girls wore tight clothes and hair gel, with their tattoos and pierced body parts on full display. They seemed barely able to contain themselves as they rattled down the stairs and through the painted glass door at the bottom.

Beyond the door beat the heart of an alternate world. Thundering music and laser lights shot intricate, ever-changing designs over every surface and person present. An odd, metal apparatus installed with rubber nozzles and portholes, about the size of a large beach-ball, hung over the center of the dance area and belched white puffs of a musky smelling incense while tendrils of vaporized dry ice crept along the dance floor like ghostly fingers. The otherworldliness of the dance club was made complete by the patrons themselves, strange children of the night who lurked in the dark recesses and writhed like snakes on the dance floor. Jeremy would not have been surprised in the least to find them hanging upside down from the ceilings as well.

Feeling conspicuously out of place, Jeremy wormed his way through the crowd to the bar on the opposite wall and slapped down a five for a beer. As he scanned the crowd, he wondered how he would identify the girl with the raven hair, even if she were here. After his eyes adjusted better to the flashing lights, he noticed an arched passageway secluded on the far side of the dance floor, and beyond, an ornate spiral staircase. Jeremy followed one particularly buxom young woman who seemed not to mind that her position on the vertical staircase and her short shirt afforded everyone below a perfect view of her thong underwear.

The basement dance area just vacated shared a vaulted ceiling with the upstairs portion of the bar. The upper room was crowded with people sitting around the tables and on the couches and stuffed chairs that lined the back wall. Along the side wall was a massive bar of black mahogany, tended by a little bald man who scurried with practiced efficiency from one mind-numbing concoction to the next. Curtains of the movie theater variety, dark and heavy, obscured what scant view of the street that might have filtered in through the painted windowpanes.

Jeremy stepped up behind a dark-complexioned, boyish man as he vacated his barstool.

"Excuse me," Jeremy muttered as they exchanged positions, their faces in proximity. Jeremy hesitated because his face rang a bell, although he could not remember from whence the bell of familiarity tolled. Intending on letting it drop, Jeremy moved past, climbed aboard the barstool and ordered another beer.

"Mr. Spires, right?" asked a voice from behind.

It was the boyish man.

"Yes, that's right."

Jeremy still could not place the face.

"Trey," he obliged.

No one referred to Jeremy as *Mr. Spires* except for the students he taught, and then only the ones who didn't know him very well.

"Hello, Trey. Please – it's Jeremy."

Instead of a traditional handshake Trey offered his fist. His shoulder-length hair was unkempt, yet fashioned as if styled by some rock star's hairdresser. A silver earring dangled from one ear lobe and a simple silver loop decorated the other. Trey was hip.

"You were one of the teaching assistants for general chemistry lab last year, right?"

"Yes, that's right," Jeremy said. "And the year before that and this year too."

"It's so cool to see you out partying," said Trey, as if somehow this astonished him.

"Yes," Jeremy said. "Even chemistry nerds have lives."

"I guess," Trey replied, suddenly distracted.

Jeremy followed Trey's gaze to see that *she* – Jeremy's acquaintance from the Singe show – had arrived, having just ascended the spiral staircase. She wore a slinky, skin-tight, black spandex outfit, cut low at the neckline, and black fishnet hose. The bare skin of her belly shone through a web-shaped hole, with the ring of her pierced navel, like a golden spider, the centerpiece of the web.

Trey asked, "You know her?"

With the exception of the angel's wings, she was dressed almost as she had been last Saturday, on Halloween. This was definitely not your typical co-ed.

"Not really," Jeremy replied. "But I'd like to."

"Well, good luck," Trey said with a wink as he turned to leave.

Jeremy glanced down at his own conservative blue jeans and golf shirt. Up against the dark angel and her radical attire, he really did look like a stuffy chemistry nerd, but what could he do? He was quite sure his closet was absent any black spandex, spider-web outfits. As he considered whether to approach her or, in his insecurity, maybe just slip out unnoticed, she suddenly looked his way as if she sensed his gaze. Jeremy turned away, but too late; he was caught. She made a beeline to where he fidgeted.

"Hi," she said with a smile. "Remember me?"

"How could I forget?"

The DJ, whom Jeremy had not noticed before now, introduced a song that erupted from the sound system even louder than the preceding tune. Jeremy had to lean in close to her face to hear her and to be heard.

"Mind if I sit down?" she asked.

"Be my guest." Jeremy watched keenly as she slid up a barstool and got situated atop the high seat. She was even more awesome than he remembered.

"So what's going on?" she asked, as she engaged him with her eyes.

Jeremy felt an overwhelming urge to compliment this beautiful creature so that maybe, just maybe, she would stay awhile. "You know I was hoping you would be here," he said. "I have to say your approach last week made quite an impression."

"Approach?" she asked, for some reason not catching his meaning.

"You do remember last weekend, don't you? The White Russian, the way you kissed me?"

"I remember the White Russian, but it was you who kissed me," she contended with a playful glimmer in her eye.

"Yeah, right, I think we both know you laid one on me, then left me standing there like a stuttering idiot," he shot back.

"It was just my way of saying thank you."

"In that case, maybe I should buy you another…"

Her dark eyes held an expression that Jeremy read as something akin to longing, excitement, and boldness all wrapped up in one.

"Yeah, maybe…" she said without committing one way or the other to his transparent proposition. After a measure of silence, she added, "You know, I was pretty messed up the other night. I'm not usually that forward."

"Well, you certainly got my attention," he said. "Are you here with anyone?"

"No, I came alone," she said and then added with a sly smile, "Say, that sounds like a pick-up line."

He didn't remind her that she had posed the identical question to him last weekend. "You should know," he said. "I imagine you've heard them all."

"Now, Jeremy, what's that supposed to mean?" she asked, putting him on the defensive.

"I'm just saying you are an attractive girl and in a place like this I'd guess that you are propositioned by a good portion of the eligible male sector – a compliment, right?"

"Whatever," she replied, her eyes averted.

"Hold on," Jeremy said, his mind catching on something she said. "I didn't tell you my name. How'd you know my name?"

She responded without hesitation. "I've always known you."

"Huh?" he asked dumbly.

"Just kidding. I guess you must have mentioned it last weekend."

"I don't think so," Jeremy said, but now he doubted himself. "I know you didn't tell me yours."

"It's Monika, with a 'k'." She turned up her drink and slammed the empty glass aggressively onto the table. "Wanna go for a ride?" she asked.

Her car, an immaculate, 1969 Mustang convertible, was parked directly in front of the old boarded up church next door to the dance club. With the firing up of the engine, a nervous excitement ignited in Jeremy. This wild and beautiful woman had picked him when she could have chosen any one of a hundred males inside, a fact made obvious by the busload of attention she commandeered as they left the bar.

"Monika, why don't we swing by my place and pick up an ice chest and something to drink. My apartment is right off the Square."

"Sounds good," she said nonchalantly. "Show me the way."

Thoughts of Jinni seeped from hidden depths and bubbled to the surface of Jeremy's conscience. What would her reaction be if she could see him now?

Something made Jeremy think of the carnival-themed pinball game he used to play with an old friend in a dark redneck bar in another town. Always late night, always the same carnie voice emanating from the machine:

Ya spin the wheel, ya take ya chances...

***

"Can I get you something to drink?" Jeremy asked as he showed his new acquaintance inside. "I've got beer, iced tea, water – or maybe you'd prefer a White Russian?"

"Water please, bottled if you have it. Where's your bathroom?"

After raiding the fridge, Jeremy turned on the stereo in the living room, plopped down in the recliner, and took a deep breath. He needed time to weigh the pros and cons of this situation, but tonight, time was flying.

Monika marched back from the bathroom. She sat down and crossed her legs jauntily. The overstuffed couch accentuated her diminutive frame. If not for her cool confidence and the sophisticated smile that graced her face, she might be mistaken for an audacious teenager.

"Nice place you've got here, Jeremy. Live alone?"

"All by myself."

"Do you know what it is to burn?" she asked, out of the blue.

"What does that mean?" he asked.

Without directly addressing his first question, Monika posed another. "Have you ever heard of the *Unreal*?"

"The Unreal? I'm not familiar... " Jeremy felt acutely uncomfortable in his ignorance.

Monika did not immediately expound, preferring instead to let him twist in the wind.

"It's a party drug," she finally said, "- the latest thing."

"Oh," he said, chastised. "The latest *illegal* thing, no doubt?"

"I really wouldn't know about that," she replied, brushing the question aside.

From nowhere, Monika produced a capsule that she laid on the coffee table. It rolled in a lazy semicircle and then back again as if moved by some invisible force.

"Why do they call it the Unreal?" The word sounded foreign coming from Jeremy's mouth.

"I don't know where the name comes from," she said. "Maybe because it's unreal how good you feel after you take it."

Jeremy held the transparent capsule up for a more intimate examination, as if maybe he could answer his own question if he looked hard enough. The fluffy powder inside possessed a lavender tint, and when he sniffed it, he detected a subtle sweetness like perfume. Jeremy wondered if some of Monika's smell had rubbed off on the capsule. The thought struck a provocative chord within him.

"So, um, what are you planning on doing with this?" he asked.

"Why, I'm planning on taking it, of course. I didn't pull it out just so you could smell it." She smiled deliciously. "What did you think?"

Monika spoke to him in an easy, familiar way, like one might address an old friend. Unfortunately, Jeremy could not reciprocate her laid-back vibe; he was wound up as tight as a tick. He retrieved his beer from the table and was surprised to find that it was empty. He didn't remember finishing it off but, in his nervousness, he must have downed it.

"What was that you said about burning?" he asked.

She laughed. "Oh, don't worry about that. That's just kind of a code name for the drug. If someone asked you, for instance, if you feel like *burning down the house*, it would mean the same thing. Really, any reference to burning or fire might carry the same connotation."

"I had no idea."

Being here with this girl was like being led to a foreign land where everything is unfamiliar and strange, but it was a place Jeremy desperately wanted to experience and understand.

She bit her lip seductively and asked, "You want to take some?"

He expected the question but was still ill-prepared to answer.

"Wanna burn?" she added.

"I don't know, Monika. What's it like?"

Monika's face shone with an inner radiance, her eyes dreamy as if she could see heaven itself. "It's impossible to describe but it's nothing like you've ever felt before. Love, peace, understanding, empathy, fearlessness, and oneness with the world – the feeling is impossible to explain, but I want to do it." She looked at him with longing eyes. "I want to do it with you, Jeremy."

"It sounds like fun and all, but I don't know…"

Jeremy needed more information and he needed more time. It would be risky taking a drug that he knew nothing about supplied by a girl he just met. What if this was some kind of ruse? What if the capsule actually contained something that would knock him out? What if she meant to take something from him?

Her tone became impatient. "Look, if you don't want to do it, then fine, but I'm quite sure I can find someone else who does. I don't have all night."

Jeremy's mind raced on the greasy wheels of rationalization. He was already taking a different kind of chance just being here now, with her. In the company of others, Jeremy had been known to say that every adventure, by definition, carries risk. The present situation was no different: dangerous, definitely, but a temptation he could not refuse.

Jeremy gave in. "Yeah, sure," he said, with bravado. "Why not?"

"You won't regret it," she said. "I promise."

"This isn't the only one, is it?" he asked, before adding on a hunch, "or have you already had yours?"

"No, I've got some more right here."

After a moment of digging in her purse, Monika produced another capsule that she popped expediently into her mouth. She chased it with a sip of water and passed the bottle over to Jeremy.

Here goes nothing, he said to himself.

His new companion watched intently as he swallowed the lavender-tinged capsule with the perfumed smell. She leaned over and kissed him, taking the initiative just as she had the night they met.

"Burn, baby, burn," he said with a grin.

"That reminds me," she said, "did you happen to see what I wrote-"

"On that five dollar bill?" Jeremy finished Monika's question for her. "It made absolutely no sense at the time but, yes, I saw it."

"It was a secret message," she said with a satisfied air about her.

"You meant it for me?"

"Of course," she replied. "It bodes well for you that you noticed."

For a while they sat together on the couch, exchanging the typical get-to-know-you information. She asked him where he was from, what he did at the Biotechnology Facility, what he planned to do when he got out, what kind of music he listened to, and so forth. For the most part, she deflected the conversation away from herself. In fact, about all Jeremy learned about his new friend was that she was 24 years old, painting was her life, and getting your belly button pierced *hurts like a mother*.

***

"I just want to check," Jeremy said.

"I don't think you'll find anything about it on the internet," insisted Monika.

As they waited for his computer to boot up, she said, "Let me," as she tugged the laptop from his lap to hers.

When the administrative password prompt appeared, she asked, "What's your password?"

"That would be classified information – here, let me..." Jeremy reached over to type it in himself.

Monika blocked his hand with hers. "No, I believe you're going to have to just trust me. What's your password?"

He said nothing, just looked at her with a dim expression.

"C'mon, give it up!" she exclaimed. "It's not like I'm getting into your bank account."

"It's *jinnigirl*," he finally said. "That's one word, lower case." He spelled it out for her.

"Jinnigirl?" she repeated tauntingly. "Who's Jinnigirl?"

"Just my password," Jeremy mumbled.

"Jinni wouldn't be your *girlfriend*, would she?"

"Something like that."

"I knew it," Monika boasted. "I saw you with her at the Singe show the other night. Where is she now?"

"She's out of town."

Monika zeroed in on his reluctance to discuss Jinni with her. It was obvious from her expression that she derived a great joy from the needling. "I suppose that explains why you came looking for me tonight."

Jeremy didn't quite know how to react. "I'd rather not discuss Jinni with you. I'm having enough trouble trying to assimilate tonight as it is."

She did not respond immediately but looked directly at him, sizing him up. He returned her gaze, hoping to get a glimpse into the inner workings of this strange and beautiful creature. What was it about her? What was that quality that so attracted him to her and at the same time intimidated him?

"Chill out Jeremy," she said finally. "If you don't want to tell me about your girlfriend, then don't. And don't worry. I'm not going to blow your cover."

"Thank you," Jeremy said, but his relief was short-lived.

"But we all must lie in the bed we make," she added with a devilish look in her eye.

He decided his best course of action was no reaction. She was just trying to get a rise out of him, and he simply would not give her the satisfaction.

Just as Monika predicted, the search engines returned no relevant links to any drug or chemical compound by the name of the Unreal.

"Wanna go for a ride?" she asked as she slid out from under the laptop.

It was the second time tonight Monika had posed the question. Jeremy had the distinct feeling much more than an innocent car ride was implied.

"Do I have a choice?" he asked, not meaning for her to answer.

As they were leaving, Jeremy's landline phone rang.

"The answering machine will get it," he said.

As Jeremy locked the deadbolt from the outside, the voice on the line pierced the door as if there were no door.

"Hey, it's me. Are you home?"

Sweet Jinni. The ice pick of guilt stabbed the heart of his conscience.

Jeremy turned away and followed Monika down the stairs and out into the night.

***

Jeremy drove his car, but he had no idea where they were going. In one fell swoop, all vestiges of control had been ripped from him by the stranger beside him who, at the moment, was digging in her purse. For a second Jeremy thought she was looking for another pill.

"I brought a CD you might be interested in hearing. Mind if I stick it in?" she asked.

"Who is it?"

"It's Singe, the band from last week."

Monika deftly adjusted the controls on his stereo – the equalizer, treble and base, the volume – like it was her own. It seemed she enjoyed her music loud, as did he.

Jeremy asked, "Do you just want to ride around, or is there somewhere in particular you wanted to go?"

Her response came as a pleasant surprise. "Do you know the way to Sticks River Road?"

Jeremy knew well the way, and as they sped down the seven-mile straight-away, he recalled the one who lived at the end of the straightaway. Grady had warned him not to go past the break in the road. The thought, however, was fleeting, as the contemplation of what he might be feeling consumed his mind.

"How long before we feel the effects?"

"It usually takes about an hour."

"It may be my imagination but I do feel a little strange, sort of on edge." After Jeremy reflected on the feeling, he added, "If this is all there is to it, I'll be disappointed."

"That's just the first sign. It won't be long now."

It wasn't long before they reached the break in the road where the straightaway became meandrous and the open fields evolved into dark forest. It was there that Jeremy's nervousness became something altogether different.

Something *wonderful.*

Like a pleasure supernova, a thousand million shooting stars of euphoria tingled up and down his spine. Jeremy saw the world with a pristine clarity, like for the first time. It was as if he had been dead and unaware of the dynamic universe that revealed itself, the veil of darkness suddenly ripped from a blind man's face. Inexpressible, just like Monika had said.

"This song!" he exclaimed through clenched teeth. "What is this song?"

"It's called *Requiem,*" she answered. "You like it?"

Burning virgin pathways in its wake, the song was bigger than life itself, a leviathan squatting on the counterweight of his soul, catapulting him to heretofore hidden and fantastic realms.

"You have no idea," he said.

"Oh, yes, I *do,*" she countered.

Monika. Jeremy felt as if she were the crucial piece missing from his life, smashing in her beauty and the essence of desire. In her, he saw what he felt; her eyes wild, her pupils black stones dilated with the high-octane excitement of the Unreal.

Monika said something but he could not hear for the music.

Jeremy reached to turn down the volume but Monika intercepted his hand with hers. She leaned over until her lips were almost touching his ear, close enough that he could feel her hot breath.

"It's just like heaven," she whispered and kissed him lightly on the neck.

They reached the end of the road after an indeterminable passage of time that could have been seconds or years, or any increment in between. With exuberance, Jeremy slid the car to a crunching stop in the gravel down by the edge of the lake. He unfolded himself from the driver's seat and stretched a marvelous stretch, arms toward heaven, every muscle clenched, back arched and relaxed with a spontaneous groan of satisfaction.

Overhead, a few billowy clouds hurried by, skimming the treetops. Above that stretched a thicker cloud sheet, solid but broken by a complex mosaic of breaks like cracks in dried mud. The cracks glowed with the light of the hidden moon. They strolled, hand in hand, down to the rickety pier. At the end of the pier they sat and dangled their feet over the edge. They laughed and talked. They flirted. They kissed.

The Unreal, as Jeremy was realizing, caused his mind to hop-scotch excitedly and uncontrollably from one subject to the next. At some point in the course of a rambling conversation – a three-way affair between himself, Monika, and his inner thoughts – he thought of Grady. Had he taken Grady's warning to heart, he would have missed this awesome experience. Thinking of Grady, in turn, reminded him of the ghost story.

"Have you ever heard of the hippie queen," he asked.

"Yes," Monika replied. "Hasn't everyone?"

Jeremy laughed. "It seems like it. Did you know that there really was a commune – and that it was in these very woods?"

"No, not really," she replied. "I thought it was just a made-up story."

"That's what I thought too, at first. But, as it turns out, the hippie queen was a real person. Her name was Claire Wales. She died, along with six of her hippie friends when their commune burned."

"How do you know all this?" asked Monika.

"I found most of it online."

"Funny that you were interested enough to look it up."

"Funny?" he asked. "Why?"

A flash of lightning, far away and benign, lit in the western sky.

"I don't know," she replied. "It just is."

Regardless of the course of their conversation, their attention invariably returned to the here and now. As they reveled in the beauty of the moment and the beauty of the world wrapped around them, the low-lying cloud curtain withdrew to reveal the upper reaches of the firmament. The moon, three-quarter's full, came into view, and with it, a massive and brilliantly-lit mackerel sky. A swath of sparkles stretched over the lake, one tiny reflected moon for each of a million water ripples. Jeremy perceived the world in all its infinite detail and shivered with exquisite delight, one tiny pleasure-laden tingle for each of a million chill bumps.

"Now do you know what it is to burn?" Monika asked.

"I do," he said to her. To the world Jeremy yelled, "Burn, baby, burn!"

On cue the distant sky responded with a double jab of a lightning bolt, low on the horizon, Halloween-orange, its spindly tendrils grasping at the malignant heart of the sky. An utterance of distant thunder of deep booming bass reverberated towards them from across the lake.

Together they watched with utter awe as the storm approached, marching steadily forward to the rhythmless cadence and gradual crescendo of growling, rumbling and, finally, crashing thunder. The two lingered until a bolt struck so close that they heard the electric *crackle*. The concurrent detonation, loud enough to wake the dead, sent them scurrying to the car. Sparse, fat drops pelted the windshield as they sped away, racing the clouds home.

Back at his condominium, Monika cut directly through his bedroom and opened the French doors that led out onto the fourth-floor balcony. Jeremy turned the corner into his bedroom and was met by a hot blustery wind and the sight of Monika. She was leaning against the rail with her back to Jeremy, the elegant lines of her body a sensual silhouette against the backdrop of the cream-colored sky.

"It's *breathtaking* out here. You can see the whole town!" she cried. "I love this."

He joined her at the balcony rail. For a good long while, Jeremy said nothing, speechless with infatuation, joy, desire and several other brand new sensations.

Suddenly Monika turned concernedly to him. "Do you smell something burning?" she asked in all seriousness.

The alarming thought that first came to Jeremy was that one of the condos below might be on fire.

He sniffed the air. "I don't smell anything. Are you sure?" he asked, before he caught Monika hiding a smile.

"I get it," Jeremy said. "We're the ones who are burning, right?"

"Wanna burn a little brighter?" she asked, catching him off guard.

"Huh?" Dosing again had not crossed Jeremy's mind, though his answer seemed somehow predetermined. "Okay."

"Wait here," she instructed.

Monika left him sitting alone at the wrought-iron table on the balcony. As Jeremy waited, the wind picked up and the chimes that hung from the overhead eave came to life, reminding him of the approaching storm.

***

"More," Monika implored.

"Didn't we just take more?" he asked.

"Aren't you up for it?" she asked deviously.

Jeremy checked his watch – three a.m. Almost three hours had passed since they arrived back at the condo. He could scarcely grasp where the time had gone. The rush of the Unreal had rendered time irrelevant. While he considered Monika's proposal, he bore witness to her magnificent repertoire of rationalizations.

"Each night is a lifetime unto itself and to give in to sleep is to die," she said. "Are you ready to die?"

Jeremy had to strain to focus his thoughts. Even here, in the grand fields of euphoria where his mind soared, there was a fine wooden box wherein his common sense lay. The lid cracked open ever so slightly, and Jeremy knew that another hit tonight was probably not wise. This would be his third, if he said yes. Besides, how could he possibly feel any better than he did right now?

Just say no.

Yet neither did he want the feeling to end.

Never say die.

He settled the issue with a compromise. Capsule in hand, Jeremy scuttled into the bathroom. He closed and locked the door behind him and as carefully as he could, he pulled apart the capsule. One half he wrapped in a gum wrapper and stuck in the back of the bathroom drawer. The other half and its measure of lavender powder, he washed down with a slurp of water straight from the lavatory faucet.

"It sure is quiet in there," accused Monika from the other side of the door. She jiggled the door knob. "What are you doing?"

"What do you think?" Jeremy flushed the toilet and, for good measure, washed his hands before opening the door to her probing gaze.

"Did you take it yet?" she asked.

"I did," he replied. "What do you want to do now?"

"Whatever you want."

If their night together had ended at that moment, it would still have been the most memorable night of Jeremy's life, but there was more to come.

Monika, unlike Jinni, slept over.

In the morning, Jeremy awoke alone with an unsettling emptiness. He did not remember falling asleep. He had not heard Monika leave and for a panicky moment considered the notion that last night had been a dream. He crawled from his bed to find that she had left a note on the bedside table, corroboration that she was real. The note read:

Jeremy-
Had a wonderful time last night
Hope to see you again soon
Love, Monika
p.s. Enjoy the cd

Underneath the note was a clear plastic case. Inside was a compact disc. Hand-written on the disc with a black permanent marker were the stacked words,

Singe
Requiem

She had left behind a copy of the mind-bending music from last night.

Jeremy hoped to see Monika soon, too, except *hope* wasn't the right word – he *had* to see her again. Unfortunately, she never got around to giving him her telephone number. Worse, she never even revealed her last name, at least not that he could remember. Recalling the night in its entirety was like recalling a year's worth of days: the memories were all in his head but not necessarily immediately accessible. Various tidbits of the night occurred to Jeremy over the course of the day – and days that followed. But he was sure that she never mentioned her last name, and he felt certain that had been purposeful on her part. In fact, the girl responsible for what was the most memorable night of his life had managed to deflect or answer obliquely every personal question presented to her. And now, like the euphoria of the Unreal, she was gone.

CHAPTER *16*

Sunday, November 9

Flames, like hot dragon tongues, licked at his body and his naked flesh blistered and peeled in the hellish heat. In the distance Jinni frantically motioned, urging him toward her, toward salvation, but his paralyzed muscles refused to cooperate. A shrill fire alarm rang relentlessly.

WITH a start, Jeremy awoke. For one confused moment he didn't know if it were dusk or dawn, or even if he had passed out of this world into the next. As the cold waters of reality rushed in, he realized the ringing was not a fire alarm but the telephone. The late afternoon light was waning and he had been in a sleep fit for the dead.

"Hello?"

"Did I wake you?" a meek voice asked.

It was Jinni.

"I was just dreaming about you," he replied groggily. "How was your trip?"

She went on to tell him all about the ceremony in excruciating detail and exuberance. He wondered if Jinni had plans for her own wedding and if he were part of those plans.

"Where were you last night, Jeremy? I left a message on your recorder."

Jeremy hadn't checked his machine.

"I guess I was at the library," he lied. "My exam is Wednesday, you know." Jeremy failed to mention how, after the weekend activities, he had decided to skip the test.

"I thought we might have dinner tonight. Want to?" she asked hopefully.

"I would, but I really need to study." Jeremy felt too drained to accept.

"Yeah, alright," she said, disappointed. "I missed you."

"I missed you too, Jinni."

Jeremy did miss her and he hated lying. And, in spite of the mind-blowing events of the night before, he still loved Jinni. Besides, he had no idea if he would ever see Monika again.

"Call me tomorrow?" Jinni asked.

"I will," he promised and hung up the phone.

CHAPTER *17*

Monday, November 10

*J*EREMY could scarcely listen during Monday's lecture, not that it would
have done much good anyhow. Comprehension of the current subject matter
hinged on having a solid understanding of the prior material and that ship had
long ago sailed. At least Jeremy knew he was not alone as his friend Tavalin occupied the adjacent seat on that same clueless dock.

Instead, Jeremy spent the hour daydreaming about Saturday night, the time
of his life, and of Monika, the new infatuation of his life. That she left without
leaving a clue as to where she could be found or even who she was only intensified his desire to track her down.

Jeremy parted ways with Tavalin and rode the elevator directly to the fifth
floor. June and two other members of Dr. Cain's inner-circle research assistants
were working in the lab when Jeremy entered. On Jeremy's approach, June
motioned him to follow her into the adjoining incubator room where they could
talk privately.

"The initial results checked out," she said excitedly. "Your mitochondrial
DNA is bigger than everybody else's, by a factor of four."

Jeremy had not expected this. June had all but assured him that the initial
assay that showed the same result must be flawed in some way.

"What could cause such a thing?" he asked.

"I don't know."

"Is the next step to determine the sequence?" asked Jeremy.

"It's already done," June announced proudly. "I ran it though the sequencer
overnight. As you know, normal human mitochondrial DNA consists of 16,569
nucleotide pairs that encode for 37 genes. Your mitochondrial DNA consists of
66,776 nucleotide pairs. There is nothing remotely similar to anything like this
in the literature."

Jeremy's head spun as he tried to assimilate the meaning behind the results.
"And you are sure about all this?" he asked.

"To be completely sure we would have to repeat the entire process from start
to finish, but I feel pretty confident what we've got is accurate."

Jeremy put great faith in June and her abilities. If she said the results were correct, he knew he could believe it.

"What's the next step?" he asked.

"Next, we determine if there are any functioning genes within all this extra genetic material."

"What else could it be, if not genes?"

"It could be that you simply have extra copies of the same genes, that some kind of gene duplication took place. Or, the extra part might consist of nonsense DNA that doesn't code for anything. In either of those cases, the functionality of your mitochondria would be the same as everyone else's. Having extra, non-functional DNA is notable as it has never been documented before, but it would be truly remarkable if you have extra, unique genes that add to or somehow change the function of your mitochondria."

He asked, "If I do have unique genes in there, could that explain my increased physical abilities?"

"As you know," June replied, "we started all this with the idea that you are getting extra energy output from somewhere. If these postulated unique genes somehow increase the energy output of your mitochondria, supercharging them so-to-speak, then we would have the answer to your question and the answer would be yes."

After the triathlon and his VO2 max endurance results, Jeremy knew there was something there, something worth researching. However, he would never have dreamed that they would make such progress after only a few short weeks.

"I don't know what I would do without you," gushed Jeremy. "There's no way I could have done any of this alone. Thank you, June, for everything."

June stood close enough that he was able to easily reach his arm around her back to her opposite shoulder and give her a good squeeze. It wasn't a full-fledged hug but at least it expressed a measure of his gratitude and affection.

"You are welcome, Jeremy. I am very excited with the results, but…" Her voice trailed off.

"But what?" asked Jeremy uneasily.

"I think it's time we confess to Dr. Cain."

Jeremy hadn't seen this coming. "I was hoping we could keep it a secret, June. Why now?"

"I don't know," she stammered, clearly uncomfortable. "What we are doing is dishonest and I'm afraid that we are going to get caught."

"All I really want to do is finish this first phase," Jeremy said, pleading his case. "If we find that my mitochondria are, as you say, supercharged due to this extra genetic material, we would have our breakthrough. Having those findings in hand would give us a lot of leverage, regardless of what we decide to do with them."

"And then we tell Dr. Cain?" she asked.

"If we were to go to Dr. Cain with findings as impressive as those, I think he would overlook the fact that we conducted the unauthorized research using his facilities."

In actuality, Jeremy could see no benefit in confessing to Dr. Cain, neither now nor later, but he needed to quell June's concerns. If this turned out to be a significant discovery, Jeremy would have to work out a plan whereby he and June would receive the lion's share of the credit, as it should be.

"I don't know, Jeremy. I've got a bad feeling about all this."

"If you can just hang in there a little longer," pleaded Jeremy, "the end is in sight."

Jeremy convinced June to go along with his plan but by the time he did he also had a bad feeling – not only for corrupting June but also concerning the bottom-line question they had yet to satisfactorily address:

What changed my mitochondria in the first place and, besides the obvious effect of increased endurance, what are the full ramifications of that change?

CHAPTER 18

Thursday, November 20

*I*T was night and Jeremy found himself, once again, on Sticks River Road. Except for the accompanying music of Singe, Monika's gift to him, he was alone in his car.

Almost two weeks had elapsed since Monika left the compact disc, along with the farewell note on his bedside table. During that time, he had become intimately familiar with the songs included on the *Requiem* compilation. Online, Jeremy could find absolutely no information related to Singe or their album except for some brief mentions in obscure blogs. Every post he read originated from someone present at the Halloween show and every blogger wanted to know where they might find a sample of the band's music. Apparently, Singe's only public performance was the one Jeremy witnessed, and the band had not yet officially released any tracks. Jeremy had no idea how Monika came to possess a copy of the album. Jeremy felt privileged, considering the rarity of the recording which now blasted authoritatively from his car stereo speakers.

Requiem was a concept album. Even though the compact disc was sectioned into tracks like any other, each song transitioned smoothly into the next with no fade-to-silence breaks in between. A reoccurring melody tied the whole of the album together. In the earlier songs, it was hidden in the underlying layers beneath the main thrust of the music or deftly obscured as an alternative version of the same melody. As the album progressed, the melody became more and more manifest until, finally, during the title-track, it burst forth unadulterated from the hidden depths at full bore.

On the night of his date with Monika, this, the most climatic song of the album, rolled around at the precise moment that the Unreal imparted that first sledge-hammer whack of exultation. Now, every time Jeremy heard that song, he thought of that night and the intrigue of that moment at the break in the road; that big-bang instant when the universe of his experience and pleasure exploded. From that moment on, he had become obsessed with the trifecta of Monika, the Unreal, and the music of Singe.

Desiring to capture every nuance of the music, Jeremy bought expensive, studio-quality headphones for listening at home. He burned multiple copies of the compact disc so as to have it as his companion wherever he might be. He ripped it to his portable digital music player so he could listen while running and while riding his bike or motorcycle. Absent Monika and the Unreal, the music of Singe became the next best thing.

From his perch atop the pier at Sticks River Landing, Jeremy stared out over the still waters of the lake. He had to think for a moment to recall that today was Thursday. Saturday night would mark two weeks since his date with Monika, and he still had not heard from her. Despite the guilt he felt for deceiving Jinni, he knew he would not hesitate to run with Monika again if she resurfaced. Sitting here, in the spot they shared, Jeremy yearned to recapture the feelings of that night, but to no avail. Restless in his frustration, he clambered to his feet and wandered aimlessly past his car, toward the back of the parking lot and the picnic tables nestled at the edge of the woods.

Without warning, a melodic chant floated in on the chilly lake breeze.

Jeremy froze.

A strange harmony of voices drifted in and out like the reception of a radio station on the edge of its range. At first it seemed the unsettling sound originated from a long way off, but then Jeremy, his fear brimming, thought that maybe its source was much closer, perhaps just ahead in the edge of the woods. All at once he sensed a presence. Was someone there, concealed in the darkness, watching him? Chills of fear prickled his spine and called every follicle to attention.

Fighting hard to suppress the urge to run, he turned and with the longest of strides hustled back toward the car. Though afraid that somebody or some *thing* might be following – for some reason he thought of Grady's devil dogs – he did not look back but focused on the goal of reaching his car.

Safe inside his car at last, Jeremy locked the doors and fishtailed off, tires spitting gravel. More than once he checked the rearview mirror to make certain no one was following. About halfway back to town his curiosity waxed and his fright waned to the point that he considered turning around. At the very least he might ride back to the lakeside and listen for the noise and scan the area using his headlights. All this could be accomplished from the safety of his car.

Then again, maybe he should just forget about it. He recalled an adage he had heard somewhere – something about stupidity masquerading as bravery. He could not help but remember Grady's vague warning of danger in Reefers Woods as well as the substantiated violent deaths – those of the hippies at their commune and the suicide that reportedly occurred in the very parking lot just vacated. There was also the case of the biologist who ventured into Reefers Woods, never to return.

At the stop sign where Sticks River Road intersected the highway, Jeremy turned right, away from home. Three turns and a couple of minutes later he wheeled past the sign for the Rose Hill Apartments. As he parked at his friend's apartment, it occurred to him that despite the name, it wasn't that hilly out here and no roses graced the landscape.

Jeremy rushed down the steps and knocked loudly, even as he opened the unlocked door of the basement apartment. "It's me," he called out. "I'm coming in."

"Yes? Oh yes, please, why don't you just barge right in," Tavalin said sarcastically. "What's gotten into you?"

"The weirdest thing just happened."

Jeremy recounted his experience at the lake.

"Satanic chants, huh?" reiterated Tavalin skeptically.

"I'm not quite sure what it was, but at the time that's what went through my head. I think we ought to check it out."

"Right now?" Tavalin asked incredulously. "I don't know, Jeremy. You know we've got class at eight o'clock in the morning."

"I know," replied Jeremy, "but it's not like you're studying anyway. How many times in your life will you get the opportunity to investigate satanic chants in the middle of the woods?"

"Any sane person would hope never to get such an opportunity." Tavalin mimed quotation marks with his fingers.

"Whoever said you were sane?"

Realizing that further argument would be futile, Tavalin sat up and pulled on his shoes.

In Jeremy's car, Tavalin continued with his token protest. "Seriously, do we have to do this?"

"I just want to see if we hear anything."

Tavalin groaned, and muttered some mostly unintelligible words, though the last few Jeremy deciphered as, "…one of your wild goose chases."

"What?" asked Jeremy with a grin.

"Never mind." Facetiously, Tavalin added, "Just get me back home in time for class in the morning, okay?"

***

When they arrived at Sticks River Landing, Jeremy swept his headlights slowly across the woods behind the parking lot. Unless one counted the pasty-white possum that gave them the evil eye before scurrying off into the underbrush, they saw nothing related to the devil or the worship thereof. Jeremy lowered his window and listened. All he heard were the typical night sounds. Tavalin chose to keep his window closed and, Jeremy noticed, his door locked.

"You know," Jeremy said a little sheepishly, "I suppose it could have been the wind whistling in the rocks."

"Or coyotes," Tavalin suggested. "Now that that's settled, can we go home?"

"Yeah, I guess so. If someone were here, they're gone now. So much for this little adventure," said Jeremy as they topped the hill and left the lake behind.

"I might get some sleep after all." Tavalin reclined his seat an extra notch and got comfortable for the ride back to town.

However, Jeremy wasn't ready to give up so easily. Without warning, he veered left onto one of the several narrow, dirt tributaries that branched off the main road. The unexpected maneuver slung Tavalin sideways against the passenger-side window.

"What are you doing?" exclaimed Tavalin. "I thought we were going home."

"Maybe what I heard originated from a point farther away then I first thought, maybe somewhere out this way."

Tavalin winced as a limb scratch-squealed up the side of the car.

"Man, you are scratching the hell out of your car. We better back out of here," he said.

"Just roll down your window and break it off."

Tavalin did as instructed and was in the process of rolling the window back up when Jeremy thought he heard something.

"Did you hear that?" asked Jeremy.

"I didn't hear anything." Tavalin replied indifferently.

Jeremy cut the engine and lowered his window.

The chirping legs of a thousand crickets greeted his ears, their grating racket magnified by the absolute darkness. Jeremy held his breath and listened. In the blackness he became aware not only of the steady drumming of his heart but also of his trepidation.

At last a *whoop* seeped in from outside, still far off but definitely human.

"There!" Jeremy exclaimed. "You heard that, right?"

"It's just a coyote, Jeremy," Tavalin insisted. "Your imagination is getting the best of you."

"I did not imagine it. Somebody's out there."

"So what if they are? Could be somebody out on a date," remarked Tavalin, who seemed bound and determined to quash Jeremy's interest. "This would serve perfectly as a lover's lane."

"Let's check it out," Jeremy said as he cranked the engine. They pushed deeper into the woods until Jeremy thought he saw a shimmering something amongst the trees. A little closer in, the red glow revealed itself as light reflected from a pair of taillights.

"Alright, just like I said, somebody's parking," said Tavalin, his voice a pitch higher than usual. "We can leave now."

"Just a little closer." Jeremy eased the car forward.

"Come on, Jeremy," grumbled Tavalin. "Let's get out of here."

Tavalin was starting to stress out, and Jeremy was about to give in except that there was something familiar about that car.

Jeremy inched closer.

"Do you see any heads?" Jeremy asked.

At the end of the road, a half-dozen cars were parked, bumper to bumper, all apparently empty, their occupants who-knows-where.

And then a startling recognition: The car last in line was a black convertible – a *Mustang*. Though it was dark and all they could really see was the car's rear end, Jeremy would have bet money the model was 1969, the same as Monika's vintage Mustang.

"Don't you think we should go home now?" pleaded Tavalin.

There was only one place to turn around but that space too was occupied by one of the mysteriously placed cars. Jeremy was forced to back his car over the considerable distance until they reached the pavement that was Sticks River Road. He swung the car around and headed back toward the lake – away from town.

"Now what?" Tavalin whined.

"Don't be a girly man, Tavalin. It's not time for class yet. I believe you said *as long as I got you back in time for class.* I want to see what those people are doing way out here at two in the morning. If you're not up for a little recognizance mission, you could always wait for me in the car..."

"I should never have agreed to come," muttered Tavalin. "When will I ever learn?"

***

"Now it's an adventure," Jeremy said as they negotiated the slick logs, underbrush and stinking mud that lined the lake shore, their only illumination provided by the crescent moon, pasted like a smile on the backdrop of the starry sky.

"These mosquitoes are tearing me up," Tavalin whispered.

"If I were you, I'd be more worried about snakes."

Tavalin chuckled and replied, "That's why I let you lead. I figure if anybody gets bitten, it'll be you."

"And don't forget about the alligators," added Jeremy, not to be outdone.

"There're no alligators out here." Tavalin spoke self-assuredly, but when Jeremy didn't answer, he asked, "Could there be?"

"You never know."

Jeremy didn't know why he enjoyed antagonizing his friend so much, but he did.

After thirty miserable minutes of tedious progress the noise in the woods was now plainly identifiable as music intermixed with voices. It sounded like a party.

Jeremy still had not told Tavalin the primary reason they were here, why he had been so dogged determined to struggle through the forest at night. Yes, he had initially been curious to identify the noise in the woods, but his new motivation was Monika, his little angel with the raven hair. That was her car and he had to see what she was up to.

Finally they emerged from the muddy hell to an outcropping of land beyond which a narrow ribbon of sand tied the water to the forest's edge. On the far side of the secluded beach, about a quarter mile in the distance, a large bonfire burned. They had found the revelers.

"Would you take a look at that!" Tavalin exclaimed. "That's wicked!"

A group of perhaps ten silhouettes danced energetically around a huge bonfire, their movements in perfect synchronization with each other but a half-count out of time with the music because of the distance from which Jeremy and Tavalin observed.

"They're having a party, mystery solved. Can we go now? I'm freezing." Tavalin turned his back as if he were about to hike back to the car.

"Hold up, Tavalin. After all that I'm not going to just turn around and leave. I want to see what they're up to."

"Why?" asked Tavalin obstinately.

"Let's just sit down and rest for a minute."

"I don't know who died and made you boss," muttered Tavalin.

After a few minutes, Jeremy said, "You know, it looks like some kind of primitive mating ritual, like something you might see on the Discovery channel, wild pygmies in the jungle or something."

"Not exactly a meeting of the Sticks River Chapter of the Satanic Devil-worshipers, is it?" Tavalin asked, not a little smugly.

"All I said was it sounded *a little like* satanic chants, but I guess it was just a weird effect of the wind and the music," Jeremy replied, and then added in jest, "although, maybe they used up all their favorite devil-chanting CDs at the beginning of the party."

The water reflected just enough starlight for Jeremy to see Tavalin roll his eyes into the white.

Jeremy still wanted to verify if Monika were here or not but there was no way to recognize anyone from this distance. "Why don't we sneak in a little closer, get a better look," he suggested.

"I don't know if that's such a good idea, Jeremy. What if they see us?"

"We'll just have to be careful that they don't."

They crept deliberately along the interface of the woods and the narrow beach, hugging the bushes. After ten minutes of stealthy approach they had closed to within fifty yards of the blaze, almost within its outermost circle of light, close enough to positively identify Monika if she were here and too close to suit Tavalin.

"All right already," urged Tavalin. "This is close enough."

They crouched behind the trunk of an ancient cedar tree, mesmerized by the unique and unusual circumstances of the night: the rhythmic oscillations of young bodies with the music; the complex patterns of shadow and moonlight on the luminescent sand of a secret beach; the black void of the lapping bay on one side and the rustling forest on the other; and the flames, a tiger that lunged time and time again toward unreachable prey, the pale-white crescent moon.

One of the young bodies, Jeremy recognized. Monika was here, just as he knew she would be. "I'm going to move in a little bit closer," he said.

"What?" asked Tavalin, and in his wide-open eyes, fear and the fire's reflection danced together. "Are you out of your mind?"

Jeremy ignored his friend and crawled, belly down, like a Marine in the sand. Twenty yards later, he stopped at a low row of prickly plants, so close to the fire that he imagined he could feel its faint heat.

Fascinated, Jeremy watched Monika's every move. She moved with uninhibited passion and grace and, despite the proximity of the others, she danced alone. Or, more aptly, her partners were the fire, the lake and the late-rising moon. She danced with the world.

The music ceased suddenly as did the writhing-dancing. Though his position in the shadows had not changed, Jeremy felt exposed. Without their previous preoccupation with the music and the dancing, they might be more likely to roam. What if one of the revelers needed to relieve him- or herself? The low bushes that concealed Jeremy might make for a convenient bathroom. He knew well enough that people who party in the woods pee in the woods. The extension of that thought ushered in a new concern: What if somebody had already tinkled over here? What if he were lying in it right now? As unpleasant as that might be he reminded himself that there were worse things than crawling in urine – like getting caught, for instance.

Just as he feared, the group mulled about, some drifting toward the lake side of the bonfire while others scuttled away toward the woods. The latter individuals reappeared after a few minutes of privacy, presumptively with relaxed bladders. Jeremy wondered if the party might be over.

After a few minutes the group began to coalesce nearer the bonfire. They talked to each other in voices too low for Jeremy to comprehend, but he interpreted the tone as one of hushed anticipation. When Monika reappeared, the others in the group settled into a semicircle facing the bonfire. Their conversations died and all became silent, save the crackling of the fire, the steady drone of the night insects, and the *swish, swish* sound of the miniature waves breaking on the sand.

Monika stood before them and began to talk.

"First of all," she said, "I want to remind you that nothing we do or say can be spoken of to anyone outside our group. Remember your vow of secrecy."

She paused, letting her admonition sink in.

"Now, a question: If you could become more than you are, more than you ever dreamed you could be, would you? Do you want to truly live? If you do, I can show you the way. Now is the quickening, the time of preparation during which we must band together for this common cause. We must not be afraid to dream or to dare to believe in the supernatural."

Monika spoke fervently – like a revival tent preacher – emphasizing, pausing, stretching out words and phrases in all the right places with a delivery as smooth as homemade ice cream. Captivated by her charisma, Jeremy wanted to believe in her and what she said even though he had no earthly idea of what she spoke.

"Something big is coming down, something awe-inspiring, something you all will be ecstatic to be a part of."

"I'm feeling pretty damn ecstatic right now!" cried one of her subjects. "Right here, right now!" The assembly clapped and whooped it up in hearty agreement.

Jeremy wondered if any of those ecstatic feelings sprang from the effects of Monika's drug of choice, the Unreal.

"But what is it?" an impetuous female voice asked. "Please, *please* tell us!"

"I can't say," answered Monika. "Now is not the time. Have faith that what I say is real and true and be patient in the knowledge that it is coming soon. Those of you who prove your loyalty to me and to the group will be rewarded beyond your wildest dreams."

So powerful was the intrigue of Monika and her words that Jeremy had to fight back the urge to rise up and run to her. He wanted to show her that *he* could be the loyal one to stand by her side. Despite the peril and despite what he risked losing, he desperately wished to join Monika and her circle of friends.

More than anything else, he wanted her.

It was then that Jeremy glimpsed movement on the forest side – the darker side – of the bonfire. He strained to make out several – five or more –shadowy figures creeping out of the forest toward the bonfire. Monika and her crew, positioned as they were on the lake side of the fire were ignorant of their approach. What if it were a pack of wild dogs or wolves or …? For the second time tonight Jeremy thought of Grady's devil dogs, and the notion raised to full staff the flag of his fright. He could not know if Monika and her friends were in danger, but he could not simply sit back and allow them to be ambushed.

But what could he do? Run screaming and waving his arms at the creatures, hoping to scare them away? If these were aggressive animals, that action might only provoke them. Or maybe he could yell out a warning, something like, *Watch out everyone, here come the devil dogs!* Jeremy imagined that any such warning that included the *devil dogs* moniker would only confuse and distract, not assist.

Helpless in his indecision, Jeremy watched as the shadowy figures moved into the outermost ring of light. When the moment of recognition arrived, Jeremy could not believe his eyes. It could not be, but yet, there they were: young children, barefooted and dressed for summer, despite the chilly November wind.

Without a word or pause, they filtered into the midst of Monika and her gang.

Stranger still, not one in Monika's group acknowledged the children in any way. It was as if Monika had so hypnotized her followers that they were oblivious to every other thing. Neither did Monika plainly respond, though Jeremy thought he heard a hiccup in her spiel when the children first burst on the scene. Of that, however, he could not be sure. She continued to speak while the others continued to listen. No one seemed able to even perceive the children who sat and stood silently among the members of Monika's group.

Just when Jeremy thought the strange procession settled, an additional visitor walked into the light to stand with Monika. Unlike the preceding children, this person was old – a woman with wispy gray hair and tattered clothing – but, as was the case with the other late-comers to the party, no one, save Jeremy, took notice.

Jeremy tuned in again to Monika's words but maintained his close scrutiny of the uninvited guests.

"Where I am going," she was saying, "where I want to take you is just like heaven. Once I locate the Source, we can all learn an alternative way – *Claire's Alternative Way.* All you have to do is trust me and believe."

Wrapped up as he was in the unfolding scene before him, Jeremy had all but forgotten about Tavalin, who had remained behind at the old cedar tree. With a *CRACK!* as loud and sharp as a rifle retort, he remembered. Every face snapped around, their features distorted in the shadows cast by the bonfire.

Jeremy clung to a meager hope that they still might not be found out. He put forth arguments, not only for his own peace of mind but also for Tavalin's.

They can't see us. It might have been anything, a deer, a beaver, a falling limb. Just sit tight, my friend, and, whatever you do, don't panic.

Tavalin panicked. Off he ran at full gallop down the beach the way they had come.

Someone from the bonfire congregation stood and yelled, "Hey you! Stop!"

There was nothing for Jeremy to do but divulge himself and follow. He sprang from his hiding place, trying as best he could to keep his face diverted from the fire's glare and the prying eyes. The last thing he wanted was for Monika to recognize him.

He and Tavalin sprinted down the beach in record time, the panic-induced adrenaline shot as effective as any synthetic, performance-enhancing drug. At the point where the sliver of beach merged into the woods, Jeremy paused and stole a look back. Three or four of Monika's minions were standing, hands on hips, halfway down the beach, apparently having given only token chase. Tavalin neither paused nor spoke, but continued his pell-mell flight, crashing noisily into the thick underbrush.

As Jeremy followed his friend into the thicket, a thousand questions cascaded through his mind. *Why clandestine meetings in the middle of the woods in the middle of the night? What were these things Monika spoke of: the quickening, the supernatural, big things coming down? What is Claire's Alternative Way? What was this thing she was looking for, this so-called Source?*

And what to make of the children he saw?

The answers quivered forebodingly, like agitated wasps ready to drop from their nest to deliver their stinging revelations.

At some point Jeremy was able to catch up with his spooked friend and persuade him to slow down. The greater danger came not from those they had left behind at the beach but rather from a collision with an unseen tree or a tumble into a hidden gully.

When Tavalin finally spoke, he delivered what might have been the understatement of the year. "Well, that was interesting," he said.

Jeremy laughed. "You could say that."

"Could you hear what that girl was saying?" asked Tavalin.

"Just a little," replied Jeremy. "What I did hear didn't make much sense."

Jeremy waited to see if Tavalin would mention the weirdest part of the whole experience – the barefooted children and the old woman that everyone else ignored.

When Tavalin didn't right away say, Jeremy asked, "What could you see?"

"I saw the same thing you did," Tavalin replied, "people having a party on the beach."

"How many would you say there were?" asked Jeremy, still beating around the bush.

"I don't know, ten or twelve."

"And you didn't see anybody or anything else come up?" asked Jeremy.

"No," replied Tavalin. "Did you?"

"I thought I heard something in the bushes, that's all."

With less mud and fewer mosquitoes, the inland route was slightly less unpleasant than had been the shoreline approach, but the forest offered no landmarks to guide them back to the car. When they emerged onto Sticks River Road, they found themselves to be a good half-mile from where Jeremy's car was parked but were, nonetheless, relieved that they were finally out of the woods.

Jeremy felt exposed in the openness of the roadway and more than a little worried that Monika's mob might come looking for the two party-crashers. Certainly they would have a good idea where to look since there was only one way in or out – Sticks River Road. Repeatedly, Jeremy turned to check for any vehicles that might be approaching from behind, imagining he heard the soft purr of a car engine or glimpsed the flash of approaching headlights. Despite his paranoia, not a soul passed their way and, in due time, they arrived back at Sticks River Landing.

They surveyed their bodily damage under the interior dome light of Jeremy's car. Mud, sweat, scratches, and ripped clothing were standard issue. Pimply splotches dotted Tavalin's face due to a mild allergic reaction to several mosquito bites. Jeremy couldn't help but laugh.

"You know," Tavalin began, "I was perfectly content back at my apartment – comfortable, clean and safe." Tavalin strained to remain straight-faced in spite of his gripes. "Now look at me: I'm muddy, bloody, tired, I itch all over, my clothes are torn, my head hurts and there's grit in my mouth. *And,* I'm still expecting some half-crazed, techno-music maniac to jump out of the woods and kill us both. So please tell me, Jeremy, why? Why me? Is your sole purpose in life to make my life miserable?"

"Come on, Tavalin. I just gave you an adventure you will never forget. We'll be a hundred years old and still talking about tonight."

"At this rate, we might not live to see graduation. Now, for the last time, will you *please* take me home?"

Tavalin did manage to extract a measure of revenge via the mud smudged on the passenger side seat, floorboard, door, dash, windshield, and sunroof and on the knobs of Jeremy's expensive stereo receiver.

The last thing Jeremy did before retiring for the night was look up an unfamiliar word Monika had used. There was no listing in an online dictionary for the word *quickening*, but the third definition listed for *quicken* seemed to fit: *to begin a period of development; come to life.*

CHAPTER *19*

Friday, November 21

NOT surprisingly, Tavalin did not make it to their eight a.m. organic chemistry class. Jeremy attended, although he had only managed three hours of sleep and was exhausted. As the professor droned on, Jeremy slouched in his chair, using the wall behind his back-row seat as a head rest. He fought mightily to hold open his eyelids over the duration of the lecture and certainly would have lost that battle except for thinking about the excursion of a few hours ago.

Jeremy was not altogether surprised to find that, more than ever, he wanted to see Monika again. Though her spiel had certainly been strange and largely indecipherable, she mentioned nothing of a negative connotation. Like the others at the bonfire, he wanted to know what it was Monika spoke of. What great event was on the horizon?

Even more intriguing, if he heard correctly, was Monika's reference to *Claire's Alternative Way*. Several questions sprang to mind: *Is this Claire the Claire Wales of hippie queen fame? If so, what is Monika's connection to Claire and to this great thing coming? What of the coincidence of Monika's and my own common interest in the hippie queen?*

Jeremy knew Grady's likely answer to the last question: *There are no coincidences.*

The only part of the experience that truly troubled Jeremy was the children and the old woman. The simple fact of the matter was that they did not belong at a bonfire on a secret beach in the middle of the night in the middle of the woods. Neither the party-goers nor Tavalin seemed to notice them. They uttered not a peep and no one spoke to them.

As Jeremy daydreamed the hour away, he tried – but could not – make sense of the things he thought he saw. *Were they not real? Was it just my imagination? Was it an hallucination? If so, where would it all stop? How will I ever again discern what is real and what is not?*

***

After class Jeremy rode the elevator to the fifth floor to speak to June.

"What happened to your face?" June asked, first thing.

Jeremy's trek of the night before had left a set of parallel scratches, like claw marks, across his left cheek. A small raisin-like bruise decorated Jeremy's forehead, front and center.

"I tried to tackle a bush with my face."

June looked questionable at Jeremy but he returned only a smile.

When she realized he wasn't going to explain further, she said, "I ran that sample of yours last night."

"Oh, that's great," replied Jeremy, happier than he let on. "Thanks."

"Is this work you also want to keep a secret?" she asked.

"It would be better if no one knew of it, yes."

Jeremy had worked all week analyzing the Unreal he saved from Saturday night. He was purposely vague when he gave June the vial of lavender powder and asked her if she would analyze it on the NMR (nuclear magnetic resonance) spectrometer downstairs. He hoped that with these additional results, he would be able to determine the chemical structure of the Unreal.

"So many secrets," June commented as she handed him the readout.

"Thanks, June. I owe you one."

Jeremy thought that he actually owed June much more than one. Though he would not have wanted to involve June in the analysis of any illegal substance, he hadn't seen any way around it. He needed the NMR data to nail down the structure of the Unreal. Of course, until he had the structure, he would not know if it were illegal or not.

Jeremy immediately went about the task of putting together all the information he now had. In an hour, he had what he was fairly sure to be the exact chemical structure of the Unreal, which he sketched out on the back side of June's NMR printout.

The next step was to try and match it up with a known compound. He searched the huge databases of known chemical structures. Though he could not find an exact match for the elucidated structure of the Unreal, the closest matches were for a group of natural compounds found in the blooms of certain water lilies. That fact, however, did not necessarily mean that the Unreal was derived from any natural source. For all Jeremy knew, Monika's drug was a product of the imagination and expertise of some chemist toiling in some clandestine lab to synthetically produce the drug Jeremy knew as the Unreal. All he knew for sure was that, for all practical purposes, the Unreal was a compound unknown and undocumented by the legitimate scientific community.

***

Later that afternoon Jeremy was in the back of his lab working and almost didn't hear the subdued knock at the door. Today, like most days that he was in the lab, Jeremy propped open the spring-loaded door of his lab with a trash can.

He peered around a stack of scientific instrumentation to find Jinni standing just inside the doorway.

"I'm so glad you're here," she said, the relief evident in her tone. "Where were you last night?"

When Jinni got a better view of him, her face lit up with astonishment. "Who did that to your face?" she asked.

"No one – actually, a bush."

"How?"

"Tavalin and I were hiking out at the lake and it was dark. We got a little scratched up, as you can see."

"Didn't you get my messages?" Jinni asked.

"I guess I didn't check the machine last night. We got back pretty late," he replied mechanically, and realizing this, added in what he hoped was a more personable tone, "I'm sorry I missed your calls."

"I'm worried about us, Jeremy." Jinni's words sprang from the overflow of her heart and, like a river, they ran: "Lately it seems like you are never at home and when you are, you claim to be tired or busy. Something has changed and I need for you to tell me what it is."

"Don't be ridiculous, Jinni. Nothing has changed," he lied. "I've just been really busy the last couple of weeks."

Busy thinking about Monika, added a voice in his head.

Jinni's intuition was dead on. For better or worse, Monika had entered the place in his thoughts that had heretofore been Jinni's exclusive niche, and Jinni sensed it.

She asked, "Was it just you and Tavalin at the lake or did somebody else go with y'all?"

"Like who?" he asked.

"Like maybe your friend June," Jinni replied cynically. "It wouldn't be the first time you sneaked out there with her."

"Jinni, you don't have to worry about June," insisted Jeremy. "She and I are friends and coworkers, nothing more."

"What time did you get home?"

"Around three, I guess. I'm not exactly sure."

"What could you possibly be doing out there that late?"

You wouldn't believe it even if I told you, thought Jeremy, though he refrained from handing out that little tidbit.

"Just killing time," he said. "I like it out there."

"You aren't still trying to find that hippie commune, are you?"

"Not per se," he replied. "I am still interested in learning what I can about the hippie queen."

"That's another thing I don't understand – this obsession you seem to have with that hippie queen girl."

"It's not an obsession. It's an interesting story that bears some investigation, that's all." Jeremy knew that, after last night, Monika's allusion to Claire only served to feed his so-called obsession. "Don't tell me you're jealous of Claire."

"I don't know what I am." Jinni gave a defeated sigh. "You exhaust me."

Jeremy took advantage of the break in the conversation to change the subject. "Tavalin and I are going to the RockFest tomorrow. You'll come, won't you?"

"Who's playing?"

"I don't know, mostly bands I'm not familiar with."

"Then why do you want to go?"

"It's free, for starters," he explained, "and some of the other graduate students will be there. Coolers and grills are allowed, and everybody sets up with tables and blankets. I think it will be fun, especially if you come along."

"I'll think about it," she said.

"Speaking of eating," Jeremy began, "How about we go get a pizza? I know this great place…"

Jinni knew it too. Jeremy always wanted to go to the same pizzeria and he always ordered the same chicken pizza with sun-dried tomatoes and mushrooms.

"I *am* hungry," she said.

Jeremy knew by the quick smile that ran across Jinni's face that everything was fine now. She was ready to move on, it seemed. For his part, he resolved to try a little harder to act as if everything was normal, even if it wasn't.

CHAPTER *20*

Saturday, November 22

*J*EREMY transferred scoop after crunching scoop of ice to the massive ice chest. After all the cans of beer were duly buried, he shut the door to the ice machine, revealing the sign on the door. "NOT FOR HUMAN CONSUMPTION," it warned in large block letters.

Tavalin raised his eyebrows questionably.

"We're not going to consume the ice, just the beer on the ice," explained Jeremy. "We'll be fine."

They exited through the side door of the Facility, which opened directly onto Grover's Field where the rock festival was to take place. Jeremy and a loose association of acquaintances and friends, mostly graduate students from the Biotech Facility, had made plans to attend. Jinni agreed to meet them there as well. The first band had already begun playing by the time Jeremy and Tavalin struck out for their saved spot, sharing the load of the very heavy cooler. It wasn't easy maneuvering through the gathering crowd.

"You could have picked a spot closer in," Tavalin groaned, struggling a little with his half of the load. "Where are you dragging me?"

"Hang in there. It's just a little bit farther. No, wait a minute; I think we're going the wrong way." Jeremy spoke with manufactured concern as he motioned back in the direction from which they had just come.

Tavalin stopped and dropped his end of the cooler and snapped back, "I hope you're kidding."

Jeremy grinned. "Why, gee whiz," he said with mock surprise. "I do believe this is our blanket and chairs right here."

"Ha, ha, very funny," replied Tavalin.

In a few minutes, June showed up.

"Hey, June, perfect timing." Jeremy had invited June but had not really expected her to show. "We just got here."

"I know. I saw you from upstairs," she said, motioning toward her window in the Facility, which, like Jeremy's, looked out over Grover's Field.

"Hello June," Tavalin said. "How are you doing today?"

"I'm okay."

Right away, Tavalin went to bat. "So, June," he said, "when are you going to let me take you to a movie or something?"

June cut her begging eyes towards Jeremy. He caught her meaning and obliged.

"Tavalin, will you do us all a favor and get the food from my car? I would do it myself but I need to talk to June," Jeremy said, then added, "about our research."

Tavalin glared at Jeremy. "I suppose," he replied.

Jeremy knew that June felt uncomfortable around Tavalin ever since he began pestering her for a date. Tavalin met June through Jeremy and that made Jeremy feel somewhat responsible for the situation. Whenever possible, he tried to help her deflect Tavalin's unwelcome advances.

After Tavalin had gone, June said, "Tavalin is like a mosquito that will not leave me alone."

Jeremy laughed. "I don't know why he doesn't just give up. I told him you weren't interested in dating him but he won't listen. I think he believes I'm trying to keep you all for myself."

June's color brightened.

"That didn't really come out right," Jeremy added quickly. "What I meant to say was that Tavalin is jealous of all the time you and I spend together."

For some reason, the look that passed across June's face made Jeremy think of the night they rode out to the lake alone.

"I don't want to make anyone angry," June said, "but Tavalin is not my type."

"Tavalin is my friend but if I were a girl and he asked me out, I wouldn't go either," quipped Jeremy.

June erupted with an infectious laugh that Jeremy caught.

Reviving their standing joke, Jeremy asked, "So have you been working this afternoon?" Not once had she answered the question in the negative.

"Why yes, I have," June replied. "How did you know?"

"Just a hunch," he replied and with as straight a face he could manage, Jeremy added, "You know it's against school rules to work after five o'clock during the RockFest."

"Yeah, right," she chortled. "You can't fool me anymore, Jeremy. I'm wise to you."

"And to think how easy you were just a few weeks ago. I would offer you something to drink but all we've got right now is beer. Someone else is supposed to bring the soft drinks."

June once mentioned her low tolerance for alcohol. She had informed him that a certain percentage of Asians, including herself, lacked the enzyme necessary to efficiently break down alcohol and therefore got tipsy extraordinarily fast.

She surprised Jeremy by accepting: "I think I would like a beer," she said, "to celebrate."

"Celebrate?" he asked. "What are you celebrating?"

"The latest results, what else?"

"What are the latest results?"

June only smiled. She was, it seemed, drawing this out on purpose, teasing Jeremy.

"Well?" he asked impatiently.

"I believe I have identified a gene in your mitochondrial DNA that is unique to you."

"Does that mean...?" he asked excitedly.

"This is it," she said with a wide smile. "This is the big discovery. There are functional genes in your extra DNA."

"Genes?" he asked. "More than one?"

"At least the one. The computer is crunching numbers on the next section of the sequence as we speak."

"What is the function of the new gene?" he asked.

"It is 97 percent homologous with the nuclear gene that codes for a certain DNA repair enzyme."

"So there's no way it could be a mutation?" he asked.

"No," she replied flat-out. "This looks like something else. I would have to say this could only be the result of the intelligent redesign of your mitochondria."

"What does that mean – *intelligent redesign?*"

"It is highly improbable that this happened by chance," she explained. "And if not by chance, then the alternative is that it is a purposeful change."

"Are scientists able to do that now, add genes to mitochondrial DNA?" he asked

"Not to my knowledge," replied June. "There's nothing in the literature to indicate that any group has obtained that capability."

"Then how did it happen to me?" he asked.

"That's what's so puzzling," she replied. "I have to say, I don't have a clue."

"It doesn't matter," Jeremy was jubilant. "We'll have millions of dollars in research grant money and years to figure out the details."

"Do you really think so?" she asked.

"I do. This is our big break, June. You did it."

"*We* did it," she said and gave him a big spontaneous hug.

Jeremy and June were sitting together in the afterglow of the sunset, alone, talking and laughing and sipping at their beers when Jinni arrived. No one else would likely have noticed the subtle look of disapproval in her expression, but Jeremy knew Jinni better than anyone else. Based on some comments Jinni had recently made, Jeremy knew Jinni had become jealous of June and all the time he had been spending with her.

Jeremy quickly leapt to his feet. "June, I'd like you to meet my *girlfriend…*"

It wasn't long before Tavalin returned and the others trickled in with additional food and drinks.

***

"What is this music?" asked Jinni.

"Why do you ask?" replied Jeremy. "Are you thinking about downloading the album?"

Jinni had long ago made obvious the fact that she did not like the loud, harsh music.

"Yeah, that's exactly what I was thinking," she replied sarcastically. "I would like to know the classification so I'll not let anyone talk me into listening to anything like it ever again."

"That bad, huh? I'm not sure what you would call it. Ask him."

Jeremy pointed to Tavalin, who was head banging in time with the music. None of the others in their little group seemed to be paying attention to the music but were instead focused on the conversation and the food and drink.

Jinni tapped Tavalin on the shoulder to get his attention. She asked, "Who are we listening to? Jeremy said you would know."

"*Cocytus,*" answered Tavalin.

"Who?" she asked. Before Tavalin could expound she added, "What I really want to know is what genre this is?"

"Rock, obviously – maybe deathcore rock," answered Tavalin.

Jeremy rolled his eyes. "He's just making stuff up. He doesn't know."

Tavalin smiled. "Wait, I know. This is alternative glam with a twist of black thrash."

"Deathcore sounds about right," muttered Jinni.

By eleven o'clock, a good five hours since they first set up in Grover's Field, everyone in their group had given up and gone home except for Jeremy, Jinni, and Tavalin. As time ticked by, the music became louder and more obnoxious until finally Jinni could take no more.

"Can't we leave now?" she pleaded.

"Okay."

"Thanks," Jinni said as she fast began clearing the picnic table of spent cups and plates of food scraps.

"Tavalin," said Jeremy. "I think Jinni and I are going to call it a night. Are you ready to go?"

"I guess," replied Tavalin, though he appeared to be a little disappointed.

Emptied of ice and most of the drinks, the ice chest was considerably more manageable now than it had been on the way in. As they walked by the back of the Facility, Jeremy glanced up at June's fifth floor lab window. Most of the lights in the building were extinguished but hers still burned brightly. Jeremy's watch informed him of the time, ten till midnight.

"That's June's lab," he told Jinni.

"She's working?" she asked.

"Yep, probably on our project," he replied. "I should probably swing by there before I go home."

Both Jeremy's and Tavalin's cars were parked out on the street in front of the Facility. They stuck the cooler in the back of Tavalin's car.

"Are you okay to drive?" Even though Tavalin got on Jinni's nerves sometimes, she was concerned for his well-being.

"I'm fine," Tavalin insisted.

As they pulled away from the curb, Jeremy asked with a grin, "So what did you think about the bands tonight?"

"They were awful!" Jinni exclaimed. "I don't know how stuff like that even passes as music."

After a short lull in the conversation, Jinni said, "You didn't tell me she was so pretty."

"Who?" Jeremy asked, as if he didn't know.

"June, that's who."

Jeremy's suspicions from earlier proved right. "You don't have to worry about her," he replied. "She's my coworker, nothing more."

"I watched you with her, before you knew I was there. I saw the way you two were laughing and talking. You were just so chummy with her."

"You don't have to worry, Jinni," he said defensively. "We're just friends."

"Don't worry?" The pitch of her voice began to rise. "What am I supposed to think? You did take her parking at the lake that night, didn't you?"

"I told you nothing happened at the lake," Jeremy replied adamantly.

"But if it did, I would never know, would I?"

"I suppose not, especially if you're going to act this way," Jeremy said. It had been a long day and he didn't try to hide his irritation. "If something had happened, I don't think I would have mentioned taking her to the lake in the first place."

"I want to trust you, Jeremy – I do," Jinni said. "But the thought of you sneaking around behind my back makes me crazy. Look at it from my perspective. First you start spending all this time with June at work. Then I find out that y'all spent time alone at the lake. Today I see how attractive she is and how comfortable you two are with each other. When I walked up, I felt like the outsider."

"June is a fine person. I'd be lying if I said she and I didn't hit it off on some level. Since we began working on this project together, we have become friends, nothing more."

"Nothing happened when y'all went parking at the lake?"

Jeremy felt as if he were fighting a losing battle.

"We've covered this ground before, Jinni. Do we have to go there again?"

By now they had made it into the parking garage where Jinni had left her car. He parked next to hers and turned his full attention to her. "Jinni," he pleaded. "Let's don't end this day on a sour note. I'm tired and you're tired –"

She cut him off. "Answer my question. Did anything happen at the lake?"

"No," he replied begrudgingly. "Nothing happened."

"Did you want something to happen?"

"You mean did I try to make a move on her?" he asked. "No, I most certainly did not."

"Did the thought cross your mind?"

Now she had him. The thought had crossed Jeremy's mind but what could he say? Could random thoughts be a violation of the terms of their relationship? If so, then to even notice an attractive girl could be prohibited.

He didn't have the energy to explain the nuances of the male sex drive to her right now. All he could muster was a frustrated, "I don't know."

They sat side-by-side but with a rift between them a mile wide.

"I found out some other stuff, too," Jinni said vaguely. She did not elaborate, only frowned at him expectantly as if she were waiting for some kind of confession.

No confession would be forthcoming. Jeremy had grown tired of defending himself and freely expressed his displeasure.

Glaring at her, he asked, "What other stuff?"

"Forget it," Jinni replied with exasperation. "I think it's time for me to leave."

She got out and slammed his car door.

Jeremy watched as she pulled away without acknowledging him. He followed her down the spiral exit of the parking garage. At the main road she turned right. A right turn would direct him toward his apartment and away from the Biotech Facility. It wasn't necessary that he drop by June's lab tonight, but if he didn't, wouldn't that only be giving in to Jinni's irrationality? Was he not allowed to interact with his coworker just because his jealous girlfriend didn't want him there? With a defiant jerk of the steering wheel he turned left, even though he knew Jinni would be watching in her rear view mirror.

On the main boulevard leading to campus, Jeremy was greeted by a long line of cars and pedestrians headed in the opposite direction. The RockFest had run its course and the boisterous hordes of deathcore rockers swarmed by like so many mindless locusts, having devoured all there was to consume at Grover's Field.

***

Jeremy easily laid claim to a parking space on the street directly in front of the Biotech Facility. When he noticed Tavalin's little yellow Honda still occupied the same spot as earlier, he guessed that Tavalin must be inside the Facility. Perhaps he had second thoughts about driving home in his condition.

Only a smattering of festival-goers remained, some still sitting in the grass or milling about Grover's Field while others drifted aimlessly by as they searched for their cars. One such couple who appeared happily lost lollygagged up the sidewalk toward Jeremy.

"Dude!" exclaimed the tall, skinny male. The greasy locks of hair that hung into his face could not obscure his bloodshot eyes. He asked, "Can you tell us how to get to the Nowhere Bar?"

Jeremy smiled at the coincidence. "Downtown, a few blocks west of the Square."

The guy looked at his companion who only shrugged her shoulders helplessly. "Can you tell us how to get downtown?" he asked unabashedly.

Jeremy pointed up University Boulevard. "Go that way, about a mile or so. When you get to the Chevron Station, take a left. When you see the Courthouse, you're in the Square."

Knowing it would be futile to try and give these two detailed directions to Bar Nowhere, Jeremy added, "When you get to the Square, just pick out somebody who looks hip and ask them where the bar is."

"Awesome," he replied as they ambled on by.

"And, dude," added Jeremy, "the name is Bar Nowhere."

Jeremy crossed the front lawn and started up the steps that led to the front doors of the Facility. At the top of the steps he paused. While Tavalin had likely gone downstairs to his basement lab, Jeremy had to entertain the possibility of an ambush. If he went in this way, he would have to pass through the lobby, one of Tavalin's favorite hiding places. Tavalin had surely heard Jeremy mention that he might stop in to see June tonight. For all Jeremy knew, Tavalin could be watching for his arrival out the plate glass windows in the lobby. Jeremy couldn't take that chance.

Stupid game, Jeremy thought as he circled around to the small parking lot and loading dock in back of the building. He stuck to the shadowy areas whenever possible, just in case Tavalin was on to him. He made it to the back door without incident but hesitated, thinking he heard someone on the other side and sidestepped just in time to avoid the door as it swung open in its outward arc. Jeremy stood with his back tight against the bricks as someone, not Tavalin, exited the building. Two steps later Jeremy recognized the short statue and bald beanie on the back of the man's head. It was Dr. Sloan, a.k.a. Skippy.

Jeremy held his position, his arms crossed in an *X* across his chest, hoping that he wouldn't be noticed, but Skippy sensed his presence. He turned and looked questionably at Jeremy.

"You almost got me," Jeremy said before Skippy could say anything. "Good thing for my quick reflexes."

Jeremy snagged the doorknob just before the door closed completely and pulled open the door. "Have a good night," he said in a jolly tone. At last glance, Dr. Sloan had not moved nor replied when the door swung shut.

At least it wasn't Dr. Cain again.

It was then that Jeremy's conscious mind caught up to something else of interest that he glimpsed in the back parking lot as he stood with his back against the wall. A pair of parking lights switched on when Skippy exited the building. Jeremy couldn't be sure because the lion's share of his attention had been focused on Skippy, but he thought he recognized the car.

Jeremy vaulted up the back stairwell to the second floor where he had a bird's eye view of the back parking lot. Skippy had just arrived at the driver's side of his car while the mystery car waited with illuminated parking lights. Jeremy knew that car – it belonged to Dr. Cain. Jeremy checked his watch. It was a quarter past midnight, not unusually late for Dr. Cain to be leaving the Facility, but, as Jeremy watched, something about the scene below struck him as odd. Only after Skippy cranked his car and switched on his headlights did Dr. Cain turn his own headlights on. And even though Dr. Cain was parked closer to the exit, he allowed Skippy to back his car out, turn around, and leave before following Skippy out.

They were leaving together.

As Jeremy walked around to the elevator, he heard a strange whirring noise. He eased around toward the front wing of the second floor in the direction of the sound. He rounded the corner to the sight of the backside of a man operating a large buffer machine. Jeremy watched until he got a good look at the man's profile. It was Grady, waxing the hallway. Jeremy ducked back around the corner before Grady saw him. He wasn't in the mood for any *Grady-speak* tonight.

As he rode the elevator up, Jeremy asked himself what reason Dr. Cain and Skippy might have to leave together. What common destination might the two men have at this hour? Jeremy could not make sense of it. *Unless...* One of his mother's many sayings came to mind:

Birds of a feather flock together.

Jeremy had long suspected that Skippy might be gay but what of the executive director? Jeremy had seen pictures of Dr. Cain's wife in his office. She was a knockout. Nonetheless, Jeremy recalled a time or two when he thought he detected a subtle prissiness in Dr. Cain's gait. There was also a definite effeminate quality about the shriek he gave when Tavalin scared him that night in the lobby.

Could it be? Could Dr. Cain be a homosexual? Though only a hunch, it was an intriguing supposition that the big boss might be harboring such a juicy secret.

Considering Dr. Cain in this new light, as a man of deceit, laid clear the path to further suspicions. What if Dr. Cain was behind what June referred to as the *intelligent redesign* of his mitochondria? Was it possible that Dr. Cain had secretly used Jeremy as his personal human guinea pig? If anyone was capable of such cutting-edge science, it was Dr. Cain, and Jeremy had always thought it strange how much time he spent in his private lab. If he had nothing to hide, why do so much hands-on work in the lab with so many capable scientists at his beck and call? Jeremy's mind ran with the idea and by the time the elevator released him to the fifth floor, he had all but convinced himself that the good doctor was responsible for the changes in his mitochondria.

Jeremy charged into June's lab, ready to run his theory by June, but the distraught expression on her face stopped him in his tracks.

"I'm afraid I have some bad news," she said haltingly.

"What is it?" he asked and grimaced at the taste of sour reflux in the back of his throat.

"He knows," she replied miserably. "Dr. Cain knows."

"What happened?"

"Dr. Cain came by and asked to see what it was I was working on. I had no choice but to tell him that it was unrelated to my official research project."

"How did he know?"

"I have no idea."

"Did you tell him any specifics?" asked Jeremy.

"No, and he didn't ask for any. He only said that *we would discuss the matter on Monday, first thing.*"

"When did this happen?" asked Jeremy. "Tonight?"

"Just a few minutes ago."

"Does he know I am involved?" Jeremy asked and immediately felt guilty for thinking of himself.

"Your name wasn't mentioned."

"June, I am so sorry," Jeremy said. "This is my fault. If you want me to, I'll talk to Dr. Cain. I can tell him the truth, that it was my idea and I asked you to help me."

"I don't see how bringing you into it helps either of us," she said stoically. "I've just got to figure out what I'm going to say on Monday."

"I'm just sick that you're the one who got caught." Jeremy literally felt like vomiting. "It should have been me."

"Don't worry about it," June said sadly. "I agreed to work on this. I knew the risk I was taking."

After a few minutes of Jeremy hanging around, trying to cheer her up, she said, "I'm tired of talking about it. We should just call it a night."

"All right then," he said, taking the hint. "Can I give you a ride back to your place?"

June lived in the large complex of dated, on-campus apartments known as the bungalows. Jeremy had offered before to give June a ride but she always declined. Tonight was no different.

"No thank you," she replied. "I've got a couple of things I want to wrap up here before I go."

"Can I call you tomorrow?" he asked. "Maybe I could take you out for lunch or something."

"Sure," she replied unenthusiastically. "If you like."

"It's the least I can do. Maybe we can figure a way out of all this."

***

Jeremy drove directly home from the Facility. He was in the shower bathing away the dirt of the now-spent day when he thought he heard a faint *ding dong* over the sound of the splattering water. The television was on in the other room and he dismissed it as merely one of those irritating commercials that mimic the ring of a telephone or doorbell as an attention-grabber.

He heard it again, past the thirty second limit of most commercials.

Not the television. Who could be here at this hour?

Jeremy hurriedly rinsed and cut off the water. Now someone was knocking loudly on the door, demanding his immediate response.

"Just a minute!" he yelled as he wiped away a portion of the water dripping from his body.

Wearing only a towel, he scampered down the hallway. "Who is it?" he asked the door.

"It's me. Let me in."

It was Tavalin. Jeremy disengaged the deadbolt and opened the door.

"What took you so long?" Tavalin asked.

"Guess."

"Oh," Tavalin said as he belatedly processed the answer based on Jeremy's dripping hair and the towel around his waist.

"What do you want?"

"Can I come in?"

"This better be important," Jeremy replied with unreserved aggravation as he motioned Tavalin into the living room.

"Do you know what time it is?" Apparently the six hours just spent with Tavalin was not sufficient for his good friend.

Tavalin checked his watch diligently. "Oh, about a quarter past one."

"I know what time it is, you idiot. I just wondered if you did."

Tavalin stood there like a puppy begging for just a little more playtime. "Umm…" was all he could say.

"Hold that thought. I'll be back in a minute," advised Jeremy as he went to throw on some clothes and brush his teeth.

While Jeremy was still in the back, Tavalin called out, "Hey, can I borrow your washing machine?"

"What for?" Jeremy asked, but couldn't hear if Tavalin responded.

By the time Jeremy came back, the washer was filling with water and Tavalin was sitting on the couch wearing only his boxers.

Jeremy shook his head in disbelief. "This I've got to hear."

"Umm, I sorta threw up after all that beer I drank and got a little on my clothes. I threw them in the wash. You don't mind, do you?"

"I guess it's better than getting it on my furniture," Jeremy muttered. "So tell me again, why are you here?"

"I just didn't feel sleepy and didn't feel like going back to my place and, yada, yada, yada, here I am." An anxious look appeared on Tavalin's face, as if Jeremy's company was of the utmost importance. "You want to order a pizza?" added Tavalin. "I'll buy."

Jeremy smiled in spite of himself at his friend's strange and unpredictable ways. And besides, he couldn't exactly throw Tavalin out of the apartment in his underwear. "I could eat," Jeremy conceded.

They ordered a pay-for-view movie, some second rate horror flick that Tavalin wanted to see. Tavalin made several trips downstairs in his underwear to watch for their pizza, just to make sure the delivery guy didn't get lost.

On returning from one such trek, Tavalin announced, "We've got company."

Much to Jeremy's surprise, it was Jinni who followed Tavalin inside. She took one step into the room and stopped. "Can we talk?" she asked. She indicated the bedroom with her eyes.

"Yes, of course," replied Jeremy. "What's wrong?"

They went inside and shut the door behind them.

"What is he doing here?" she whispered.

"With Tavalin, I have learned to expect the unexpected. Did he tell you why he's walking around in his underwear?"

"Yes," Jinni replied. "Why don't you give him some clothes?"

"Why would I want to deprive you?" asked Jeremy with a smile. "It doesn't seem to bother him. He's oblivious."

"If only I could be so oblivious…"

Their laughter faded into the void of a self-conscience hush, forcing Jinni to address the elephant in the room. "You're probably wondering why I'm here," she said.

"You could say that…"

"Yes, well, it's just that…" she stammered a bit before she began. "I just felt so bad for the way I behaved. I shouldn't have jumped all over you like I did."

"It's okay, really," Jeremy said.

Jinni's apology actually made Jeremy feel worse. She had been right to be suspicious – only the target of her jealousy was misplaced. While kissing June had crossed his mind that night out at the lake, he had resisted. Monika, not June, was the other woman.

"I don't know what's gotten into me lately," Jinni said. "I've been feeling a little insecure."

Jeremy didn't know what to say. "Maybe it just means you care for me."

"Or, maybe I just need more hugs," she said with puppy dog eyes.

"C'mere," Jeremy said as he guided her into his open arms.

"You feel so good," she said. "I don't want us to ever fight, okay?"

"Fine by me," agreed Jeremy.

"So," began Jinni, "Did you see her?"

Jeremy fought to suppress a smile. "Just for a second," he replied. "I didn't stay long."

Jinni had come here to apologize for being jealous but she still had to know if he spoke to June.

"She said you were pretty," added Jeremy.

"She must be a really sweet girl."

Jeremy thought it best not to comment. Anyone could see that Jinni's issues with June remained. Jeremy wondered if the real reason Jinni dropped by unexpectedly at one-thirty in the morning was not to apologize but to check up on him. Maybe she thought she might catch June and him together. If that were the case, then Jinni must have been surprised to find Tavalin, not June, parading half-naked around his condo.

"Why don't you stay?" asked Jeremy as they exited the bedroom. "We ordered a pizza."

"I might stay for a few minutes," Jinni replied as she sat down on the couch.

In a few minutes Tavalin appeared and plopped down unceremoniously across from Jinni.

"Where's that pizza?" asked Jeremy.

"Don't know. Are you sure you gave him the right address?" asked Tavalin.

"I'm sure."

"You know, on second thought, I really should head on out," announced Jinni. "It's late."

Jeremy escorted Jinni downstairs but only as far as the front stoop because his feet were bare. He waited while she walked to her car and watched her drive away.

"What did she want?" asked Tavalin when Jeremy returned.

"I think she came here to check up on me."

"Why?"

"It's a long story."

Jeremy did not want to get into the whole parking-at-the-lake-with-June bit, especially considering Tavalin's feelings for June.

"I'll be back."

Tavalin got up and disappeared again, presumably to wait downstairs for the delivery guy. Twenty minutes later he strutted into the living room with the pizza in tow.

They ate gustily, despite the fact that the pizza arrived cold.

Ironically, but predictably, it was Tavalin who fell asleep first, still clad only in his boxers, his bony frame curled up in a tight fetal position on the couch. Jeremy placed a blanket over his friend, more to hide the spectacle than anything else. The second pay-for-view movie was almost over before Jeremy fell asleep in the recliner.

CHAPTER 21

Sunday, November 23

JEREMY, still in his recliner, awoke with a bitter taste in his mouth and a thumping in his temple. Tavalin was sacked out on the couch. Jeremy started to wake his friend so that he could finally be rid of him but remembered Tavalin's clothes, still in the washing machine, still wet. Jeremy put the clothes in the dryer and dozed on his bed until the buzzer roused him.

"Wake up!" Jeremy demanded as he tossed the warm clothes in Tavalin's face.

Tavalin groaned loudly in protest. His first words of the morning were, "Oh, my poor aching head."

In jest Jeremy asked, "Do you want a beer? Or maybe some warm whiskey? You know what they say, hair of the dog."

"Shut up," Tavalin pleaded. "Or maybe you want me to throw up again?"

"I dried your clothes, by the way."

"Thanks," Tavalin said but didn't seem inclined to make any effort to move.

"So you should probably get dressed and, you know, take off."

"What, you're throwing me out?"

"All good things must come to an end."

"Alright already," Tavalin said as he sat up.

"You don't look so good," Jeremy jabbed.

"Looks can be deceiving, but in this instance I have to say they are not. I feel like I got run over by a concrete truck."

Tavalin dragged himself first to the bathroom and then to the kitchen where he helped himself to a giant glass of water. "You got any aspirin?" he asked.

"Ibuprofen, on the counter."

Before Tavalin could leave, the phone rang.

"Hello?"

"Mr. Spires?"

It was a man's voice, unfamiliar.

"Yes?"

"Mr. Spires, this is Lieutenant Sykes down at the police station. I have your address listed as 111 Townview. Is that correct?"

"That's right. What's the problem, officer?" Jeremy had a sick feeling in his stomach.

"We need you at the station, Mr. Spires. I'm sending a car over right now."

"What for?" Jeremy asked, but the line was dead.

Baffled, he checked out the breakfast room window and discovered the police car already parked in the tow-away zone at the front door of his building.

With saucer-sized eyes Tavalin asked, "What's going on? Was that the police?"

Almost immediately came the inevitable banging on the door.

Jeremy opened the door to the sight of two uniformed officers.

"Jeremy Spires?" asked one of the cops.

"The one and only," replied Jeremy, trying to be upbeat though he felt anything but.

"May we come in?"

Since they asked, Jeremy knew he didn't have to let them in but could think of no reason why he shouldn't. "I guess so," he replied and stepped back from the door.

The policeman in the back looked especially nervous as he held his right hand close to his holstered gun like a gunslinger in a spaghetti Western.

Not a good sign, Jeremy thought.

"Are you alone?" one of them asked.

"No. My friend is in the kitchen."

"Tell him to come out."

Tavalin took an uncertain step out from around the corner as he was well within earshot. "Hello," he said, but the quiver in his voice belied the casual greeting. At least he had finally pulled on his clothes.

"Come out where we can see you." The policemen studied Tavalin as he skulked into the living room. "Anybody else back there?"

Jeremy replied, "No, it's just us."

"Do you mind if we verify that ourselves?"

"I guess not."

One cop stayed with Jeremy and Tavalin while the other disappeared into the back bedroom. In a moment he came back up the short hallway and made a quick scan of the front bedroom, including the balcony and the closet.

When he had rejoined the rest of them, Jeremy asked, "What's going on, officer?"

"We need both of you to come with us downtown, if you don't mind." The cops were all business.

Jeremy didn't know how to react or what to say. In the end, he shrugged and said, "Let me get my keys."

Jeremy didn't like the way the world looked from the back of the squad car. Tavalin appeared utterly terrified.

***

Once inside the police station, they escorted Jeremy to a small office and asked him to have a seat. They took Tavalin somewhere else. Jeremy clasped his hands together on his lap after he noticed their slight shake. One of the officers stayed behind, leaning against the wall by the door in silence except for annoying little gum-smacking sounds. After only a minute or so, an older man entered the room and sat down behind the desk.

"Hello, Mr. Spires. I'm Lieutenant Sykes." The policeman tried to smile, but the expression looked to Jeremy more like how a dog might bare his teeth at an adversary.

"I'd like to ask you a few questions. Do you mind if I record this conversation?"

Lieutenant Sykes placed a small, black tape recorder on the cluttered desk. He was a compact man, with a prominent jaw and a mustache that tweaked up and down over his upper lip in syncopated time with the cadence of his speech.

"I don't know," replied Jeremy audaciously. "Why don't you tell me what's going on?"

"I get to go first. What did you do last night?"

"I went to the rock festival on campus."

The young, gum-smacking cop flipped open a wire-bound notebook and pulled the cap off a pen with his teeth.

"Alone?"

"With a small group of friends."

"Do your friends have names?"

"Why do you want to know?"

"Just a couple of quick questions, please. I'm trying to establish your whereabouts last night. What are your friends' names?"

Jeremy rattled off the names of several of his fellow graduate students who were there, including June Song. "Also, Tavalin Cassel – he's in the other room – and my girlfriend, Jinni Malone."

Now the gum-smacker was scribbling in his little notebook.

With an almost imperceptible nod, Lieutenant Sykes motioned the other officer out of the room.

Jeremy's mind reeled, groping at the possibilities. *Why am I here?*

"What time did you leave the RockFest?" asked Lieutenant Sykes.

"A little before midnight."

"Where did you go after that?"

"I dropped my girlfriend off at her car, which was parked on campus. Then I went to the Biotech Facility for a few minutes, and after that I went home to my apartment."

"Why did you go to the Biotech Facility?"

"I dropped in to speak to my coworker, June."

"What was she doing there?"

"Working in her lab."

"Was she alone?"

"Yes."

"What time would you say you parted company with Ms Song?"

"Must have been around half past twelve."

"After that?" asked the lieutenant.

"After that, I went home."

"Did you see anyone else in the building?"

"The janitor was waxing one of the hallway floors."

"Do you know his name?"

"Grady."

"Last name?"

"I don't know."

"Anybody else?"

"Don't think so."

"What about your boss, Skip Sloan?"

Jeremy wondered how the cop knew that Dr. Sloan was his boss and that he had run into him last night.

"Oh yeah, I passed him coming out of the back door of the building on my way in. Also, I'm pretty sure I saw Dr. Cain's car in the back parking lot at that same time."

"Where did you go after you left June's lab?"

"Home."

"And did you notice anything unusual when you left or at any time while you were on campus?"

"No, nothing sticks out."

"What time did you get home?"

"Best guess, a quarter till one. I didn't notice exactly."

"And what time would you say your friend Tavalin arrived at your apartment?"

"Approximately one fifteen."

"Did you leave your apartment at all after that?"

"No."

"Did you see or talk to anyone else after Tavalin arrived?"

"No," answered Jeremy, but quickly corrected himself. "Actually, I did. My girlfriend, Jinni, stopped by for just a few minutes."

"When?"

"Around one-thirty, maybe a little later."

"Why did she come over?"

"Jinni came over because she wanted to apologize over a little tiff we had earlier."

"You had an argument?"

"More like a small disagreement."

"About what?"

"About nothing really – something she thought I did. You know how it can be sometimes." Jeremy thought that maybe he could use the battle between the sexes to make an ally of the Lieutenant.

"I really need to know what the argument was about," insisted the cop.

"Like I said, it was no big deal. She thought I was flirting, that's all."

"Flirting with whom?"

Jeremy hated being forced to divulge his private affairs with this stranger, especially since he had no clue why he was being made to do so in the first place.

"I'm sorry, Lieutenant, but I would really like for you to tell me why I am here."

"Please, sir, bear with me. It's crucial that we get through all this."

Jeremy glared at the policeman.

"Now, who did your girlfriend accuse you of flirting with?"

"June."

"And were you?"

"Was I what?"

"Were you flirting with her?"

"Like I told Jinni, June is my friend, nothing more." The cop was punching the same provoking buttons as had Jinni the night before.

"Alright. It's time to tell you why you are here…"

***

When Lieutenant Sykes broke the dreadful news, Jeremy's reaction was one of absolute horror and shock. He sat perfectly still, frozen with his mouth agape, staring back at the bad news bearer, waiting for the smile and the punch line that would not be forthcoming.

"How – how – how could this be?" Jeremy stammered. "Was there an accident?"

"No, she was murdered – slaughtered like a pathetic animal."

Jeremy's jaw dropped farther but no words emerged. He shut his eyes to implore God or fate or whatever to take it back, to carry him back to his previous world and away from this one. Like a child, alone and afraid, he repeated the mantra: *It's only a dream, wake up, wake up! It's only a dream, wake up, wake up!*

But all to no avail. When he opened his eyes, nothing had changed.

"Ms Song's body was discovered early this morning."

With acute self-consciousness Jeremy realized the cop was studying him, watching his reactions, reading his expression. How was one supposed to react when told that his good friend had been murdered?

"You might very well have been the last person to see Ms Song alive."

It took Jeremy a further moment to process the trappings of the policeman's statement. "You mean the last person *besides the killer* to see her alive, am I right?"

The cop slid a piece of paper to Jeremy's side of the table. "Do you recognize this?" he asked.

Jeremy studied the roughly-drawn symbol. It appeared gratuitously cryptic and dark, like something an aspiring Satanist might create to impress his friends.

"No, I don't think so," he replied.

"Are you sure about that?"

For the next hour Sykes made Jeremy hash and rehash every detail from the night before. It was the longest hour of his life. The cop's last request had been that he identify the remains at the morgue.

Only when they performed the dreaded act of pulling back the sheet did Jeremy understand the significance of the roughly-drawn symbol presented to him by Lieutenant Sykes: For reasons only a madman could understand, the strange symbol had been etched into her forehead. As disturbing as the spectacle was, Jeremy could not look away. And later, try as he might, Jeremy could not exorcise the grisly image of June's mangled body from his mind.

***

The following hours Jeremy spent alone at his condominium in a daze. Denial reigned supreme with one reoccurring thought cycling endlessly around his head: *I can't believe she's dead.*

It was late in the afternoon before Jeremy was able to summon Tavalin on the phone. When he answered, Tavalin's voice sounded far away like he was halfway around the world instead of halfway across town.

"Is she really gone?" he asked, uncharacteristically subdued.

"What did the cops ask you?" asked Jeremy.

"Where I was, who I was with, did I see anything suspicious and did I have any idea who could have done it – all the usual police stuff. The only weird thing was the drawing. Did they show it to you?"

"Yes, twice." said Jeremy.

"Twice?" asked Tavalin. "What do you mean?"

"I saw it once at the police station and then again at the morgue. It seems the killer carved the symbol into her forehead."

A protracted silence ensued while Jeremy waited on his friend to respond. "You still there?" Jeremy asked.

"You did recognize it, didn't you?" asked Tavalin.

"No, I don't think so. You did?"

"I had a pretty good idea where I saw it before but I wasn't sure until I looked it up online."

"Well, what is it?" asked Jeremy impatiently.

"Are you at your computer?" asked Tavalin. "Go to the events calendar on the University web page. Click on the *RockFest* link and under that you'll find all the links for the bands that played. Choose *Cocytus*."

"Hang on." Jeremy moved to his desk and navigated to the *Cocytus* link. Heavy metal music, obnoxious and loud, spewed from his speakers. As fast as he could reach for the volume knob, he turned it down.

"Now click on the *compilations* link."

"I really don't feel like doing this right now," complained Jeremy. "Can't you just tell me?"

Tavalin continued, ignoring Jeremy's complaints. "Under the *compilations* link, select their latest, *Aliens of the Armageddon*."

"Could they have come up with a cheesier title?" asked Jeremy as he scanned for the link. "Here it is."

"Now click on the thumbnail of the album cover to enlarge it," instructed Tavalin.

The album cover contained an over-abundance of the dark-side elements one might expect, considering the compilation's title. Demonic creatures with their requisite hoods and scythes stood on a carpet of human skulls in a ruined post-apocalyptic world, all in shades of black and white. The symbol of interest was inscribed within the circle of the full moon, and, as such, highlighted in yellow.

"Do you see it?" asked Tavalin.

"That's it, isn't it? How did you find it?" asked Jeremy of his friend.

"Did you happen to notice the design on the backdrop of the stage last night?"

"I suppose I didn't," replied Jeremy.

"Basically, take the moon with the symbol inside and blow it up to a diameter of thirty or forty feet, paint it on the backdrop with luminescent paint and hit it with black light," said Tavalin. "I don't know how you missed it."

Jeremy's phone beeped in his ear. "Tavalin, can you hang on? I've got another call coming in."

Jeremy clicked over to Jinni's voice on the other line.

"Hey," he said. "Did you hear about June?"

"Yes, Jeremy," Jinni replied. "I'm so sorry. Are you okay?"

"I'm fine – listen, Jinni, can I call you right back? I've got Tavalin on the other line."

"No need – I'm driving over right now."

"See you in a minute."

Jeremy clicked back over to the other line. "Tavalin?"

"I'm here," replied Tavalin.

"Any idea what the symbol might signify?" asked Jeremy.

"That I don't know."

"How did the police react when you told them?" asked Jeremy.

"Are you crazy? I didn't tell them anything."

"Why not?"

"For starters, I didn't like the way they treated us, dragging us down there and asking a thousand questions. They made me feel like a criminal. Also, I couldn't be entirely sure the symbol was the same until I looked at it again online."

"You probably should have told them anyway," chided Jeremy. "It might help them figure out who the killer is."

"June is dead and nothing I say or don't say to the cops is going to bring her back. I'm not equipped to handle joy rides in the back of squad cars and interrogations down at the station. Call me apathetic, but if I never deal with the police again, it'll be too soon."

"I suppose I can't fault you for that," agreed Jeremy. "I wasn't exactly thrilled with the morning's activities either. But as far as feeling like a criminal, I wouldn't worry about that too much. I think that's just how they conduct these interviews."

"If you want to tell them about the symbol, go right ahead," said Tavalin. "Just leave my name out of it."

When Jinni arrived, Jeremy told her everything that he knew, including the connection of the strange symbol and the band. On studying the Cocytus website, they discovered that Tavalin had been correct when he identified their genre of music as a subcategory of rock known, ironically, as *deathcore*.

CHAPTER 22

Monday, November 24

*J*EREMY might have skipped his eight o'clock class had he been able to sleep in. That, however, proved to be impossible as his mind flipped relentlessly through its rolodex of recollections – memories of June. The pleasant memories he relived; the vague memories he revived as best he could; the scarcity of the memories he regretted; that there could never be a new memory made enraged him. Jeremy slept fitfully throughout the night and woke up well before the late November dawn.

The morning air was seasonably cool, but it felt cold as hell as Jeremy rode his Hayabusa to campus. He expected a certain level of activity at the crime scene, but in no way did he anticipate the pure pandemonium that greeted his sight as he closed in on the Facility. Police cars, news trucks and a plethora of University-logoed vehicles had transformed the street in front of the Facility into a parking lot. A virtual army of city cops, highway patrol officers, and University policemen guarded and patrolled every intersection, sidewalk, and doorway. A crowd of onlookers milled around behind the sawhorse and yellow tape barricades that had been erected around a large portion of Grover's Field. Imbedded within the crowd were the news crews with their lights and cameras and microphones stuck in people's faces. On the other side of the barricades were ten or more forensic lab workers wearing white coats and latex gloves as they sifted through the abundance of trash left over from the RockFest. It certainly was not the image the University suits wished to be beamed from the booms of the satellite news trucks to the four corners of the earth.

After taking in the other-worldly scene outside the Facility, Jeremy wandered inside. The stairwells to the upper floors of the Biotechnology Facility were cordoned off and a campus cop stood guard at the elevator. The ground floor and its classrooms, however, were open for business.

He got to his classroom fifteen minutes early and mumbled a hello to the two students already there. He took his accustomed seat in the back and, with dread, turned his attention for the first time to the University newspaper.

"MURDER IN GROVER'S FIELD" read the prominent headline. The

article offered nothing Jeremy didn't already know and included most of everything he did know, including how her body was mutilated and some internal organs removed. There was, however, no direct reference to the symbol engraved in her forehead nor any mention of the band who called themselves Cocytus.

CHAPTER 23

Tuesday, November 25

BY Tuesday, the third day after June's murder, the activity around campus and the Facility had settled down. Around lunchtime the police reopened the upper floors of the Facility. Needing something other than the murder to occupy his mind, for once Jeremy wanted to work. Early that afternoon as he sat at the console of his primary instrument, a state-of-the-art UV spectrophotometer, Grady popped in.

"I heard what happened to June," Grady said. "I know you two were close and I'm sorry."

"Did you know her?" asked Jeremy. He would have been surprised to learn that Grady spoke to anyone besides him, as skittish as he was.

"I knew her enough to know that she had a kind heart."

"Yes, she did," concurred Jeremy. "I'm going to miss her."

"I wouldn't."

"What?" asked Jeremy with indignation.

"I'm not being disrespectful," added Grady hastily. "All I'm saying is maybe she's better off – she's been released from her cocoon."

Jeremy glared into the black of Grady's sunglasses but all he could see was the reflection of his own annoyed face. "Just once, Grady, I would really like it if you would just talk in an understandable way. Is there any way you could do that for me?"

"Our bodies are like cocoons – just a few silky threads wrapped around our souls to tether them to this earthly plane. One day, the threads break and the soul is freed to roam the hidden realms. We should not mourn June's passing for death is not the end."

"For June's sake I hope you're right," said Jeremy, "but as for me, I'd just as soon keep my cocoon anchored right here in this world for as long as possible."

"You should be careful what you wish for, Jeremy. Some things are worse than death. Remember that."

CHAPTER 24

Wednesday, November 26

*I*T was Wednesday, the day before Thanksgiving and the campus resembled a ghost town. The undergrad students had all gone home for the long holiday. The upper floors of the Facility, however, bustled with activity as the professors and grad students tried to make up for the time lost earlier in the week.

Jeremy, too, was hard at work in his lab when Jinni called.

"Are you sure you'll be okay alone?" she asked.

Jeremy's parents, who lived a few hours south of Destiny, were gone on vacation, a Caribbean cruise.

"I'm sure," he replied. "I could use a little down time."

Jeremy declined Jinni's invitation to spend the holiday with her at her family's home. Feeling as he did, he had no desire whatsoever to spend the next day and a half pretending to be cordial. Ever since June's death, Jeremy could do little more than go through the motions of his life. He attended his morning classes and showed up for the labs he taught and zoned out in front of the television at night. Although every conversation at the Facility gravitated to the murder, he had little to say. On the outside he wore a brave, even nonchalant face but underneath it all he had done nothing but think about June and the waste that was her death. He felt awful.

"I should be back by Friday afternoon," said Jinni. "You can call me if you like."

It was mid-afternoon when Tavalin unsuccessfully tried to sneak up on Jeremy while he worked.

"Don't even think about it," warned Jeremy. "I'm really not in the mood."

"I had to try," Tavalin quipped.

"Have you heard anything else about the investigation?" asked Jeremy.

"Just what I've seen on television," replied Tavalin. "Did you see our good friend Lieutenant Sykes' interview on CNN this morning?"

"Wow, CNN?" exclaimed Jeremy. "No, I didn't see it. What did he have to say?"

"Not too much," replied Tavalin. "He didn't look very comfortable with all the questions they were asking. I must say I thoroughly enjoyed seeing him on the hot seat. Now maybe he knows how we felt."

"So they still don't have a suspect?"

"Apparently not. Sykes appealed for anyone with information to come forward. He said that someone at the RockFest must have seen something."

"Did they mention the symbol at all?" asked Jeremy.

"No, but certainly they've figured out by now where it came from."

"You would think," agreed Jeremy.

"Think of all the time that and the other mutilation took," said Tavalin. "Why would anybody go to all that trouble?"

"They wouldn't," began Jeremy, "unless that was part of the motive. Take away the mutilation and maybe that takes away the reason the sicko killed June in the first place. It had to be one of Cocytus' drug-crazed fans gone bonkers."

"Maybe you should go back down to the station and explain it all to Lieutenant Sykes," Tavalin joked. "It sounds like you've got it all figured out."

"I hope I never have to talk to that man again."

CHAPTER *25*

Thursday, November 27

O N Thanksgiving Day, Jeremy turned on the television, expecting nothing more exciting than the pre-game parades. When he surfed by the cable news network, he learned of what the talking heads described as a *shocking new revelation in the slaying of June Song*.

It took the media exactly four days to learn of the symbol carved into June's forehead and how the killer carefully removed her internal organs, including her heart. All morning long, Jeremy watched the news shows as each of the various experts claimed his or her fifteen minutes of fame. Medical examiners rotated through to discuss the technical details of human dissection. The criminal psychologists discussed the mindset and motives of the textbook mutilator-killer. Authorities on the occult were conjured up, strange characters who either studied these shady factions or else had been cult members themselves. The symbol itself was the centerpiece of most of the discussions.

They even showcased an interview with the drummer of the band, Cocytus, who maintained that the symbol was meaningless. He said that he and his band mates had essentially cut-and-pasted the elements of the symbol's dark-themed imagery from various sources they found on the internet. He seemed most uncomfortable when asked to explain the source of the band's name.

Sheepishly, he answered, "Cocytus is a name for the lowest level of hell. I can only tell you that we ran across the term one night and thought how bitchin' it sounded." At that he covered his mouth and, to someone off camera, muttered, "Sorry," before continuing. "I know how it might sound suspicious or whatever, but that's about all the thought we put into it. We never expected anything like this to come of it."

For his final comment, the drummer read a disclaimer, obviously composed by someone other than himself: "We, the members of the band Cocytus, have never, nor do we now, condone the use of any of our copyrighted symbols in the commission of any crime. We truly hope that the person or persons who are responsible for this heinous crime are brought to swift justice. Thank you."

The pundits on television mostly ignored the idea that the symbol was meaningless. They surmised and supposed and hypothesized all manner of meanings and innuendos that could and should be derived from the symbol. Jeremy suspected that the media moguls were happy to stretch out this sideshow for as long as people would turn on their televisions to watch. No one, it seemed, truly gave a damn about the death of his friend June, except as a sensational tragedy to exploit.

Around lunchtime, Tavalin called. "Have you seen this?" he asked.

"Regrettably, yes," replied Jeremy. "It makes me sick at my stomach, but for some reason I can't stop watching."

"That's why they keep playing it," said Tavalin, mirroring Jeremy's opinion. "They keep it rolling because it pumps up their ratings. And, get this – I read online that Cocytus has had over a million downloads of their songs since their connection to the murder became public."

"I'm sure they must hate that," added Jeremy facetiously.

Changing the subject, Jeremy asked, "So why aren't you spending the holiday with your mom? Judging by how often she calls, I would think that you two must be close."

Because Tavalin seemed uncomfortable speaking of his mother, Jeremy often brought up the subject, if for no better reason than to try and figure out why his friend seemed loath to enter into a discussion of her.

"I really have no desire to visit my mother," replied Tavalin. "She's a manipulative, mean-spirited bitty, and that's putting it nicely."

"Where did you say she lived?" asked Jeremy.

"I didn't. She moves around a lot."

"She sounds like quite the character," said Jeremy.

"What are you going to do this afternoon?" asked Tavalin, taking his turn to change the subject.

"The smart thing to do would be to study, especially since I skipped the first exam," replied Jeremy, "but we'll see. I'm good at finding other things to distract me."

As it turned out, this afternoon's distraction had to do with a certain girl burned to death back in 1969. Monika's mention of Claire at the secret beach rekindled Jeremy's desire to look for more information on the hippie queen. The most promising avenue of investigation seemed to be Claire's artwork, though before tonight, the only example Jeremy had been able to find was a low-resolution thumbnail of a painting that only served to tease.

Long after the last football game ended, somewhere in the far reaches of the world wide spider web of the internet, in a footnote to a footnote, Jeremy's perseverance finally paid off: One of Claire Wale's paintings – a composition entitled *Wicked Water* – would be on display tomorrow night as part of an art showing at the local gallery.

CHAPTER 26

Friday, November 28

*I*T was about eight p.m. on Friday when Jinni called, having just returned to town from visiting her family. She suggested they swing by Holgram's Department Store to take advantage of their after-Thanksgiving sale.

"We'll have to hurry," she said. "They close at nine."

"I would go, but there's somewhere else I need to go tonight."

"Where?" Jinni asked.

"It's a surprise."

"What about Holgram's?" asked Jinni. "I can't miss this sale."

"Do this thing with me and I promise I'll take you shopping in the morning."

Jeremy picked Jinni up a few minutes later and drove her downtown. The art gallery was located just off the Square.

"What are we doing here?" she asked, when she realized where he was taking her. "I know you – you aren't that much into art."

"I guess you don't know me as well as you think," he teased.

The gallery consisted of a single room, narrow and deep. Jinni stopped to admire a sculpture showcased near the front while Jeremy made his way systematically along the perimeter, scanning the paintings hung on the walls until he found the one in particular.

Coming into the gallery, Jeremy had a theory as to why there might be a market for the artwork of Claire Wales. Dead artists command higher prices for their limited-supply pieces but in Claire's case it was her story that really got the buyers juiced. The hippie queen died almost forty years ago, but her story had a life of its own. Who could resist the legend of a talented young artist who painted scenes of her wilderness home and died shortly thereafter in an all-consuming fire? There would always be some local hippie-turned-baby-boomer in the know ready to snatch up anything of hers that came up for sale. That was what Jeremy had come up with before he had seen one of her paintings in person. However, standing in the presence of Claire's creation raised his understanding to a new level.

A river bank separated the scene into roughly two halves, the forest side and the river side. The forest, full of dark green hues and darker shadows, stood in sharp contrast to the bone-white tones of the sun-draped boulders and roiling water. The river crashed headlong into the house-sized rock strategically placed in the middle of the channel. A sheer rock wall, the top of which extended beyond the scope of the painting, formed the backdrop. Immediately, Jeremy recognized the setting: this was, no doubt, a representation of the rapids of The Devil's Crotch.

While he had certainly enjoyed the scenery of the river and the surrounding forest, Claire's oil painting added more to the reality than Jeremy bore witness to before. Though hard to describe, part of this *more* was a hazy atmosphere and a certain quality of green iridescence that permeated the piece. The net result was a scene so lush and serene that it might have been from a primordial rain forest.

But it was the melancholy child that was the source of the emotional reaction stirring within him. The child, hauntingly beautiful, stood straight and still, veiled in the murky shade that surrounded her. Except for a contradictory purple flower stuck between the dark locks of her hair, she appeared as an integral part of the shadows, camouflaged within the gloominess. In her eyes a terrible sadness pulled at him like the gravitational suction of two black holes. Jeremy longed to assure the child, to comfort her, to gather her up in his arms and run with her, the way a loving brother might save his young sister from a burning house.

Jinni brought him back. "I really like this one," she said, having approached from behind.

Jeremy asked, "Do you recognize the scene?"

"Is it Sticks River?"

"Very good. How did you know?"

"It looks like The Devil's Crotch," she replied without missing a beat.

"You'll never guess the artist."

"I have no idea." Jinni tried to make out the signature in the bottom right corner.

"Claire Wales," obliged Jeremy.

"Who?"

"You might know her better as the hippie queen."

"I should have known this had something to do with her." Jinni studied the painting for a bit before adding, "But I have to admit she's very good."

"I wonder how much something like this costs?" Jeremy was picturing how awesome the painting would look on his living room wall.

"It's not for sale, but I can tell you it is one of the more expensive pieces in the gallery."

Jeremy twirled in the direction of the nasally voice. A well-groomed man with a diminutive frame had sidled up behind them. He wore a dated sports jacket and a white dress shirt open at the neck to reveal a large quantity of chest hair. Jeremy thought his style looked a bit like someone out of the '70s, reminiscent of a young Burt Reynolds or Engelbert Humperdinck. The man admired the painting for a long moment before directing his attention toward them.

"Are you connected with the exhibit?" asked Jinni.

"I am," the man replied. "Allow me to introduce myself. My name is Quinton Gordy. And you are…?"

"Jinni," she obliged.

"Charmed, I'm sure." Borrowing a custom from a more genteel time, he held Jinni's hand and lightly kissed it.

Jeremy introduced himself. The man's handshake revealed his hand to be extraordinarily soft and silky, like the hand of a well-pampered woman.

"I gather that you own at least some of these lovely pieces?" Jeremy asked the question even though he recognized the name as being one of the contributing collectors.

"I am only the humble caretaker. Works of art are meant to be shared, not owned."

"Is this one yours, Mr. Gordy?" asked Jeremy.

"Please, call me Quinton," he said. "And, yes, it is mine, I'm happy to say. I consider it the crown jewel of my collection."

"What do you know about the hippie queen?" asked Jeremy.

Quinton laughed. "Ah, I see you have heard the circulating stories. I know a great deal about her painting techniques but I'm afraid I know only as much – or little – about her personally as the rumor mill allows."

"Jeremy's interest in the hippie queen almost did me in," interjected Jinni.

"Pray tell, how so?" asked Quinton.

"Coincidentally, it was right here," she said as she pointed at the painting. "We almost drowned, right here in The Devil's Crotch."

The collector returned a puzzled look.

Jinni asked, "You are familiar with The Devil's Crotch, are you not?"

"No, I can't say that I am," he replied. "Please, enlighten me."

"The Devil's Crotch," Jeremy replied, "is a set of rapids on Sticks River. Jinni and I navigated them, so to speak, by canoe."

The collector turned back to the painting, rubbed his chin and muttered, more to himself than anyone else, "A real place – that explains a thing or two…"

Jeremy and Jinni looked on curiously.

Eventually, Quintin turned back to them and said, "I suppose that explains why the artist entitled this particular piece *Wicked Water*. I had no idea that the title referenced the proper name of the rapids, but I am very grateful to have learned this. Now, if you will, what were the circumstances of your visit to The Devil's Crotch?"

"Jeremy took me through the rapids all because he wanted to find the old ruins of the hippie queen's commune," said Jinni, "and almost drowned me in the process."

"That's quite the story," replied Quintin, clearly impressed. "Does the painting do the scene justice?"

"Absolutely," replied Jeremy. "I actually snapped some photos when we were there. I could send them to you if you want me to."

"Yes, yes," the collector replied enthusiastically. He retrieved a business card from his front shirt pocket and handed it to Jeremy. "Feel free to contact me anytime."

"I can email them to you tomorrow," said Jeremy.

"Wonderful."

"What is your interpretation of the child in the painting?" asked Jeremy

"The interpretation of art is subjective," replied Quintin. "Don't ask what she means to me. True meaning is found in the eye of the beholder."

"You know this painting better than anyone," said Jeremy. "Why don't you give us your expert interpretation? Being a student of science, my leanings are not of the artistic slant."

Quintin smiled. "We all have an artistic slant, no matter our vocation. What I can tell you is that the child is common to many of Claire's paintings. Mine is not the only example of the nymph in the shadows."

Jinni asked, "How did you happen to obtain one of her paintings?"

"Actually, it's a little surprising." The collector lowered his voice a notch. "It seems every year at the local flea market one surfaces. I got mine for a good price before the other collectors wised up to the pattern. Apparently, back in the day, Ms Wales used to peddle her paintings around town. No one really knows how many might still be out there. My fear is that a masterpiece could be melting away in some hot, humid attic, its value unbeknownst to its owner. My hope is that even the ignorant masses would see the appeal of these paintings and not expose them to ruinous conditions."

Jeremy asked, "If you don't mind my asking, what might one expect to pay for one like this?"

"If you can find one for less than six to eight thousand dollars, I would say snatch it up."

"Well, that leaves me out," Jeremy muttered. "I guess I'll have to settle for adoration from afar."

"Oh, you never know. The annual flea market commences a week from tomorrow. You could get lucky."

"Only if you are not there to bid against me," Jeremy remarked.

The collector laughed. "Well, it was nice meeting you all. I should get about the business of packing up. Closing time is upon us."

Before they left, Jeremy snapped a few pictures of the painting, including some close-ups of the child in the shadows.

***

Back at Jeremy's condo, they settled in to watch the tail end of a big game on television. Unlike most girls of Jeremy's acquaintance, Jinni understood even the nuances of football and enjoyed watching it almost as much as did Jeremy. However, as entertaining as the double-overtime finish should have been, Jeremy could only think of their trip to the gallery and Claire's painting. He replayed their conversation with the collector, and as he did, he reflected on one particular word Quintin used in reference to the child in the painting: He called her a nymph.

Speaking of nymphs…

Grady first made mention of nymphs in Reefers Woods, a statement Jeremy judged at the time to be completely ridiculous. Before tonight, Jeremy only had a vague sense of the term's meaning, but after seeing the dreamy little girl, he had a clearer picture. If ever there was a nymph, she was it. And, consistent with Grady's pontifications, she existed as part of Reefers Woods, even if it was the version of Reefers Woods that sprang from the imagination of the hippie queen.

That Jeremy had witnessed children (nymphs?), creeping enigmatically from Reefers Woods to join in at Monika's bonfire, was too much of a coincidence to ignore – but were they even real? Did anyone else present at the bonfire see them or was he the only one? After Jeremy dropped Jinni off at her house, he immediately rang up Tavalin.

"Are you awake?"

"You know I never sleep," replied Tavalin. "What's up?"

"The reason I called…" Jeremy paused before reloading the sentence. "I'm calling because I've been meaning to ask you something – something about that night at the beach on the lake."

"What is it?"

"Did you, by any chance, see anyone at the bonfire besides the ten or twelve people who were dancing when we first arrived?"

"No, I don't think so," replied Tavalin before adding, "I do remember you asked me a similar question that night. What gives?"

"Some of what I'm about to tell you might sound a little crazy," cautioned Jeremy. "You remember after they quit dancing and that girl started to speak…?"

"I do."

"Well, I saw, or I thought I saw, a group of young children and an old woman walk out of the woods to mingle with the others around the bonfire. They didn't say anything and nobody else seemed to take notice. Did you see them?"

"No, Jeremy, absolutely not. Are you off your rocker?"

"I know how it sounds but I saw them, as clear as day."

"You *are* crazy," said Tavalin. "Think about what you are saying. It makes no sense for children to be out there in the first place."

"Maybe you just couldn't see from where you were," said Jeremy, grasping at straws. "Maybe your view was hindered?"

"I could see just fine." Tavalin was adamant. "They weren't there, plain and simple."

If Tavalin did not see them, Jeremy did not want to dwell on this any more than he had to. "It must have been some weird trick of the shadows," replied Jeremy flippantly. "I'm glad that's settled."

In reality, nothing had been settled in Jeremy's mind, other than the observation that he, Grady, and Claire might or might not have seen young children lurking about Reefers Woods.

Surprisingly, Tavalin did not pursue the subject. Instead, he asked, "What are you doing tomorrow?"

"Nothing exciting. Jinni is coming over first thing. I promised I'd go shopping with her."

"In town?" asked Tavalin.

"Yes. She wants to be at Holgram's as soon as the doors open."

"That sounds pretty dull, but then again, I hear that's exactly what married men do."

"I'm not married," replied Jeremy.

"You might as well be."

"You just wish you had a girlfriend."

Jeremy had not meant to counter with a remark so close to the truth, and he immediately felt bad for having said it.

"Any plans for tomorrow night?" asked Tavalin, seeming not to notice the zinger.

"I'm not sure but I'm pretty sure I'll be with Jinni."

"Wouldn't you rather go out on the town?" asked Tavalin. "It is Saturday night, you know."

For a moment Jeremy considered his friend's proposition, not because he wanted to go out with Tavalin but because of a certain someone else he might meet up with if he happened to find himself at a place called Bar Nowhere on a Saturday night.

When Jeremy did not respond, Tavalin added, "If you change your mind or Jinni goes home early, call me and maybe we can do something."

"I will, but don't count on it."

"Like I said," replied Tavalin despondently. "You might as well be married."

Just before Tavalin hung up, he said, "Let me know if you see any more children who aren't real."

Reefers Woods – August, 1969

(Thirty-nine years ago)

The King's Pinnacle

As soon as she heard the growl of the rapids, Claire's anticipation caught fire. Now at least she could focus on this new liquid sound and try to ignore the maddening slosh-slosh sounds that emanated from her canteen with every step. The walk, made more difficult by the large number of limbs brought down by the remnants of Hurricane Camille, took longer than usual. For the duration, Claire kept telling herself it would be better if she waited. By the time she arrived at the rapids she was bursting in her desire. She spread her beach towel on a large flat rock overlooking the tail end of the white water and removed her shoes. When she finally drank, she shuddered a bit at the twang of the homemade wine. Though necessary, ingesting the lotus within an alcohol-laden drink was her least favorite part of the process. The alcohol in the wine served to extract the intoxicating ingredient from the roughly 20 blooms required for the desired effect.

Claire jiggled the canteen and watched with crossed eyes as the last drop of her purple concoction dripped onto her eager tongue. Now all she had to do was relax and enjoy the day and her surroundings. Her present location was the rockiest area within Reefers Woods and the only place she knew where deposits of the King's Yellow pigment could be found. The dominant feature of this setting was a sheer-walled rock formation that bordered the river and rose to a height well above the tops of the tallest trees. So unusual was the topography that she gave it a name. Initially, Claire referred to the area as the King's Yellow Pinnacle, *but the moniker soon got shortened to the* King's Pinnacle.

The sunshine caressed Claire's body while she waited. She knew the routine well. The first shot across the bow was characterized by nervousness and a slight wooziness. It would only be a few more minutes before the everyday world was transformed into a burning new world of euphoria.

Finally, the moment Claire had been waiting for arrived. The first two hours were the most intense part of the trip, and were defined by her love of everything under the sun. She loved the river and the rocks and the towering walls of the King's Pinnacle *and the sky and the trees and how it felt to comb her fingers through her hair. She marveled at the working of her mind and whatever else she saw or heard or felt or thought. She climbed down to hang her feet in the ice-cold river and made short excursions into the woods. Wherever Claire happened to be at any given moment was the most excellent place in the universe.*

As morning turned to early afternoon, she settled into the less intense but still surreal phase of the lotus experience. Claire had wandered a few hundred yards from the river when a slight, out-of-place movement caught her eye. A boy, no more than ten years old, was quietly watching her from the shadows. At first she wondered if perhaps the boy was akin to the mysterious young girl who had been known to make her appearances to Claire at times like this.

"Hello."

When he spoke, Claire assumed the boy to be real.

"Are you lost?" she asked. She could not imagine why else a child of his age would be this deep in the forest.

"No," he answered indignantly. "I know my way home."

"Where do you live?" she asked.

"Over yonder."

The boy pointed away from the river in the general direction of the road. Still, his presence here surprised Claire because there must be at least four miles of heavy forest in between here and the road.

"Do your parents know where you are?"

"I stay with my uncle but he don't care where I go." The boy stared at the ground and shifted his weight from one leg to the other. "I don't like it too much where he is anyway."

"Why not?"

"I just don't," he replied meekly. In a stronger voice he added, "I like the woods better."

Claire knew something about an unhappy home life. "You know what? I like the woods too."

At this the boy smiled. It wasn't until after they walked back to the river and sat down in close proximity that she noticed his strikingly-blue eyes. The boy saw her see them and averted his gaze.

"What are you staring at?" he asked defensively. "Haven't you ever seen a Negro with blue eyes?"

"They're beautiful," replied Claire in all sincerity.

"Most everybody just makes fun of them."

"They're probably just jealous."

She and the boy shared a comfortable rapport, so much so that Claire thought that perhaps he had been sent to her for a reason. He did seem to know his way around, and she could think of no better person to help her search for any undiscovered lotus habitat. She took him by their picked-over lotus swamp so he would know what he was looking for. She also showed him the commune so he would know where to find her. Portraying his good manners, the boy removed his muddy shoes before entering the hippies' abode.

"This is groovy," he exclaimed as he padded around in his socks, looking at everything.

Claire smiled to herself. She was pretty sure the word "groovy" was a new addition to the boy's vocabulary. He had picked it up from her.

After he left, having assured her that he knew his way back home, Claire got out her painting supplies and a fresh canvas. Painting solely from the vivid memories she had burned earlier in the day, she reproduced the scene from the King's Pinnacle, *as she had seen it through the prism of the purple lotus experience. She worked obsessively until the painting had taken on all the splendor of its final form. All, that is, with the exception of the melancholy child, whom she would not think to add in until a later date.*

CHAPTER *27*

Saturday, November 29

"**D**ON'T you want to come in with me?" Jinni asked. "You know, you could use some new clothes."

"If you don't mind, I'd rather wait out here." Jeremy plopped down on the sidewalk bench.

Jinni smiled. "Why does that not surprise me? I shouldn't be long."

Jeremy loved this town, peculiar name and all. Destiny had somehow managed to preserve a certain quaintness that one might associate with an earlier, simpler time, when America was defined by the sum total of thousands of small, prosperous towns such as this. The shops and restaurants that lined the covered sidewalks were unique to Destiny, bearing names like Smitty's and Miley's Grocery and Holgram's Department Store. While not overcrowded, the streets and shops were full of activity. There were soccer moms with shopping bags, babies in jogging strollers and toddlers with ice-cream-sticky hands. A smattering of senior citizens, primarily tourists and well-to-do retirees moved to town, also mulled about. Jeremy, however, found that he was most interested in the co-eds sauntering about on legs the same gold as the Indian summer sun.

Jeremy squinted as one petite young lady approached from the sunny end of the sidewalk. Obscured as she was by the backdrop of bright sunshine, he could not easily discern her features, but there was something about the deliberate way she walked that caught his eye. Trying not to stare as she drew closer, he looked away, toward the Courthouse in the center of the Square. After a handful of seconds, Jeremy sensed her in his peripheral vision. She was nearby and she had stopped, presumably to window shop. Why else would she be standing so close?

As she dawdled, Jeremy sneaked a peak. Seeing her face above him here in the bright of day seemed so unexpected and out of context that he thought he imagined her. Reflexively, he stood up.

"Monika?" It was all he could think to say.

She was real and she was smiling.

"What are you doing here?" he asked dumbly.

"Good to see you too," she said sarcastically. "Don't I get a hug?"

Jeremy leaned awkwardly in and stiffly accepted her embrace. His insides quivered in extreme anxiety. Worlds would collide if Jinni were to catch him talking to Monika.

"How have you been?" she asked.

Jeremy fought the urge to turn tail and run, reminding himself that Jinni was shoe-shopping. In all likelihood, she would be inside for a good while longer.

As casually as he could fake, he answered, "Fine, I guess."

"You look good," she said.

"You do too," he admitted.

"Have you been missing me?" she asked and flashed a mischievous grin.

Honestly, Jeremy had missed Monika but this didn't feel like the proper time or place to speak of it, but neither could he bring himself to lie and say that he had not.

"Because I've missed you," she added boldly. "I want to see you again."

Jeremy did not allow himself to even consider the unexpected proposition. "I can't do that, Monika. It wouldn't be right to betray Jinni's trust – not again."

He also could not contemplate the longing in her eyes. He lowered his gaze to his shoe tops and absent-mindedly pawed one sneaker at a dirty spot on the concrete.

"I don't understand," said Monika, clearly taken aback.

"I have obligations." Jeremy's words sounded stupid to him but they were, more or less, accurate. In the wake of June's death, he felt more obligated to do right by Jinni. Losing June made him appreciate Jinni all the more.

Monika, however, did not give in so easily. "Don't you remember our night together?" she asked. "Don't you remember the majesty?"

Jeremy stared at the scuff mark on the sidewalk.

"Yes, I remember," he replied as he raised his eyes to meet hers. "I remember *everything*."

"Tell me then, how can you not want to be with me now? Tell me truthfully that you don't want me and I'll leave. That's all I'm asking."

Jeremy knew the right course of action. Still, he could not bring himself to dismiss the one who stood before him. What did he do to deserve this dilemma? Was there any way to resist the allure of this woman?

"I can't deal with this now," he said. "Jinni is right inside."

Just then the door to the store opened, spooking Jeremy. "I've got to go."

He lurched away, almost colliding with the woman leaving Holgram's. Thankfully, she wasn't Jinni but he kept moving anyway. Without looking back, Jeremy slid into the ice cream shop two doors down. At the counter he ordered a double scoop of chocolate ice cream on a waffle cone. When the little bell on the shop door tinkled softly behind him, he turned to look and wasn't entirely surprised to see that it was Monika. She joined him at the counter.

"I'll have what he's having," Monika said without directly acknowledging Jeremy. She sat down at one of the tables by the plate glass window that looked out onto the sidewalk.

Jeremy paid for their ice cream. As he handed over Monika's cone, he noticed the silver ring on the slender forefinger of her outstretched hand. The scene triggered a memory of their first encounter that night at the Singe show, only then it had been a White Russian that passed from his hand to hers. With parted lips and a steady gaze, she took a slow, deliberate bite from the crown of her ice cream. Fittingly, the visual also took him back to the first night they met, back to that first ambush of a kiss.

Jeremy felt as if it were not the ice cream but he who was melting.

Frantically, Jeremy debated what to do next. He certainly wasn't comfortable hanging out with Monika with Jinni two doors down, but neither did he relish the image of him running from Monika like a coward. In the end, and in spite of the peril, Jeremy joined Monika at her table. At least they were no longer parked at the front door of Holgram's Department Store.

"What if you just give her some?" asked Monika.

Though Monika did not explicitly say, Jeremy knew exactly to whom and to what she referred. Even so, it was a radical suggestion.

"Who, Jinni?" he asked.

"Why not?"

"I can think of several why-nots," he asserted. "The question is why her? Why Jinni?"

"As it turns out," replied Monika, "I have some very special friends I would like you to get to know. I'm gathering that you and your little girlfriend are a package deal. Give Jinnigirl a little taste of the Unreal and she'll understand. It could be you and her, and me, and the others, all together as one big happy family. She can become one of us."

What does that mean, "one of us"? wondered Jeremy. *Am I already one of them?*

He laughed uncomfortably. "I don't think that would work. I'm pretty sure Jinni wouldn't try it and, even if she did, I don't think I could talk her into joining your little group."

As soon as the words came out, Jeremy wondered if he had given something away. He could not let on that he had, in a sense, already met Monika's *special friends* on the secret beach.

"You might be surprised what Jinni would agree to if she were to develop a taste for the Unreal."

"Even if Jinni could handle being around the two of us," said Jeremy, "I don't think I could handle being around the two of you."

"Why, Jeremy?" Monika's gaze flittered over his face, probing his expression for the answer. "You still want me, don't you?"

Jeremy hesitated, and his hesitation gave him away.

Monika laughed exultantly. "You don't have to answer if you don't want to. I know what your deal is. You want to have your cake and eat it too. Jinni's the good girl and I'm the bad. You want us both."

"It doesn't matter what I want," replied Jeremy, not bothering to differ.

"I don't know why not," countered Monika. "If what you want doesn't matter, then tell me, what in the world does matter?"

Not knowing what to say, Jeremy said nothing at first. Then, of all things, the gist of something Grady once said to him came to mind. "Maybe doing the right thing trumps doing what we want."

Meanwhile, Monika dug something out of the front pocket of her jeans. "Here," she said. "Take this."

It was a folded square of aluminum foil, about the same dimensions as a postage stamp, but lumpier.

"What is it?" he asked.

Suddenly, Jinni stepped into view. She was immediately outside on the sidewalk, walking, and at the same time, trying to peer through the glare to the inside of the plate glass window.

Monika pressed the foil into his palm. "Just take it," she insisted.

"I've got to go," Jeremy rocketed from his chair, banging his knee painfully on the underside of the table.

Monika squeezed in one more sentence just as he got to the door. "You know where to find me."

Jinni had her hand on the handle as Jeremy aggressively swung open the door and limped outside.

"Hey, watch out!" exclaimed Jinni.

"Oh, hello," Jeremy said as if surprised to see her. "Are you done shopping already?" He put his arm around Jinni, not as a loving gesture but to influence her away from the ice cream shop.

"I thought I might find you in there." Jinni eyed his ice cream cone. "That looks yummy."

"You can have it," Jeremy said as he practically jabbed the cone at her face. "Enjoy," he added as he led her down the sidewalk and away from his dark angel.

Just when he thought he had gotten away clean, Jinni asked, "Were you talking to that girl in the ice cream shop?"

"Not really," replied Jeremy. "Just small talk, that's all."

Certain that Jinni saw something or at least sensed his deceit, Jeremy waited for the additional questions and accusations that most certainly would be forthcoming. To his surprise and great relief, Jinni made no further mention of the girl in the ice cream shop.

It was only after they turned the corner to the sight of his condo that Jeremy calmed down enough to reflect on Monika's insight. Monika was right – he did want both of them, Jinni and her, a greedy desire that would never be compatible with reality. But his dark angel raised another interesting point. What if he did turn Jinni on to the Unreal? If he did, and she accepted, it might bring out the bad girl in Jinni. Then he would have his good and bad girl, all wrapped up in one. As Jeremy fingered the little folded square of aluminum foil in his pocket, Monika's words reverberated in his mind:

You might be surprised what Jinni would agree to if she were to develop a taste for the Unreal.

***

That night in bed, Jeremy revisited his chance meeting with Monika. He took great delight in how she came right out and said she wanted to see him again. In a million years he would not have expected her to admit to that, even if it were true.

You know where to find me, she had said. Jeremy knew she meant Bar Nowhere. He also knew *when* to find her there. *I'm there most Saturday nights,* she had remarked before the Singe show on the night they first met. Seeing how Saturday night was happening right now, Jeremy wondered if hooking up with her would be as easy as it was the last time. The recollection of that wild night out with Monika triggered an almost overwhelming urge to seek her out again.

If I get up right now, I could be there in twenty minutes.

Jeremy's only defense was to fill his mind with thoughts of Jinni. Like everyone, Jinni had her faults but the good in her far outweighed the bad. She was kind, compassionate, quick to listen and slow to anger. Perhaps most importantly, she opened herself up to him. When he peered inside Jinni's glass-house heart, Jeremy could see that she loved him completely and without pretense. At times he wondered why she had chosen him to be the one she loved but he could never muster the courage to ask. He was afraid she might not know why either and he didn't want to get her thinking.

Jeremy felt proud how he had stuck up for Jinni this morning but he knew Monika recognized his ligering desire to be with her again. Certainly, the prospect of another romantic interlude with his dark angel tweaked his fancy, but it was not the only facet of his attraction to Monika. He was equally enthralled by her secrets. He wanted to know what she spoke of on the beach that night, and he wanted to uncover the nature of her connection to the hippie queen. Adding to the overall intrigue was the parting gift she so deftly pressed into his palm at the ice cream shop. What he would ultimately do with the contents of that shiny little package, now tenuously stored in the back of his sock drawer, was anybody's guess.

Even as he drifted into slumber, Jeremy continued to wrestle against the inexorable pull of Monika. For once in his life, he must choose wisely. He wanted to do the right thing, but could he realistically break free from his attraction to her? Could the ocean tides ever cease to be pulled by the moon's gravity?

I, the ocean; Monika, the moon.

Yet, the tides wax and wane day after day, perpetually drawn by the moon but satisfied to be separated from it. And does not the earth hold the oceans close to her bosom? Does not the gravity of the earth render the influence of the moon negligible?

Jinni, the earth.

It would be disastrous for that chasm of separation to vanish; calamitous to allow the oceans to touch the moon and so, too, it must be for Jeremy and this other woman.

Though I may be drawn to Monika, I must never again touch her.

With that last conscious thought, Jeremy fell into sleep.

CHAPTER *28*

Sunday, November 30

*S*TUDYING was the last thing in the world Jeremy wanted to do.

Tavalin had called at ten o'clock on Sunday, waking him. Though he agreed to the study session, Jeremy had no desire to subject his mind to the throes of organic chemistry this morning. He might have turned down his friend had Tavalin not suggested they first meet at the drive-in for an early lunch.

When Jeremy arrived, Tavalin was waiting for him. Jeremy parked his car, got out and slid into the passenger seat of the little yellow Honda.

"What are you having?" asked Tavalin

As Tavalin barked his order into the speaker box, Jeremy's mind was occupied not with the food and not with organic chemistry. He was thinking of the hippie queen. And though, admittedly, at least some of his interest in Claire sprang from Monika's connection to her, and though he had resolved not to seek out Monika, he could see nothing wrong with seeking out Claire.

"Do you have any money I can borrow?" asked Tavalin. "I don't have enough."

"And if I don't, what are you going to do?" asked Jeremy contemptuously.

"I guess I just assumed you could spot me a couple of bucks."

"Here." Jeremy tossed some crumpled bills onto Tavalin's lap.

The next obvious step for Jeremy's quest for Claire was to find her grave, but who would possibly have that information? The students at the University had a tradition of passing along the hippie queen ghost story to incoming students. Could it be possible that there existed a contingency of students who were familiar with the ghost story and who also knew the location of her grave?

"Somebody knows," muttered Jeremy under his breath.

Tavalin, who had been occupied with the carhop, passed a grease-splotched bag over to Jeremy and asked, "What are you mumbling about over there?"

Jeremy recalled having mentioned the hippie queen a time or two in Tavalin's presence but his friend never seemed much interested.

"You remember that hippie queen ghost story, right?" Jeremy asked.

"Yeah, I guess," replied Tavalin. "What about it?"

"Do you think there's anything to it?"

"Why do you care?"

"I think the story is fascinating," replied Jeremy. "I'm especially curious to know if she really is buried somewhere in or near Destiny. If so, I'd like to take a look at that sculpture that supposedly appeared on her grave from nowhere."

"Is that right?" Tavalin seemed more interested in his hamburger than anything Jeremy had to say.

Jeremy stopped short of mentioning Grady, even though it was he who had informed Jeremy of the Reefers Woods connection and juiced Jeremy's interest in the ghost story. Jeremy also didn't dare bring up Monika's role in all of this. After her reference to Claire's Way and the rest of her intriguing spiel at the secret beach, how could he *not* want to investigate the hippie queen?

After eating and drinking for a few minutes in silence, Tavalin spoke up. "If you really want to see her grave," he said nonchalantly, "I know where it is."

Jeremy was flabbergasted. "Why didn't you say so before?"

"I'm saying so now," replied Tavalin with a smirk. Without elaborating, he took another large bite from his burger.

"Well," prodded Jeremy. "Are you going to tell me where it is or not?"

"Would you like me to show you?"

"Take a wild guess," replied Jeremy sarcastically.

***

Tavalin wouldn't say where he was taking Jeremy.

When they turned out Sticks River Road, Jeremy asked, "Is Claire really buried out here?"

About two or three miles past the *Keep Out* sign at the break in the road, Tavalin pulled onto the shoulder. A narrow lane, barely discernable, jutted off into a grown-over field.

"Think you can find your way back here later?" asked Tavalin.

"Aren't we going in now?" asked Jeremy.

"This is as far as I go."

"What do you mean?" asked Jeremy.

"This is as far as I go," repeated Tavalin as he worked to turn the car around in the limited space.

Jeremy looked over at his friend, trying to get a read on his evasiveness, but Tavalin only stared straight ahead, pretending not to see him in his peripheral vision. It was obvious that he was holding something back.

"Out with it, Tavalin. Why won't you go out there with me?"

"It's creepy out there, okay? I'm not especially fond of going to deserted cemeteries in the middle of the woods, that's all."

Jeremy's first impulse was to poke fun at his friend's nervousness but thought better of it. Only after he actually laid eyes on the grave would he give Tavalin the hell he deserved for being afraid.

Jeremy studied the nearby landscape. Most notable was an oddly formed pine tree with three trunks. "I can find it," Jeremy replied confidently as he committed the three-in-one tree to memory. "Do I just follow the road in? How far do I go?"

"It's a long way, at least two or three miles, I would say. And it's not much of a road. I doubt you want to drive your car all the way in. You go until you see an old gate on the left. There might even be a sign that says *Eternal Springs*. Just follow the path on the other side of the gate. The cemetery is at the end of the path, just behind some old church ruins."

"Eternal Springs?" Jeremy asked. "What's that?"

"There used to be a settlement there a while back, 100 years ago or something like that. It's gone now."

Back at the drive-in, Jeremy said, "I think I'd rather go to the cemetery instead of studying. You understand, don't you?"

"I understand that if we don't study today, we'll regret it for a long time because there is no way for us to pass if we don't. We might fail even if we do study."

Tavalin was adamant and, for once, he was right. Jeremy gave in and spent the next several hours holed up with his friend in one of the small study rooms in the library. Though Jeremy intended on returning to the cemetery, the days were short this time of year and by the time they wrapped it up, it was too late. Though disappointed, he thought it best to postpone the trip.

Claire would have to wait.

CHAPTER 29

Monday, December 1

O N Monday morning Jeremy arrived at the elevator to find a cluster of graduate students, also just out of class, attempting to get upstairs to their respective labs for work. A University police officer was checking identification cards against the printed sheet he held.

"All non-faculty personnel who work in this building have permission to take the day off," the officer said. "That's straight from the chairman of the department."

Jeremy heard this and had already begun to walk away when the officer spoke again, louder this time.

"You're free to leave *after* I see your ID," he said.

Jeremy turned, looked at the cop, raised his eyebrows, pointed a finger at himself and mouthed, "Me?"

To which the officer responded resoundingly, "Yes, you."

He studied Jeremy's student identification for a moment then punched the elevator *up* button on the wall behind him.

"You can go on up, Mr. Spires. Fifth floor, right?" the officer asked. Before Jeremy could answer, the guard pushed the fifth floor button.

"Thanks," Jeremy said, glad that his section of the building seemingly had not been deemed pertinent to the investigation but disappointed that he might have to work today after all.

The elevator door opened to two more men in uniform who somehow already knew who he was.

"Step this way, Mr. Spires," one of them instructed and directed Jeremy toward Dr. Sloan's office.

Much to Jeremy's chagrin, it wasn't Skippy Sloan who sat at the desk; it was Lieutenant Sykes. He did not stand when Jeremy entered the room, nor did he offer his hand to shake.

"Have a seat, Jeremy. I have a few questions."

"Okay," Jeremy said in an uncertain tone.

"If you don't mind, I'm going to be using this." The cop indicated to a small tape recorder on the desk. The little red light was already on. "State your name please."

"Jeremy – Jeremy Spires."

Jeremy caught himself leaning forward in a posture that reflected his tense mindset. He forced his shoulders back, took a deep breath and tried to relax.

"For the record, can you affirm that you are here of your own volition?"

"My own volition?" asked Jeremy. "I don't know about that. I was headed home when one of your partners-in-crime directed me up here." Jeremy spoke jokingly and smiled, as he tried to lighten the mood.

"Let me reword that," the cop said in a tone that was not pleasant. "You understand that this is a voluntary meeting."

"Yeah, I guess."

"Let's get started." Lieutenant Sykes picked up the pen that was lying on the open page of a small notebook. "Can you think of anyone who might have had a reason to want to kill your coworker, June Song?" he asked and clicked the mechanism of the pen: *Click-click.*

"I can't imagine anybody even getting mad at June. That's what's so weird. I never heard her say a cross word, much less get mad at anybody."

"What about a jealous boyfriend?"

Jeremy thought of how she rebuffed Tavalin's advances but kept that information to himself. Tavalin was not only his friend; he was also his alibi.

"As far as I know she didn't have a boyfriend."

"Did you ever go out with her yourself?"

"No, not really," Jeremy answered, remembering the night they had gone to Sticks River Landing, the night they almost kissed.

The lieutenant perked up at this and not in a good way.

"What do you mean, not really?"

"I mean we went out as friends only."

"I've seen pictures of the young lady. She was an attractive girl. You're telling me you never made a move on her?"

"You know I've got a girlfriend, Lieutenant."

"Answer the question please."

Today felt totally different from their other talk a week ago. The prior meeting, though nerve-racking, had, in retrospect, been casual and unscripted, more like a simple conversation between two men. The current meeting felt contrived, as if the script were being read straight from the manual of standard operating police procedure.

"No sir, I never made a move on her," Jeremy replied and sighed deeply. "And you're right, she was an attractive girl. She was my friend and I still can't believe she's dead."

"Did Ms Song have a key to your lab?" Sykes asked, switching gears.

"No," answered Jeremy. He wondered where this line of questioning would lead.

"And the door to your lab is kept locked?"

"The door closes and locks by itself."

"So you would agree that if Ms Song were in your lab on the night that she was killed, someone with a key must have let her in?"

"What would make you think she was in my lab that night?" asked Jeremy.

"Hang on, I'll get to it. You previously told me that you spoke to her on Saturday night."

Lieutenant Sykes paused, waiting on Jeremy to verify the statement. Jeremy did not break eye contact but maintained his silence. He felt as if he were under attack or was about to be, and his passive-aggressive tendencies were rising to the surface.

"Well?" prodded the policeman.

"I'm sorry. Did you ask a question?"

The lieutenant tapped an angry-sounding *rat-a-tat-tat* rhythm with the pen on the surface of the desk. "You previously told me that you spoke to Ms Song on Saturday night. Is this an accurate statement?"

"Yes, it is."

"Where did this exchange take place?"

"In her lab down the hall."

"Did she leave her lab at any time while you were there?"

"No."

"What did you talk about?"

"Nothing in particular," replied Jeremy.

"Nothing to indicate that she was concerned for her safety?"

"No."

"Any indication that she had had any sort of disagreement or argument with anyone?"

Jeremy hesitated before answering. It was that very night, the night of June's murder, that Dr. Cain had confronted June over her use of his lab for the unauthorized research. Could he have been so angry as to kill June over that? It didn't seem likely. Besides, if Jeremy mentioned the secret work he and June were doing, he would be opening himself up to a whole slew of uncomfortable questions and to much closer scrutiny from the police. He finally decided to keep the subject under wraps, at least for the time being.

Jeremy replied, "No arguments with anyone that I am aware of."

"When you entered the building, which door did you use?"

"I came in the back door," answered Jeremy, perplexed.

"But didn't you park your car out front?"

"Yes." Jeremy realized that someone else must have provided this information to the police and, trying to be preemptive, explained, "You might be wondering why I went all the way around to the back door when the most direct route would be to simply go in through the front door."

"Yes, that was my next question."

"I noticed that my friend's car was parked down the street and I was trying to avoid him."

"Who were you trying to avoid?"

"Tavalin Cassel. It's a little silly, actually. I thought he might be hiding in the lobby. I was afraid he might try to scare me."

"I don't understand."

"Let me explain. I made the mistake of sneaking up on Tavalin a time or two inside the Facility and scaring him, you know, just for kicks. He returned the favor. After that, the whole thing got out of hand. Now, every time I enter the building, I worry that he is lying in wait for me. For that reason, I try to be unpredictable when choosing my route in. That's why I walked around to the back door of the building the night of the murder – simple as that."

Lieutenant Sykes glared at Jeremy as if he didn't know whether to believe him or not. Meanwhile, the pen in his hand, which seemed to be operating independently from the man, tapped out rhythms that would make a drum major blush.

"You also were observed, and I quote, 'sneaking around in a suspicious manner'. Do you claim that behavior to be similarly motivated?"

"We refer to it as *the game*," said Jeremy, trying to add credence. "It's just our on-going, tit-for-tat practical joke."

A fat bead of warm sweat gathered at the base of Jeremy's armpit and ran down his side. Everything he told the cop was true but he knew it must sound suspicious. "If you don't believe me, you should ask Tavalin. He'll back me up on this."

"That's the problem I'm having with you, Mr. Spires. Every part of your alibi is dependent on your friend Tavalin. I'm sorry to have to tell you this, but his credibility is questionable at best. That boy is as crazy as a road lizard. As for you, my impression is that you're hiding something."

"I'm not hiding anything, Lieutenant."

"Our forensic team found a tuft of hair caught in the window in your lab. It belonged to Ms Song. Can you tell me how it might have gotten there?"

"She's visited my lab plenty of times. I'd be surprised if you *didn't* find any of her hair in my lab."

"We found a *tuft* of hair, along with some tissue caught in the window's hinge. It could only have gotten there at a time when the window was open."

For many years, before it became the Facility, the building housed the since-relocated biology department. On its reincarnation as the house that Cecil Cain built, the outer design and construction of the original building remained intact. Included in this vintage design and retained in the new facility were windows that opened outward like miniature French doors.

"Did you ever have an occasion to open the windows in your lab?" asked Lieutenant Sykes.

"Maybe once or twice."

"How about Saturday night, the night June was killed? Did you open them then?"

"I told you, I didn't even go in my lab that night. After I left June's lab, I went straight home."

"You sure about that?" The cop's manner changed from methodical complacency to glaring ferocity. "You wouldn't be lying to me, now would you, Mr. Spires?"

Jeremy's fear and frustration boiled over. Venomously, he asked, "What exactly are you getting at, Vick?" Jeremy only knew the lieutenant's first name because he had overheard someone at the police station using it. "Why don't you just cut to the chase?"

"The autopsy results show wounds on the body that are consistent with a post-mortem fall from your window. June was thrown out the window of your lab into the dumpster, sometime between one and five a.m. on Sunday," growled Sykes. "This was an inside job and you are slap-dab in the middle of the inside. *That*, Mr. Spires, is what I'm getting at."

Jeremy's heart lost count for a second before resetting itself with slower, more powerful strokes. He could not quite fathom this turn of events. Were they really going to try to pin June's murder on him?

"I don't know anything about that," Jeremy retorted. "We aren't even supposed to open those windows," he added without reason, as if this provided some sort of defense.

"Jeremy, you have to realize that I'm in one hell of a tight situation. Someone threw a dead girl out your window right into my lap. I need answers and I need them now!"

"I didn't do it, I swear. I have no reason to kill June or anybody else."

"I want to believe you, Jeremy, I really do. But you've got to face the music. Your alibi is dependent on your friends and you were in contact with the victim on Saturday. Practical jokes aside, you were observed behaving in a suspicious manner around the time of her death. Furthermore, I believe you had a thing for Ms Song. Why else would you spend all those late hours with her? Maybe she rebuffed your advances. Of course, these things are circumstantial and would mean a lot less if it weren't for the physical evidence found in your lab. Put it all together and you are a suspect."

"Anybody with a key could have done it," whimpered Jeremy. If the lieutenant's intentions were to wear him down, he had succeeded. Jeremy felt defeated and spent.

A fine sheen of sweat had popped out on the lieutenant's forehead. "Alright then," he said, "let's pretend for a second that I believe you. Help me out – help yourself out. You know most if not all of the persons who have access to your lab. If you didn't do it, who did?"

Grady.

His name popped into Jeremy's mind of its own accord. Of all those who had a key to Jeremy's lab, Grady stood out as the oddball. He had also been in the building that night, waxing the hall floors.

Tell him about Grady.

Jeremy opened his mouth but no words escaped. For over a week, ever since June's death, Jeremy had felt numb. He hadn't even cried for June. Now, sitting here under the duress of the interrogation, it all hit home. June was dead. June was dead and he was here because they thought he did it. How was an innocent man supposed to react when accused of killing his friend?

Say something. The silence is damning.

But try as he might Jeremy could not perform like some trick pony for the police or anyone else. For the moment he couldn't think of himself. And, as convenient as it would be, he could not in good conscience sic the cops on Grady.

Instead, Jeremy retreated to some faraway recess of his mind, away from the four walls of this dreary little room, away from the straight-back chair that held his board-rigid body, and away from his own vacant gaze to a bittersweet place swelled full with images and sounds of his late friend June.

"There must be something more you can tell me."

The sound of the lieutenant's voice brought Jeremy back.

"No, that's it."

"Are you sure that's all you want to tell me?" asked the persistent cop.

"Yes."

Sykes returned a blank stare and clicked the pen's mechanism repeatedly in and out, in and out: *Click-click, click-click, click-click.*

Jeremy began to wonder if all the tapping and clicking was an interrogation technique. He pictured a young, pimply-faced Sykes, sitting in one of his police academy classes, eagerly studying the chapter titled, "Fifty ways to legally torment a suspect."

The lieutenant turned off the tape recorder. "Jeremy," he began, "Let me give you some friendly advice. Don't try to fool me. You might think I'm just some incompetent, small-town cop, but I've been in the game for a long time. I know when people are lying to me and I know when I'm not getting the whole story."

"I'm not hiding anything from you," insisted Jeremy. "I've got nothing to hide."

"Well, we'll just see about that." The cop's tone had changed to one of imminent dismissal and Jeremy gladly stood up, ready to leave.

"And, just so you know…" continued Sykes, "We are expected to report our progress to the media. I will not give out your name in the form of any official statement but it's not unusual for leaks to occur in high profile cases like this. Don't be surprised if your name surfaces at some point, even before being formally charged."

"That's just wonderful," Jeremy said sarcastically. He picked up on the Lieutenant's choice of words, *before being formally charged*, as if Sykes fully expected Jeremy to be arrested eventually.

He was halfway out the door when Lieutenant Sykes added, "And Jeremy, one more thing."

"What's that, boss?" Jeremy asked facetiously.

"Stay in town."

***

Later, Jeremy would not remember leaving the Facility and driving back to his condo. He simply found himself at home in the middle of a dizzying reality: June was dead. He was a suspect.

Where do I go from here?

He dreamed of escape. Why not vanish into the night? Why not hide out somewhere far, far away, somewhere where his troubles could not find him? Jeremy pictured himself traveling the country, camping, exploring, living life by the seat of his pants. But he knew if he ran now, his fate would be sealed. He would be presumed guilty and could never stop running.

Where, then, do I go from here?

Jeremy had no answers, only questions. He felt lost. And so he sat, alone, elbows propped on the desk's edge, bowed head held in his hands and tousled hair licking out between the slits of his clutching fingers.

In a sudden, unbridled expression of frustration, Jeremy screamed, "Let me OUT!" The echo of the last syllable lingered, ringing in his ears and burning in the back of his throat.

I gotta get out of here…

Downstairs, the automatic garage door squeaked grudgingly upward, replaced from the bottom up with an ever-widening crease of sunlight of the purest white. The hyper-sport street bike glistened like the lips of a sorority sweetheart: curvaceous, candy-apple red, sexy. Jeremy straddled the seat and worked at the straps of his helmet, his face obscured behind its polarized visor shield. He engaged the starter and with only a slight twist of the throttle the 1300 cc engine growled to life, greedy for more high-octane gasoline. Jeremy shared in its gluttony, desired its brain-sloshing power, and craved the speed it would soon deliver. Here, however, just off the downtown Square, was not the place nor were the oak-lined streets that comprised the outskirts of Destiny.

The place was Sticks River Road, his raceway and shrink. The time was now. Man and machine, together as one aerodynamic entity, blasted down the straight-away, the roar of the engine an accompaniment to Jeremy's throat-wrenching screams, the countryside blurring by ridiculously fast, at times in excess of 160 miles per hour.

By the time he arrived at the lakeside, Jeremy had managed to work off at least a measure of his frustration. For a good long while he sat in the grass staring at the expanse of Sticks River Lake. When he could no longer bear thinking about June and Lieutenant Sykes, he turned his thoughts to other things. He thought about the significance of this place to him, of Monika and of the hippie queen. Jeremy remembered the three-pronged tree that marked the entrance to the lane that presumably led to Claire's grave. A trip to see Claire's final resting place might be the perfect reprieve, but he would have to hurry if he wanted to make it to the cemetery before dark.

***

It had rained a good bit as of late. Jeremy rode slowly, trying to keep from sliding over in the muddy sections. The Hayabusa was not made for off-road riding, but at least he could pick and choose his line through the ruts and mud. With the conditions as they were, only a four-wheel-drive vehicle could have navigated through this mess. Had he brought his car, he would not have gotten far.

After a solid hour of slow-going, Jeremy finally arrived at the remnants of a sign and a gate. Kudzu vines had spun their way up the sign, mostly obscuring its declaration. Knowing what he thought it was supposed to say made it easier to discern the phrase amidst the vines, *Eternal Springs Church*. The gate was closed. A narrow, but well-beaten path wound around the gate and up a substantial hill. It was getting late and the light was failing. He would have to hurry to beat nightfall.

After retrieving his digital camera from one of the small saddle bags that hung from either side of his motorcycle, Jeremy legged his way up the steep path. There was absolutely nothing to indicate that it led anywhere. There was no evidence of a church or a cemetery, only deep woods getting deeper, and it had become noticeably darker. If there were people buried way out here, it was a hell of a place to wind up.

For a moment Jeremy considered where his body's final destination might be. He looked down at his legs as they lumbered autonomously toward this evening's goal, as unrelenting and unstoppable as his own eventual date with death. It was weird, thinking of the time when his soul could no longer lay claim to this body.

Just when Jeremy thought that the sign was nothing but a ruse, he came to something. If he had not been looking for it, he might have missed the crumbling structure wedged into the biomass. Large trees towered above while thick underbrush snuggled up tight to the peeled-paint walls. The church was fast going the way of the rest of the settlement, dust to dust. Jeremy followed the skinny dirt path that snaked around the back of the church. It led to the base of a knobby hill and split the difference between the two sides of a break in a wrought iron fence. The gate that had once filled that void was long gone. As he topped the hill, he was blinded by the almost horizontal beams of the setting sun. Jeremy shaded his eyes as if saluting.

The cemetery was utterly deserted, devoid of any living souls, save Jeremy. It was situated on a high point in the landscape although most of the long views were blocked by the scattered cedar trees on the hilltop. Sheets of Spanish moss hung like heavy beards from every limb. So prolific was the moss that tufts and clumps had spilled from the trees and draped itself over the ground, the fence, and every other available surface. Even the tombstones wore coats of the gray-black material.

Many of the tombstones were broken or lying prone like disjointed segments of a sidewalk. The engravings were reminiscent of kids' scribbles – names and dates, scratched in the soft palate of freshly poured concrete. Seeing the dilapidated condition of the grounds and the markers pained Jeremy. Was no one left who cared for those buried here? Were their lives so meaningless? These had once been living, breathing people, unique persons who presumably loved and were loved. Were they now nothing?

Jeremy followed the dirt path to its conclusion and found what he came for: The final resting place of the fabled hippie queen. The headstone read:

Claire Wales
1947 – 1969

Unlike the rather ordinary headstone, the sculpture beside the grave was breathtaking. The monument consisted of two sculpted figures – an angelic creature and a woman of exquisite beauty posed together in a lover's embrace. Spanish moss wrapped the angel's shoulders like a tattered shawl. According to local lore, the sculpture appeared mysteriously sometime during the year after Claire was buried, and no one seemed to know how it came to be placed here. How unbefitting it seemed for such an elegant and finely crafted work as this to have been placed here, in the middle of nowhere.

A multitude of candles decorated the grave site. Many were burned to nubs while others appeared brand new. One was held by an empty whiskey bottle caked with frozen streams of multicolored wax. Others appeared as if they had sprouted of their own accord from the black, humus-rich soil. Tossed coins littered the ground. Layer upon layer of graffiti had been indiscriminately penned, painted, or scratched on the headstone. Most prominent were the words *Hippie Queen*, which had been painted in white on the headstone. In stark contrast, the sculpture remained pristine, as if invulnerable to any such disfigurement.

If the rumors were true, who cared enough to go to the trouble and expense to place such a sculpture, yet had declined to step up and accept Claire's unclaimed body? The monument was not inexpensive and getting it here had been no meager task.

It did not take long for the sun to fall away, and although Jeremy had his digital camera, he had failed to bring a flashlight. It would be completely dark soon, especially once he got back to the tree-covered trail. Before he left, he captured several images of the gravesite, including the sculpture. Halfway between the church ruins and the missing gate to the graveyard, Jeremy snapped what he thought might be the best photo of the batch, an all-encompassing shot of the cemetery, backlit by the soft, failing light of sunset.

Jeremy could see, but just barely, as he hustled back down the hill, all the while trying to ignore the anonymous rustles in the woods.

Guided only by the bouncing beam of his headlight and the single tire track laid down on the way in, the ride out of the woods was more treacherous than the ride in had been. In one particularly slippery section, the rear end of the Hayabusa got away from Jeremy and he and the made-for-pavement bike plopped down in the muck. Though not hurt, he suffered through a few minutes of suspense as he could not immediately get the motor cranked.

When the engine revived, Jeremy still had to get the heavy bike out of the mire. He walked alongside, riding the clutch and doing the best he could to keep the bike upright. With every step forward, the mud threatened to pull the tennis shoes from his feet with a sucking sound like that from a toilet plunger at work. The spinning rear wheel sent clumps of mud skyward while gravity brought them back to earth with an ongoing series of sodden *plops*. By the time Jeremy emerged onto drier ground, he and the motorcycle were covered, head to toe and front wheel to back in the sticky red goo. With some sense of relief, he remounted and continued his slow progress out of the woods, but he did not relax fully until he finally arrived, the better part of an hour later, back at the blacktop.

***

Jeremy stopped at the antiquated self-serve car wash located at the intersection of Sticks River Road and the edge of town. The high-pressure sprayer removed the greater part of the caked-on mud, but it would take a good deal more tender loving care to restore the shine to his motorcycle.

Back at home, after his own fairly high-pressure shower, Jeremy called Jinni at work and gave her the one-minute version of the interrogation he had endured earlier in the day. She insisted on coming by after her shift.

While he waited for Jinni to arrive, Jeremy conducted an Internet search and was surprised to discover a photo of a sculpture on display in the Louvre that was identical to the one at Claire's gravesite. Jeremy learned that the sculpture, carved by Antonio Canova in the late sixteenth century, depicted a scene from a particular classical myth. In the story, Eros, the winged being, becomes infatuated with the beautiful human, Psyche, but is forbidden from acting on his passion. Eros disobeys, and in an attempt to keep his forays to visit Psyche a secret, he comes to her only in the darkness and dead of night.

Before Jeremy could learn how the story ended, he was roused by an obnoxious but familiar squealing sound. The door to Jeremy's condo fit too tightly within its frame and protested loudly each time it was opened or shut. Jinni must have used her key to get in. He jumped up and turned the corner to the hallway just in time to collide with a big hug. In Jinni's hair he caught a whiff of that distinctive hospital smell, a combination of odors derived from disinfectant, rubbing alcohol, and sick people.

"Are you alright?" she asked.

Jeremy returned a half-hearted smile and asked in jest, "Will you come and see me after they put me in jail?"

They walked into the living room and sat together on the couch.

"You feel like talking about it?" she asked.

"About what?" he quipped.

"Don't be obstinate," she replied. "I want to know what the police said."

Jeremy filled in the details of the unexpected meeting he had with Lieutenant Sykes.

"So you see," he said, "whoever killed June had access to my lab. That puts me on a very short list of suspects."

"What are you going to do?" she asked.

"Short of figuring out myself who did it and informing the police, I don't know."

In the ensuing quiet, Jeremy became aware of the music leaking from his stereo speakers. "Do you recognize this song?" he asked.

Jinni cocked her ear and said, "Wait, don't tell me...it's that band we heard on Halloween, right? With Tavalin?"

"That's right – Singe," he replied. "Good guess."

"It wasn't a guess," she contended. "They have a very distinctive sound."

What Jinni did not know was that, whenever he heard this song, it triggered a recollection of a very specific time and place and experience, that of his first night out with Monika. She was riding shotgun in his car, just over the threshold of the break in the road when this song and the Unreal kicked in. The music meant far more to him than Jinni could possibly fathom.

"How do you like this song?" he asked deviously.

He thought of the chance meeting with Monika in the Square and the words she chose to describe that night and how her eyes sparkled when she asked, *"Don't you remember the majesty?"*

As he listened to the song he loved, Jeremy wondered if he dared dream of experiencing the majesty again. In a strange way, the music of Singe had become tightly entwined with Monika and the Unreal. Monika, Singe, and the Unreal – any one by itself might have been resistible. As a trinity, they were an awesome force to be reckoned with. Yet, for all its significance to him, the music had absolutely no effect on Jinni.

"It's okay I guess," replied Jinni dispassionately. "I really don't understand why you like it so much."

It annoyed Jeremy that Jinni did not understand, and it frustrated him that he could not explain his obsession with the music. He also would not be relaying the comeback line that popped into his mind:

Monika understands.

"How about Dr. Sloan or Dr. Cain?" asked Jinni, oblivious to his hidden thoughts. "Can you think of any possible motive either of them might have?"

Jeremy hesitated before answering. If he planned on telling Jinni about the undercover research and how Dr. Cain confronted June over it the night of the murder, now was the time.

"Well?" she asked.

"Jinni, there is something I need to tell you about June and me – what we were doing all those nights…"

Jinni's eyes narrowed in a suspicious gesture.

Before Jinni could jump to any unfounded conclusions, he explained: "June and I were using Dr. Cain's materials and equipment for an unauthorized research project I dreamed up. That's why I was spending so much time with June. It's just as I said all along, we were working, just not always on our *official* project."

"What exactly were you working on?" asked Jinni skeptically.

"We were trying to figure out the reasons behind my sudden increased endurance."

Jeremy told Jinni the whole story, how he had recruited June and how they had discovered the anomalies in Jeremy's energy output and, finally, how Dr. Cain confronted June on the night she was killed.

"Does Dr. Cain know of your involvement in the undercover project?" asked Jinni.

"I don't know. According to June, my name never came up. Apparently, he didn't give details as to what he knew; he only said he knew something and that they should discuss it later."

"If he does know that you were in cahoots with June, don't you think it would be better for you to volunteer that information to the police rather than waiting for them to hear it from Dr. Cain?"

"I'm afraid it's too late for that," replied Jeremy. "It seems to me that, if Dr. Cain knew of my involvement, he would have already told the cops. I might as well keep quiet now and hope the subject never comes up."

"If Dr. Cain somehow did know all about the project, would that be motive enough to kill June?"

"I just don't know," replied Jeremy.

"What about Dr. Sloan?" she asked. "Any reason to suspect him?"

"No, no reason other than the fact that he's a little weasel," replied Jeremy. "I did notice that Dr. Cain seemed to be waiting on him to leave that night in the back parking lot of the Facility. That was a little strange, I thought."

"What can I do to help?" asked Jinni.

"Just keep on doing what you've been doing," he replied. "Keep on believing in me and I'll be fine."

"I just wish you weren't involved."

Jeremy dredged up an old saying his mom recited whenever the going got tough: "This too will pass," he said. "The truth will come out in the end."

"I hope you're right."

After Jinni left, Jeremy donned his headphones and cued up the music of Singe on his portable music player. Even though it was still early, he crawled into bed. It had been a long day and he needed to digest all that had happened. As he lay on his back, safely tucked under the covers, he tried to review the interrogation in his mind. He needed to come up with a rebuttal to the accusations of Lieutenant Sykes. Jeremy realized he had done a poor job defending himself this afternoon, so shocked was he to learn that he was a suspect. He worried that he might never be able to convince that bull-headed man of his innocence.

However, as he lost himself in the music, his mind drifted from that chore. Instead, Jeremy thought of his excursion to the cemetery and pondered the enigma of the sculpture placed over Claire's grave. And, as the song sequence of the Singe album built from one to the next, Jeremy could no longer thwart his thoughts from turning to that night – the night of his life – at the break in the road. A stubborn notion insisted that there was something familiar about the re-occurring melody that permeated the Singe album, but for the life of him, he could not put his finger on it.

CHAPTER 30

Tuesday, December 2

*A*BOUT nine p.m. the following night Jeremy strolled casually down the fifth-floor hallway of the Facility. His reasons for being there, however, were anything but casual.

June kept a separate notebook containing all the metabolism results and notes gleaned from their undercover research project. Whenever possible, Jeremy stored the notebook in the relative safety of the desk drawer in his lab, dropping off the notebook on his way out. On those nights that June worked alone or was the last to leave – as she had on the night she died – she usually stowed the notebook in the back of her bottom desk drawer.

Jeremy could think of at least two reasons why he needed to get his hands on that notebook. First of all, he hoped to avoid having to defend himself, either to the police or to Dr. Cain, on the subject of their secret research. Secondly, not only did he – and June – conduct the research, he also happened to be the subject of the work. Certainly if anyone could lay claim to the notebook, it was he.

Over the past couple of days Jeremy had made several passes by June's lab, waiting for an opportunity to access her desk. On those prior occasions, the door to the lab was either closed or there was simply too much ongoing activity to risk going inside. Tonight, the door was wide open and the hallways quiet.

Jeremy stuck his head in to find no one immediately visible in the lab, though whoever left the door open must be somewhere nearby. This was, however, as good an opportunity as he would get. Moving quickly, he slipped into the lab and sat on the lip of June's chair. He bent over and dug around in the deep drawer the best he could, considering the stuffed condition of the space.

Where is it?

Like a gopher from a hole, Jeremy raised his head and looked about. Despite his swelling apprehension, the coast remained clear. He ducked back down and began pulling materials from the drawer onto the floor.

It took a solid minute to confirm that the notebook was not there.

He began to hurriedly pile the papers and other paraphernalia back into the space but was interrupted by the gruff sound of someone clearing his throat.

That someone wore a pair of men's black dress shoes and was standing right behind him. Jeremy slowly lifted his gaze past the slack cuffs to the imposing figure in the white lab coat. Jeremy did the best he could to hide the guilt he felt as he made eye contact with the last person on earth he wanted to run into.

"Is there something I can help you with?" Dr. Cain asked accusingly.

"Hello, Dr. Cain. I was just looking for the watch I misplaced – I thought maybe I left it when I was working up here with June." It was a feeble excuse.

"I don't think it's appropriate for you to be snooping through June's personal belongings, especially considering the circumstances," retorted Dr. Cain.

Hoping to remind his boss that there once was a time when his presence here was legitimate, Jeremy said, "You know, June and I were able to finish up the viral prep that she and I were working on before she – well, you know…"

"Died?" Dr. Cain had no trouble articulating the word even if Jeremy did. "Yes, I know. June informed me of that at least two weeks before she *died*."

Jeremy could think of only one reason why Dr. Cain would make an issue of Jeremy's hesitancy to speak directly of June's dying. He, like the police, must believe that Jeremy had something to do with her murder, and he meant to rub Jeremy's nose in it.

"I was just making sure you knew," mumbled Jeremy.

Jeremy waited for Dr. Cain to say something. The crushing silence forced Jeremy to carry the conversation. He asked, "Will you be reassigning June's research to someone else?"

"To tell you the truth, I really haven't given it much thought."

"Well," Jeremy began, trying in vain for some sort of reconcilement, "if there's any way I can assist you, let me know. I would be glad to work with whoever takes over June's project."

"I don't think that will be necessary," came the curt reply.

"Well then, allow me to clean up my mess here and I'll be on my way." Jeremy reached down to put the rest of the papers back into the drawer.

Pointedly, Dr. Cain spewed the words, "If you don't mind…," and placed a surly hand on Jeremy's shoulder.

There was no mistaking the threatening intent of the gesture. In an evasive motion Jeremy twisted from Dr. Cain's grasp and stood up. Executive director or not, Jeremy could no longer conceal his fast-rising anger.

"You know, Dr. Cain, I am just as devastated as I'm sure you are over what happened. June and I were the best of friends."

"For your sake, I hope you can convince the police of that."

Jeremy stood defiantly in the face of the executive director's accusations, wanting to lash out but trying to hold back. In a quivery voice, Jeremy finally said, "I didn't do it."

"I think you should leave now." The flush of Dr. Cain's face matched his red hair.

Jeremy maintained his position in the face of his accuser. Enunciating every word for emphasis, he said, "*I did not do it!*"

In a growling tone, Dr. Cain said, "Get the hell out of here."

"Whatever you say, *boss,*" replied Jeremy with a tone absent any deference whatsoever.

Jeremy high-tailed it out of the lab, sorry that he had ventured here in the first place but more sorry he had been caught. For perhaps the first time, Jeremy realized the magnitude of the trouble he was in. Would everyone turn against him?

***

Back at home, Jeremy found it difficult to settle his emotions. He paced from one room to the next and fretted over the confrontation he had just endured with Dr. Cain. Why did he not think of a better excuse to be snooping about June's desk beforehand? He should have prepared for the possibility that someone might confront him. Still, Jeremy was astounded to receive such a hostile response from the executive director.

Jeremy wondered if his days at the Facility were now numbered. Had the countdown to the day he would receive his termination letter begun? Jeremy assumed his standing in the department to be primarily dependent on his status as a suspect in June's murder. In spite of the bad blood just spilled between him and Dr. Cain, Jeremy could see no reason why he could not continue in the pursuit of his degree, once all this was behind him.

And, after everything, Jeremy had failed to place his hands on June's research notebook. Unfortunately, he could only assume that it would eventually wind up in the hands of the police. Once discovered, with Dr. Cain acting to decipher it, they would figure out that the work contained in it was unrelated to June's official research. And, because it also contained annotations in Jeremy's handwriting, it would only be a matter of time before they connected him to it. The police would then, no doubt, work to weave those findings into the larger tapestry of their case against him.

In retrospect, Jeremy realized he should have been forthcoming with the police regarding the unauthorized research. He considered whether or not he should come clean with them now but decided it was too late for that. He could only hope that they would discover other clues and that those would lead them in the direction of the real killer.

But what if they don't? he asked himself frankly. *What if they continue down this path and charge me with June's murder?*

Shell-shocked at what he saw as a progression toward that, the worst possible outcome, Jeremy stared blankly off into space. If they charged him, what would he do? Would he face it? Would he run? There were no easy answers.

When the focus of his eyes returned, his gaze settled on the short stack of papers in the tray of his printer. Absentmindedly he retrieved the pages and thumbed through them. They belonged to the purple lotus article, the one authored by Claire, her boss – Dr. Nevins – and the other person whom Jeremy knew nothing about, Maurice Anthony.

The article contained two reproductions of photographs. One was a close-up of a purple lotus bloom. In the caption of the other picture, a wide shot of a swampy area awash with the plants, he noticed something quite intriguing; something he had missed before. The caption read:

Figure 2: Habitat of newly discovered variant of the water lily family, Nymphaeaceae.

The base word of *Nymphaeaceae* was, coincidentally, *nymph*, one of the same words Grady had used in reference to the strange goings-on of Reefers Woods. However, that wasn't the point of primary importance. Several weeks had passed since Jeremy first read the article. At that time, he had assumed it to be largely irrelevant to his quest to unlock the mystery of the hippie queen. She discovered some new plant – so what?

Now, however, realizing that the terms *lotus* and *water lily* refer to the same family of plants shed a blinding new light on the subject. Jeremy's prior analysis of the Unreal had turned up a potential connection between it and certain compounds found in the flowers of water lilies. Initially, he assigned no significance to that finding, but remembering the Unreal's lavender (purplish) tint and perfumed (flowery) smell and learning that Claire discovered a purple *water lily*, or *lotus*, in Reefers Woods, begged the question: Could the purple lotus discovered by Claire, the hippie queen, be the source of Monika's Unreal?

Reefers Woods – September, 1969

(Thirty-nine years ago)

The Fruit

What in the hell is this?

Claire couldn't believe her weary eyes. The sun was rising, and she and her mates were just going to bed after partying all night. On her bed was what could only be described as a small branch. From its leaves and purple flowers she easily recognized that it came from a lotus plant. Judging by its size, it came from a quite large specimen, bigger than any she had ever seen. Her first reaction was one of anger at the boy. Certainly he had left it here for her to find, but why did he damage what was obviously such an unusual and pristine plant? All she needed were the blooms.

Carefully she picked the flowers and placed them with the other blooms on the drying tray she kept hidden on the floor behind her bed. None of the others, save the boy, knew of Claire's growing stash of the dried flowers. She expended a great deal of time and energy canvassing the woods and, though they worked independently of each other, she employed the boy to do the same. He worked diligently and became quite good at finding and harvesting the increasingly hard-to-find blooms. She paid him in the currency of hard candy, chocolate and soft drinks.

Earlier in the summer, the supply of healthy plants and of the flowers they produced was plentiful. Most of the lotus plants grew in a series of shallow backwater pools in a location the hippies called the main swamp. Initially, Claire and her friends had more than enough flowers to meet their requirements, but as the summer of the first harvest wound down, so did the availability of the blooms.

Now it was September and the hippies could no longer indulge them-selves as frequently as they had become accustomed. They spent more and more time scouring the swamps for the dwindling supply. Inevitably, the plants and their habitat suffered, so much so that Claire declared the swamps off limits to everyone, save herself. She could only hope that the plants could rejuvenate themselves and that next year's harvest would not be impacted.

Claire undressed for bed. When she went to move the plant from her bed, it hung on something. What she saw next did not compute. Concealed under her pillow was some sort of strange fruit, about the size of a large orange, but deep purple and with a slightly oval shape. Astonishingly, the fruit was connected to the limb of the lotus plant, as if it had grown there.

Is this some kind of joke? *she asked herself.*

Was this really a fruit produced by one of her lotus plants?

Had she only been exposed to the lotus plants for this one growing season, she might have come to the conclusion that she and her friends simply picked every lotus bloom before it had the chance to begin to mature into fruit, but that was not the case. She first discovered the swamps late last year, after the plants had grown unimpeded all summer, and in all that time, she had not once come across anything resembling this.

Where in God's name had the boy found this?

Claire could not wait to find out, but when she went into his room to rouse him, she found his bed empty and neatly made. The boy was not there.

CHAPTER 31

Wednesday, December 3

*J*EREMY studied Claire's article well into the wee hours of Wednesday morning. He had missed the lotus-lily connection on his first read-through and he did not want to overlook any other important details, but nothing else popped out.

Even after he turned out the light, he could not get to sleep for thinking about the possible implications. If the Unreal was in fact derived from the purple lotus, who figured it out? Who knew where the lotus fields were located, and who was aware that the blooms of the plants possessed the euphoria-inducing drug? Might Monika have accomplished all of this or was someone else supplying the Unreal to her?

The morning sunlight, sliced by the slats of the vertical blinds, summoned Jeremy to the waking world. He had not meant to sleep all night on the couch. The music of the antiquated clock radio in his bedroom was barely audible and had not been enough to wake him on time. Jeremy had missed his organic class but he didn't really care. This morning he had in mind a task separate from his school work.

Without bothering to shower or shave, Jeremy got dressed and left his condo. He rode his 'Busa past the Facility and parked on the sidewalk beside the biology building. He wanted to look up Maurice Anthony, the last of the three authors listed in the purple lotus article, as he was the only one about whom Jeremy still knew nothing.

Even though it had been two months since his one-and-only visit to the biology department, Ms Lang, the perky old secretary, recognized Jeremy the moment he walked into the front office of the biology department.

"I knew you'd come back for me." Ms Lang smiled and flipped her gray hair back in an exaggerated motion. "No one can resist my charms for long."

"You've got that right," replied Jeremy, playing along. "I only hope you think of me half as much as I do you."

"Flattery will get you anything you want," she said, clearly enjoying the banter. "Now, tell me, what is it that you want?"

"Like last time, just to borrow your key to the old file room in the basement..."

"Be my guest."

After spending half the morning in the musty old file room, Jeremy finally hit pay dirt. Just as he suspected, Maurice, like Claire, worked under Dr. Nevins. He attended the University for two years, starting in the fall of 1969 and, like Claire, did not receive a degree. The handwritten notes scribbled at the tattered base of his transcript were almost illegible. Jeremy worked to decipher the words but the best he could come up with was, "Student disappointed on 9/1."

It wasn't until Jeremy solicited Ms Lang's help that they were able to figure out what it actually said: "Student *disappeared* on 9/1."

"That's odd," commented Ms Lang. "What could they mean by that?"

"I'm not sure," replied Jeremy, "but I've got to go now. Thanks again, Ms Lang."

He hustled out of her office with his head down and his mind racing. Though he chose not to disclose it to Ms Lang, the annotation on the transcript jostled something in Jeremy's memory.

Back at his condo, Jeremy searched though the folder containing the archived articles he had printed out that included any news that happened in or around Reefers Woods during the last 40 years or so. Specifically, he was looking for those that told of the two men who, separately, ventured into Reefers Woods but never returned, at least not alive. The first he ran across told of one who committed suicide in his car at Sticks River Landing. Jeremy put that article aside and skimmed the headlines of the other articles until he found the one that read, SEARCH SUSPENDED FOR MISSING HIKER. The hiker, who disappeared in the same general area, was last seen on September 1, 1970. Though the article included only sketchy personal information, it gave enough: He was a biologist – actually, a graduate student – who worked at the University. Below that, written in the stark contrast of black over white was the missing hiker's name: Maurice Anthony.

This explained the note – *student disappeared* – scribbled at the bottom of the transcript from the biology department. Maurice Anthony, the biologist who worked under the same research advisor as Claire, was the same Maurice Anthony who went missing late in the summer of 1970 while hiking in Reefers Woods.

On a roll, Jeremy directed his attention to the suicide victim claimed by Reefers Woods. It didn't take much investigation to reveal that the deceased, a Dr. Zachary Taylor, also had a connection of sorts to Claire and the other hippies. He was identified in several of the earlier articles as the medical examiner at the time of the commune fire. It had been his job to identify the victims' burned bodies.

According to the old newspaper article, the medical examiner shot himself in December of 1970, two months after Maurice Anthony disappeared. Claire and the other hippies met their demise on December 21, 1969. Was it only happenstance that all these people – Claire and the hippies, the biologist, and the medical examiner – died in Reefers Woods during the span of one year? The only obvious common thread that wove all this misfortune together was the area itself.

A superstitious man might steer clear of Reefers Woods. Jeremy wondered if his interest in the area might also end badly, especially in light of Grady's warnings, but it was far too late for Jeremy to divorce himself from his interest in Reefers Woods.

***

There was only one means to prove Jeremy's hypothesis, one method to verify that Monika's Unreal heralded from Claire's purple lotus: Analyze the purple lotus for the presence of the Unreal. But to do that, Jeremy would first have to find the purple lotus. He carefully reread Claire's article but it gave no specific location of the lotus swamp other than its placement somewhere within Sticks River National Forest.

If Jeremy meant to prove his hypothesis, he would have to find the purple lotus on his own. He needed maps, detailed enough to demarcate any wetlands within Reefers Woods. Jeremy searched on the web, starting with keywords *Sticks River National Forest Maps*, until he uncovered a site that offered high resolution aerial photographs of the area. Best of all, he could view them for free.

Jeremy spent the next hour poring over the overlapping slides. The bird's-eye view made it easy to follow the ribbon of Sticks River Road from Grady's house to the gravel parking lot of Sticks River Landing. By zooming all the way in, even the rickety old pier was discernable on the high-resolution photograph. Jeremy retraced the route of his and Tavalin's trek along the shoreline from Sticks River Landing to the secret beach. Sticks River flowed into the lake a few miles north of the beach, and he easily pinpointed the rapids of The Devil's Crotch at the only place where the river split in two. It required a little more time to pick out the interiorly-placed cemetery and the ruts that linked it to Sticks River Road.

The most useful feature was that the coordinates of any spot on the map could be ascertained. In this fashion, Jeremy was able to record the latitude and longitude values for a handful of sites that might potentially harbor Claire's purple lotus. Among these were several small inland lakes and a string of swampy areas that roughly paralleled Sticks River. He should be able to navigate to each water body of interest by plugging the coordinates into his portable GPS unit.

The only problem Jeremy could foresee was the likely difficulty of passage through the rough terrain and dense forest. With a chuckle he wondered if he might bump into Maurice Anthony, still lost after 40 years inside Reefers Woods. It occurred to Jeremy that Anthony might have gone there for the same reason that Jeremy now contemplated going. At the time he disappeared, Anthony and his boss were writing the paper that would be published sometime the following year. Might he, in his capacity as a biologist, have ventured into Reefers Woods to search for the purple lotus swamps first discovered by Claire? With Claire dead, might he have gone there to obtain additional lotus samples for their research? Though pure conjecture, Jeremy thought the scenario to be reasonable. What better reason could Maurice Anthony have had for traipsing around Reefers Woods?

In lieu of all the work laid out before him, Jeremy wondered why he couldn't just ask Monika if she knew of any connection between the Unreal and the purple lotus blooms. If she did, and admitted as much, he would have his answer and would have saved himself a heap of trouble. As reasonable as this idea seemed on the surface, Jeremy had to acknowledge the pitfalls of any contact with Monika. Just being in her presence, as he had been in the ice cream shop, was almost more temptation than he could resist. In the end, Jeremy decided against contacting Monika as he did not want to risk letting Jinni down again, loving her as he did.

Reefers Woods – September, 1969
(Thirty-nine years ago)

The Child

It was September and, as the summer wound down, so did the availability of the purple lotus flowers in the swamp. Fortuitously, with the boy's help, Claire Wales had amassed a nice stash of the flowers and, for her, the summer of the lotus marched on. More mornings than not, she still afforded herself the luxury of the drink made from the special tea bags, the ones that lent a deep-purple hue to her mid-morning pick-me-up.

It was one such morning that Claire, having separated herself from her friends, was sitting in the shade of a willow tree down by the river. It was during times like this, when she was alone and the woods were still and quiet, that her little friend would make her appearances.

From the beginning, Claire recognized that the lotus, though primarily a euphoric, possessed hallucinogenic properties as well. During the summer, this hallucinogenic component had been largely insignificant, most often manifested as a glimpse of movement where there was none or where none was expected. It also seemed to present itself in her peripheral vision. Every time Claire turned to look directly at the disturbance, nothing ever was there.

Nothing, that is, until a few weeks back. At the time, she had been alone in the woods, tripping on the Unreal. Much like prior instances, she sensed an out-of-place movement in the bushes. This time, however, when she looked, something – or actually, someone – was there. Though largely hidden, Claire perceived a young child watching her from the shadows. When Claire shifted her position to get a better view, the child simply melted into the background like she had never been there at all. Even after two additional and equally brief appearances, Claire chalked the sightings up to just another strange but harmless upshot of the lotus experience.

As the stream of days trickled into October, the child's visits became more frequent and of longer duration and Claire began to entertain a particularly intriguing possibility:

Might she be real?

To begin to believe in the child was a natural progression. It might have been easier to do so except for one caveat of which she constantly reminded herself:

Remember what else you saw.

Claire had glimpsed other apparitions in the woods, frightening images that she immediately pushed aside. As much as she longed to embrace the child as real, she did not want to lend any credibility to the existence of these other creatures. She feared that, if she allowed the child to become real in her mind, the others might spring to life as well. Besides, if the child were real, then the circumstances become even more mysterious, considering what Claire realized for the first time today:

She looks like me.

Today the child was a little less hidden, or it might have been how the light hit her face that revealed more details than before, but, whatever the reason, this was the first time Claire noticed that the child looked like she did as a little girl. In her lotus-amplified dreams that night, when the child made yet another appearance, Claire advanced it one step further. In her dream she thought:

I am the child. The child is me.

With that revelation, Claire awoke and sat straight up in bed. She wondered if the lotus juice were altering her mind permanently, and if so, was it necessarily a bad thing? The presumed answer to the latter question, at least tonight's answer, was a resounding no, for it was at that instant that she hit upon a most intriguing idea. Why not include the child in the background of some of her paintings?

Even though it was the middle of the night, Claire dragged her easel from the corner and feverishly mixed some paint on her palette. In the flickering light of a kerosene lamp, she carefully blended a likeness of the child into the background foliage of one of her most recent compositions. The result so pleased her that she did the same to several of her other paintings. Claire had never thought her work good enough to put up for sale, but tonight she decided that it might be time to try.

CHAPTER 32

Wednesday, December 3

*F*ROM his sock drawer it whispered his name; softly, no louder than the slight sound made by his bed covers as he tossed and turned.

Jeremy...

Every day Jeremy accessed the dresser for clean clothes to wear and every day he was reminded of what he had buried inside. When he thought of the Unreal tucked into the recess of the drawer, he could not help but think of the girl secreted away in the dark alcoves of his mind. It was she who had passed the Unreal to him at the ice cream shop and it was her voice – Monika's voice – that whispered to him now.

Jeremy...

A stray impulse advised him to just get it over with, one way or the other. Having the Unreal in the condo only fed his desire for Monika, as his desire for her and it would always be tied together. He should take it or flush it – right here, right now.

Just take it.

Jeremy wanted to take it but at the same time he feared where it might lead him if he did. If he allowed himself to come under the influence of the Unreal, would he once again betray Jinni and seek out Monika?

Flush it.

If he did – and if he avoided Monika as he had promised – he would be flushing away his last opportunity to burn with the ecstasy of the Unreal. Even if he never freed the Unreal from its sock tomb, what would be the use of throwing it away? If only for future study, it had value. It would be foolish to toss it.

Save it, then.

Straddling the middle of that uneasy truce, Jeremy tried to settle down into sleep. He assured himself that, in time, he could learn to live in peace with the temptations it presented.

Thump-thump. Thump-thump.

Like a tiny tell-tale heart, the capsule was alive.

Go away, Jeremy pleaded. He cradled his pillow over his ears in an effort to block out the sound, but to no avail. The drumming originated not from inside the drawer but from inside his head. He knew this, but the knowledge was worthless. Jeremy tried to turn his twisted mind back toward the things that mattered; back toward that which is sane, back toward that which is real.

Do it for Jinni.

He focused on the ceiling fan above his bed and its slow-twirling blades. If he could not remove this wanton craving from himself, perhaps he could remove himself from it.

My mind has wings.

In his mind, Jeremy manufactured a mountain meadow. Rays of the yellow sun warmed his face. Water gurgled from a nearby stream. Far away, a hawk cried out. Brightly colored wildflowers decorated the landscape and pearly bouquets of clouds adorned the sky. The sweet fragrance of flowers rode piggy back on the breeze. Jinni was there and they sat together on the ground, their feet bare upon a soft carpet of clover. He watched as her hands tied together a necklace of flowers with unhurried grace.

A gift for you, she whispered, and gently placed it around his neck.

All was bliss inside his daydream.

As Jeremy admired the daisy-chain necklace he thought how the flowers were familiar to him, although he didn't immediately know how so.

In the distance, but not so far away as before, the hawk cried out: *Har!*

These flowers, so familiar.

Again, the hawk cried out, closer this time: *Har! Har!*

Oh my gosh. All at once Jeremy recognized those flowers. They were purple, identical to the purple bloom in the hair of the melancholy child in Claire's painting.

Har! Har!

The proximity of the hawk's shriek startled Jeremy. He turned to see it on the ground right behind him.

Jerrrr-re-my, it cried in its sing-song voice.

"Bug off, you." Jeremy was getting ticked off. "This is my daydream."

The ornery bird held its ground. *Come with me!* it demanded. The hawk sounded like Monika.

"Leave me alone," Jeremy pleaded. "I made a promise to Jinni."

Jeremy turned back toward Jinni but she was gone. When he looked again, he found that the appearance of the hawk had changed. Its feathers had been replaced by hair – silky human hair, black as night.

Don't you want me?

"Yes." The affirmation spewed spontaneously from his lips, muting what he meant to say, overriding any utterances of reason.

That shook Jeremy from his reverie. He had lost control of his daydream somewhere along the way. He must have been falling asleep and dreams, as a rule, don't follow the dreamer's script. Thankfully, Jeremy found himself back in his bed, back in reality. But after a few minutes, just when he started to relax a bit, the original distraction returned.

Thump-thump. Thump-thump.

In frustration Jeremy stripped the bed of its covers and pillow. He stomped out his bedroom door, slamming it shut in his wake, and relocated to the couch in the living room.

What, he wondered, had happened to him that a figment of his imagination could chase him from his bed? What of the other symptoms of an unstable mind, the voices in his head and the ultra-vivid dreams? What of the amazing disappearing children in the woods?

"God help me," he muttered.

Reefers Woods – November, 1969
(Thirty-nine years ago)

The Longing

During the latter stages of the autumn of '69, the blue-eyed boy had begun spending some nights at the commune. From what Claire could gather, he was troubled by his home life, and when he had asked if he could stay over one night, she had reluctantly agreed. Allowing a minor to stay with them invited trouble with the law, especially without proper permission. But he had begged and said that his uncle, or whomever it was he stayed with, didn't care one way or the other. Claire certainly never meant for it to become a regular occurrence, but by the time November rolled around, the boy slept at the commune more nights than not.

Meanwhile, as the hippies' supply of lotus flowers dwindled away, so too did the idyllic peace and harmony fade. While Claire had her personal cache of lotus to quell her need, she did not share, nor did she dare tell anyone else of it. In the beginning, she, too, tried giving it up, just to see what might happen, but it didn't take long to acknowledge that mistake. Almost immediately, she began to feel grumpy, mean and mad. Nothing satisfied. Every day was defined by a growing, unappeasable want. Sleep ran from her. After only 13 days, her disgruntlement intensified to the point that she felt as if life were not worth living.

One dose of the lotus relieved her suffering, but her friends' ordeal worsened. Claire bore witness to the rising melancholy, angst and paranoia of the other commune members. Short of giving up some of her lotus, which was out of the question, she could do nothing but stand helplessly by. Except for the young boy who, to her knowledge, had never eaten of the lotus blooms, each of the other members lived out his or her own version of unrequited desire.

Claire had hoped that, in time, their harrowing symptoms would lessen, but indeed, they did not. Yet no one would leave the commune lest they miss out on the upcoming lotus season, still months away. They seemed intent to ride out the storm, come hell or high water.

Hell came.

CHAPTER 33

Thursday, December 4

*I*T was Thursday afternoon, less than 24 hours since Jeremy first conceived of a foray to Reefers Woods to look for Claire's purple lotus. While in the process of programming coordinates into his GPS unit, the phone rang.

"Do you have your television on?" Tavalin's tone carried a burden of ill omens.

"What is it?" asked Jeremy as he punched the buttons that summoned the talking heads of CNN.

"It's bad," replied Tavalin. "Brace yourself."

Jeremy looked and listened in disbelief at the prime-time news report. The anchor, an attractive brunette and one whom Jeremy had seen and admired before, was talking about the murder case. In the upper right quadrant of the screen beside her flowing hair was a still image of Jeremy's face. She was speaking of *him*.

She was saying, "…we have breaking news in the brutal mutilation and murder of June Song, the case that has, for the past ten days, gripped the nation. Jeremy Spires, a coworker of the deceased, has been identified by a reliable source as a person of interest in the case. No charges have been filed and no other details have been released. Though we don't yet know much about Mr. Spires, we do have an acquaintance of his on the telephone…"

"Hello?" asked the pretty anchor. "Can the caller hear me?"

The caller was a classmate of Jeremy's whose name he scarcely recognized, certainly not someone who had any intimate knowledge to pass along to all the inquiring minds. About all the anchor could pull from the conversation was that Jeremy always sat on the back row and that he mostly kept to himself. Though they did not say it, Jeremy was waiting on them to refer to him as a *loner*, that term that always seemed to apply to serial-killer types with no prior arrest records.

"Are you still there?"

Jeremy recoiled at the sound of Tavalin's voice. He had forgotten that he still held the phone to his ear.

"I'm here," replied Jeremy flatly. He felt dead and utterly devoid of emotion.

"What are we going to do?" asked Tavalin.

"We?" asked Jeremy. "They didn't mention your name too, did they?"

"No, but I've got to believe it's only a matter of time before I get sucked into this too. We already told the cops we spent most of the evening and night together."

Jeremy wanted to tell Tavalin not to be worried if only to shut him up, but to do that Jeremy would have to pretend not to be worried himself. "You're probably right," he said.

"Jeremy?"

"Hang on..." Jeremy was trying to hear what the eye-catching anchor was saying about him now. As he watched, she no longer struck him as bubbly and insightful, as she once did; he now saw her true colors. She was a gossip and an instigator, and Jeremy could hardly stand to look at her and her perpetually glossy lips.

"Can I ask you a question?" asked Tavalin hesitantly.

"What?" asked Jeremy, still not paying full attention to his friend.

"You didn't do it, did you?"

The newscast cut to commercial.

"Do what?" asked Jeremy.

"Kill June."

"Tell me you're not serious."

"Not really." Tavalin waited a few seconds before qualifying the remark. "I was just checking to be sure."

As the top of the hour rolled around, the newscast replayed the worst part of the coverage, Jeremy's face. The three o'clock anchor's lead-in was, "What does this man, Jeremy Spires, know about the gruesome death of June Song? That seems to be the question everyone is asking..."

"I've got to get out of here," Jeremy said, as he killed the power to the television set. "Let's go to Cooter's."

"When?"

"Right now."

***

Jeremy set out for the bar on foot. He desperately needed a reprieve and hoped that, for starters, the mile-long walk would help burn off the energy of his pent-up anxiety, but he could not easily release from his mind the spectacle just witnessed. It mattered little that, technically, the term *suspect* was never used in reference to his standing with the police. Based on the news report, millions of viewers would undoubtedly judge him as guilty. Jeremy was afraid that he had become, for all intents and purposes, the presumed mutilator-killer in the highly publicized ritual murder of June Song.

As Jeremy walked self-consciously through the Square, he read his name on the lips of the passer-bys, and every gaze that met his eyes harbored knowing looks and accusations. Sidewalk traffic gave him wide berth. Who wouldn't shrink away and shield their children from him, the infamous hometown murderer and mutilator?

While perhaps the downtown scene was not quite as portentous as he imagined, Jeremy feared that his future could unfold exactly as he imagined. Even Tavalin had felt compelled to ask if he were the one who killed June. If Tavalin, his closest ally besides Jinni, had been swayed so easily by that juggernaut of influence, the media, what chance did Jeremy have among the minions of society?

Though the walk over did little to relieve Jeremy's worries, he could try to smother them inside the smoky atmosphere of Cooter's or drown them inside the golden amber of a cold draught beer – or two or three.

Cooter's Pool Hall served the indigenous population. It stood defiantly as the last bastion of the common drinking man in a town that catered to the educated, the artsy and the upper middle class. The décor, if one could use a word like that for a place like Cooter's, was bare-bones. Lighted beer signs hung from the walls, attached to their respective electrical cords like neon dogs on dust-laden leashes. On the cheap linoleum floor stood an array of pool tables, as precisely aligned as the members of a marching military band. Illumination for each green-felt playing surface was provided by fluorescent lights encased in low-hanging *King Cobra Premium Malt Beer* housings. Out of the old, beat-up juke box in the corner blared an endless stream of tunes by the Allman Brothers, Lynyrd Skynyrd, and Stevie Ray Vaughn.

Jeremy was already well into the first pitcher of beer by the time Tavalin walked in, his head on a swivel.

Tavalin greeted Jeremy with the question, "What are you going to do?"

"Nothing, other than play pool and drink this beer." Jeremy desperately wanted to escape the news of the afternoon, not rehash it.

Tavalin bided his time until midway into their fourth game, when he delved in again. "Why do they think you did it? What happened to the cops' random killer theory?"

"I guess that was my theory, not theirs. They found some hair and skin stuck in the window of my lab. They think she was thrown out my window into the dumpster. If that is true, then whoever did it must have had a key to my lab."

"What about your alibi? You and I were together all night. There's no way you could have done it."

"That's not how the cops see it," replied Jeremy as he circled the table. "Corner pocket," he announced, and with the subsequent *slam* of the eight ball impacting the back of the called pocket, won another game. "That's three to one," he jabbed. "Loser pays."

"Yeah, yeah," complained Tavalin. "We need more quarters."

"Grab another pitcher while you're at it."

"Another pitcher and I'll lose what little game I've got."

Understandably, Tavalin's speech sounded a wee bit garbled. This would be their third shared pitcher on empty stomachs. Jeremy watched with amusement as Tavalin crept slowly back from the bar like a wannabe acrobat on a tightrope, trying not to spill the full-to-the-rim pitcher. In spite of his best efforts the beer sloshed out with every step, soaking his hands and leaving a wet trail across the floor.

"Hey man, don't waste it," Jeremy ribbed.

Tavalin stopped and spitefully sucked a couple of gulps straight from the spout while more of the golden liquid dribbled from his chin and hit the floor. "Oops," he said disingenuously.

"That's disgusting," Jeremy chided.

"Don't worry. The alcohol will kill the germs."

Jeremy inserted the quarters into the slots of the slip-slide mechanism of the pool table. After some fumbling he succeeded in unlocking the balls and used the triangle rack to set the balls for the next game.

"You were saying?" prompted Tavalin.

"The cops might be trying to discredit my alibi," said Jeremy. "They think that maybe you are covering for me." Jeremy didn't state the other obvious possibility but Tavalin came up with it on his own.

"Or that we both are guilty?" Tavalin was livid. "Did they mention that possibility as well?"

"Not exactly."

"If they try to pin this on you, it will only be a matter of time before they try to tie me into it too," whined Tavalin. "I've already told them that we were together all night."

"You're right."

"What are we going to do?" asked Tavalin pitifully.

"Hopefully the cops will find someone else to harass, someone else who has a key to my lab," Jeremy replied. "Shoot."

"You won, it's your break," Tavalin said.

"I don't care. You go ahead."

Jeremy took his turn sitting down and refilled his mug with more beer. Tavalin carefully lined up his shot but to no avail. He miscued, launching the cue ball, which flew off the table and hit the floor with a loud *thump*. Its momentum ran out at the boot of a local yokel with a steely-eyed glare and a skinhead haircut.

"He's gonna kick your butt," Jeremy called out as Tavalin made his way over to retrieve the ball.

"Sorry," Tavalin implored the man.

On his return Tavalin scolded Jeremy, "I'm pretty sure he heard you. If you don't watch out, somebody's gonna kick both our butts."

"He knows I was just kidding around."

"He wasn't laughing."

"You're the one hitting home runs. This ain't no baseball game, you know." Jeremy knew proper English but didn't always choose to use it.

"Are you hungry?" Tavalin asked.

"Getting there."

"Let's get some chicken at the Chevron."

"Alright," agreed Jeremy. "But we've got to finish off this beer first."

"I think I've had enough beer. Let's take off."

"You're just scared of ole baldy over there."

"*Shhhh.*" Tavalin shushed his friend.

***

"If it really was an inside job, who might the killer be?" asked Tavalin, as he and Jeremy began the trek to the Chevron station. They wisely decided against driving after all the beer they had just drunk.

"Dr. Sloan and Dr. Cain have keys, but if I were a betting man, I'd put my money on Grady."

Jeremy aired his theories to his friend, the same theories he had refrained from revealing to Lieutenant Sykes. Were it not for the lubricating effects of the beer, he might have abstained from telling Tavalin as well.

"Who?" asked Tavalin.

"Grady."

"Who's Grady?"

"The janitor."

"The one with the dark sunglasses?" asked Tavalin.

"Yes, him."

"What makes you think he might be involved?"

Jeremy recounted the details of the day he met Grady broken down on the side of the road, how he cooked the meal for the two of them, and finally how he warned Jeremy to never go past the break in the road, "Or people might get hurt."

"That's it?" asked Tavalin skeptically. "You think he killed June just because you disregarded the *Keep Out* sign?"

"No, there's more to it than that," replied Jeremy defensively. "He said some other things that didn't exactly make sense."

"Such as…?" Tavalin performed an out-with-it, rolling-wheel motion with his hand.

"He told me the old hippie queen ghost story," said Jeremy, "only his version was a little different from the one I had heard before. It's funny how that story seems to follow me around. Anyway, soon after that, he started working at the Facility."

"And you think he did that on account of you?"

"It seems too big a coincidence to think otherwise," replied Jeremy.

"What could he hope to accomplish by working in the same building as you?"

"That, I don't know for sure," Jeremy said. "But he is always giving me all this lofty-sounding advice and popping up in strange places, like he's watching me."

"He is odd," agreed Tavalin, "what with those dark, wrap-around sunglasses he wears 24-7."

"You know why he wears them?" asked Jeremy.

"Nope." Tavalin gave his friend a querulous look. "Why?"

"It's to hide – get this – his ultra-blue eyes."

"Blue eyes?" asked Tavalin. "You don't see that every day with a person of his coloring."

"I am aware. He also said it was very important that I didn't tell anyone."

As soon as the words escaped Jeremy's mouth, he felt bad for telling. He always strived to keep his word, even for something as trivial as this. Even though it shouldn't matter that people learned of Grady's blue eyes, Grady seemed to think it very important that no one find out. Regardless, Jeremy had promised not to tell.

"You know it's curious that his eyes are blue," began Tavalin, "but why go to all that trouble to conceal them?"

"That I don't know," replied Jeremy, "but it is another example, I think, of his unconventional behavior."

The Chevron station sat on a prominent corner in the small town. Instead of walking the extra half-block to the crosswalk at the light, they choose instead to jaywalk. As they began a quick sprint to the other side Jeremy's feet got tangled and he fell down in the middle of the street, directly in front of traffic that was forced to stop while he struggled to his feet and hustled to the other side.

"You know it's not that funny," Jeremy complained as Tavalin burst out laughing.

After making a pit stop in the bathroom, they went inside and ordered. They sat at one of the booths in the back of the store and quickly got to work on their fried chickens-on-sticks and potato logs.

As Tavalin was chewing the last of several humungous bites, he revived the subject of the murder. "But why would he kill June?" he asked.

"I have no idea why anybody would want to kill June. All I know is that of the very few people that have access to my lab, Grady strikes me as the weird agent of the bunch. If he really is crazy, we might never understand why he would do such a thing. He did say that if I crossed over the break in the road-"

"People could get hurt." Tavalin finished Jeremy's sentence for him. "And June got hurt."

They sat in silence for a minute or so, digesting the Grady-as-a-suspect theory as well as the food.

"Did he ever mention me?" asked Tavalin. "I've been past the *Keep Out* sign a time or two myself, you know."

"Hey, that's right. And," Jeremy added ominously, "if you remember, you are the one who took me out there in the first place. If anyone should be next on Grady's hit list, it's you."

"Oh, shut up. I'm not scared of that man."

"So you don't think Grady could have killed June?" asked Jeremy.

"I didn't say that," replied Tavalin. "What did the cops say when you told them?"

"I didn't tell them anything," replied Jeremy. "I figure they can find their own suspects."

"The suspects are you and, by extension, me," Tavalin said.

"One problem is that we both dropped by the Facility the night of the murder."

"As did Grady," added Tavalin.

"And don't forget I saw Dr. Cain and Dr. Sloan loitering around the back parking lot as well. Everyone who has a key to my lab was there that night."

"I guess we're lucky the killer took the time to mutilate the body," said Tavalin. "Neither of us were in the building long enough to carve on her and remove her heart."

Tavalin's callousness angered Jeremy. It didn't feel right to refer to June's mutilation as lucky for anyone. He hoped with all his heart that hers was a painless death and all those other atrocities came after.

"In the meantime, we need to account for as much time as we can on the night of the murder. We need proof that we quickly returned to your condo. Did you tell the cops we saw your downstairs neighbor?" asked Tavalin.

"I don't remember seeing any of my neighbors that night," replied Jeremy.

"I did," said Tavalin. "I talked to the guy who lives on the ground floor – Glen, I think – briefly while I was downstairs waiting on the pizza."

"That's good. That should help to verify our alibi. Do you think he'll remember talking to you?" asked Jeremy.

"He ought to. All I had on were my boxers."

"Oh yeah, that's right," said Jeremy. "And Jinni came by around the same time. She can vouch for us."

"The pizza delivery guy should vouch for us too. I gave him a generous tip."

"What did you give him, a whole dollar?" quipped Jeremy.

"I gave him a five."

"You sure the pizza delivery guy wasn't a hot chick? I've been a witness to your tipping and it is never generous. It only rises to the level of barely sufficient when a pretty waitress is involved."

"No, no it was a guy," countered Tavalin. "And he will remember."

"You must have still been drunk – that's the only explanation."

"Yeah, yeah, yeah," replied Tavalin derisively.

Once outside, meaning to take quick leave of his friend, Jeremy said, "I'm going home now."

"You aren't going back to Cooter's?" asked Tavalin. "What about your car?"

"My car is safely parked back at my apartment. I walked to the pool hall before."

"I didn't know I was going to have to hike all the way back to Cooter's by myself," complained Tavalin. "What will I do if that skinhead dude is waiting for me?"

Jeremy laughed. "I guess you'll find out when you get there."

"Thanks a lot, Jeremy. I guess you screwed me again."

"I'm too tired to spar with you or the skinhead dude." Jeremy held his hand up in a parting gesture and turned toward home.

From behind, Tavalin's voice: "Keep me informed!"

Jeremy waited at the intersection for the light to change. He had learned his lesson: No more jaywalking. He looked back over his shoulder just in time to see Tavalin re-enter the Chevron station. What was he up to now? Jeremy felt guilty for implicating Grady, even if it had only been to Tavalin. The light turned, but Jeremy was already headed back toward the Chevron station. He needed to make sure Tavalin kept all this to himself.

Jeremy had just drawn even with the farthermost bank of gas pumps as his friend exited the front door of the station. Tavalin had a drumstick in one hand and his mobile phone in the other. Preoccupied as he was with his chicken and his conversation, he did not notice Jeremy right off. When he did look up, his expression showed his surprise.

An over-sized SUV, driven by the tiniest of girls, eased by and briefly eclipsed Jeremy's view of his friend. When he could see Tavalin's face again, the phone had disappeared from his ear.

"I thought you were going home," Tavalin said.

"I thought you were headed back to Cooter's," countered Jeremy.

"I decided to get some dessert," replied Tavalin. "This chicken is delicious."

"Who were you talking to?" asked Jeremy pointedly.

"When?" asked Tavalin dumbly.

"Just now, on the phone." Jeremy pointed at Tavalin's right hand. "And I must say I've never seen anybody holding fried chicken and their cell phone in the same greasy hand."

"Oh, right," replied Tavalin sheepishly. "I guess I wasn't thinking." Tavalin held the chicken leg between his teeth while he wiped his phone with the tail of his shirt.

Jeremy waited until his friend removed the drum stick from his mouth, and again asked, "Who were you talking to?"

"My mother," replied Tavalin. "I was talking to my mother."

"About what?" asked Jeremy.

"You don't want to know," answered Tavalin in that same exasperated tone he always used when the subject of his mom came up.

"I don't care, as long as you don't mention what I said about the janitor to anyone."

"Why not?" asked Tavalin. "What's the big deal?"

"I'll feel guilty if the police target him because of something I said. Grady might not have the resources to defend himself properly, and one vague threat does not a murder suspect make. We should just let the police do their own thing, at least for now."

Tavalin said, "Better for them to target him than you – or me."

"We'll be fine – we didn't kill June. If Grady had something to do with it, the police can figure it out by themselves. For all we know, my illustrious boss, Skippy Sloan, might be the culprit, not Grady. Just don't mention what I said to anybody. Okay?"

"I heard you the first time," grumbled Tavalin.

"And please don't mention his blue eyes to anyone," added Jeremy. "I promised not to tell."

***

As Jeremy trudged home, the excessiveness of the evening weighed heavily. Too much beer, fried food and tongue-wagging only served to add a splitting headache, indigestion and guilt to his list of woes. The headache and the indigestion would fade but Jeremy knew that words, once released, cannot be rescinded and tend to roam.

Though he singled out Grady as the prime suspect, in reality Jeremy had no idea who might have killed June. Four persons had access to the lab – Grady, Dr. Sloan, Dr. Cain and himself. Lacking other evidence, all Jeremy had to go on was each person's prior behavior and his very subjective impression of each individual's personality. Why pick on Grady? On the surface, Grady was at least as good a man as the others on that list. He was certainly not pretentious and petty like Dr. Sloan, and he had never laid his hands on Jeremy in anger as Dr. Cain had the other night. Furthermore, as far as Jeremy knew, Grady didn't slam pitchers of beer at pool halls and unjustly accuse others of murder in an attempt to save his own skin. Jeremy cringed to think that perhaps he had picked on Grady because he was an easy target.

So what? asked a voice in Jeremy's head. It was the voice of self-preservation. *So what if the police learn a little about Grady's weirdness?*

The voice of his conscience countered: *It's okay if you think Grady is weird but, without hard evidence, you shouldn't say anything to anybody.*

Would you rather I go to jail for a crime I didn't commit?

It would be easier for you to live in jail than for you to live with the knowledge that you had a hand in an innocent man's demise.

But I don't know Grady is innocent.

But neither do you know he is guilty. You don't know who is innocent or who is guilty. That's the whole point and that's why you should just keep your mouth shut!

Both of you, shut up! screamed a third voice that approximated Jeremy's regular mental voice.

About that time, Jeremy arrived at the front stoop of his condo. He wondered if it were normal for the voices in one's head to argue among themselves.

Having arrived back in the sanctuary of his home, Jeremy engaged his tortured mind with his laptop, starting with his email. Lying in wait was a message sent earlier in the day by Quintin Gordy, the art collector. One week had passed since Jeremy met the collector. As Jeremy had promised, he sent Quintin the pictures he took of Sticks River, including those of The Devil's Crotch rapids.

Quintin's reply was written more like a formal letter than a typical email:

> *Dear Jeremy:*
>
> *It was my bona fide pleasure to make the acquaintances of you and your lovely friend, Jinni. Many thanks for the pictures you sent. I was thrilled to see for the first time the setting of my Claire Wales' "Wicked Water" painting. Were it not for you, I would never have made the connection between her title and The Devil's Crotch. Your information is much appreciated and I owe my new-found enlightenment all to you!*
>
> *I thought you might be interested to know that, true to form, there will be a Claire Wales' painting for sale at the annual art extravaganza, otherwise known as the Destiny Flea Market. I ask that you don't broadcast this information since I, of course, plan on placing a bid on it.*
>
> *I have already seen the piece and find that it is an excellent representation of Claire's work. For your viewing pleasure, I have attached a photo of that painting, as well as a photo of Claire's "Wicked Water" composition, which you so admired the night of the showing.*
>
> *Sincerely, Quintin*

Jeremy opened the attachments and was pleasantly surprised to find two high resolution photographs, one of each painting. Evidently, Quintin spared no expense in either his artwork or his photography equipment. The real shocker, however, was the subject matter of the newly-surfaced painting, entitled *The Ends*, which Quintin hoped to obtain.

The depiction was of a graveyard on a knobby hill. Cedar trees, overrun with Spanish moss, were scattered over the landscape and the silhouettes of tombstones punctured the ground-hugging haze like skyscrapers of a distant skyline. An aged but intact wrought-iron fence traced the perimeter of the cemetery.

At the slice in the fence where the gate had been, a child stood, holding a purple flower. Dark hair spilled out onto her slender shoulders. The invisible hand of the wind held her hair and contrasting white dress afloat and, like a ghost, she seemed to hover at the gateway. She was beautiful and utterly innocent, yet she harbored an expression of terrible sadness and longing. As Jeremy gazed wistfully upon the image of the child, he perceived in her demeanor the most heartrending aspect of all: she knew. The dark forces of the graveyard had her and she, though as innocent as the sacrificial lamb, understood, and had resigned herself to this terrible fate.

The cemetery, absent the child, was a familiar scene to Jeremy as he had taken several photographs from the same exact perspective. Claire's painting was undoubtedly of the Eternal Springs Graveyard, the very one Jeremy visited on Monday, three days prior. Ironically, Claire had chosen as a subject the place in the world where she would come to be buried. This was the surprise.

Jeremy compared his photos to the painting and marveled at how little the cemetery had changed in the nearly 40 years since the hippie queen put the scene down on canvas. As he studied the images, he noticed one particularly intriguing detail. Had he not been to the cemetery and taken the pictures, he could not have known at what he was looking, but there, in the background, far removed from the viewer's vantage point and rising ever-so-slightly above the clutter of so many tombstones, were two protrusions, so inconspicuous as to almost be invisible.

And though the implications were baffling, Jeremy could not deny that the two protrusions were, in fact, wingtips – the wingtips of a certain angel.

***

How did one explain the inclusion of Eros' wingtips in her painting of the cemetery? How could someone compose a painting that included a monument placed *posthumously* over her own grave? Did this mean that Claire did not die after all in the commune fire? Her death and burial in Eternal Springs Cemetery seemed to be a well-documented fact, at least as far as the newspapers and the official county records were concerned.

If one did not subscribe to conspiracy theories – and Jeremy decidedly did not – the only other plausible explanation was that the painting was a fake and that someone other than the hippie queen composed the painting. While Jeremy did not know much about how easy or difficult it might be to imitate someone else's painting, he knew exactly who would know: Quintin Gordy, the art connoisseur. And, not only would Quintin likely know the finer points of artist authentication, he would also likely be grateful to be made aware that he might be about to place a substantial bid for what could be a forgery.

Jeremy checked the phone book but could find no listing for the collector. He did, however, have Quintin's email address and promptly shot off a message:

> Quintin:
> *How difficult would it be to manufacture a fake Claire Wales' painting?*
> *How do you make sure of a painting's authenticity before buying it?*
> *Just wondering,*
> *Jeremy*

The collector's reply came back within the half-hour:

> Jeremy,
> *Based on the painting technique alone, I am 99% sure that the cemetery painting (The Ends) is an authentic Claire Wales' composition. Every artist has a distinctive pattern of brush strokes and style that is very difficult to copy. Having studied many of her known works, I am quite confident that this particular painting is indeed authentic.*
> *I am curious as to why you might pose such a question. Perhaps you could elaborate?*
> *Quintin*

Using instant messaging, the ensuing exchange occurred in real time:

Jeremy: *Is there a means to be absolutely sure it is authentic?*
Quintin: *Claire often used paints derived from natural sources. This is one reason why her work attracts so much interest. There are certain pigments she used that are completely unique to her compositions. A positive test for those specific pigments would satisfy the other 1% of uncertainty. Does this answer your question?*
Jeremy: *Without elaborating, I would suggest that you go forward with the pigment tests before you purchase this particular piece, just to be sure.*
Quintin: *As for waiting to purchase the piece, I'm afraid it is too late for, as of this evening, it belongs to me. The seller unexpectedly accepted my early bid and the transaction is complete. As for the additional testing, perhaps I will take your*

advice, as your insight has been beneficial to me in the past. I'll let you know the results of the pigment tests as soon as I am able to complete them. Perhaps then you'll tell me what this is all about.

Thinking that he owed Quintin an explanation, Jeremy began typing out his reasoning, but stopped mid-sentence. Quintin was perfectly happy with his acquisition – or at least had been before now – and Jeremy had no desire to play the role of spoil sport. Jeremy used the delete key to chomp up what he had begun to write. Even though he had good reason to believe the painting was a forgery and he would very much like to discuss the matter in depth, telling Quintin at this time would only make the kind collector worry. Jeremy decided it better to just wait, as they could not know the answer for sure until after the pigment tests were completed. And, as they say, ignorance is bliss.

There was one more question Jeremy wished to ask the collector, but he did not know if Quintin would be inclined to answer.

As politely as he could word it, Jeremy asked: *This is none of my business, and if you don't want to tell me I would understand, but I was wondering how much you paid for the painting?*

Quintin replied: *12K.*

Jeremy knew Quintin had likely anted up handsomely for the painting, but twelve thousand dollars was a good bit more than he had expected. For Quintin's sake, Jeremy hoped that he was wrong and the painting was not a fake.

On the other hand, if the painting proved to be authentic, Jeremy would be forced to consider the intriguing notion that Claire – the queen of the hippies – had somehow managed to survive the fire.

CHAPTER 34

Friday, December 5

THE early tinges of dawn lent a pinkish hue to the lake as Jeremy paddled north along the shoreline. He was glad he thought of the two racked canoes stored in the back of the Sticks River Landing parking lot and, better yet, glad he remembered the combination to the lock that secured them. The by-water approach would save close to two hours of hiking each way.

As he paddled, Jeremy's thoughts ran over the variety of issues he faced. He felt guilty for skipping his organic lecture today, the last class of the semester, but after having been outed on the national news yesterday, he had no desire to show his face on campus. The make-or-break final exam was scheduled for next Friday, giving him exactly one week to prepare. While the test seemed insignificant compared to his legal troubles, failing the course would not help matters.

The police had not contacted him since Lieutenant Sykes' interrogation five days ago, but Jeremy knew they would be doing everything in their power to gather more evidence against him. That they had not already searched his apartment underscored his standing as a person of interest and not yet a full-fledged suspect. Jeremy cringed at the idea of a bunch of strangers rifling through his apartment and his personal belongings. Except for the prize tucked away in the back of his sock drawer, he had nothing to hide. He should, however, probably move the Unreal out of his apartment.

Maybe you should just take it – that would get it out of the apartment.

He tried to ignore the wayward thought, although he had to admit that would serve the purpose.

Jeremy paddled until he reached a point about three miles past the secret beach, not far from where Sticks River emptied into the lake. Using his GPS unit to guide him, he walked overland until he closed in on the waypoint he had first pinpointed using the aerial photos of this part of Sticks River National Forest. Jeremy could not assume that he would find any blooms this late in the season but he hoped to be able to find at least some remnants of the lotus plants.

The target he chose to survey first looked to be one of the largest inland bodies of water in Reefers Woods and was located less than a half-mile from the lake's edge. In actuality, it consisted of a series of interconnected swamps with the outflow of one feeding the next and the next on down the line. When he arrived, Jeremy was surprised to find a very narrow but well beaten path that roughly followed the perimeter of the swamp, though at times it seemed to lead directly into the black water. One such trail came to a dead-end at a pool of water filled with lily pads.

Could it be this easy? he asked himself. *Could this be Claire's lotus?*

He had no way of knowing if these were the Reefers Woods variant of the purple lotus or some other run-of-the-mill variety, and frankly, he had no idea how to tell the difference. There did not seem to be any blooms on any of the plants, which had seen better days. No doubt the cold weather killed them off each year, and while it had been a warmer-than-average autumn, the temperature had certainly dropped to or below freezing on several occasions.

Just when he had all but given up on finding any trace of a lotus bloom, Jeremy glimpsed something floating out in the water. Squinting against the morning sun, he strained to discern if it could be what he came to find. It might be nothing more than a curiously-shaped leaf, one of many dead leaves that floated on the surface of the back water. Reaching it would be no simple task but something told him to go for it anyway.

A downed tree bridged the gap between the bank and his objective. Jeremy climbed aboard the trunk and rocked it up and down a time or two. Despite its crumbly-rotten appearance, it seemed sturdy enough. Step by shaky step he inched down the length of the log. After progressing about halfway down the log, the inevitable slip occurred. Jeremy lost his balance and tumbled in. The shock of the icy water induced in him a sharp inhalation, followed up by a long exhaled *Ahhhh!*

Waist-deep in the water and chilled to the bone, there was nothing left to do but stay the course. Each step propelled Jeremy into slightly deeper water and each step brought the icy liquid in contact with a virgin sliver of his stomach and back. When he could reach it, he gingerly picked the instigating item from the water. Though not attached to any plant, lotus or otherwise, and far from pristine, it did appear to be a flower of some sort. More black than purple, and wilted, Jeremy wondered how his eyes happened to latch onto this and if indeed it could be the source of Monika's Unreal. He would not know the answer to the latter question until he had time to analyze it back at the Facility. At least he had something to show for his effort.

***

Knowing exactly which compound he was looking for greatly simplified the analysis. Late Friday night, using an instrument known as the gas chromatograph-mass spectrometer, or GC-MS for short, Jeremy confirmed that the bloom he collected that morning from the swamp did indeed contain a small portion of the compound Jeremy knew as the Unreal. Without a doubt, the source for Monika's Unreal was Claire's purple lotus bloom.

All at once, Jeremy made a connection he should have noticed long before now. A common theme of Claire's paintings was the dark-haired girl-child. While Jeremy could not yet guess what the child represented, he could now extend a theory as to the meaning of the ever-present flower – the *purple lotus* bloom. What better explained Claire's preoccupation with the flower except that she knew of its euphoric effects? One could even surmise that this was the reason she established the commune in the first place. Hippies were known for, if not defined by, their desire to experience altered states of consciousness. The Unreal certainly accomplished that end. Jeremy could well understand the appeal of moving into the wilderness with a few like-minded friends to be near the lotus swamps and the Unreal they provided.

The current existence of the Unreal capsules testified that this knowledge of the lotus and its effects did not die with Claire and the hippies. Someone was currently aware that the purple lotus contained a euphoric-inducing drug; that someone also knew how to extract it as the lavender powder with a perfumed smell.

This led Jeremy to the next series of questions. Who bridged the gap? Forty years had passed since Claire first discovered and partook of the lotus. Was the knowledge somehow passed down over all that time or was it lost and later rediscovered? Finally, how was it that Monika seemed to have a steady supply of the Unreal? What was her connection to all of this?

Conceivably, it could be that Monika knew little or nothing of the Unreal's origin, but this Jeremy doubted. At the bonfire on the secret beach – which, incidentally, was not that far from the lotus swamps – Monika mentioned *Claire's Way*. Monika obviously had knowledge of Claire and was familiar enough with Reefers Woods to host the bonfire get-together within its confines. And, she maintained some type of authoritative role over the others who were present at the beach that night. If anyone were handing out capsules of the Unreal that night, it had to be her. All evidence seemed to indicate that Monika knew exactly where the Unreal came from and had ready access to it.

What he did not understand was how Monika became interested in the hippie queen and her lotus in the first place. How did she learn of the special effects of the lotus? Jeremy, too, had worked at digging up any and all information he could discover about the hippie queen and the lotus but he had never run across any reference to its psycho-activity. He only figured it out by starting with the Unreal and working backwards.

Jeremy thought of how Monika introduced him to the *burn* terminology used when describing the Unreal experience. Because of the perpetuated ghost story, many persons knew of the fiery demise of the commune and that Claire and her friends burned, literally. Might the terminology have been coined in reference to the burning down of the hippie queen commune? Could it be a coincidence?

That he had figured out the connection between the lotus and the Unreal gave Jeremy a giddy satisfaction. He wanted to track down Monika, if only to inform her that her secrets were falling, one by one, but, in light of his obligation to be true to Jinni and to avoid Monika and her temptations, that option was off the table.

But, boy oh boy, wouldn't I love to see the look on Monika's face...

During the daylight hours, Jeremy assured himself that all this time and effort spent researching the hippie queen, the Unreal, and now the lotus was harmless. He was, after all, only satisfying his curiosity – a purely intellectual exercise. If anything, his quest had been therapeutic. If not for the distraction it provided, he might have gone mad with only June's murder and the subsequent police inquisition to dwell upon. Sometimes, however, when the hour was late and his thoughts unfettered, he could not deny that this might only be a justification to pursue Monika and the Unreal.

Could he really hope to ignore the emotional side of this so-called intellectual endeavor, especially when these feelings were intermingled, as they were, with an unhealthy dose of obsession? Simply put, could he tread so closely to the edge of temptation and not go tumbling over?

CHAPTER *35*

Friday, December 5

JEREMY lay alone, spread-eagle in his bed.

All about him, the nighttime world was alive. Jovial ghosts frolicked on the ceiling and walls, a product of the wind-whipped trees and the light cast by the gothic-styled street lamps on the street below. Directly above, the blades of the ceiling fan stirred the air in endless circles. To Jeremy's left stood a wall of glass, French doors flanked by windows that opened onto the outside balcony. Wind chimes, a gift from Jinni, trembled in the breeze from their position high on the corner eave. Dissonant notes tinkled forth sporadically, accompanied by the hiss of leaves, dry and dead, swirling on the floor of the balcony.

As Jeremy watched the mesmerizing motion of the silvery gongs and listened to their somber song, his restless mind gravitated to a familiar preoccupation. Try as he might, he could not forget the booty in the back of his sock drawer, that hot coal of smoldering temptation. In spite of his good intentions, the preoccupation turned into anticipation. Tonight, Jeremy knew, the inevitable fire would burn.

After tonight, with the Unreal disposed of, perhaps he could finally cast thoughts of it and Monika aside. One final indulgence, he assured himself, and everything could go back to the way it used to be. After tonight, he would rededicate himself to Jinni.

Jeremy rose in harmony with multiple facsimiles of himself, shadows cast at various angles by the street lamps outside. These human-esce forms joined with and became an essential part of the elaborate bedroom screen show, ever-changing with the other night shadows. Hurrying now, in sharp contrast to the time before spent waiting to fall asleep, Jeremy collected the blue jeans and sweatshirt crumpled on the floor beside the bed. Clothes in hand, he maneuvered across the room, making for the light switch. Blinded by the darkness he snagged his little toe on the leg of his weight bench.

A flip of the switch and the shadows recoiled, only to regroup outside on the balcony. Jeremy sat on the wobbly weight bench, bent over and checked to make sure his little toe was still attached at the point of an acute throbbing pain. The nonsensical childhood rhyme – *and this little piggy went wee, wee, wee, all the way home* – pinged through his brain.

Jeremy pulled on his clothes and, from the back of his sock drawer, retrieved his aluminum-foiled prize. The rising tide of vivacious energy washed away any residual sleepiness and lent him a keen agility and coordination of body. He spun through the apartment with an efficient grace in preparation for the night, in anticipation of the outside world. He gathered his wallet, keys, two beers from the fridge, and a coat from the entrance closet and bolted out the front door onto the stairwell, negotiating the stairs two at a time, his sneakers echoing a rhythmic *thump, thump, thump* all the way down. Jeremy pushed through the door at the bottom and into the garage, jumped into his low-slung sports car, activated the garage door remote, turned the ignition and dug through the compact discs scattered haphazardly throughout the car as the door slowly raised.

Finally, he freed the Unreal from its wrapper and washed it down with a slug of beer.

Jeremy punched the clutch, shifted to reverse, and man and machine eased backwards out of the garage. At long last, he raced forward into the night, the dual exhausts emitting a long, guttural exhalation of burned over gasoline in his wake. In the rear view mirror he watched the garage door descend on the only light apparent in the entire condominium complex, squeezing the brightness and then obscuring it completely.

And, as that first Singe song began to play, an imperious expectation ripped through the catacombs of his mind.

Burn, baby, burn.

***

Killing time, Jeremy drove around Destiny and the University, jamming to the music of Singe and dreaming of the immutable event coming down the pipe. Last time it took about an hour from ingestion to blast off. After forty-five minutes, he turned onto Sticks River Road and drove toward the lake. The seven-mile straightaway before the break in the road was mostly flat with the exception of a single but significant hill and it was there, at the top, where Jeremy turned off the main road onto the gravel service road. Up ahead, the TVA microwave tower loomed impressively in the backlit sky, beacon blinking.

A giant Cyclops, its red eye winking.

The free-wheeling association and the sheer velocity of his thoughts made him wonder if the raging elation of the Unreal might be imminent.

At the end of the service road, Jeremy stopped the car, got out, stretched, and walked over to the chain link fence that encompassed the base of the tower. With hands on hips, neck craned and mouth agape, he studied the imposing structure. The steel girders of the tower were framed together like from a child's erector set.

On top, along with the beacon, were four microwave transmitters, shaped like nurses' caps. Jinni, his nurse, came to mind, and he wondered what she would think of him if she knew what he was up to tonight.

When the puny breeze that whispered through the pine boughs took pause, Jeremy noticed a subtle on-and-off electric buzzing. It was the sound of the beacon blinking. As he listened and focused in on the corresponding flicker of the beacon, he was reminded of the disorienting strobe lights at Bar Nowhere. That, in turn, reminded him of Monika, a dangerous subject under the circumstances.

Don't go there, Jeremy. Monika ain't nothin' but trouble. For some reason, this particular voice in his head sounded like Grady's.

Jeremy turned his attention back to the tower and wondered what the view might be from on top. He had also wondered, in vain, what the view might be from on top of the sheer rock walls of the monolith that bordered The Devil's Crotch. He and Jinni had failed to find a way to scale those walls, but this tower was made for climbing. His eyes found the ladder rungs that ran up one leg of its four legs, a bridge between the earth and the sky.

Like a stairway to heaven.

Though he was not ready to commit to climbing the tower, Jeremy allowed himself to mull over the logistics involved. Would it be possible to get inside the enclosure? Three strands of barbed wire stretched across the top of the fence at a 45-degree outward tilt to dissuade would-be intruders. Jeremy climbed up and managed to swing a leg over the top of the barbed wire and, with much straining, leveraged the rest of his body to a precariously-balanced position on top of the fence. As he assessed the only harm done, a three-cornered hole torn in the crotch of his jeans, a voice from his childhood recited:

The cows are getting out, Jeremy. Don't let the cows out.

Before he could decide if he had the guts to proceed, the sound of crunching gravel alerted him to an approaching car. Spooked, Jeremy leapt from the fence and quickly legged his way back to his car. He arrived at his still-open, driver's-side door at the same time the blue lights ignited on top of the police cruiser.

The policeman stepped from his car and cautiously approached. "I need to see your license and proof of insurance."

"What's the problem, officer?"

"The problem is that you're not supposed to be out here."

Jeremy dug the two cards from his wallet and handed them over. "I didn't see any *Keep Out* signs or anything." It occurred to Jeremy how he never heeded a certain other *Keep Out* sign, the one at the break in the road.

"Wait here." The cop walked back to his car and sat inside.

As Jeremy waited nervously for the policeman to finish checking his documentation, he thought about the hole in the crotch of his pants. Would the cop figure out how they got ripped? Had the cop seen him on top of the fence?

Don't let the cows out.

This was actually the more critical concern – not that his boxers showed through the hole in his jeans. No, this time, the cows represented his tenuous hold on his good sense. Jeremy checked his watch – one hour gone. Last time, right about now, the Unreal impacted his psyche with a force like God's hammer. For four weeks running, not a day passed that he did not remember and wish to relive that feeling. That it might descend upon him right now, in the company of the law, terrified him.

When the patrolman returned, Jeremy struggled to maintain control. The goblin of the Unreal, though still caged, was able to thrash madly about and sling all sorts of fearful and bizarre thoughts into Jeremy's frontal lobes. Shaky-scared, Jeremy mostly avoided eye contact and answered the handful of questions thrown his way by *no, sir* and *yes, sir*.

Finally, the words Jeremy longed to hear:

"You're free to go – but don't let me catch you up here again."

"Yes, sir."

At the main road, the policeman turned left, toward town. Jeremy turned right, toward the lake. By the time he passed Grady's house and the break in the road, Jeremy was finally able to put the confrontation behind him and relax. His thoughts rotated back to what he was, or was not feeling. It was here, at the break in the road, where he had made his first acquaintance with the Unreal, but that was then. Tonight's experience, at least thus far, fell far short of his expectations.

Just give it a little more time, see what happens.

By the time he reached the lake, almost two hours had elapsed since he swallowed the capsule. Jeremy felt stuck, so close yet unable to cross over into the promised land of ecstasy he remembered and so deeply desired. Desperate to alter his mindset, Jeremy got out of the car and walked down to the rickety old pier where he attempted to guide his thoughts toward the positive. There was, after all, so much to be thankful for, so much to love.

His thoughts, however, had a mind of their own. He could not help but consider the contrasting backdrop on which all worthwhile things shine – the end. Days pass and youth does not last. Friends fall away. Lovers leave. Every personal relationship is ultimately doomed, if not by immediate circumstances, then by death. Life and every part of it will expire. There will come a day when the sun burns itself out. Even the universe is doomed, the manner of its demise the only debate; not whether death but whether death by big crunch, freeze or rip.

Jeremy considered the brutal duality. Everything has a beginning and an end. The joy of any moment must be coupled with the wretched knowledge that the moment must end and the joy will pass. In his frustration he finally concluded that the only way to avoid despair is to live in the here and now. He should take advantage of his limited, and therefore priceless, time. Now he had his youth. Now he had the world and the sun and the universe.

What he didn't have at the moment – what he burned for – was Monika. Why was it right to be with Jinni and inherently wrong to run after Monika? Who defines right and wrong anyway? Why not chase down Monika tonight and let the chips fall where they may?

As Jeremy walked back to his car, he wondered if he would have been better off never to have met Monika in the first place, never to have become privy to her secret ways. But it was too late for that. He could never go back.

***

Jeremy drove back to the downtown Square and wheeled into the alleyway that led to Bar Nowhere. Monika's Mustang was conspicuously positioned in front of the old boarded-up church. The only empty parking space on the whole, jam-packed street was right behind her car, which Jeremy interpreted as a sign. He parked, killed the engine and, as he checked his wallet for cash, something slipped out into his lap. It was a photograph he had saved of Jinni and him.

Jinni, while attractive in her own right, did not possess the raw, exotic beauty of Monika. Few girls could measure up to Monika in that department. However, what Jeremy could plainly perceive was that Jinni's attractiveness extended clear to the core. Her splendor sprang from the physical, yes, but much more in the way she looked at him. The picture in his hand offered indisputable proof of the pure adoration and love Jinni held for him and him alone.

Jeremy considered, perhaps for the first time, the preciousness of Jinni's love. Guiltily, he grasped the magnitude of his infidelity and deceit, starting with the night he took that wild ride with Monika to the lake and, ultimately, to bed. That had been traitorous enough but his two-timing behavior extended far beyond the confines of that single night. For weeks now, he had relived their night together in his mind. He also had to admit that his investigation of Claire and the Unreal was really just an excuse to pursue Monika and her props – her sex, her drugs, and her rock-and-roll. Looking at the photograph, he could no longer deny what he was doing to Jinni. Truly it was Jinni, not Monika, who deserved his love and commitment – but he still craved Monika.

Jeremy sat in his car, at the impasse. In a flash of a brainstorm, he knew what he needed to do. The plan, now emerged, was nothing short of radical.

A loud rap at his window jolted him from his reverie. Jeremy recoiled at the face, frightening and grotesque, mashed up against the glass, inches from his own face. However, when the person pulled back and offered a smile, Jeremy recognized him as Trey, his undergrad acquaintance with the rock star good looks. Jeremy remembered he had bumped into Trey upstairs in Bar Nowhere the last time he was here.

Trey's roll-down-your-window gesture unfroze Jeremy.

Before the window was all the way down, Trey greeted him with an enthusiastic, "Dude!"

"Hey man," Jeremy said in a good-will attempt to match Trey's gusto. "What's up?"

"It's all good." Trey took one look at Jeremy and added, "You look like you've been having a good time yourself."

Jeremy wondered if Trey could tell so easily that he had taken something, especially considering how little affected he felt by it.

"No, not that much really," Jeremy muttered. "I was just about to head home."

"Why?" asked Trey. "You just got here."

"Yeah, I was thinking about going in but I changed my mind."

"You sure?" asked Trey, and with a straight face added, "The party is unreal in there right now."

Jeremy tried to discern if Trey's use of the term *unreal* was purposeful or not. No matter, he had already made up his mind. "I guess not."

"Alright, man," replied Trey. "You gotta do what you gotta do."

Jeremy punched the button that raised the window and pulled away from the curb, away from Bar Nowhere, away from Monika and away from the possibility of another hit of the Unreal. Following his conscience, Jeremy headed home.

CHAPTER *36*

Saturday, December 6

*J*INNI arrived at Jeremy's place the following evening, armed with a gourmet meal picked up from Mario's and two rented DVD movies.

"What's all this?" she asked.

Jeremy had not thought to put away the slew of maps of Reefers Woods he had printed out. "Just some aerial maps I found online."

"Of what?"

"Reefers Woods."

"Why am I not surprised?" Jinni took it upon herself to examine a couple of the maps. In a lower, almost inaudible voice, she added, "You and your obsession."

Twenty minutes into the first movie, the phone rang.

Jeremy answered, "Hello?"

"Jeremy?" asked a feminine voice.

"Yes?"

"Do you know who this is?"

"Uh, huh," he replied affirmatively. It was Monika.

"What are you doing?" she asked.

"Um, not much," he stammered nervously. "Just watching a movie." Jinni looked at him with casual interest from the other end of the couch. He pressed the earpiece of the phone firmly, almost painfully, against his ear in an effort to block the sound of Monika's voice from Jinni's ears.

"I heard you came by Bar Nowhere last night," she said. "Were you looking for me?"

"Maybe," Jeremy replied vaguely. He knew that Monika assumed that to be the case, even without asking. Of course he could not very well elaborate, not with Jinni staring a hole through him.

Sweetly, Monika asked, "So do you want to meet up with me, maybe do something?"

Jeremy tried to maintain a calm demeanor but on the inside he was sweating bullets.

"Right now?" he asked.

"Sure, why not?"

"Now's not the best time for me…"

"Aw, come on," she pleaded. "Perhaps we could burn something or the other."

"I better not."

"If you are going to turn me down, you're going to have to do it to my face," she said. "I'm coming up."

Jeremy's blood pressure shot through the roof. "No, no," he replied hastily. "That won't work." He thought Jinni had to realize he was trying to hide the other side of the conversation.

"Then you'll have to come to me," insisted Monika.

"Where are you?" he asked.

"I'm at the fountain behind City Hall," she said. "You know the place?"

"Yes," he replied. The fountain was plainly visible from his balcony. "I'll be there as quickly as I can."

"Jeremy?"

"Yes?"

"Hurry, okay?"

"Yeah, okay," he mumbled and hung up the phone.

"Who was that?" Jinni asked.

Jeremy couldn't tell for sure if Jinni picked up on his nervousness but there was no turning back now. He had to come up with a lie, and it had to fit in with his side of the conversation with Monika.

"That was Tavalin," he improvised. "Wouldn't you know it – his car has broken down and he needs my help."

"Where is he?"

"Out in the county, north of town," Jeremy said. "He walked to a gas station and left his car on the side of the highway."

"What's he doing up there?" she asked.

"I don't know," Jeremy answered. "I didn't ask and he didn't say."

"Why doesn't he get someone at the gas station to help him?"

"He said there's no mechanic there and you know he would never pay for a tow."

"How long is this going to take?" she asked.

Jeremy uneasiness grew as Jinni ran down her list of twenty questions. "Not sure, but knowing Tavalin it might take a while. He asked me to bring some tools and a tow rope. If we can't fix it, we'll have to tow it back to town."

"You know, my SUV would pull his car a lot easier than your car. Why don't we take it instead?"

"Thanks, Jinni, but I'd really hate to drag you into this." replied Jeremy. "Hopefully, we can get his car running and he can just drive it home."

"I really don't mind…"

"You're a sweetheart," Jeremy said, brushing aside her suggestion. "Perhaps you'd like to take the movies home with you?"

"No," replied Jinni. "I'd *like* to wait and watch them with you."

"Believe me, so would I. I just don't know how long this might take."

"When will you know?"

"I'll call you when I get an idea."

As they exited his apartment Jeremy cast a wary eye down the stairwell shared by his condo and the two units below. He was terrified at the thought of running into Monika with Jinni in tow. They paused at the front entrance to the building. Jinni's vehicle was parked out front while Jeremy's car was downstairs in his garage.

"I'll call you," he said and gave her a hug.

Jeremy knew, judging by her lethargic response, Jinni was not happy with the night's turn of events, but he had no choice. He had to tend to Monika.

"Goodnight," Jinni said blandly as she walked out the door.

In keeping with the charade, Jeremy threw a socket wrench set and some other miscellaneous tools into the back of his car. As he backed his car out from his garage, he thought he could just make out the silhouette of someone sitting on the rim of the fountain.

He circled around to the front of the building to make sure Jinni was gone. When he did not see her white SUV, he whipped into the parking area that wrapped around the back of his building and parked next to Monika's Mustang. Jeremy worried that Jinni had seen through his lies and was afraid that she might drive back by to check up on him. His safest bet would be to marshal Monika into his car and vacate the area as quickly as possible.

Monika, however, was in no hurry. There were exactly seven concrete steps that led from the fountain to the lower level of the parking area where he waited. Jeremy knew there were seven steps because, in his extreme impatience and paranoia, he counted each one as Monika glided down as deliberately as a beauty pageant contestant.

"Get in," he said in a tone made gruff by his high anxiety.

Monika looked a little surprised at his manner but did not hesitate to climb into the passenger seat and shut the door.

"Hey you," she said sweetly. "Wanna burn?"

"Maybe," he began, "we should just ride around for a bit and talk."

"Alright," she replied. "That sounds good – for starters."

"So whatever happened to the little package I passed to you at the ice cream parlor?"

Jeremy steered the car and its incriminating human cargo away from his condo and away from the well-lit downtown area. "I took it," replied Jeremy with a smile. "Last night."

"Did you come looking for me last night?" she asked.

"I wouldn't say I was necessarily looking for you," he replied, "but I did drive by Bar Nowhere."

"I didn't see you inside," she said.

"I didn't go inside," he said. "How did you even know I came by?"

"A little bird told me."

"Who, Trey?" asked Jeremy, following a hunch.

"Trey?" she asked. "Who's Trey?"

"Never mind."

Any one of several persons outside the bar could have seen him. He wondered if maybe Monika had employed one of the members of her secret group to watch for him. He did not know whether to be flattered or creeped out.

"Did you see my car?" she asked.

"I did."

"So why didn't you come in and say hello?"

"I don't know," Jeremy replied. "It was late and I was tired…"

Cunningly, Monika placed her hand lightly atop Jeremy's right hand as he operated the gearshift. He did his best not to show it on the outside but his insides quivered in response to her touch.

She asked, "So, are you tired now?"

"A little." When he answered, Jeremy's voice cracked, having reverted, along with his willpower, back to the days of his adolescence.

"Wanna burn?" she asked.

Tell her no, pleaded an inner voice.

Jeremy did not know what to feel when it came to Monika. It seemed like every time he resolved to move on, she reappeared.

Damn this infatuation, this obsession.

He knew that it was in no one's best interest for him to yield to her again. Less than 24 hours ago, sitting outside Bar Nowhere, he promised to put aside all thoughts of Monika and the Unreal.

When he stopped at the deserted four-way stop, Monika lifted his hand from the gearshift lever and held it in both of hers. She looked sweetly into his eyes. He knew she was trying to seduce him, just like old times. But was that such a travesty? How could he turn down this beautiful girl who wanted to be with him?

What to do, what to do? The voice in his head reached a fever pitch. *Say something – anything!*

Finally, he blurted out, "I'm engaged."

This was the radical plan Jeremy hatched last night, his resolution to commit himself once and for all to Jinni. He had even gone so far as to purchase a ring from the downtown jewelry store, even though he probably could have found a better deal elsewhere. In spite of that fact, the declaration just delivered to Monika was not true. Jeremy had purchased an engagement ring, but Jinni, as of yet, was unaware. He had intended on presenting it to her tonight.

"What?" Monika asked, clearly taken aback. "Don't tell me…"

"That's what I wanted to talk to you about." Jeremy removed his hand from Monika's double-fisted grip. "I'm getting married."

Monika looked at him slyly as if she sensed his deception.

"So you see," he continued, "I have commitments and I can't drop everything just because you appear out of the blue."

That should have been enough. Jeremy thought he had said the one thing that would discourage Monika. Certainly, after this verbal slap in the face, she would let him go.

"What if I told you it would be different this time?" she asked.

"What do you mean?" asked Jeremy.

"What if I told you I wanted to be your girlfriend?"

Jeremy stopped just short of laughing out loud. "Really?" he asked.

"Yes," she replied in all seriousness. "Really."

"Girlfriend?" Jeremy's curiosity was stoked. Even if he didn't plan on accepting her proposal, he could not wait to hear where Monika was going with this. "Why now?" he asked.

"I just don't think we've given this a chance to run its course."

"And what would that entail – your being my girlfriend?"

"That's a dumb question," she replied. "I suppose it would be like you and what's-her-name." Monika smiled and added, "But without the ring."

"Maybe if the circumstances were different…" he replied in a last-ditch effort to resist the onslaught.

"Couldn't we just have one more night tonight?" Monika's hand slithered over the console to rest on the inside of his thigh. "No one would have to know."

All he had to do was say no but it was that all-too-familiar voice of his insatiable longing, that virus of his mind that overrode everything else. Not coincidentally, the words mirrored those just spoken by Monika.

Just one more night, it said. *No one would have to know.*

He wavered. He wavered, and she recognized it.

"I know you want to kiss me," Monika said huskily.

And so, under the light of a lone streetlight at the deserted four-way stop, only hours after buying Jinni's engagement ring, Jeremy succumbed to his dark angel's embrace.

***

When Jeremy looked up from the kiss, headlights had unexpectedly appeared in his rear view mirror. Jostled by the realization that they were not alone in the world, Jeremy pulled smartly away from the four-way stop.

"Now what?" he asked.

Monika handed him a little lavender capsule and said, "I want to go for a ride on your motorcycle."

"You mean the crotch rocket?" he quipped.

"Crotch rocket?" asked Monika. "Interesting connotation."

Monika pointed to his clasped hand. "Aren't you going to take that?" she asked.

With nothing in the car to drink, Jeremy took a second to gather extra saliva in the back of his mouth. "Are you serious about riding the motorcycle?" he asked after he dry-swallowed the capsule.

"Dead serious," she replied.

"I don't think you know what you are getting yourself into."

"Maybe not," she said, "but I'm willing to take the chance."

"Right now?"

"I don't see why not."

Against his better judgment Jeremy retraced their route back to his condo. In kissing Monika and accepting the Unreal she offered, he felt obliged to do her bidding. Back at his condo, he waited impatiently for the garage door to raise itself.

Once inside the garage, Jeremy took a good look at Monika and the clothes she had on. She wore faded blue jeans and a shirt just short enough in the front to show off her belly button ring. Her pants fit nicely, tightly, and a sunflower with yellow-orange petals and a big black *(dilated)* center adorned the front of her white tee. Even though the night was unseasonably warm, she would need more clothes to offset the wind chill on the back of the motorcycle.

"You're going to need a jacket," he said.

"I didn't bring one."

As much as he wanted to get on the bike and vamoose, he had to say, "Hang on, I'll run upstairs and get you one."

Right on his heels, she said, "If you don't mind, I need to use your bathroom before we go."

"Sure, okay." Jeremy tried to hide his reluctance. He felt very uncomfortable taking Monika upstairs with Jinni only ten minutes out the door, especially considering that Jinni had a key to his condo.

While Monika peed, Jeremy retrieved a coat from the entrance closet. He was happy he remembered to grab his music player and the headphones from his bedroom.

"What's this?"

Monica had returned from the bathroom and promptly discovered the two photos lying on Jeremy's computer table. He had printed hard copies of the photos that Quintin had emailed to him, photos of the two Claire Wales' paintings.

"Do you know what you're looking at?" he asked.

"I believe these would both be paintings by a certain Claire Wales, am I right?" Monika spoke boastfully.

"Ah, so you do know something of the hippie queen after all."

"A little bit," she admitted.

Jeremy responded with a wry grin. "I figured as much," he said without elaborating. Now was not the time to mention what he knew of the connection between Monika's Unreal and the hippie queen's lotus blooms.

Jeremy traipsed over to where Monika stood and peered over her shoulder. She was studying the photo of Claire's cemetery painting, *The Ends*. He asked, "It's the young girl that makes the paintings, don't you think?"

"I suppose," she replied noncommittally.

"You're the artist," Jeremy said, pressing her. "Why do think the child appears in Claire's paintings?"

"I doubt that anyone can look at a painting and fully know the mind of the artist," she replied, "but I do have a theory."

When she didn't immediately expound, Jeremy said, "I'd like to hear it."

"Promise not to laugh?" Monika asked.

"Absolutely."

"I believe the child represents the hippie queen as a child and everything that is beautiful and sacred about childhood. The child is Claire before she lost her innocence."

"But the child looks so sad," he said. "Do you think that means Claire had an unhappy childhood?"

"No, that's not it at all. The child, or her childhood, is lost to her but at the same time she is the child." Deflating her air of assuredness a bit, she added, "Anyway, that's my theory."

Jeremy wondered if Monika's interpretation might be more a projection of her own psyche rather than that of the hippie queen.

"I suppose we would all like to recapture certain aspects of our childhoods," Jeremy said, trying to keep Monika talking. "I know I had some fun times growing up."

Monika bit: "I think you are missing the point. What is lost is so much more than just a few fun times. Consider a child's zest for life. Everything is new and fascinating. A child can truly live in the moment, putting all worries aside. There are no devious intentions, no hidden agendas. Everything a child of a certain age thinks and does springs from a pure heart. That, the innocent heart of a child, is what the hippie queen yearns to recapture."

"Impressive." Jeremy patted his hands together in quiet applause. "I wish I could look at a painting and see so much. I guess that's why you're the artist and I'm just a wannabe scientist."

On a roll, Monika didn't stop there. "I think that's one reason why we are drawn to the Unreal. For a short time we forget our worries and beat back our self-consciousness. We can allow ourselves to be excited about life and more open to what this world has to offer."

"Too bad the trip only lasts for a few hours." Jeremy smiled to himself and thought how he might not be artistically inclined but he had succeeded in getting Monika to talk. For once, he thought she had revealed a part of her real self to him. "Speaking of which," added Jeremy as he indicated the door. "We should probably get going before it hits."

Downstairs in the garage, Jeremy asked, "Have you ever been on a racing bike?"

Jeremy maneuvered the motorcycle through the narrow space between the car and the garage wall.

"I've ridden motorcycles before," she replied nonchalantly as she picked a dead leaf from the inside of her helmet.

"This is not your everyday motorcycle," he said. "This is a Hayabusa or 'Busa for short, arguably the fastest production motorcycle in the world."

"Well, la-dee-da to you," she said.

Jeremy ignored her sarcasm. "Couple of things – first thing is hang on tight – real tight. We don't want you to fall off the back when I take off. The other thing is that, if the bike don't lean, the bike don't turn. So don't fight the lean. Got it?"

Jeremy could not help laughing gustily at Monika, who, with difficulty, had donned her headgear and stood, alien-like, with the oversized helmet perched atop her petite body.

"What is so funny?" she asked.

"You are," he replied. For the first time Jeremy thought he saw a chink in her heretofore impenetrable armor of self-assurance.

On the firing up of the engine Monika wrapped her arms around his waist and molded her body delightfully tight against his. As they waited to merge into the string of cars looping round the downtown square, Jeremy's worrisome feelings dogged him. Sitting still under the bright streetlights, he felt more exposed than ever. What if Jinni were still out and about? What if she caught him with Monika?

As best he could manage, Jeremy willed a mental about-face. If he were going to do this, he could not worry himself sick. It was the sing-song voice of the carnie pinball machine of days past that advised: *Ya spin the wheel, ya take ya chances…*

And so, as in a school-boy's dream, Jeremy cruised the Saturday night streets on a tricked-out motorcycle with a girl as wild and beautiful as Aphrodite, the glory of the moment made sweeter by the promises of the Unreal, which hovered just beyond the teetering precipice of anticipation.

"Faster! Go faster!"

Monika screamed with a wonderful, unbridled enthusiasm. Had it been Jinni's arms wrapped around his waist, she would probably be urging him to slow down.

That was the difference between Monika and Jinni. Of course, if Monika truly wanted speed, there was only one place to be.

Jeremy took advantage of the opportunity to be heard at the last stop sign before Sticks River Road. "Are you ready?" he asked.

"I think so," she replied.

Monika's pupils looked engorged, like maybe the Unreal was starting its inevitable surge through her brain, which made Jeremy think that perhaps he too was starting to get off.

"One more thing-" Jeremy pulled out two sets of ear-bud headphones and handed one to her. "For our listening pleasure…"

"What is our pleasure?" she asked.

"You know."

She smiled a perfect little smile. "Yeah, I guess I do, don't I?"

He tucked his into his ears and waited until Monika got hers positioned. He felt for the play button on the digital music player he had tucked away in his coat pocket. When the music of Singe began to play, Jeremy threw one last look at her, gave the *thumbs up* gesture and slid the protective visor over his face. Monika followed suit.

"Burn, baby, burn," he muttered, even though neither he nor Monika could hear his voice over the music.

As best he could, Jeremy fought back the urge to immediately rocket out of the gate. He kept the considerable forces of acceleration available to him tamped down and built their speed slowly and deliberately, a patient lover. But when the song he loved kicked in, there could be no holding back. He downshifted to third, released the clutch and goosed the throttle to the engine's 11,000 rpm rev limiter. Despite their velocity, the front wheel lifted more than a few inches off the ground, a testament to the power of the engine beneath them. Despite the wheelie, Jeremy did not back off the throttle, a testament to the invincibility that he felt.

Never before had Jeremy taken a passenger as fast as this. It was almost a spiritual experience, he and Monika and the speed of the bike in simultaneous climax with the ecstasy of the Unreal and the song he loved.

***

Just inside the outer boundary of Reefers Woods, on the far side of the first hill past the *Keep Out* sign, they came upon the oddest of sights. There, on the edge of the road were two individuals, a young boy and a grandmotherly figure. The woman's hand was clamped onto the boy's arm as she dragged the reluctant child along the roadside in the direction of the lake.

Jeremy slowed, but the motorcycle was on them and past in an instant. As he applied heavy pressure to the brakes, he felt Monika's body press into his back. Only when she dug her fingers into his side did he think to shut off the music.

When she could make herself heard, she asked in a voice muffled by her helmet, "What is it? Why are you stopping?"

Jeremy did a u-turn in the middle of the deserted road and raised his visor. "I'm not sure," he replied. "I thought I saw something back there."

He drove past the skid mark painted on the pavement, turned around and drove slowly back toward the lake. When Jeremy got back to the spot where he thought he saw the two figures, he swung the bike around so that the headlights shone into the thick underbrush. There was no sign of anyone or anything out of the ordinary. Nobody was there.

Jeremy let loose a nervous little chuckle. It wasn't the first time he had experienced a hallucination in Reefers Woods. Interestingly, he was pretty sure the old lady beside the road tonight was the same one who appeared with the children at the bonfire during Jeremy's prior hallucination. In each instance, it seemed highly improbable that any of the actors could be real.

Maybe, he thought, *that's why they call it the Unreal, because it can make you see things that aren't really there. A small price to pay...*

"What did you see?" asked Monika.

"Nothing," he finally said, satisfied that no one was here besides Monika and him.

"What did you *think* you saw?" she asked.

"I guess it was just a couple of deer," Jeremy said. With that, he lowered his visor, cued the music and pointed the motorcycle in the direction of the lake.

The Unreal dressed up every passing notion with the same cutting-edge fascination. Every detail of the world and the way he moved through it inspired in him a love of the world. Where Monika was concerned, the effect was multiplied. On arrival at the lakeside, they dismounted and, with an all-consuming infatuation, Jeremy watched as she released her raven hair from the confines of her helmet and her elegant beauty to his sight.

"Monika, while I'm thinking about it, I wanted to ask you about the Unreal you left with me before, in the ice cream shop-"

"What about it?"

"Like I told you, I took it last night but I never was able to fully get off. I felt something, maybe like how it is right before it hits, but nothing close to the way it feels right now. It was extremely frustrating, let me tell you."

"I don't know, maybe it was just a weak dose. Believe me, I know how awful it feels to be on the verge, to want more and not have it. What I don't understand is how you managed to leave Bar Nowhere last night without coming inside for more." she said. "All you had to do is come to me."

"It wasn't easy."

Thinking about it now, Jeremy wondered if Monika might have purposely provided him an inadequate dose of the Unreal at the ice cream shop so that he would be forced to seek her out for more. But could she really be so conniving? Would Monika use the Unreal as a way to entice him back to her? It seemed a little farfetched, but somehow, Jeremy didn't doubt it.

Monika surprised him by asking, "Those weren't deer you saw back there, were they?"

Jeremy had all but forgotten the hallucination as his fractured wits had since rambled over and through at least a dozen other subjects. "How did you know?" he asked.

"I could tell," she replied. "What did you see?"

"If I tell you, you might think I'm crazy."

"Try me."

After a brief hesitation, Jeremy confessed. "For a second I thought I saw an old woman and a boy right there beside the road but I'm pretty sure I imagined the whole thing."

"That is weird," she agreed, "but not unprecedented. I've seen some things out here too."

"Really?" he asked. "Like what?"

Jeremy didn't mention how he experienced a similar hallucination at the secret beach because he didn't want Monika to know he had been there that night, spying on her and her group.

"I'd rather not talk about it right now," she replied, shutting down the subject.

Before his Unreal-fueled thoughts rocketed off to parts unknown, Jeremy realized something else about tonight's hallucination. Didn't the towheaded boy on the edge of the road look a little like he did as a child? Perhaps, he thought, as in a dream, his mind inserted the stored image of his childhood self into his hallucination. After all, dreams and hallucinations must be related, both being spontaneously created by the mind. The main difference, Jeremy thought, is that dreams are drawn from the sleeping mind while hallucinations spring from a mind awake.

Jeremy felt compelled to share his insight. "You know," he said, "maybe hallucinations are nothing more than dreams you have when awake."

"Maybe," Monika replied distractedly as she was busy performing a ballet in the empty air, like a student practicing her Karate moves.

"Speaking of hallucinations and such," she asked, "Can you see the trails?"

Trailing the movement of Monika's arms and hands were images of the same, left behind like slow-fading streaks made by shooting stars.

"Yes, I see them," Jeremy replied.

"You know," she said, "maybe all this is nothing but a dream."

***

Only after the most intense portion of the rush passed did they hop back on the 'Busa and return to town. Jeremy drove directly to the fountain where Monika's car was parked and pulled into the adjacent space.

"Aren't we going up to your place?" asked Monika.

Trying hard to resist that urge, Jeremy circled the wagons of his disjointed thoughts around Jinni. He tried to remember the reasons behind last night's landmark decision to buy the engagement ring. He tried to imagine the glee that would surely flood Jinni's face when he presented his gift to her. Distracted as he was by Monika's allure, he tried to remember the love he had for Jinni.

With a welling up of his will, Jeremy stated, not asked, "Why don't we pay a visit to the mermaid." He led the way up the steps to the fountain.

Monika, pinpointing the reason they came here instead of going upstairs, asked, "Are you still planning on getting married?"

"That's the assumption I'm operating on."

Monika looked him square in the face and said, "I think you're making a big mistake."

Speaking frankly, Jeremy said, "I don't think you are capable of understanding what Jinni means to me – and, more importantly, what I mean to her. Jinni loves me."

"If she means so much to you, how come you are out with me?"

"You started it," Jeremy countered, but he knew she had him. "I was with Jinni before, when you called."

"I called, but nobody forced you to spend the last five hours with me," she contended. "Nobody forced you to kiss me."

Jeremy sighed. "I shouldn't have done that. And, as much fun as all this has been, this has got to be our last hoorah. Starting right now, I have to do what's right."

After a thoughtful pause, Monika said, "You know, she could be out with someone else right now. Maybe she's lying to you, just like you lie to her."

"I don't think so," retorted Jeremy. "I know I can trust her – Jinni's the most honest person I know."

"What about me?" asked Monika. "You don't think I'm trustworthy?"

"You must be joking." Seeing the hurt look on Monika's face forced Jeremy to elaborate. "You're just so damned secretive, Monika. How can I trust someone who reveals nothing of herself?"

"What if I told you I've had a crush on you since I first saw you at the Singe show?" Monika asked. "What if I told you I love you?"

Jeremy would have been no more surprised had he seen extraterrestrials dancing to the beat of *Blondie's* song *Rapture* above them on the roof of City Hall.

He asked, "If this is true, why am I just finding out?"

"I don't know," she replied. "Maybe it's because you had a girlfriend. Maybe

I just wanted it all to be strange and mysterious. I guess I was just playing a game with the assumption that, in the end, I would win my prize."

"Me?" asked Jeremy. "I'm your prize?"

Monika stared at her feet, avoiding eye contact as if embarrassed, while Jeremy glowed with delighted pride at the words uttered by this beautiful creature. His deepest, most secret desire – her profession of love – had come true.

Jeremy could do nothing other than give in to the emotions rising within him. He reached out to Monika and caressed her hair until she raised tear-shiny eyes to meet his. Self-conscious and vulnerable, she buried her face in the crook of his neck and hugged him like never before. He reveled in the deliciousness of the moment and wished for time to stand still.

"So do you forgive me?" she whispered.

"For what?" he asked.

"For the way that I am."

"You don't have to apologize for the way that you are," he said. "I just want you to let me know *who* you are."

Monika's expression gushed happiness as she led him by the hand to the stone rim of the fountain. For a time they sat together with the voluptuous mermaid and the fine mist that drifted onto them from her graceful streams.

It was Monika who eventually broke the silence. "Now what?" she asked as she bit her lip in a highly seductive gesture.

"Umm...," was all Jeremy's indecision allowed him to utter.

"I thought maybe..." Monika's words trailed off but her eyes, uplifted toward his condo, finished the sentence for her.

More than anything, Jeremy wanted to invite Monika to spend the night but he could not allow that yearning to interfere with this decision set before him.

Jinni or Monika: One to keep and one to lose.

"We should call it a night," he said stoically. "It's late and it looks like I've got a lot of thinking to do."

Jeremy followed Monika and her pouty silence down the steps. They kissed a long goodnight at her car.

"Are you *sure* you want me to leave?" she asked.

"Well...," he replied, waffling, but in his heart of hearts he knew this choice should not be relegated to the heat of this particular moment. As difficult as it was, he would take the honorable course. He would not be with Monika again unless he first broke it off with Jinni.

"Yes," Jeremy finally said. "Just go, okay? We can talk later."

It was all he could do not to chase like a dog after her car as she drove away.

When she was gone, he bypassed his motorcycle and returned to the fountain. As he sat with the mermaid, the weight of a thousand questions pressed down upon him. In spite of Monika's alleged affection for him, could he trust her? What if he inspired not her love, but her competitive spirit? What if Monika said what she said just to see if she could win out over Jinni? Or, what if Monika was sincere but her feelings sprang not from her heart but from the repercussions of the Unreal? In the stark light of tomorrow, she might feel nothing for him at all.

Whatever, Monika's true feelings and motivations remained a big unknown. The sure bet would be to stick with the original plan, to give Jinni the engagement ring and, hopefully, to live happily ever after. Jinni's love for him, he knew, was real.

Jeremy stared glumly at the cascading water of the fountain. He felt very alone. To the mermaid he remarked, "Looks like it's just you and me, kid." Jeremy smiled an empty smile that garnered no reaction from his fish-tailed friend. She was immune to his indiscretions. He could not lie to her as he had to Jinni, or become unduly fixated on her, as had been the case with Monika. Neither could the mermaid assist him in his dilemma.

Jinni or Monika: One to keep and one to lose.

Jeremy stood to leave, but something made him stop and reexamine the figure of the fountain. Something in the mermaid's expression rang familiar but the déjà vu escaped him before he could reel it in. He shrugged it off and trudged down the steps to his motorcycle. It was time to call it a night.

As he rounded the front of his condominium, Jeremy noticed with a start what looked like Jinni's white SUV parked in the small parking lot out front. A sinking sensation reminded him that he had promised to call her to let her know what was going on. That was hours ago. He had completely forgotten.

Jinni had a key to his apartment, and if that were her vehicle, she was most certainly inside waiting on him. It didn't matter that she was upstairs – he couldn't let her see him like this. Jeremy cruised slowly by, struggling to positively identify the car in the poor predawn lighting. The *Lifehouse* bumper sticker on the back verified his worst fear. It was definitely Jinni's vehicle.

Just as he accelerated, intending to get the hell out of dodge, he saw her, sitting quietly on the front stoop. Alone, still, and silent, Jinni reminded him of a cat sitting on its haunches and here he was, a careless little sparrow ambushed by the vigilant hunter.

Jeremy waved a stupid little wave and grinned a stupid little grin. He slowly turned his motorcycle around in the street and parked beside Jinni's car. Stalling, he gathered a few miscellaneous papers from his saddlebag, thinking perhaps papers in hand might lend some flimsy legitimacy to the lie he had yet to create. He needed something, anything, to help explain away where he had been all night, but his mind was as blank as the black, starless sky.

Jinni stood, hands on hips, as he lollygagged up to the stoop.

"Why didn't you call me?" she asked in a tone carefully measured.

"I'm sorry, I forgot."

All true, so far.

"Where were you?"

"At the lab?" For some reason Jeremy's response came out more like a question than an answer.

"Don't lie to me Jeremy. Where have you been?"

"After I left the lab, I rode out to the lake. With all that's happened I guess I just needed some time alone."

Jinni peered deep into his eyes, trying to decipher the strangeness that resided there. Jeremy diverted his gaze to hide his transgression, but it was no use. Some things you just can't hide.

"What's wrong with your eyes? Did you take something?" she asked incredulously.

"I can explain," he replied, even though he had no idea how. "Why don't we go inside where we can talk?"

Jinni looked past him at the headlights of an approaching car. Jeremy heard the rumble of its engine but didn't turn around, at least not until the vintage Mustang pulled alongside them and stopped. Jeremy's eyes widened in a look that must have been pure horror as the tinted window slowly lowered, revealing the face of his dark angel.

"Hey Jeremy, I think I left my purse in your car," was all Monika said but it was enough – more than enough – for Jinni.

Jinni screamed, "Who the hell is that?" Without waiting for his response, she slapped him hard across the face, ran to her car and squealed away in a cloud of vaporized rubber.

Jeremy stood in shock as her car careened down the street and out of sight.

"So I guess that must have been your fiancée, huh?" Monika asked, a little too nonchalantly. "What did you say her name was?"

"Jinni," he answered numbly. "Her name was Jinni."

Jeremy waited at the top of the stairs while Monika retrieved her purse.

On her return, she asked, "Are you okay?"

"Yeah."

"I'm sorry about all this," she said. "I guess I wasn't thinking."

"It's not really your fault," he said, though he was thinking the opposite. "Don't worry about it."

"Do you want me to come up?"

"That's probably not the best of ideas, but thanks for asking."

"Alright, then." Monika stood on her tip toes to kiss Jeremy on the cheek. "See you later."

Jeremy arrived upstairs to find the door to his condo unlocked and the stereo on. If this were not Jeremy's life but a movie scene, the soundtrack provided by the long-forgotten song could not have been more fitting:

Farewell, my dearest friend
This is it, the bitter end
Turn the page, close the door
Our Eden is no more…

Besieged by a wave of grief, Jeremy collapsed in the middle of the living room floor, buried his face in his hands and cried.

When the song was over and after Jeremy had gathered himself as best he could, he considered calling Jinni – but what would he say? What *could* he say? Finally, after much debate, he decided to wait. He needed time, rest, and a clearer mind to figure out the best approach to manage this dreadful situation.

As he readied for bed, his mind went to task. What justification could he possibly give to explain his actions? In spite of all tonight's misdeeds – lying to Jinni, taking the Unreal, and kissing Monika – he had managed to resist Monika's final offer and had sent her home. Tomorrow, couldn't he simply try to explain it all to Jinni and somehow make her understand that, despite all, he never intended to do her wrong?

However, as Jeremy measured the strength of his arguments, he knew deep down that he had done more than enough to deserve Jinni's wrath. It didn't matter that Monika started all this four weeks ago with the kiss at the Singe show. It made no difference that Monika rushed everything along at breakneck speed, including the giving away of herself while Jinni insisted on saving herself until marriage. It meant nothing that he felt awful for not being able to deflect Monika's advances. Even the engagement ring held no sway. No matter the circumstances, it was he who betrayed Jinni's trust. He was the one who went to Bar Nowhere looking for Monika that fateful evening and accepted all she had offered. He opened the door to Monika and she had been stuck inside his head ever since.

Truly, there was no justification for what he had done.

✱✱✱

More than anything, Jeremy wanted to put to bed – figuratively and literally – this disaster of a night. Despite the stress, or perhaps because of it, he fell asleep almost as soon as his head hit his pillow.

Jinni was a vision, angelic in a flowing white gown. Jeremy stood proudly by her side at the altar. Multicolored light streamed in from all sides through huge stained glass windows. Throngs of candles flickered from ornate candelabra and the sweet fragrance of flowers filled the sanctuary. The families sat down front, hers on the left and his on the right. Presiding over the ceremony was the preacher from Jeremy's childhood church. He looked the same as he did the last time Jeremy saw him, even though that had been some fifteen years prior. Tavalin stood as the best man. All present were dressed to kill, all shining and smiling in black suits and white dresses.

All, that is, save Grady. The attire he had chosen for the occasion included a wide brimmed hat and dirty overalls absent any underlying shirt. He stood in the midst of the properly seated guests, sticking out like an insulting middle finger. Why, Jeremy thought, must Grady always ruin everything? A stinging sensation on his arm brought Jeremy back to the task at hand. Jinni had pinched him as the preacher prompted him to recite his vows.

"Jeremy, do you take this woman to be your wedded wife, to have and to hold, for better or worse, for richer or poorer, in sickness and in health, till death do you part?"

He faced Jinni and gazed into her sky-blue eyes and in all sincerity answered, "I do."

Detachedly he watched as something stirred in her eyes. Black swirled with the blue like mud into clear water. Jeremy glanced at the preacher to his left and at Tavalin to his right, but neither man seemed to notice the storm brewing in his bride's eyes.

Jeremy blinked once, twice and again. All about, change was afoot. The sanctuary had become dirty and dilapidated. Light no longer streamed in through the stained glass windows, darkened as they were by drapes of grime. The flower bouquets had become rotten and were grown over with thick colonies of black mold. The few stubby candles that still burned emitted more black smoke than light. The guests' formal wear was tattered and soiled as if they had just endured a bomb blast.

Fluttery movement summoned Jeremy's attention back to his bride, whose gown and hair gathered life from an air draft. Jeremy could not see her features because her hair, now black-hole black, veiled her face. So similar were her hair and dress in color and motion that he could not tell where one stopped and the other began. Despite the ambiguity, he knew that it was Monika who stood in Jinni's place.

The wind intensified in sound and fury. All manner of debris – loose papers, dirt, and leaves – careened wildly through the air. Sparing no one, the wind whipped every person's hair and clothes into frantic motion. Yet, only Jeremy seemed alarmed. He looked to the preacher, but he had been replaced by a woman with wild eyes and wiry gray hair and an aura steeped in wickedness. Jeremy watched in disbelief as she seemed to be suspended on the bellows of her dress as it flapped violently in the wind. No part of her body touched the floor.

The old woman and Monika spoke in unison. They said, "With this ring, I thee wed."

How he knew he did not know, but it dawned on Jeremy that the levitating woman was none other than Claire Wales, the hippie queen. She had not died in the commune fire after all.

Jeremy jerked his hand from Monika's grip but it was too late. She had already slipped on the ring. Thorny projections on the inner surface of the ring dug into his flesh like anchors. With revulsion he watched the blood run down his finger, spiral down his forearm and drip from the point of his elbow. Jeremy tried to remove the ring but it wouldn't budge, even with the blood as a lubricant. Beside him, Tavalin jumped and screamed like a cheerleader in a rapturous state of celebration.

Jeremy looked to Monika who seemed unaffected, if not amused, by the spectacle. She spoke to him in a soothing tone. "Listen to the music," she said. "It helps you to become."

"What music?" Even as the words formed on his lips there was music. Jeremy recognized the pounding music as that of Singe and the melody, none other than the song he loved. His eyes followed the source of the music to the balcony. The members of the band were there, clad in black and perched among the steep amphitheatre seating like four crows in a tree. The congregation rocked in their seats, head-banging to the beat.

Jeremy's attention revolved back to the master of ceremonies. Claire was saying, "… let no man or god put asunder. You may kiss your bride!"

Jeremy opened his mouth, meaning to voice his objections, meaning to give lip-service to his confusion, but his words were stifled by a consummating kiss.

Everyone in the sanctuary erupted in applause, save Grady, who was the only one who remained unchanged, in his original clothes and holding his original stance in the middle of the church. Impossibly, his hat remained stuck to his head in spite of the windstorm.

Grady spoke in still quiet voice that Jeremy somehow heard despite the ruckus. "The task falls to you," stated Grady.

"What task?" asked Jeremy.

"You must destroy the Source."

Before Jeremy could ask any more questions the church began to spin, slowly at first and then faster and faster like some twirling fair ride. The words of the carnie pinball game resonated in his brain: Ya spin the wheel, ya take ya chances. The guests laughed and screamed with glee but Jeremy felt no thrill, only a sickening sensation of impending doom. A force tugged at his body and sucked him down a dark drain, spinning and falling, five words in his head repeating: Till death do you part, till death…

CHAPTER 37

Sunday, December 7

*L*ATE in the morning, Jeremy awoke, soaking wet. His mind, like a malfunctioning computer, crunched only confusion. He did not comprehend that his drenched sheets derived from his own cold sweat, nor could he readily accept the transition from the spinning church to his bed.

Gradually, as he moved toward a more cognizant state, Jeremy realized that the ceremony was only a dream. There was no dilapidated church, no thorny ring, and no evil-scary hippie queen floating about. He did not wed Monika when he meant to marry Jinni. He could relax and let go that feeling of impending doom.

Can I now?

As the paint brush of his recall colored in the blank spots, his anxiety found a new home. He had invited Jinni over last night to give her the engagement ring – to ask her hand in marriage. It was supposed to be a beautiful and sacred night that they both would fondly remember for the rest of their days. Instead, he shot an arrow, loaded with the poison of his deceit and unfaithfulness, through Jinni's heart.

He had to call her. Jeremy didn't know what he would say or even what he hoped to accomplish, but he had to at least try to apologize. He gave himself twenty minutes to shake off the cobwebs before dialing her number. As her phone began to ring, that same feeling of impending doom from the dream returned. Two rings… three…four… Coward that he was, Jeremy's hopes rose when it appeared that Jinni would not pick up.

Just when he was sure her voice mail would answer, he heard the familiar *click* of a connected line. Jeremy likened the sound to the *click* of a gun's safety disengaging.

Jinni's voice: "What do *you* want?"

"Can we talk?" he asked tentatively.

"If we must." Jinni's tone was hostile.

Jeremy could hear outdoor sounds in the background on Jinni's end. "Where are you?" he asked.

"I just got out of church."

"Listen, if now is not a good time…"

"Let's just get this over with," insisted Jinni. "What's her name?"

"It's Monika," Jeremy replied, meaning to answer her questions in a forth-right manner. "Don't ask me what her last name is because she never told me."

"How long has this been going on?"

"I went out with her once before, a few weeks ago."

"Where did you meet her?"

"At the Singe show."

"The one I went to?"

"Yes, Halloween night. If you remember, I went to the bar to buy the first round of drinks. The line was long and she asked me to get her a drink."

"And you paid for it?"

"No, she did."

Jeremy remembered how he had saved the five dollar bill Monika gave him that night, the one with the repeated words lining the borders of the bill, *burn baby burn baby burn...*

"And then what happened?"

Jeremy could see that the full disclosure route would not likely lead to redemption. "I don't see how these details are going to help the situation," he replied.

"You're the one who wanted to talk," said Jinni, unrelenting.

"I really just called to say that I'm sorry and to tell you that nothing of conse-quence happened between her and me last night."

Jeremy chose carefully his wording so as not to lie. It was true that nothing of consequence happened *last night*.

"So that whole lie you cooked up about Tavalin's car being broken down – you did that just so you could get rid of me."

"When she called, Monika threatened to come up to the condo and so, yes, I lied. I intended to tell her to get lost. I was trying to do the right thing. It just didn't exactly work out like that."

"Did you kiss her?"

"Yes, but that was as far as it went."

"And you did drugs with her, right?"

"Yes, but nothing illegal."

"What was it, then? It wasn't aspirin that made your eyes look like they did."

"It's called the Unreal."

"Can you hold on a minute?" asked Jinni. "You'll never guess who just walked up."

Jeremy heard Jinni's muffled voice in the background, asking, "Is that really you, Grady?"

After a long pause, Jinni came back on the line. "Okay, I'm back."

"Was that Grady you were talking to?" asked Jeremy. "My Grady?"

"In the flesh."

Jeremy wanted to ask what Grady was doing there but Jinni quickly revived the prior, unpleasant subject.

"Let me get this straight," she said. "You lied to me to get me out of your apartment, you met up with this girl, spent all night out with her, did some weird drug with her, kissed her – and yet you claim that *nothing of consequence* happened?"

"More could have happened, had I been willing." For the first time since the interrogation began, Jeremy replied in a less than conciliatory tone.

"More?" Jinni was livid. "Tell me this, did *more* happen the other time you went out with her?"

"I don't see how any of this is helping..."

"Were you intimate with her?"

Though he knew it was coming, this was the question Jeremy most feared. "Jinni," he pleaded, "please believe me when I say I didn't plan for any of this to happen."

"I can't believe what I'm hearing." Jinni was almost wailing. "Why, oh why did you do it?"

"I don't know," he replied truthfully. "Somehow I just got sucked in. The thing is, in spite of it all, I never stopped loving you."

"Don't!" she demanded. "Don't you dare say that! You don't know what love is. Love is keeping your word and being loyal no matter what. I loved you. What you gave to me was considerably less."

"I'm sorry," he said, realizing that Jinni's expression of her love for him might forever be relegated to the past tense. "I don't know what else to say."

"You can say goodbye."

"Jinni, don't-"

"You wear me out," Jinni said with a lifeless tone. "Have a nice life."

The line went dead. Jeremy had entered into this lion's den of a conversation not knowing what he hoped to accomplish. Being disemboweled by the lion, however, was not it.

CHAPTER 38

Monday, December 8

MONDAY night, before Jeremy went to bed, he flipped on the television. Ever since June's death three weeks ago, and especially for the past four days since he had been identified as a person of interest, Jeremy found himself obsessively checking the news stations for any freshly-disseminated information. The breaking news of this moment provided a shock that Jeremy did not anticipate. Apparently, no longer would he be of consideration in the murder, at least according to the anchor's breathless spiel.

He was saying, *"...repeating the top story of the hour, there has been a break in the much publicized murder of graduate student June Song. It is now believed that a janitor who worked in the same building murdered Ms Song. We have just learned that the alleged killer has himself been found dead by apparent suicide and that certain, unspecified human remains, presumably from the murder victim, were discovered at the scene. An anonymous source connected with the local police department in Destiny informed CNN that while DNA tests on the remains have not commenced, the evidence strongly suggests that the janitor was indeed the perpetrator of this horrific murder. The motive for the killing is unknown at the present time..."*

Immediately, Jeremy rang up Tavalin at home. Together they listened in on the unexpected development.

"That's it, then," remarked Tavalin when the segment was done. "You're off the hook."

It wasn't until Jeremy hung up the phone that Tavalin's words sank in. The ordeal was over. A part of Jeremy felt like jumping for joy because this meant he was free from all the accusations. In an instant, the news stripped away the possibility of his arrest and punishment for a crime he did not commit.

As for Grady, Jeremy now perceived him as the evil, despicable man that he was. Never again would Jeremy foster anything but hatred and disgust for the man who murdered his good friend June.

The worst of what Jeremy felt was a devastating wretchedness for June. She had undeservingly been snatched away from this life and nothing, not even the killer's demise, could bring her back from the great beyond.

Chapter 39

Tuesday, December 9

FOR several days running, Jeremy had attempted to contact Jinni but she refused his calls. By the time Tuesday afternoon rolled around, after the last in another spate of rejected phone calls, he had had enough.

Angry and frustrated, Jeremy swung by Tavalin's apartment and convinced his friend, who was studying, to take a break. Over a hamburger and French fries at the local dive, Jeremy purged, filling Tavalin in on the details of his infidelity with Monika and subsequent breakup with Jinni.

"Why didn't you tell me more about this Monika girl before?" asked Tavalin.

"Because I was afraid you might accidentally say something in front of Jinni," replied Jeremy. "I know how that mouth of yours operates independently from your brain."

"And yet, it was your own stupidity that got you caught. All you had to do was call me the night you got caught and let me in on your lie."

"I told you before, I did try to call but you didn't answer. And," Jeremy added, "you never did call me back, either."

"I tried to call you, just as I'm sure Jinni did. You said you went to the lake. You were out of range. Admit it, Jeremy. This time, it's all your fault."

"Yeah, I guess. But it's only been four days. Jinni still might come around."

"Face the music, Jeremy. Jinni ain't coming back."

"You might be right."

"So what about this other girl?" asked Tavalin. "Are you going to go out with her again?"

"I don't know," replied Jeremy. "Monika isn't the easiest person in the world to track down."

"Maybe she'll show up again, like she did before."

"I probably don't need that complication in my life right now anyway," Jeremy said, for some reason feeling it necessary to downplay the desire he felt for Monika.

***

Late that night, Jeremy was roused from his recliner by a knock on the door. The fisheye lens in the peephole distorted her face, but not so much that he didn't recognize his uninvited guest.

"May I come in?" Monika asked when he opened the door.

Jeremy stepped aside and invited her in with a sweep of his hand.

"Where's Jinnigirl?"

"I have no idea," Jeremy replied. "I don't think we have to worry about her dropping by tonight – or, for that matter, ever."

"Because of me?"

"I believe you already know the answer to that question."

Monika slung her arms around his neck. "Are you mad at me?" she asked.

"No," he replied. "I knew the chance I was taking."

"Did you get the ring back?"

"I've got the ring."

Jeremy did not bother to tell her that Jinni never even knew he bought the engagement ring.

"Look on the bright side," she quipped. "Think of all the money you saved."

He asked, "So, did you mean all that stuff you were spouting at the fountain the other night?"

"Why would you think that I didn't?"

"It just seemed a little surprising."

"Why?"

"Because it's difficult to think of you in the role of my girlfriend when you still haven't told me one solitary thing about yourself."

"I always mean what I say," declared Monika. "What do you want to know?"

"For starters, how about your last name?"

"It's Lyons," she replied. "Satisfied?"

"How about a phone number?" he asked.

"I'm signing up for a new mobile phone tomorrow. As soon as I have my new number, I'll give it to you. What else?"

"Where do you live?" he asked.

"It's a really tiny place way out in the sticks. I can take you out there sometime but your place is ten times nicer. Now," she added, "I've got a question of my own."

"Shoot."

"What about Jinnigirl? Is she really out of the picture now?"

For better or worse, Jeremy's dilemma had been settled. "Yes," he said. "That bridge has burned."

"Burn, baby, burn," added Monika.

"Ha, ha, very funny." Jeremy was not nearly to the point of being able to make light of Jinni's departure, although he had to admit that Monika's presence made the transition more bearable.

"Speaking of getting things out in the open…" he began, "Though I never could wring out any of your personal information, I did manage to learn a thing or two about your little pick-me-up."

"You mean the Unreal?"

"I know where it comes from."

Jeremy shook his head knowingly. For once he loved this game, playing as such from a position of strength.

"What are you waiting for?" she asked. "Let's hear what you've got."

He opened the bay doors and let the first bomb drop. "I am aware of the connection between the hippie queen – Claire – and the Unreal. I know the Unreal comes from the flower of a certain water lily, the purple lotus discovered by Claire in the swamps of Reefers Woods, to be exact."

Monika glared at him. "How in the world did you come up with that?" she asked.

"I figured it out." Jeremy grinned some more but did not immediately elaborate.

"I need for you to tell me what led you to believe such a thing." The muscles in Monika's jaw clenched and unclenched while she waited for his answer.

Jeremy related the chain of events, beginning with how he had elucidated the chemical composition of the Unreal and ending with his trip to the lotus swamp in Reefers Woods. The evidence linking the Unreal to Claire's lotus was definitive and undeniable.

"Well, well, well…" Monika's indignation had all but disappeared.

"Furthermore," he continued, though surmising, "I believe you are intimately involved in the production of the Unreal from the purple lotus."

"C'mon, Jeremy," she said. "All this is news to me. As far as you know, all I did was buy a few pills from some dude on the street corner."

"Oh shut up," he said. "Can't you for once just come clean with me? I'm right, aren't I?"

"I suppose it's possible."

He interpreted the twinkle in her eye as acknowledgement. Finally, Monika had admitted a secret to him.

"Now," Monika added, "tell me how you managed to locate my lotus swamps so easily."

"Aerial photos turned into maps, online. From above, it is easy to spot any standing water. Then, I just programmed the coordinates into my GPS unit."

"I never thought of that," Monika said, clearly impressed.

"I guess I also hit it lucky in that I found a lotus bloom in the first swampy area I visited."

"I'd like to take a look at those online maps you used."

"Remind me later and I'll show you," he said.

"No, right now," insisted Monika. "I want you to walk me through the whole process."

"Why?" asked Jeremy. "You obviously already know where to find the lotus plants."

"There's never enough, and it seems you've hit upon a really efficient system to locate more places in Reefers Woods where it might grow."

Jeremy duly fetched his laptop and his GPS unit. He showed her how to pinpoint even the smallest bodies of water within Reefers Woods while Monika sketchily described the process she employed to harvest the blooms and extract the Unreal.

"How did you ever get interested in all of this to begin with?" he asked.

She replied, "When I first moved to town, somebody told me the hippie queen ghost story. I can't really explain it, but something about that story captivated me. I was drawn to the hippie queen."

"That's like me," interjected Jeremy.

Monika continued: "I wanted to get to know Claire and, over time, I even wanted to be like her. I researched her, like you did, and eventually ran across the publication that documented her lotus discovery. That led me to Reefers Woods and, after a long time searching, I finally found the lotus swamps."

"That still doesn't explain how you knew about the effects of the lotus," Jeremy said. "Her publication said nothing about that."

"Once I found the swamps and saw all those purple flowers, I knew what to do. I can't tell you how I knew – I just did."

Jeremy could not help but wonder if this were the whole story. "Did you just pop some flowers in your mouth or what?"

"I know it sounds suspect. There is no rational explanation."

Monika leaned in and spoke in a lowered voice. "I wouldn't tell just anybody this but it's like there really is some part of her that lives on, like a ghost or a spirit or something. I believe Claire passed along the information to me."

"Interesting – a new twist on the old hippie queen ghost story."

"Did you tell anybody else about the lotus – what it is or where to find it?"

"Nope."

"Are you sure?" asked Monika. "It's very important you tell me the truth."

Jeremy was adamant. "I said I didn't."

"Not even Jinnigirl?"

"Not even Jinnigirl," replied Jeremy.

"I have another question." Monika's gaze was direct. "How is it that you came to spy on me and my friends at the lake that night?"

Sheepishly, Jeremy responded, "You know about that?" He had been waiting for the right time to bring up the subject but he never expected Monika to beat him to the punch. "How did you know it was me?"

"I saw you, that's how," she replied. "Did you hear what I was saying out there?"

"A little but then I got distracted. What little I did hear I didn't understand."

Monika seized on his first statement. "Distracted by what?"

"It doesn't really make much sense."

"Tell me anyway."

"Alright then, if you insist," replied Jeremy. "Right after you stood up to speak, I thought I saw a group of people, kids primarily, wander from the woods to stand with you and the others around the fire."

Monika's reaction was more restrained than he expected.

"Really?" she replied. "Did your friend see the children too?"

"No. That, and the fact that no one in your group acknowledged them was how I knew it must be a hallucination."

"Why didn't you just tell me this before?" asked Monika.

"I wasn't sure how you would react. I thought you might be angry for my spying on you."

"Actually, I'm impressed that you managed to find us that night." Her tone was almost indifferent. "But I'm even more impressed that you saw the children."

"Because it proves I'm certifiable?"

"Because," she said and, pausing for effect, added, "I saw them too."

Eyes narrowed, Jeremy asked, "This is a joke, right? You're just trying to mess with my mind."

"It's the truth."

"Prove it, then." Jeremy had already mentioned the children but not the old lady. "Tell me, did you see anyone besides the children?"

"Yes," replied Monika confidently. "There was this one old woman too."

Jeremy tried to understand this unexpected turn of events. "This doesn't seem at all surprising to you. Why?"

"Because this is not the first time I've seen things like this in Reefers Woods," replied Monika. "And I know that, on rare occasions, others might have seen a brief flash, kind of like you did the other night on the road, but what is surprising is that, besides me, no one has ever been able to see to the extent that you did at the bonfire."

Jeremy asked, "What does it all mean?"

"For starters, it means you and I must be different from everybody else."

"And beyond that?" asked Jeremy.

"That's what I would like to explore."

Monika pumped Jeremy for details, insisting he divulge everything he saw and heard around the bonfire. However, when Jeremy requested some clarification from her – what she meant by *Claire's Alternative Way* and *the Source* and this *big thing coming down* – Monika refused to elaborate, claiming that Jeremy knew just as much as did the rest of her group. She said that he, like the rest of them, would learn more in due time.

Abruptly, Monika stood up. "It's getting late," she said.

Though Jeremy assumed Monika would hang around for a while longer, he did not push for her to stay, nor did he ask when he might see her again. He supposed he could mark it down as one last goodwill gesture toward Jinni. It had only been three days since they broke up. At the very least, his conscience could be reassured in that he did not invite Monika over tonight nor did he insist she stay.

Monika left Jeremy with plenty to ponder. Before tonight, he had largely made peace with the idea that the children around the bonfire were figments of his imagination. Hallucinations and flashbacks were a well-documented effect of other psychoactive drugs. Why shouldn't something as powerful as the Unreal be capable of spinning out an imaginary child now and then?

However, Monika's claim to have experienced the *same* hallucination changed the game completely. Generally speaking, when more than one person perceives the same thing, it is real, and though the children's presence might be hard to explain, he could take solace knowing that he wasn't completely bonkers if Monika saw them too. Finally, Jeremy wondered what significance, if any, could be attached to the identities of the visitors. Why did it happen that it was an old woman and children who showed up at the secret beach that night?

Jeremy recalled how the hippie queen had seen fit to include the so-called melancholy child in her paintings. For her settings, Claire used actual places in Reefers Woods, such as the cemetery and the river rapids. Could the girl-child of the paintings be just as real in Claire's mind as were the settings in which the child appeared? Was it possible that Claire, like Monika and him, had been privy to the now-you-see-them-now-you-don't children of Reefers Woods and that the girl in her paintings was a representation of the same? Maybe Claire could be added to the short list of those with the ability to perceive what most everyone else could not.

Though Jeremy had entertained the notion that there might be some grain of truth to the ghost stories associated with Reefers Woods, he now realized he never truly bought into it. It had been more like a game of pretend and, as such, capable of inducing little more than a persistent – but detached – curiosity. He fancied that he would relish a supernatural encounter, whatever that might entail. But, like a child, who in principle believes in the tooth fairy, might not be especially thrilled to wake to the sight of a strange creature in his room, Jeremy admitted his growing consternation. He revisited the question Grady had posed:

If your eyes could be opened to truths and realities you never knew existed, would you want to see?

Once upon a time, Jeremy had answered an adamant *yes* to that question but now he wasn't so sure. Closer, as he was now, to more substantial proof of supernatural goings-on in Reefers Woods moved him beyond curiosity and, unexpectedly, toward fear.

CHAPTER 40

Thursday, December 11

O N Thursday Jeremy got up early and relocated to his lab. Do-or-die time had arrived. After a whole semester of procrastination, he finally felt motivated to study. He had twenty-four hours left before the final exam, one day to pay the devil his due.

Around nine a.m., as Jeremy sat at his desk, Skippy Sloan slithered in. "Read this," he said and handed Jeremy a set of papers. "I should be back with the chickens in a couple of hours."

"Chicken?" asked Jeremy. "Are we having a picnic?"

Dr. Sloan, as always, ignored Jeremy's levity. "Read the procedure and you'll understand."

"Dr. Sloan," began Jeremy, "I have my final exam tomorrow. Couldn't this wait until after the test?"

"No. It can't."

When Skippy returned, rolling the ice chest into the lab, it was almost two o'clock. He did not bother to explain why he was three hours late.

Jeremy was to isolate the two primary proteins found in skeletal muscle, actin and myocin, from the half-dozen chickens in the cooler. He guessed the procedure would take at least a couple of hours. Unfortunately, the protocol required that all grinding of the meat and extraction of the muscle proteins be performed in the confines of the cold room – essentially a walk-in meat locker – located in the back of Jeremy's lab.

Jeremy tugged on the door handle to the cold room only to discover that it was locked – again. "Won't I ever learn?" he muttered to himself as he dug for his keys. It wasn't the first time today he had yanked on the unyielding door. The design of the door was such that it swung shut and locked of its own accord, requiring that the key be used for every entry.

Despite the sweater Jeremy wore under his lab coat, the near-freezing temperature of the cold room necessitated frequent breaks. During one such interlude, he opened the door to the unexpected sight of someone bent over his desk. It was Tavalin, rifling unceremoniously through a drawer.

"What do you think you are doing?" asked Jeremy.

"Oh, there you are," replied Tavalin. "What are you doing in there?"

"Isolating actin and myocin from chickens," Jeremy replied without elaborating. "What are *you* doing? Snooping through my stuff?"

"I'm not snooping. I'm looking for a calculator."

Jeremy pointed to a calculator in clear view on top of his desk.

"Can I borrow this?" asked Tavalin. "I can't find mine."

"You came all the way up here for that?" asked Jeremy.

Tavalin did not respond as he disappeared out the door.

As Jeremy wrapped up his work in the cold room and was about to wash his hands, his eye caught on something way down in the sink drain, something shiny. Lacking a better tool, he poked a disposable glass pipet into the drain. Predictably, the brittle glass snapped. Bits of glass together with the mystery object tinkled farther down into the darkness of the drain. Though Jeremy still had not gotten a decent look at it, it sounded like a dime.

Oh well, he thought. *Hardly worth taking the drain apart.*

Jeremy used the extendable water sprayer that was mounted overhead to wash the leftover meat particles off the stainless steel counter, which, by design, drained directly into the sink. Finally, Jeremy followed the detailed procedure posted over the sink which detailed the steps required to fully clean and sterilize the workspace so that no remnants of tissue or other contaminants remained.

Chore completed, Jeremy moved to his desk and began to study, but like an annoying song stuck in his head, he could not quit thinking about that dime in the drain. For a half hour or more he fought the wayward thought.

So what? his mind screamed in desperation. *It's a dime, for God's sake.*

Or is it?

Finally, Jeremy had had enough. Seeking to break the chain of this aberrant mind game, Jeremy vacated the lab and walked across Grover's Field to the Student Union. There he stopped by the bookstore for a snack.

"That'll be two dollars and twenty cents," the cashier said.

Jeremy handed over three dollar bills and waited as she scooped his change from the register.

"Sorry," she said as she gave him his change. "I'm out of quarters."

Jeremy looked down at the eight coins in his palm. "Dimes?" He held his ground a little too long as there were others in line behind him.

"Yes, dimes," she said, perplexed at his reaction.

***

In Grover's Field, Jeremy sat down on a bench to take care of the business of his snack. The sun was setting and it was chilly out, though not as cold as the cold room had been. As he ate each of his peanut M&M's, methodically eating the chocolate shell first before crunching the nut, Jeremy realized that he was very near the spot where they had set up for the RockFest. He recalled the laid-back vibe and how he and June had sat together in the sunshine, laughing and talking. He remembered how she spoke of Tavalin's unwelcome advances and smiled when he replayed her words in his mind.

Tavalin is like a mosquito, June had said. *He will not leave me alone.*

A vision of June's face appeared in his mind, the way she was on that day, the last afternoon of her life. It was how he would always remember her, sitting beside him, a red scrunchie holding her brown hair back from her face. He had complimented her silver earrings, engraved with a crescent moon face and tiny stars. As the recollection focused in Jeremy's mind a shudder rippled through his body.

He catapulted from the bench and hurried back inside the Facility, straight upstairs and into the cold room in the back of his lab.

Using a wrench Jeremy wrestled loose the U-shaped trap under the sink, soaking his hands and arms and the base of the wood cabinet with the potentially toxic water. He found nothing of interest in the trap, only glass fragments and some black cruddy material. Like a mechanic checking beneath a car, Jeremy slid on his back into the cabinet and peered awkwardly up the conduit that led to the sink. Finally, he saw it, hanging precariously on a seam in the pipe just out of finger's reach. He tapped the pipe, gently at first then more forcefully until the object dislodged and fell, landing like a wet kiss on his neck.

Eagerly he examined the object and, just as he expected, found it to be an earring, a silver disc engraved with a crescent moon and tiny stars. It had to be June's.

Unexpectedly, a voice from above asked, "What's that?"

Jeremy jumped, bumping his head on the edge of the metal drain pipe. "Ouch!" He squinted upward to see his friend standing over him. "Thanks a lot."

"Gotcha," Tavalin said triumphantly. "Score another one for me."

"And score one cracked skull for me. That really hurt."

"Let me see."

Jeremy crawled out and parted his hair at the point where the throbbing originated. He could feel a knot rising.

"I don't see any blood," Tavalin said callously. "You'll live."

"This game is getting old. Why don't we call a truce?"

"I don't think so."

"We could limit it to after-hours only," suggested Jeremy.

"Rule number one," said Tavalin. "The game is always on."

"How did you get in here anyway?" asked Jeremy. "The door closes and locks by itself."

Tavalin jingled keys in Jeremy's face. "You left them on the countertop beside the door."

In good humor, Jeremy replied, "A mistake I shan't make again."

"You found something in the drain?"

Jeremy replied hesitantly, "Yeah, I did." He could not right away judge the significance of his find but something told him to keep it to himself. He saw no need to divulge anything to Tavalin right now.

"What is it?" asked Tavalin.

"Just an old earring."

"Any idea whose it is?"

"No, not really."

"Let me see."

"What I really need is for you to take a look under here." Jeremy indicated the space from which he had just emerged. "I bet you could show me how to put this drain pipe back together. You're good at stuff like this."

Tavalin, usually easily distracted, doggedly insisted, "I want to see that earring."

Now that Tavalin had sniffed out Jeremy's reluctance to reveal it, Jeremy had no choice but hand it over to his overly curious friend.

Tavalin flipped it over and over in his hand. When he looked up, he asked, "Can I have it?"

Jeremy, perplexed at the request, asked, "Why would you want it?"

"I've been thinking about getting an ear pierced. If I do, I'll need some earrings."

"I don't think so." Jeremy tried to snatch it from Tavalin's hand but missed. He did, however, manage to grab hold of Tavalin's pinky finger, which he sadistically bent backward. "Give it back," insisted Jeremy.

"Ouch, ouch, ouch!" Tavalin tried to resist but the pain won out. The earring tinkled when it hit the concrete floor.

"Thanks," Jeremy chortled victoriously as he scooped it up. "When you get your ear pierced, maybe then I'll let you have it."

Jeremy couldn't think exactly what all the implications might be but something told him that this finding was of extreme significance. How did it get into the sink drain in the cold room? The door to the cold room could only be opened using the key. If he was correct in his belief that June was wearing the earrings that afternoon in Grover's Field, then she must have been in the cold room at some point between that afternoon and the time that her body was dropped into the dumpster later that night.

Jeremy recalled the day that Grady had been working and asked if there might be any trash in the cold room. In the course of the ensuing conversation, Jeremy learned that Grady did not have a key to the cold room.

But if neither Grady nor June had a key, how did June's earring end up in there? Did someone besides Grady kill June? Was Grady framed and also murdered? Was Grady one of the good guys after all?

This was the last thing Jeremy wished to learn. With every fiber of his being, he wanted to be over and done with June's murder. It had wrapped itself up so neatly. Grady, assumedly because of his guilt over having killed June, had committed suicide. Justice had been served with no loose ends. There would be no trial and Jeremy was off the hook.

But now, in light of this new information, Jeremy knew he was not done. As much as he might like to toss the earring and move on with his life, he could not. He had to investigate further. He needed to find out who, besides him, had a key to the cold room.

The Biotech Facility upheld a strict access policy because the labs typically held expensive equipment and dangerous chemicals. Keys were given out sparingly, only to primary users of a particular lab. Everyone had to first fill and sign a special form that assigned responsibility for the lab and all its contents to the holder of the key. Jeremy had been granted one key to the small lab where his desk resided, one key to get into the building and one key to the cold room. When he needed access to any other lab, he had to arrange with someone who had official access. The policy produced complaints among the grad students, but in the post 9/11 world, security concerns at the University had become much more of an issue than before.

Before Jeremy left the building, he checked Mrs. Reese's office on the second floor. In her capacity as the department coordinator, she was the one who issued keys to the graduate students and she should know who else had keys to the cold room. Jeremy arrived to find her door locked and the lights out. He could try again to track her down tomorrow after his test.

CHAPTER *41*

Friday, December 12

*T*HE exam was brutal. Jeremy could only hope that everyone else did as poorly as he did and that the test would be graded on a curve. Beyond that, there was nothing he could do. After he turned in his test, he went upstairs to see if Mrs. Reese was in. As he cupped his hands to cut the glare to her darkened window, someone addressed him from behind.

"If you are looking for Mrs. Reese, she's out of the office today."

Jeremy turned to see a big-boned woman with a friendly face. He recognized her as one of the secretaries that worked across the hall.

"Do you know when she'll be back?"

"I expect her back early next week," replied the secretary. "Is there something I can help you with?"

"I'm trying to find out who might have a key to a certain door in the building. Do you have that information?"

"No, sorry," she replied. "The only other person who might be able to help you out is Dr. Cain but only if it is an emergency."

"That's okay." Jeremy had not had any contact with Dr. Cain since their confrontation that night in June's lab and he definitely would not be calling the executive director for this or any other reason. "Thanks anyway."

Jeremy rode the elevator upstairs to his lab and opened the cold room door. As the rush of icy air slapped him in the face, he stopped to look closely at the key and the lock it fit. The key was not a regular key. Like the keys commonly used to unlock the doors of drink or other vending machines, it was cylindrically shaped. The keyhole in the handle of the silver-steel door was circular, or more precisely, Q-shaped. This was not a key that could be easily duplicated.

He rummaged through the cabinets in the cold room until he found the owner's manual. According to the documents, the cold room lock came with only two keys. Jeremy had one, but who had the other? Was it naïve of him to think that whoever had the other key was responsible for murdering both June and Grady?

Jinni seemed to have a soft spot in her heart for Grady and he thought that she might relish hearing that Grady might not have killed June after all. That was before he remembered that he could no longer lay claim to Jinni's ear – or her love.

Never intending to stop, Jeremy took a detour through Jinni's neighborhood on his way home from the Facility. Even though he knew Jinni was lost to him, it gave him a measure of comfort, however bittersweet, just knowing that she still roamed the world, even if it were down paths that did not cross his own. Rubbernecking as he passed by her house, he was surprised to spy Jinni's white SUV parked in the open garage. She must have taken the day off. Without forethought, Jeremy backed up and pulled into her driveway.

What are you trying to prove? he asked himself as he sat in the hush of his car's interior. *What will you say?*

Despite not having an answer to either question, he exited his vehicle and made a beeline for the front door. Nervously he rang the doorbell. Jeremy noticed a slight dimming of the light in the peephole. Someone was on the other side looking out. He waited but the door did not budge. "I know you're in there, Jinni. Can you open the door, please?"

Jeremy knew that she could hear him and that she stood mere inches away on the far side of the door. He waited for some sort of acknowledgment. When none seemed forthcoming, he tried again. "All I'm asking for is a couple of minutes of your time."

If Jinni would allow him, he would give her a proper apology. That was about all he could hope for at this stage of the game; that, and one last chance to gaze upon the sweetness of her face.

He waited in vain. He did not want to beg and badger and was about to give up when a different tactic occurred to him, slipping in between the bars of his better judgment. Hoping to appeal to Jinni's compassion, or at least her curiosity for his dilemma, he announced, "I thought you might be interested to learn that Grady could not have killed June after all. No one knows this, but I found June's earring, one she wore the night she was killed. Grady could not have killed June because he didn't have a key to the cold room. I'm trying to figure out who else might have a key. I was hoping you would let me in so I could run a few of my theories by you."

Jinni's voice from the other side: "I don't care about all that right now. I want to know about you and Monika."

"We went through all that already."

"Have you seen her again?"

Jeremy did not have a leg to stand on. "I'm not going to lie to you. I didn't try to contact her but she showed up at my door a couple of nights ago. But that's not really important right now. I came over here to apologize for everything and to tell you I'm sorry how it all worked out."

"When she showed up at your door, did you let her in?"

"I couldn't just tell her to go away."

"Go away, Jeremy."

Apparently Jinni meant to show him how to get rid of an unwanted guest outside one's door. He pleaded with her, "Jinni, please-"

Go away," insisted Jinni. "I've got nothing more to say to you."

"Fine," muttered Jeremy.

As he drove slowly from Jinni's neighborhood, Jeremy could not help but feel saddened by the state of his life's affairs. His graduate school career had taken a turn for the worse, thanks to the failing grade he just assured himself for the organic chemistry course. Secondly, the discovery of June's earring meant that he was not yet finished with the nightmare of her death and its investigation. And, finally, there was the small matter of his ex-girlfriend, Jinni Malone. For good reason, Jinni hated him and it seemed nothing in this world would ever change that.

***

Lying in bed that night, Jeremy could not sleep for thinking of Jinni. He still could not comprehend how it happened that he lost her mere hours after he purchased her engagement ring. Ironically, he had never been closer to committing the rest of his life to Jinni than that evening, five days removed. It was just a little thing, but had Monika not called or even if she had waited until the subsequent night, Jeremy would have had time to give Jinni the ring.

He remembered with a rueful smile how he had struck up a conversation with the mermaid of the fountain after Monika drove away, right before he ran into Jinni. If only he had lingered at the fountain a few extra minutes, Monika would have found him there instead of sharing the front stoop with Jinni. Even before Monika returned, Jeremy was in trouble with Jinni, as he could not hide the glow of the Unreal burning within him. However, he would not have lost Jinni over that alone. Jinni vanished from his life at the precise moment that Monika pulled up to the curb and showed herself.

Two more minutes with the mermaid of the fountain might have changed the entire course of his life.

It's the little things that kill, he thought.

But there was something else. Jeremy recalled how, at the fountain that night, he had noticed something familiar in the mermaid's expression, some connection to something else somewhere else…

And now I know what it is.

Jeremy had not had the inclination to deliberate the matter that night because of the debacle on his front stoop, and for whatever reason, he hadn't thought of it since.

Jeremy scrambled from bed to his computer and pulled up the file with the pictures he had taken the day of his trip to the cemetery. He thumbed through the thumbnails until he found one of the close-up shots of the sculpture at the hippie queen's grave. Although he didn't have a photo of the mermaid for direct comparison, he knew he had his eureka moment. The expression on the face of Eros' lover – the lovely Psyche – looked just like that of the mermaid, too much so to be a coincidence.

(*There are no coincidences.*)

The two sculptures must have a common origin.

The next day Jeremy paid a visit to city hall, and in short order someone looked it up and was able to provide him with the name of the local artist who sculpted the mermaid back in the late sixties. Her name was Veronica Gilmore. Jeremy looked up the name in the phone book, and while there was no listing for that exact name, he dialed the first entry of only four *Gilmore* listings for Destiny.

As luck would have it, the woman who answered was the daughter of Veronica Gilmore. The daughter informed Jeremy that her mother had been in the Destiny nursing home for several years and that she would certainly not mind if he paid her mom a visit to discuss her work.

"One thing you should know," warned the daughter. "My mom has Alzheimer's disease."

Despite the warning, Jeremy paid a visit to the nursing home that very afternoon. As the attendant walked Jeremy down the hallway, Jeremy asked what he could expect from the ailing patient.

"Ms Gilmore probably won't say much of anything and even if she does, don't expect her to discuss any current events with her," explained the attendant, "and by current events, I mean anything in the past 30 years or so."

As it turned out, this served Jeremy's purpose well because what he wanted to find out occurred well over 30 years prior.

When Jeremy first sat in the rickety chair beside Ms Gilmore's bed, she was withdrawn and downcast. However, once Jeremy breeched the subject of her years as a sculptress, she livened up. Veronica Gilmore loved to talk about her work. Jeremy thought he might mention that to her caregivers on the way out as a way to brighten the last days of a sweet old soul.

Mrs. Gilmore remembered being commissioned by the city to sculpt the mermaid of the fountain, and when Jeremy brought up the Eros and Psyche replica, her face positively glowed.

"That one," she said, "was my greatest creation."

Jeremy had finally, it seemed, found the one person in the world who best knew who was responsible for placing the monument at the grave of the hippie queen – if only Ms Gilmore's riddled brain could recall…

"Ms Gilmore," he began, "do you remember who hired you to fashion that particular sculpture?"

Jeremy took out a pen and paper to write down her reply but as it turned out, he didn't have to, for he had heard the name before.

"Why of course," she replied. "Zachary – Dr. Zachary Taylor."

Jeremy recognized the name from the old newspaper articles. Dr. Zachary Taylor was the medical examiner in 1969, the same man who was responsible for identifying the burned bodies from the commune fire and the same man who later committed suicide in Reefers Woods.

Mrs. Gilmore's face clouded over with concern as she added, "You won't tell him I told you, will you? He gave me an extra 75 dollars not to tell."

"I won't tell him, Mrs. Gilmore," replied Jeremy as reassuringly as he could. "I promise." Jeremy saw no need to remind the old sculptress that Dr. Taylor had been dead for almost 40 years.

CHAPTER 42

Saturday, December 13

*L*ATE that Saturday night, Monika appeared again at Jeremy's door. "Wanna burn?" she asked.

As Jeremy weathered the mental maelstrom of the Unreal, he presented the request, not for the first time, but for the first time tonight. "I want to know what that party on the beach was all about. I want to be a part of your circle of friends. I want in."

"In due time, my dear Jeremy. You'll just have to be patient with me on this."

"What is the Source you spoke of on the beach that night?"

"I can't tell you."

Jeremy refused to give in so easily. "If you won't tell me what it is, can you tell me if you have found it yet?"

"You know just as much as the others. If I told you more, it wouldn't be fair to everyone else."

Monika told him this, that he knew just as much as the others, meaning to make him feel better. Jeremy saw it differently. He was no more privileged than her other friends, none of whom he had yet met. He wanted to know her friends, her plans, and her motivations. He wanted her to open up to him like Jinni used to do, but it just wasn't happening.

"I thought since I am your so-called boyfriend, I'd get a little special treatment," Jeremy said cynically.

She flashed a shrewd smile. "You're getting plenty of special treatment."

It had been Monika who had first described their new affiliation as *boyfriend/ girlfriend*. However, except for more frequent stopovers, Monika was the same as she ever was – unreadable, distant, and secretive. Still, Jeremy could not envision a time or a circumstance in which he would not open the door if it were she who knocked, precisely because she was the same as she ever was – exotic and strange and irresistible as hell.

"How about a hint?" Jeremy wasn't willing to give up just yet, and as they say, the squeaky wheel gets the grease.

"All right then, a hint," she said. "Let me think."

Jeremy waited with bated breath.

After a long pause, Monika said, "When the time comes, you will become, and time will come."

"What does that mean?"

"It's a riddle," she replied. "You figure it out."

"One more time?" he asked.

"When the time comes, you will become, and time will come."

He said it over and over again to himself, memorizing it. "Is that it?"

Monika nodded, looking proud. "That's it."

"Not much of a hint," Jeremy muttered.

"Actually, I have to say it's a damn good hint. You may not understand it now but after the ceremony it will make perfect sense."

"Ceremony?" Jeremy asked. "What ceremony?"

From her expression Jeremy could tell that Monika had let something slip. This might be more of a hint than the actual hint.

"You'll see," she said.

"When is this *ceremony* going down?" he asked pointedly.

"When the time comes."

Jeremy looked at her in a way that he hoped communicated his growing frustration.

"Let's go to bed," she said.

He consented, even though he was not sleepy in the least.

It wasn't until the following day that Jeremy remembered the dream he had had the night Jinni caught him, the dream with the wedding *ceremony*. In it, he had married Monika. In it, she had said, "Listen to the music – it helps you to *become*." Tonight, Monika mentioned an upcoming *ceremony*, and, as part of the riddle, she spoke of his *becoming* – whatever that meant – just as she had in his dream.

Coincidence? Jeremy asked himself.

There are no coincidences.

CHAPTER 43

Sunday, December 14

SUNDAY morning, Jeremy logged on to discover an email from Quintin Gordy waiting for him:

> *Jeremy:*
> *The pigment tests are complete. Much to my relief, the tests verify that "The Ends" is, without a doubt, an authentic Claire Wales' composition. Now, if you will indulge me, I am quite curious to learn how you came to doubt its authenticity.*
> *Sincerely, Quintin*

Jeremy was floored by the unexpected results. How could Claire paint a portrait that included the wingtips of the angel that adorned her own grave? To accept Quintin's assertion that the painting was not a fake forced Jeremy to consider the other possibilities. Could Grady's insinuation – that Claire did not die in the fire – be true after all? Did Claire, as the hippie queen ghost story insisted, still roam Reefers Woods?

Before he jumped to any unfounded conclusions, Jeremy thought of one thing he needed to check. What if, despite the legend, the sculpture was *not* mysteriously placed at her grave after her death but was there beforehand? In that case, Claire was only painting what was in plain view before her death.

Luckily, there was a way to check this theory, the most obvious explanation of all. From the oft-referenced manila folder of newspaper articles, Jeremy retrieved the one that contained the photo taken at Claire's graveside wake. By comparison with his own photographs of the gravesite, Jeremy verified what his gut already knew to be true. There was no sculpture at Claire's grave at the time of her interment.

Would it be reasonable to believe that Claire faked her own death? It occurred to Jeremy that in order to pull this off, Claire would only have had to fool one person – the medical examiner, Dr. Zachary Taylor. Could it be a coincidence that it was he who was responsible for the sculpture secretly placed at Claire's gravesite or were his actions manifestations of a guilty conscience? Might the medical examiner have knowingly misidentified the crisped remains of the victims so as to make it appear that Claire died in the fire when, in fact, she survived?

CHAPTER 44

Monday, December 15

FIRST thing Monday morning, Jeremy called the office of the department coordinator. For some reason, he was surprised when she answered the phone. Fumbling over his words a bit, Jeremy asked Mrs. Reese who had the other key to the cold room.

After looking it up, she told him that the other key was just where it was supposed to be, hanging in the lock box that held all the extra keys. She informed him that the policy called for at least one spare key to each lock to be kept safely stored in the lock box.

"Would it be possible that someone could access the lock box without your knowledge?" asked Jeremy.

"Absolutely not. We have safeguards that make such a breech impossible."

Jeremy remembered something the big-boned secretary from across the hall mentioned on Friday and knew exactly what his next question would be. "What about Dr. Cain? Is it true he also has access to the lockbox that holds the keys?"

"Yes, of course, but he's the only one."

"Thank you for your time, Mrs. Reese." Jeremy hung up before the department coordinator could pose any questions of her own.

The cat was now out of the bag. Jeremy knew Mrs. Reese to be one of the meekest, most conscientious persons he had ever met. While she was in charge of all the extra keys, including the cold room key, Jeremy knew she could not be involved in any underhanded deeds, and certainly had no hand in June's murder.

That left the executive director as the lone suspect for he was the only person left with access to the other cold room key. But what conceivable motive might Dr. Cain have for killing June? He knew June had been using his lab for unauthorized purposes, an offense which might, at the very most, be grounds for dismissal from the department. It seemed unlikely that Dr. Cain would go so far as to kill her over such a thing.

But why, then, might Dr. Cain have had a reason to take June's life? What motivates a man to murder? Jeremy surmised two common incentives, money and passion. Obviously, whoever killed June did not do it to steal money from her. Could Dr. Cain and June have had an affair? Based on her character Jeremy knew this could not be a possibility. June spoke of Dr. Cain respectfully but never hinted at any personal knowledge of the man. Jeremy thought back to the times he had seen them interact in the lab. Dr. Cain treated June just as he treated every other grad student that worked in his building. Based on personal experience, Jeremy's impression was that Dr. Cain regarded grad students about as unemotionally as he might regard a piece of laboratory equipment, nothing more than a means to an end. If there had been more between June and Dr. Cain, Jeremy would have picked up on it.

What, then, might Dr. Cain be passionate about? What floated his boat? Based on the many nights Jeremy observed him working in his private lab, it must be his research. He was already successful but perhaps he was not satisfied. He had not yet made the finding that would catapult him into the company of the world's most elite scientists.

Something else to consider was the notebook that went missing from June's desk, the one that contained all the notes pertaining to his and June's undercover research project. It was surprising to Jeremy that no one – neither the police nor Dr. Cain – ever brought up the subject of the notebook. If the police were in possession of it, certainly they would want to quiz Jeremy on its contents. But if Dr. Cain was the one who removed the notebook from June's desk, what possible motive might he have for not informing the police of its existence?

Jeremy could think of only one reason why Dr. Cain would not want to show the notebook to the police. Perhaps, he meant to lay claim to the groundbreaking research within the notebook, a theory which also supplied a motive for June's murder. Dr. Cain could not take full credit for the work unless June was out of the way.

Straight away, Jeremy rang up Tavalin's lab.

"I need to run something by you," said Jeremy. "Meet me on the roof?"

"Okay."

Tavalin had a habit of exploring every nook and cranny of his surroundings, and it was he who first discovered the deserted rooftop lab. According to the notes they found scattered about, it had once housed research on certain explosive compounds, hence its isolated location. Jeremy and Tavalin utilized it as their private getaway.

After stalling for ten minutes, Jeremy took the back stairwell up and through the door that led onto the roof. He weaved his way to the far side of the massive air conditioning units, silenced for now by the cool air of December. In case of toxic fumes, he held his breath and picked up his pace past the long row of vent hood exhausts. When he reached the lab, he forcefully slung open the door and burst through to the other side. Tavalin, who was leaned back in an old straightback chair, almost fell out of his seat.

Pleased to see that his ploy had the intended effect, Jeremy laughed and said, "I had to get you back for the other day in the cold room."

"That's just great," muttered Tavalin as he tried to recover from the scare. "That better not be the only reason you asked me up here."

"No," replied Jeremy. "I've got some serious news."

"What?" Tavalin sat straight in his chair, at attention.

"Do you remember the earring I found in the cold room?"

"Yes."

"I'm pretty certain that it belonged to June and that she was wearing it the night she was killed." Jeremy spoke in a lowered voice even though it was entirely unnecessary in the rooftop lab.

"So what if she lost an earring during the course of the crime?" asked Tavalin. "We already know she was thrown out the window of your lab."

"Yeah, but here's the kicker: I don't think Grady had access to the cold room. He had a master key that opens my outer lab door but the cold room is self-contained. It came with two keys and I have one of them."

"If Grady didn't have the other key, who does?"

"It's actually in the lockbox with all the other extra keys locked away in that closet-like room inside Mrs. Reese's office. She told me that the only other person with access to both the closet and the lockbox is Dr. Cain."

"Dr. Cain," Tavalin repeated contemplatively. "I knew there was more to that man than meets the eye. Of course you know it would be next to impossible to get the police to investigate him, considering his position and all."

"Also, considering they've already closed the case," added Jeremy. "The police want it to be over, I'm sure." Jeremy jumped off the counter and asked, "Do you want a Coke?"

"If there's any left," replied Tavalin with a guilty grin.

They had installed an undersized refrigerator in the lab, and while Jeremy tried to keep it stocked with soft drinks, Tavalin tended to sneak up here on his own time for the free beverages.

Jeremy opened the fridge to reveal Tavalin's transgression. "One?" There's only one left? I put a twelve-pack in day before yesterday."

"I can't help it," Tavalin whined. "I'm addicted."

"What would you do if you were me?" asked Jeremy as he took a big swig from the last Coke. "Would you tell the police about the earring?"

"No way," Tavalin replied as he instinctively smacked his lips. "I would keep my mouth shut. You tell them about that earring and all you've done is eliminate Grady as a suspect. Then it would all come back to you. My guess is that the balance of your life would be spent on death row. Now, if you had some other evidence against Cain…"

"I don't."

"Then my advice is to keep the information to yourself."

"And let Dr. Cain get away with it?"

"What choice do you have?"

Jeremy rubbed his eyes with the palms of his hands. "I suppose you are right. The smart thing to do is to just sit on it for now."

"The smartest thing to do would be to go home right now and get rid of that earring before it comes back and bites you on the butt."

CHAPTER 45

Tuesday, December 16

"ARE you a vampire or what?"

Monika laughed as Jeremy welcomed her inside with a hug. "Not that I know of," she replied. "Why?"

"Because the only time I ever see you is late at night when you come over here. I don't think I've seen you once during the daylight hours."

"You bought me a chocolate ice cream cone that time, downtown," she said. "That was during the day, so I can't be a vampire."

"Maybe *creature of the night* is a better term."

"Oh, shut up."

"Kidding aside, I'm really glad you came because I have come across the most amazing bit of information."

"What is it?" asked Monika.

"Brace yourself," Jeremy began. "I believe that Claire – the hippie queen – did not die in the commune fire."

"How in the world did you come up with that?" asked Monika.

"It all began with the painting of the cemetery, the one Claire titled *The Ends*. If you remember, it is a depiction of the very cemetery where her grave is, or should I say, her *alleged* grave. I visited the graveyard and snapped several pictures, some with the exact same perspective as the painting. I compared my photos to Claire's painting and discovered two tiny details on the painting that gave it away."

He paused for effect. Monika was piddling with her music player, preoccupied, or so it seemed. After a moment she looked up.

"I'm listening," she said.

"The monument over her grave is a replica of a late 16th century sculpture by Antonio Canova and depicts a popular character, Eros, from the classical myths, embracing his forbidden lover, Psyche. Eros is portrayed as an angelic being with his unfurled wings held over him."

"How do you know all that?" asked Monika.

"I looked it up online," replied Jeremy. "If you look closely, you can just make out Eros' wing tips in her painting, sticking out from among the other graveside monuments. That means the painting was composed *after* the angel monument was erected, *after* the fire and *after* Claire's supposed death."

"I don't buy it," said Monika.

"Why not?"

"Maybe it's something that just happens to look like the tips of angel wings," she suggested.

"I don't think so." In short order, Jeremy produced the two photos for comparison. "Why don't you judge for yourself?"

Monika barely glanced at the photos before handing them back to him. "That's an interesting theory," she said.

"Why don't you give me your theory?" Jeremy was becoming irritated at her indifference.

Monika's lips parted as if she were about to speak but pursed them shut before any words could escape.

"What were you going to say?" prodded Jeremy.

"Just that…" Monika pulled her words back again.

"Out with it, soul sister."

After another pause, Monika finally finished her thought. "I was going to suggest that maybe it's a fake. What if someone other than Claire painted it?"

"That's what I thought too, at first," he said, "but they can tell if it's a forgery or not."

"Who is *they?*" she asked.

"You know, the experts in the field."

"Yeah," she said with a snicker. "The experts. Do you know any?"

"As a matter of fact…" Jeremy was about to tell her all about Quintin Gordy and how he believed the painting to be authentic when Monika cut him off.

"This painting, *The Ends*, did it by chance just change hands?" asked Monika.

"Yes, it did." Jeremy studied her with a curious eye.

"And I imagine it fetched a pretty penny, say somewhere in the neighborhood of $12,000?" Monika could barely contain her laughter.

"What have you got up your sleeve this time?" he asked.

"Oh, about $12,000, less a small processing fee paid to the middle man," she replied smugly.

"I don't understand," Jeremy said. "You owned the painting?"

"You always say I never let you in on my secrets," replied Monika with a gleam in her eye. "Here's a nice juicy one for you."

"I'm listening."

"You tell anybody and you're dead meat," she cautioned.

"I won't tell."

Monika surveyed his face for a moment before saying, "The hippie queen didn't paint it – I did."

"You?" Jeremy was thoroughly confused. "How? Why?"

"For the money, dummy. It's a little scam I began after I found out how much Claire's paintings fetch."

"I'm not sure I believe you."

"It doesn't matter what you believe. I painted it. I named it. I pocketed the money for it."

"But how were you able to fool everyone?" asked Jeremy. "These collectors really know their stuff."

"What can I say?" she replied boastfully. "I studied Claire's subject matter and her techniques. It took a little doing, but as it turns out, I'm quite good at mimicking her work."

Jeremy shook his head. "So I'm dating a con artist..."

"If Claire's spirit is alive and working through me, then the paintings aren't really fakes, are they?"

This wasn't the first time Monika had voiced a similar notion. Before, when he had asked her how she knew that the lotus blooms harbored a euphoric drug, she suggested that the hippie queen communicated this to her. Even though she said it as if she were joking, Jeremy got the impression that on some level Monika really believed that the hippie queen's ghost was working through her. True or not, there was no doubt that Monika *wished* it were true.

"I only hope no one else notices those damned wing tips," she lamented. "It's not like me to make such a rookie mistake."

"I wouldn't worry too much about it," said Jeremy. "One would have to be familiar with both the cemetery and the painting and, even then, they might not figure it out."

"You figured it out."

Jeremy allowed himself a prideful smile. "I did, didn't I?"

"Hopefully, whoever bought it wouldn't want to know, not after dropping that wad of cash," said Monika. "I know I wouldn't."

"You're probably right about that."

Jeremy didn't mention that he knew who bought it and that Quintin Gordy was no fool.

"I could never make that kind of cash with my own stuff," Monika was saying, "although obviously I would prefer to be able to sell my work under my own name."

Jeremy remembered what the collector had said, how it seemed that every year another Claire Wales' painting surfaced as if from nowhere.

Every year...

"You've done others, haven't you?" he asked.

"You find something that works, you stick with it," Monika replied slyly. "I've done several now."

"So all this time we could have been discussing Claire's paintings," he said. "Of course, I've only seen two of them-" Jeremy stopped himself. "Actually, I suppose I've only seen one that was Claire's – unless that one is a fake too."

"Which one are you talking about?" asked Monika.

"The one entitled *Wicked Water*."

"That one," said Monika, "is real."

Reefers Woods – December 21, 1969

(Thirty-nine years ago)

A Noncommittal Wind

Psssst.

Something disturbed the child's sleep. He turned over in his bed without opening his eyes. The others in the house kept odd hours and the plyboard walls of his room were anything but soundproof.

Noises that sounded like a knock-knock at the door roused him to full wakefulness. He lay alone in bed, frozen in the uncertainty of the moment.

"Is someone there?" he asked in a voice too soft to penetrate the door even if someone were there. In his imagination monsters clamored on the other side.

He waited. The odd whistling and popping noises persisted to the point where he could no longer ignore them or wish that they would just go away. It was only after he stood that he smelled smoke. He flung open the door to find a monster – not the one he had imagined but a perilous foe nonetheless. The fire leapt toward him in fits and starts, seeking out the oxygen that had been holed up in his room.

"Claire, help!" the child screamed.

There was no response except for the crackling and groaning of the house being consumed by the fire.

"Help me Claire!" he screamed again, but still, no human response.

The flames chased him toward the only escape route left, the window over his bed. Frantically he unlatched the lock but the window wouldn't budge. By standing on the bed, the boy had unknowingly thrust his head into the thickest layer of smoke nearest the ceiling. Quickly he became disoriented as the fumes did their duty. In a last ditch effort of coherent thought, he shoved his body into the window and through it, landing in a shower of glass on the ground outside. Bleeding and coughing, he crawled away from the burning structure and collapsed in the underbrush.

Get up! His mind screamed at his body but it refused to move. He must warn the others before it was too late but the toxicity of the smoke rendered him dizzy and weak. Try as he might, he could not muster the strength.

Please God, save the others, he prayed.

As he lay in the bushes, unable to move and barely able to see, a shadowy figure slid in between the boy's line of sight and the window through which he had escaped. For a moment he thought that it might be God manifest, that the Creator had answered his prayers and had come to save him and the others from the burning hell. The figure stood very still and very close to the flames that flapped wildly from the broken window. The boy's tunnel vision squeezed down to a pinhole and still this person only stood calmly by. The final thought that meandered lazily across the synapses as he blacked out was that maybe this person was the furthest thing from God.

When the boy came woozily to, all was dark and quiet. Shakily he rose to his feet. With a double-fisted death grip, he clung to a sapling until his dizziness eased and his vision cleared. What had been his home away from home had been reduced to a skeleton of blackened bones. In shock, he walked the perimeter of the ruins. Red embers like the eyes of demons winked with the whims of a noncommittal wind.

Where is everyone? *Grady asked himself.* Are they all dead? Where is Claire?

Dead?

CHAPTER 46

Sunday, December 21

"**I**'VE got something you want."

Monika appeared at Jeremy's doorstep in the waning moments of Saturday, the eve of the winter solstice, after having been missing in action since Tuesday. She did not offer any explanation or apology for her absence, as was typical for his new so-called girlfriend. Jeremy had no choice but to take it – and her – in stride.

"Interested?" She presented her closed hand but did not reveal what it held.

"Have I ever turned you down before?" he asked.

"If it makes you feel any better, nobody ever turns me down." She handed over two lavender-tinged capsules.

"Two?" he asked. "Did you mean to give me two?"

"Think you can handle it?"

"Whatever." Jeremy's flippant façade belied the unease he felt. He had never taken two hits of the Unreal simultaneously.

On nights like this, time flew by in elated leaps and bounds, and even though he was pretty sure he had never felt better than he did right now, Jeremy began to dread the inevitable comedown. He hated that the thought crossed his mind, but there was no denying the brutal dichotomy of it all. The pure joy of any moment must be coupled with the despair of knowing that the moment will pass. The bitter end always comes, even for life itself.

"Are you up for a walk?"

The question seeped in from some faraway place, so Jeremy thought, until he realized that Monika was sitting right beside him on the couch.

"Hello," he said reflexively.

Monika laughed and asked, "Is there anybody in there?"

Jeremy gathered his wits as best he could.

"A walk, you say?"

***

They took the sidewalk that led from the front of Jeremy's condominium to the downtown area. An eerie fog had descended on the town, wrapping halos around the gothic-styled street lamps. As they approached the backside of City Hall, the sound of splattering water beckoned.

"Let's stop and say hello to the mermaid," suggested Jeremy.

"Okay, but we can't stay long."

Monika stepped up onto the rim of the fountain. "Do you have any change?" She accepted a penny and tossed it in.

"What did you wish for?" he asked.

For a moment, Monika's face was obscured by the steam that drifted up from the fountain like a phantom. "To never die," she said.

"Good one, ditto for me." Jeremy threw in a penny of his own.

Monika checked her watch. It required several tries at different angles before she got the right light. "We need to go," she said.

"Why?" asked Jeremy. He couldn't think of a better place to be than right here.

Monika smiled. "The time has come."

They moved on from the fountain, past the Square shops, restaurants, bars and banks, talking and laughing all the way to the alleyway that housed Bar Nowhere.

"The bar is closed, you know." Jeremy spoke as if this thought had been simmering in his mind all along, as one who was with it. In reality, he was so tripped out on the drug that, despite its proximity, no thought of the nightclub had crossed his mind before they arrived at the deserted alley.

"I know," she replied.

"So what are we doing here?"

"It's a surprise."

Monika stopped in front of the old boarded up church next door to *Bar Nowhere.* "Wait here," she instructed.

"Where are you going?"

"Inside," she replied. "I'll be right back." Monika stepped through the darkened entrance to the nightclub.

Jeremy trotted up the steep grass bank and onto the small courtyard of the old church. He discovered a bench beneath a hickory tree with U-shaped branches hung low. Jeremy envisioned young children, climbing and swinging, bending the branches as they waited for church on a thousand Sundays past.

Why, he wondered, *had the church been abandoned? Where had all the children gone?*

On a whim, Jeremy, who as a child had been quite an accomplished tree climber, started up the tree. The branches were numerous and closely spaced and he rocketed upwards with an almost superhuman strength and agility. Jeremy stopped when he heard a voice filter up from the street below. When he looked down, he was surprised to see the height he had attained.

For a moment or two after Monika exited the nightclub, Jeremy simply watched her from his position in the tree. Monika looked up and down the alleyway several times before calling for him again.

"Jeremy?"

Instead of answering he gave a little birdcall, "Ca-cooooo!"

"Jeremy, where are you?" she asked snappily.

Louder this time: "Ca-coo! Ca-coo!"

"Quit fooling around Jeremy. I've got something I want to show you."

"Yeah I know, it's a surprise," he stated in a conversational tone that somehow allowed her to pinpoint his position high above the street.

"You are crazy!" she cried. "Come down before someone sees us."

"Come and get me," he kidded.

"Are you a man or a monkey?"

Jeremy humored her by hanging from one arm and scratching his armpit with the other when he reached the lowest branch. From there he dropped safely to the ground. Ironically, he slipped on the steep grass bank at the border of the church lawn and the alleyway, arriving at street level with a scraped elbow that bled but didn't hurt at all.

Inside, the nightclub was void of people and strange in its silence. The scant light provided by a string of haphazardly-placed light bulbs could not overcome the reign of shadows in this dark place.

"Is it okay to be in here?" Jeremy quizzed.

"Shhhh," Monika hissed softly through puckered lips.

Like an obedient puppy he followed her across the basement portion of the bar, up the spiral staircase to the upper level, around the periphery of the balcony which overlooked the dance floor, and finally up several more steps which led into the DJ's booth, a small glassed-in perch from which the sound and light systems were operated. Jeremy, his Unreal-racked mind working furiously, thought perhaps Monika intended to crank the music and the lights for their own private dance party, but she bypassed the stacks of compact disks and electronic equipment. Her hands settled on an area along the back wall of the booth.

With a nerve-grating wood-on-wood *squeak*, she slid back a section of the wood paneling to reveal a dark crawl space. Jeremy knew at this point he probably should be asking questions but, not wanting to spoil the intrigue of the moment, chose instead to let Monika play out her surprise. Using a small penlight that she produced from who-knows-where, she squatted and shuffled duck-like through the diminutive passageway, leaving Jeremy alone to ponder this girl and the ultimate destination toward which she strived and to wonder at the depth of his desire to follow.

"Come on," she urged from somewhere within the wall.

Jeremy obliged and, on hands and knees, crawled into the void.

The first thing he noticed as he negotiated the tunnel-like passageway was the smell: The smell of stale cigarette smoke and beer gave way to a musty aroma like that of an old house, rank with the odor of wet and decomposing wood.

He called out for his dark angel. "Monika?"

"You can stand up now."

Jeremy's acute disorientation was gradually replaced with awe as his eyes took in, and his mind digested, the abrupt and unanticipated change in surroundings. He found himself in a large, cavern-like area – the sanctuary, he realized, of the old church next door to Bar Nowhere. The light that filtered in through the huge, stained glass windows, though dim, was bright compared to the pitch black of the crawl space. Besides the inevitable decay that accompanies the neglect of disuse, the interior of the church appeared largely intact. They had emerged in the choir loft in the front of the sanctuary, directly behind the altar. Even the organ and piano remained, silent in their cubbyholes on either side of the choir loft.

"How did you find out about this place?"

"I have my ways," she replied hazily. "Pretty cool, huh?"

Jeremy's attention had been directed outward, toward the back of the sanctuary. With a start he discovered the huge crucifix that loomed over them from behind the choir loft. Jesus hung on a cross of wood, his face a portrait of silent agony. Blood tears streamed from his rolling eyes.

Jeremy became uneasy and forced his gaze and thoughts away from the crucifix.

"Come on, there's more." Monika lit the wick of a long, slender candle, and used it to light more candles, prepositioned in holders around the stage, altar, and front pews.

They walked up the carpeted aisle, through the heavy wooden doors at the back of the sanctuary, and up a dark stairwell that led to the balcony. Monika paused periodically to light additional candles, illuminating their pathway as they progressed. As Jeremy paused to take in the sanctuary from the upper seats of the church, his attention once again focused on the crucifix. Strangely, but certainly an aberration of either the lighting or of his mind, the Christ appeared to have taken on a translucent quality. Jeremy blinked twice, shook his head in incredulity, and turned his back. He followed Monika to a creaky door in the back of the balcony and beyond, where pigeons *cooed* and a cool draft blew. The box--shaped stairwell culminated in the open air of the bell tower.

Jeremy ducked his head as he passed through the small door that led outside. The balcony platform was narrow, with no more than two feet of clearance between the bell housing and the rail. They were high, above the upper-most boughs of the tree that Jeremy had just scaled. In the distance he could make out the lights of his hilltop condominium. His top-floor unit, like the belfry, stood head and shoulders above most of the other downtown buildings laid out in between.

More and more, Jeremy got the feeling that Monika left nothing to chance, that she manipulated every circumstance to some preconceived end. Through that lens, even the first night they met warranted a more close-up examination.

"Do you remember the night we first met?" he asked.

"Of course I do."

"Why did you kiss me, a total stranger, like you did?"

"Was it so bad?"

"No, no, it was well received on my part. I don't know why but, looking back, it all seems a little premeditated. Are you sure you didn't target me?"

Monika laughed. "Target you? No, not hardly. I checked you out and liked what I saw – spur of the moment, as they say."

"Spur of the moment?" Jeremy remembered their rendezvous one week later at Bar Nowhere. "How was it you knew my name before I told you?"

"I made it my business to know."

Though Monika continued to dole out answers, her responses were tepid and vague. She seemed pre-occupied, distant; a world away.

"Are you okay?" Jeremy asked.

"Never been better," she replied, but Jeremy thought he saw a truer answer stated by her expression of melancholy, a look her face carried often.

Jeremy felt an overriding affection for Monika, but instead of a hug, he ventured an intimate question.

"Do you believe in God?" he asked.

It seemed a relevant query, considering the setting.

"No." Monika answered swiftly, as if she were ready for the question. "I think God is a figment of man's imagination, a fairy tale made up by people afraid to face their own mortality."

"Does that mean you don't believe in heaven either?"

"No, I don't," she replied, "at least not in the traditional sense. I believe we can make our existence on earth to be just like heaven."

She turned from him deliberately as if to say, "Subject closed." With glazed eyes, she stared out over the quiet town, lost again in her secret thoughts.

Movement in the alleyway below caught Jeremy's eye. A group of dark figures had congregated near the door of the bar. They stood still and quiet, in an ethereal hush. The first thought that came to his mind was that the children from Reefers Woods had shown up here. Jeremy poked Monika to alert her to their late night company.

"Good," she said. "They're here."

"Who?" whispered Jeremy, but Monika did not respond as she passed through the doorway that led downstairs.

The ten or so individuals below stood still and compliant, like lambs to the slaughter. One, Jeremy recognized: Trey, the lab student with the rock star good looks, was here. These must be the constituents of Monika's group, and tonight must be the night of the purported ceremony. After Monika let them in, Jeremy had nowhere to go but down. As he descended the candle-lit stairwell, his feelings flickered between giddy anticipation and apprehension.

***

Jeremy stood off to the side as, one by one, the members of Monika's group popped out of the crawl space that connected Bar Nowhere to the church. He was surprised to recognize the two faces belonging to the singer and bass player for Singe, but the only person who really acknowledged Jeremy at all was Trey.

"Word," Trey said, pausing just long enough to offer his trademark fist bump.

Not knowing exactly what the greeting meant, Jeremy nodded his hello.

Jeremy sat at the far right side of the second pew. A significant space separated him from the others, who were clustered together closer to the center. Jeremy felt like an outsider; a man apart. So quiet was the church that he heard the sound of the candle flames fluttering in Monika's wake as she passed by.

Monika appeared small, almost childlike, standing beside the massive altar. She placed her hands over an unidentified article covered with a white cloth and set upon the altar.

"It is good news that brings us together tonight." She paused theatrically as she looked out over her querulous flock. "This is the time you've waited for."

As Jeremy scrutinized the profiles of the other faces, he could see that they were completely taken by her. Monika owned them, much like she owned him. From the instant Monika applied that fateful kiss to his unsuspecting lips, she had him. He wondered if tonight would mark another sea change in his life.

"Tonight you shall become more than you are, more than you ever dreamed you could be. Tonight you will be changed, and together we will embark on the path of Claire's Alternative Way."

Monika was perfectly at ease as a public speaker and, if anything, her charisma multiplied in the group setting. There were twelve in her audience, but Jeremy suspected that she would have been equally at ease speaking to twelve thousand.

"You will become one with this world; indeed, you will become gods of this world, for I have finally found the Source. Tonight, we shall all become one with it."

Monika's reference to the Source made Jeremy realize, with a jolt, that all of this – the dark church, the ceremony, and Monika at the altar – was eerily similar to the wedding dream he experienced last Saturday night.

Monika continued: "However, I have decided not to betray the nature of the change until after the ceremony. You must, therefore, submit to me and to Claire's Way as an exercise of faith. But don't worry. It is more awesome than you could ever imagine, and I'm so excited that we have all finally arrived at this moment in time."

The substantial mental overhang of the Unreal made it difficult for Jeremy to process all the incoming information. Grady had once warned Jeremy to *beware the point of no return*, and though Jeremy had not known before what that meant or if it meant anything at all, he was pretty sure the point of no return was fast approaching.

Meanwhile, the Monika show marched on. Done, it seemed, with words, she turned her attention to the object enshrouded on the altar. Like a magician, she pulled away the white linen cloth to reveal a silver challis. The subsequent production she made of the folding of the cloth reminded Jeremy of the Catholic rite of Communion.

"Prepare your hearts for what is to come," she announced grandly.

Monika grasped the two wing-like handles of the challis with both hands and presented it to the group, holding it over her head like a trophy.

"I think it would be appropriate for Trey to go first," she said. "As most of you know, he has been of utmost importance in the operation of the affairs of our little group and I would like to show my appreciation by letting him begin. After his turn, I will call the rest of you up in no particular order."

"Trey, would you please join me at the altar?"

"So you'll know what to say...," she said as she handed him a piece of paper. "Place your right hand on the Bible."

Trey did as he was instructed.

"Begin."

Trey began to read:

"With God as my witness, I give over everything that I am, my heart, mind and soul to Claire's Way and to the one who stands before me now. I also pledge my loyalty and my everlasting friendship to my fellow eleven group members. I swear that nothing shall ever come between us, neither angels nor demons, neither the present nor the future, nor any powers, neither height nor depth, not anything else in all creation, not even the love of Jesus Christ himself."

Jeremy recognized part of the oath as coming from the Bible, except Monika had twisted it around. Why did she have to bring God and Jesus into this anyway? Before, Monika told him that she didn't believe in God, but if that were true, why did she feel the need to have them swear on the Bible? Why was the ceremony held in the church and why did she have them recite a vow that essentially disowned God? Jeremy did not know if God was real or not, and he wasn't prepared to make a final judgment on that very important question tonight, but one thing he did know: All this was making him extremely uncomfortable.

"Drink," Monika said to Trey, "and freely receive all the powers inherent in the Source." As Trey drank from the silver cup she offered, she added, "Together we shall burn."

When he was done, she said, "I love you, Trey."

"I love you too, Monika."

"Call me Claire."

Trey didn't miss a beat. "I love you too, Claire." His ears-wide smile could not be missed as he returned to his seat, even in the low light of the candles' glowing tongues.

"Jeremy, would you please join me at the altar?"

Jeremy's stomach lurched. Why did he have to be next? Slowly he rose from the pew and watched his feet walk the short distance to the altar. He could not shake this feeling of trepidation, that this was wrong, and that he shouldn't be here – but it was too late. Wasn't it he who wanted to become a party to Monika's secret group? He had asked for this. He couldn't back out now.

Or could he? Grady had told him to fear the point of no return and had warned of losing things he didn't even know he had, or something to that effect. Jeremy had scoffed at Grady and his seemingly nonsensical advice. And yet, as Jeremy stood here with his hand on the Bible and his heart in his throat, Grady's words fit. There could be no doubt that he now stood at the proverbial fork in the road.

Movement on the wall caught Jeremy's eye. The see-through Christ was trembling. Logically, Jeremy knew it had to be the well-documented hallucinogenic effects of the Unreal, nothing more than a waking dream. Unfortunately, logic had little to do with the fear and apprehension growing exponentially within him.

Monika offered him the parchment that held the words of the oath. He accepted, but with an uncertain hand. Solemnly she raised the cup up and out from her body to a position even with his chest. Jeremy peered inside the shadowy innards of the challis to feast his eyes on the mysterious elixir known as the Source. Except for a faint, fruity-fermented odor that wafted up to meet his nostrils, discernment was impossible. The liquid looked like used motor oil, though even the crystal clear waters of Sticks River would have likely appeared just as black in this light-deprived space.

"Begin," Monika instructed as she raised her serious gaze to meet his.

"With God as my witness..." he began shakily, "I give over..."

Jeremy froze, unable to continue. He felt as he had as a child in first grade, called upon to read aloud but stuck on some indecipherable word. As the pause stretched longer, the tension mounted.

"Jeremy?" Monika (the teacher) asked, shaking him from his trance. "Are you alright?"

"Yes – I'm sorry. I lost my train of thought."

She looked questionably into his eyes.

High on the wall behind her, the movements at the Crucifix were multiplied. The Jesus figure seemed to be writhing in savage pain, just as one might expect from a man nailed to a cross.

Forget the Crucifix, he told himself. *It's not real.*

Jeremy took a deep breath with no resultant calming. "May I start over?"

"Sure," she said hesitantly.

He looked down at the paper he held and tried to speak but the frog in his throat allowed only a raspy whisper to escape.

"Take your time," Monika said, visibly concerned.

I can do this.

Jeremy cleared his throat and began again.

"With God as my witness, I give over everything…"

He stopped again and looked up just in time to see the look that flashed across Monika's black-ice eyes, a frightfully malevolent presence no dainty twenty-something-year-old girl had any business owning.

His blood ran cold. "I don't feel so good," Jeremy said.

He blinked and she blinked and the evil look vanished. "What's wrong?" Monica asked with connived innocence.

"I feel a little woozy. Is there a bathroom I can use?"

"In the vestibule." Monika pointed to the doors at the back of the sanctuary. "But I'm not sure you want to go in there. It's nasty and there is no running water."

Jeremy turned abruptly from her, bumping the challis and spilling some of the blackish liquid.

"I'm sorry," he said as he wiped his hand on his shirt tail and walked away from the altar. "I'll just be a few minutes. Y'all go ahead."

The farther Jeremy got from the altar and that whacked vow of allegiance to Monika's so-called Alternative Way, the faster he walked.

This is not right.

This ceremony, these strange vows, and the way the Messiah on the cross kept wavering and writhing: all wrong. But could it just be his imagination getting the best of him? Jeremy didn't know. Once upon a time he had a method: Anything that didn't fit into his preconceived notion of what was reasonable – the illogical, the supernatural, even God – was swept under the rug of rationalization. Somewhere along the way he lost his frame of reference. No longer could he tell the difference between what was real and what was not.

From nowhere, the song Jeremy loved began to play, and he faltered.

From behind him, familiar words: "Listen to the music, Jeremy. It helps you to become."

It was Monika's voice, though Jeremy could not be sure if she spoke out loud or if it were only his mind replaying his dream.

My mind has wings.

The song he loved summoned him back to that first night in the time of his life, back to that exquisite moment at the break in the road when his mind opened to a brave new world. In an instant, Jeremy relived that night and all its lures: his adoration for Monika, the ecstasy of the Unreal, the way the song stimulated new reaches of his mind and the indescribable confluence of the three. He remembered the feeling of her hot breath on his neck and the words she whispered in his ear:

It's just like heaven.

Jeremy's progress up the aisle slowed to a crawl. Could he walk away? The biggest part of him longed to turn around and take the vow, to enter into the mysterious intrigue of Claire's Alternative Way, to accept on faith this gift Monika offered, to once and for all give himself away to her. And maybe, just maybe, he was taking this all too seriously. Perhaps this ceremony was more a joke than anything else, something Monika dreamed up purely for theatrical effect. After all, wasn't the whole purpose of an initiation to make the prospective member uncomfortable? Didn't the Greek-system pledges have to endure hell-week and make oaths of allegiance just like this? Maybe this was no more sinister than the process of joining a fraternity at the University.

But he could not shut his mind's eye to that look Monika betrayed at the altar. Often, Jeremy had taken note of a certain faraway look in his dark angel's eyes. Eyes are the windows to the soul, as the old saying goes, but Monika veiled hers in secrecy. Try as he might, he had not been able to decipher what lay beyond the veil. This was, in part, what attracted Jeremy to her in the first place. It was certainly what drove him to investigate the origin of the Unreal she provided and to deepen his quest for the hippie queen she referenced. He yearned for Monika to open up to him, to show what she had secreted away. Jeremy had always imagined beautiful things concealed there, an extension of her stunning physical gorgeousness. Now he wasn't so sure.

It's just like heaven, Monika had said, not only that night at the break in the road but also at the bonfire to describe Claire's Way. It occurred to Jeremy that a distinction could be made between *just like heaven* and *heaven* and he wondered if the two states might be mutually exclusive.

"Jeremy! Are you listening to me?"

"I can't do this," he blurted out. "I'm sorry."

Every head snapped around to stare at him, the dissenter.

"It's too late to back out now, Jeremy," asserted Monika coldly. "You know too much."

"Too much about what?" Jeremy asked. "I could care less what you and your group are up to. Why shouldn't you be allowed to carry on, to take your Unreal and have your secret meetings? There's no reason why I would want to hinder you. Live and let live, I always say."

"You can never go back," she said. "Take the vow or face the consequences." Monika's gaze pierced the space between them like lasers.

"What consequences?"

Monika held her position behind the altar clutching the silver challis. "The time has come," she said.

Jeremy had missed it earlier, back at the fountain, but now recognized this as a reference to the riddle:

When the time comes, you will become, and time will come.

He still had no idea what it meant except that the moment of reckoning had arrived. Now, *the time had come*, but it was the next line of the riddle that really had him worried. If he recited Monika's vow and drank from the silver challis, *what* would he become?

When he didn't respond, she tried a more amiable approach: "Lighten up, Jeremy. It's me, your girlfriend. You're supposed to trust me." In a louder voice she asked, "Anybody else in here having second thoughts?"

When no one responded, Jeremy retorted, "I'm sure none of them want to face the aforementioned consequences."

"Do you?" Monika asked forebodingly.

Jeremy had had enough. "To hell with all this," he said. "I'm leaving."

Menacingly, Monika responded by saying, "Don't let him leave."

By now the male members of the group were standing. Trey eased out of his pew and into the aisle while the others fanned out behind him like the living dead. Jeremy backed slowly up the aisle. Why had he telegraphed his intentions? He should have run when he still had the chance. Better yet, he should never have come here in the first place.

"Y'all don't have to do this," he insisted.

"You and you," barked Monika at two of her henchmen, "Guard the exit."

Jeremy held his hands up as he retreated, like a hiker might move away from a bear encounter – no sudden movements – all the while furiously thinking of what his next move might be.

"Come on, Jeremy. Think about what you are turning down." Monika flipped back to the soothing tone. "Join us and become what you were meant to be."

Two of Trey's burly brethren joined him and the three of them crept slowly up the aisle. Jeremy moved backwards in lock-step, keeping about 15 paces of separation between them.

"Last chance," warned Monika. "Don't be a fool."

Jeremy made one last appeal, this time to Trey. "Trey," he pleaded. "This is crazy. I've got nothing against you."

"If it were up to me, I'd have cut you loose a long time ago," Trey said. "Just take the oath and drink the juice and everything will be copacetic."

"I'm afraid I can't do that."

"Then I'm afraid I'm gonna have to take you down," replied Trey unmercifully.

Jeremy glanced around, looking for something – a loose board, a Bible – anything he might be able to use as a weapon.

As his desperation increased and the hopelessness of his situation became apparent, Jeremy's thinking mind gave way to instinct. Lacking any obvious viable options, he succumbed to that adrenaline-pumping, last resort, nuclear option of survival – fight or flight.

Jeremy bolted. He burst through the swinging doors at the back of the sanctuary. Passing by the boarded-up front doors, he charged up the first flight of stairs that led to the upper seats of the church. As he lunged up the second flight, the pounding sounds of his feet on the steps were joined by those of his pursuers. They were already in the lower stairwell, not more than a few seconds behind. Jeremy broke into the openness of the upper seats of the church. He could hear shouts coming from the sanctuary below. In the midst of it all, he also heard the music, playing even louder than before. In an instant he realized that he was near the source of the music. It was coming from the balcony. Jeremy thought he might run into the members of the band as they had been in his dream, perched like black birds in the balcony, but instead he glimpsed a jam-box as he sprinted by.

I remember now.

The song Jeremy loved played on but it became something altogether different, no longer a wire around his heart. In that instant he knew where he had first heard it, and it was neither that night with Monika at the break in the road nor at the Singe show. Even in the midst of his pell-mell dash for the creaky door at the back of the balcony, his panic faded into peace; inexplicable soothing peace.

He knew exactly what he had to do. He also knew that there was a chance that he wouldn't make it, that this might be the end-game but somehow he was fine with that too. In seconds flat Jeremy glided up and around the box-shaped stairwell, out the undersized door and into the open air of the bell tower.

Calmly and deliberately Jeremy climbed onto the rail and, without a moment's hesitation, sprang out into space, his target the crown of the tree he had scaled earlier. He flew through the air, a bat out of hell ready to seize hold of any part of the old rugged tree that might arrest his fall. Small branches snapped as he tore through, scratching at his face and arms, but doing nothing to slow his acceleration. Finally, a brain-rattling collision bled away most of his momentum. Jeremy grabbed at what he could not see and tumbled down a bit farther before finally coming to a precarious rest. It took a moment for him to understand that his view of the world was inverted. His knees were draped over a small limb that supported most of his weight. His right hand gripped the tree's trunk while his left arm dangled freely.

Luckily for him, this tree, despite the lateness of the season, had not yet shed its leaves. Through a space in the brown foliage he clearly saw Trey and his companion as they burst out onto the bell tower balcony. Jeremy could only hope to remain hidden from their sight.

"Where did he go?" Trey shouted breathlessly. He did a quick scan of the scant perch. The bell housing and the small roof offered no place for a grown man to hide.

Jeremy did not move and did everything he could to stifle his heavy breathing. His position was not more than 20 feet below where they stood.

"He's not here," answered the other one.

"I can see that, you idiot. Did you see him enter the stairwell?"

"I saw the door swing shut. I can't say that I actually saw him go through it."

"He tricked us, the sneaky little bastard. He didn't come up here at all. Go, go!"

With that they disappeared from Jeremy's view. He breathed a sigh of relief. Had they been one second closer, they would have heard the cracking of the branches as he fell. Slowly Jeremy pulled his battered body to an upright position. He had to get down and away before they realized what had happened.

***

Jeremy climbed down the tree without a hitch. As he trotted down the deserted alleyway, he ran over a short list of options. His first thought was to contact the police but he wondered if any provable crime had even been perpetrated. Sure, he had been chased and threatened but the only bodily harm inflicted was from the jump. The police would likely rule no harm, no foul. He considered calling Tavalin to ask for a ride but did not want to involve his friend in this unless he absolutely had to. As for hiding out at home, Jeremy knew he could not count his condominium as refuge. However, it might be feasible to retrieve his car from his garage *if* Monika and her crew lingered in the church. Conversely, if they quickly realized that Jeremy had escaped the church, they could conceivably hop in a car and beat him home.

When Jeremy reached the main thoroughfare, he glanced one last time over his shoulder. The alleyway remained dead quiet.

What to do?

Jeremy opted for his car. He turned toward home and sprinted down the sidewalk at full tilt, his progress measured by the passing of the gothic street lamps. As he passed each light, his shadow trailed at first before drawing even and finally accelerating past. At the next street light, a new shadow racer gave chase and, like the one before, started slow but won the rigged race in the end. His Birkenstocks slapped the concrete, an audience of one clapping for the assured victor – the shadow racer. Surely he was leading Monika in the race back to his apartment, and he hoped that she, unlike the shadow racers, was not bound to win in the end.

As Jeremy entered the Square he was confronted by high-beamed headlights that pained his dilated pupils. It was the first sign of life since he escaped the old church. Very slowly, too slowly, it approached. Jeremy slowed to a brisk walk and kept a wary eye on the car, ready to react to any threatening action. The car passed without incident.

Two blocks down on the right was his condominium building. He could make out no obvious activity there or in the adjacent parking area. Up to this point, Jeremy had chosen speed over stealth, but he didn't feel comfortable taking the direct approach home from here. Instead, he veered right and cut in front of City Hall and sneaked down the hidden steps that led to the fountain. From the fountain he could see the back side of his building, including the closed garage door on the ground floor and his top-floor condo. The window shades in the living room of his unit were partially open and the lights were on. Jeremy usually made a point of turning out the lights when he left home but on nights like tonight, with the Unreal burning brightly in his brain, routines were easily forgotten. In fact, not only did he not remember if he turned the lights off, he also had no specific recollection of locking the door when he left. What if they were already waiting for him inside?

Jeremy hated all this uncertainty but it didn't matter. He needed transportation. The garage door remote was in his car so he would have to enter through the front of the building. He cut across the public parking lot that bordered the back of his building, using the smattering of parked cars for cover. He crouched at each vehicle and watched for any movement before darting to the next bumper.

A black Dodge Magnum with tinted windows occupied the first parking space in the lot, directly behind and facing his garage door. If someone meant to stake out the back side of his building and garage, that would be an ideal location. Actually, he thought, if someone were only watching his building, they would probably not park quite so close. The Dodge Magnum was better positioned for an ambush, especially if the target were someone entering or leaving by way of the garage. Jeremy lingered but his internal clock urged him on. He had already wasted too much time watching and waiting.

Jeremy sprinted past the suspicious car and along the side of the building. He peeked over the head-high retaining wall, pulled himself up and over and landed squarely on the brightly illuminated front stoop. Once inside the common entrance, he opted to go downstairs, directly to the garage. He would have liked to go upstairs and gather a few things but that was a luxury he could not afford. He had his wallet and car keys and his cell phone and that should be enough. When he got to the bottom of the long, steep stairwell, he unlocked the door to his garage, turned on the light and locked the door behind him. Jeremy felt better, now that he had made it this far; in a couple of minutes he would be free and clear.

Suddenly, a sound like stampeding horses echoed down from above.

They're here.

The heavy pounding of feet on stairs spurred him to frantic action. He had to get out. In his renewed panic Jeremy reconsidered his plan. If he had to outmaneuver and outrun he should take his motorcycle, not the car. As he made for his beloved crotch rocket, he caught sight of his hiking boots and his backpack, which lay exactly where he had dropped them after the camping trip with Jinni in September. He heard men's voices, loud and urgent, followed by a sharp *CRACK* like the sound of a door being broken down. Jeremy tore off his Birkenstocks, slipped on the boots without tying the laces and as quickly as he could, strapped on the bulky backpack. He grabbed his helmet, strapped it on and punched the button on the wall. With a series of loud squeaks and clanks, the chain drive raised the garage door, its progress painfully slow.

Jeremy jumped onto the bike and dug frantically in his pocket for the key. On the third try he got the key into the ignition and fired up the engine. If his pursuers hadn't heard the garage door, they certainly heard the engine's snarl. As usual, there was just enough room for the bike to squeeze out between the bumper of his car and the wall, but this time the bulky backpack got hung up. Jeremy lurched and jerked, trying to break through but could not. By now a panic of epic proportions threatened to render him helpless. Time was running out. He couldn't go forward so he pushed himself backwards until he and the backpack broke loose. Jeremy fell flat on his buttocks while the motorcycle rolled forward and fell over just outside the garage.

Without the encumbrance of the motorcycle, Jeremy slipped easily through the space between his car and the wall. Under other circumstances it might have been a strain to lift the 500 pounds of motorcycle, but not tonight. In one quick, almost effortless motion he righted the bike. However, getting the engine to crank again was a different matter.

The carburetor must be flooded.

Jeremy punched the starter button again and held it but like the doomed character in a cheap horror flick, he could not get it to crank.

Well, I guess this is it, he thought fatalistically. *I'm a dead man.* He could not believe that this was what would get him caught.

He forced his thumb off the starter button, trying to give the uncooperative engine a respite, but he couldn't wait long, terrified that he might be on the verge of being caught. Just as he tried again, two lights as startling bright as a prison searchlight popped on. It was the Dodge Magnum and its blinding headlights took dead aim at his corneas. Jeremy jumped violently, almost upsetting the bike again. He hit the starter button desperately, like a monkey on crack.

The Magnum swung out of its parking space with a subtle squeal of its front tires on the slick concrete. He caught a glimpse of the driver, a young male with tousled hair and a deadpan expression. Jeremy expected the car to mow him down or mash him against the concrete wall until his guts spilled out, but those weren't the driver's intentions at all. The car whipped around in the opposite direction and scooted off down the street. Jeremy realized that the driver had the look of someone who had been asleep – perhaps a bar patron who passed out in his car after a night out on the town.

Then, when all seemed hopeless, the most beautiful sound – the engine sputtered to life. Miraculously, all this commotion had yet to attract any of Monika's goons. Perhaps they had taken the stairs down and were stymied by the locked door that led into the garage. Jeremy stabbed the gearshift down to first. A right turn would have led away from the scene and was the safer choice but his curiosity got the best of him. He turned left onto the street that ran alongside his building.

As Jeremy topped the small incline that bordered the condominium, a light swept across the faces of the houses that lined the street opposite his building. A split-second later he saw more of the same and recognized them for what they were – flashing blue lights. At the stop sign he was baffled to see that there were two police cars parked at the curb in front of his building. Why were *they* here?

Was this Dr. Cain's handiwork? Had he framed Jeremy in the same manner that he had presumably framed Grady? Did he know that Jeremy suspected him? Maybe he got word that Jeremy had been asking about the cold room keys. If Dr. Cain framed Grady, couldn't he just as easily plant some damning piece of evidence on Jeremy?

Jeremy made sure he came to a complete stop at the stop sign. As he stared squarely at the front door to his condominium, the uniformed policeman exited. Jeremy eased out into the street, turning right, away from his building and the cop. As he made the turn, the officer's arm went up in a waving motion. He wanted Jeremy to stop. Pretending to misunderstand the gesture, Jeremy returned a friendly little wave as he completed the turn and headed off down the street, not too fast and not too slow.

The road dropped off at a steep angle, quickly obscuring Jeremy from the policeman's view. Jeremy accelerated down and away, using a higher gear than normal to reduce the engine noise. Halfway up the next rise, he took a quick left turn into a church driveway. If he could get to the outlet on the far side of the church grounds, he might be able to buy enough time to get out of town.

The church road ran up a long gradual rise, affording Jeremy a good view of the road from which he had just turned. He zipped past the church and the small cemetery. There was a single speed bump that he only remembered after the shock wave initiated in his tailbone, propagated up his spine and terminated painfully in his brain. Jeremy slowed as he approached the outlet onto the public road. One more turn and he would be home free.

Jeremy checked his rear view mirror one last time before he exited the church grounds. With all that had already happened tonight, he was numb to the scene unfolding behind him. First one and then the other police car slid around the corner, blue lights flashing and sirens wailing. Jeremy watched detachedly, as if those were not rear view mirrors mounted on his handlebars but rather two tiny televisions and these were not real policeman but stunt men shooting a staged chase scene.

When the reality of the situation sank in, Jeremy's reflexes took over. He turned left and gunned the throttle. He realized that by running, he was digging himself a deeper hole with the law. But if it was as he feared, and the police believed that he, and not Dr. Cain, killed June, the legal repercussions of running were inconsequential compared to those associated with the charge of murder. He needed more time to implicate Dr. Cain. It would do him no good to get corralled now.

A hundred bicycle rides had left Jeremy intimately familiar with every side street, short cut and cut-through in the small town, but this knowledge merely leveled the playing field. These were city cops and this was their turf. His only chance was to get out of Destiny and away from its confining streets. Jeremy's was the ultimate road machine but he needed wide open spaces to exploit his advantage. If he could just make it to Sticks River Road, he could outrun them, and at the end were hundreds of square miles of wilderness in which to hide.

Two miles down the road, Jeremy turned right onto Sticks River Road. The police cars were still in hot pursuit but he felt confident that he could distance himself from them now. The initial portion of the road ran through a residential section with a number of intersecting streets. Jeremy held back a bit, inasmuch as 80 mph could be construed as holding back. He topped the last hill before the long flat straightaway, ready to open it up. But there was a problem: more blue lights. Unlike the ones that tracked him from behind, these were stationary. It was a roadblock, perhaps a half mile down the road.

The sun had stagnated somewhere below the eastern horizon but the car's headlights illuminated the crucial details. A lone officer had staked out a position just in front of the right front bumper of his squad car. He stood staunchly, holding a make-my-day pose, and in his right hand, the requisite make-my-day revolver. His left hand fervently motioned for Jeremy to stop with a gesture similar to the Nazi salute.

Heil Hitler! Heil Hitler!

Jeremy slowed to half his prior speed. The police cars were right behind him now. He was trapped.

Or not? asked a rogue voice in his mind.

The car was positioned so that Jeremy's right lane was completely blocked; however, there was sufficient room for a motorcycle to pass by in the left lane, in front of the police car. As for the gun, he didn't think policemen were allowed to shoot at people except in self-defense.

As he approached within a couple hundred feet of the roadblock, Jeremy still did not know if he would stop or try to get through.

What to do, what to do?

Based more on impulse than careful consideration, he went for it. That open space in front of the police car begged to be breeched. Jeremy downshifted and accelerated. He tried to telegraph his intentions to skirt the roadblock by hugging the left edge of the road, a line that would leave plenty of leeway between the bike and the roadblock cop. In as much as it was possible, he did not want to threaten the officer. Jeremy felt a little safer with his helmet on, although it would probably offer scant protection from a bullet.

At less than a hundred feet Jeremy caught sight of something laid across the road. He had seen enough police chase scenes on television to recognize it as some type of tire-puncture strip. It extended from the middle of the road and disappeared in the grass on the left-hand shoulder. No wonder that side seemed so inviting – Mr. Make-My-Day planned it that way. Jeremy leaned hard to the right and careened recklessly across the road, directly in front of the gun-welding cop who, thankfully, instead of shooting, dove for cover. The motorcycle left the road on the right shoulder, passing within inches of the rear bumper of the squad car.

Jeremy overshot the smoothest part of the shoulder and could do little more than hold on for dear life the bike bumped inelegantly over the rough ground. Gradually he coaxed it out of the clumpy grass and back onto the shoulder proper. He endured one more moment of concern as the front wheel struck a discarded cardboard beer box, which burst open on impact. The rear end fishtailed danger-ously in the loose dirt before he finally managed to finesse the motorcycle back onto the pavement.

In a burst of exhilaration and horsepower, Jeremy launched his beloved 'Busa down the straightaway with a ferocious roar. Now they would have to play by his rules. In his wake, twelve empty beer bottles bounced and rolled across the blacktop, clinking like chimes.

***

Jeremy had hoped that the roadblock would delay the chase cars longer than it did, but they took the same route around it as he had and promptly rejoined the chase. He estimated his lead to be about 30 seconds. He didn't know how fast their souped-up cruisers could go, but he could go faster. In the past, Jeremy had gone as fast as 160 mph down this same stretch of road, and he was confident that would be more than enough to maintain his cushion. But as he punched through the 120 mph mark, he realized something was amiss. It felt the same way it did when riding in the turbulent cross-winds behind an eighteen-wheeler on the interstate, only worse. It was the bulky backpack. While he lay flat on the gas tank in the usual aerodynamic position, the backpack extended up into the wind stream. The uneven air flow was destabilizing the bike. As Jeremy increased his speed, the effect worsened until he felt as if the vicious wind might rip him from the bike like an ill-secured mattress from a pickup truck.

Jeremy now feared the police would catch him before the break in the road, some five miles distant. As the blue lights in the rear view gradually gained ground, a plan of sorts came to him. It hinged on spotting the old three-in-one pine tree in time to make the turn while maintaining enough lead to turn off the road undetected.

By the time Jeremy reached the *Keep Out* sign at the break in the road, his buffer zone had shrunk to almost nil. He would have to take full advantage of his familiarity with the area if he meant to shake off his pursuers. His lead gradually increased as he negotiated the curvy section of Sticks River Road and after a few minutes he could no longer see their lights. Jeremy had no way of knowing if the cops trailed by one, two or three curves, but he knew that time and speed were of the essence.

As he wound farther and farther down that crooked road, he became more and more worried that he had already passed the landmark pine.

Suddenly, inexplicitly, the words that went with a childhood game entered his mind and began to repeat: *Red Rover, Red Rover, send Jeremy right over...* Curiously, the voices – and there were several – were like those of young children. That made sense, inasmuch as Red Rover was a child's game. Why or how he heard the voices made no sense at all.

An instant later he saw them in the beam of his headlight. As dreadful and impossible as it seemed, a string of children, holding hands, had formed a barricade across the road. They were chanting, *Red Rover, Red Rover, send Jeremy right over...*

Jeremy braked – hard – but it was too late. Just before impact, he shut his eyes. He would rather die than witness the carnage the speeding bike would certainly inflict on their fragile little bodies.

One second passed... nothing. Two seconds... Jeremy opened his eyes to see nothing but the empty road before him. He checked behind but his vision could not penetrate the trailing darkness. The children were nowhere to be seen.

There was, however, something there, something of utmost importance, standing like a sentinel in the shadowy edge of the forest: the three-pronged tree. Had it not been for the red-rover children in the road, Jeremy would have passed by the tree and the skinny ruts that lay beyond it. Were it not for the hallucination, or vision, or whatever the children were, he would have missed his turn.

Jeremy veered off the pavement and into the woods. If there was a way to turn off his headlights, he would have done so, but, as a safety feature, the lights on the 'Busa were designed to stay on. The only way to kill the lights was to kill the engine and at fifty yards in, that's what he did. He didn't have to wait long. The two police cars whizzed by, blue lights blazing. Just as they passed his position, their brake lights activated. Jeremy winced, fearful that they had spotted him. After a tense few seconds, the brake lights blinked off and the taillights disappeared over the next hill.

Jeremy waited, half expecting to see headlights reappear but none did. He relaxed for the first time in a long while, counted to fifteen, cranked his motorcycle and headed into the forbidding darkness of Reefers Woods.

On the other side of the first significant mudhole, Jeremy cut the engine again. He checked the coverage on his mobile phone – one bar. He hated to stop but if he were going to call Tavalin, he had to do it now before going deeper into the woods and farther away from any towers. He needed information. Coincidentally, his phone showed two recent missed calls from his friend. Had Tavalin already heard what was going on? Did everyone know? Jeremy hoped against hope that his picture would not once again be making the rounds on the national news outlets.

Jeremy kept a nervous eye trained down the muddy lane in the direction of the main road while he waited for the call to connect.

"What have you heard?" asked Jeremy.

"About what?" asked Tavalin.

"The cops are after me," replied Jeremy. "They raided my apartment a little while ago."

"No way!" exclaimed Tavalin. "Why?"

"My guess is that Dr. Cain has something to do with it."

"Are you sure it's him?" asked Tavalin.

"No, but somebody must have told the police something. If I'm right and Dr. Cain killed June, it would make sense that he would try something like this. Just find out what you can and I'll try to call you back in a day or two."

"Where are you right now?" asked Tavalin.

"I'm hiding out in Reefers Woods."

Tavalin asked, "Where, exactly?"

"It's probably best if you don't know."

"What if the police come to me with questions?" asked Tavalin. "What should I say?"

"If they ask about the earring, tell them the truth."

"What is the truth now, Jeremy?"

"What's that supposed to mean?"

"It means I sometimes wonder about you," replied Tavalin. "It's obvious to me that you have been keeping secrets from me, starting with June. I know you two were up to something. I just don't know what exactly. And how about last night? I tried to call you but you didn't answer your land line or your cell phone. Where have you been all night?"

"I really don't have time to get into all this right now, Tavalin. I promise I'll fill you in when I get a chance."

"I thought we were friends." Tavalin's tone was subdued and self-indulgent.

"We *are* friends, Tavalin." Jeremy struggled to conceal his impatience. "Right now, I need for you to be a friend and give this message to the police: Tell Lieutenant Sykes how I found the earring in the cold room drain, which proves that someone other than Grady killed June. Tell him I said to check out Dr. Cain's alibi. Tell him I'm innocent."

"I will," replied Tavalin. "But when this is all over, I expect answers."

"I've got to go now," announced Jeremy. "I'll call you when I can."

"Alright…"

"Thanks, Tavalin, for helping me out."

"Yeah. I guess you owe me one."

When Jeremy arrived at the kudzu-entwined gate and sign, he stopped, but not for long. On his prior excursion to the cemetery, he had parked his motorcycle here but tonight Jeremy forged on. The street bike almost got hung up as he squeezed it between the end of the gate and an unforgiving bush. With great difficulty, Jeremy manhandled the motorcycle up the narrow, steep trail. When he finally arrived at the graveyard, he hugged the perimeter of the wrought iron fence until the dense growth of the forest made further progress unattainable.

After moving a few items from his saddle bags to his backpack and turning the fuel cock beneath the gas tank to the closed position, Jeremy laid his hyper-sport honey on its side and covered it with limbs and dead leaves. It felt as if he were burying alive a good and trusted friend. Working frantically in the dim light of an overcast dawn, he backtracked, scratching at and covering over as best he could the intermittent tire tracks. As he worked, a soft but steady rain began to fall. With any luck, the shower would wash away his tire tracks, not only on the immediate trail but also those left behind on the log road. When Jeremy finally took leave of the area, he remembered the small packet in his backpack that unfolded into what its label described as an *emergency poncho*. Though flimsy and likely susceptible to tears, he was delighted to have it as well as the other supplies inside the backpack.

Unfortunately, Jeremy did not have his GPS unit but he did find a compass tucked into one of the outer pockets of the backpack. Using that and the knowledge of the area derived from his prior forays into Reefers Woods, he set off on a westward heading in the general direction of the river.

Reefers Woods – December 21, 1969

(Thirty-nine years ago)

Whoop Juice

It was December and Claire's summer of love was but a distant memory. The swamps had been devoid of the lotus blooms for almost two months and her fellow hippies' discontent decayed into suicidal depression and disagreements that she feared would soon erupt into physical violence.

At first Claire thought it best to let them tough it out until spring when the lotus would grow again and the heavenly bliss of the summer could be reborn. She began to worry, however, what might happen when the new lotus crop began to emerge. She imagined her friends, these hippies-turned-maniacs, descending on every young plant, destroying the very object of their desire. She had discovered the purple lotus and it was her responsibility to preserve it.

Although she could not have predicted this outcome, she now realized that it had been a mistake to involve the others. These people, once her friends, had become a liability. They could not stay and yet neither could they be allowed to leave because they knew the secret of the lotus. Therein lay her dilemma.

It had been easy enough to get everybody drunk on the whoop juice. Claire showed up with a new five-gallon bucket and six bottles of liquor on the evening of winter solstice, December 21, 1969. Her fellow hippies watched with mild interest as she stirred up two gallons of grape Kool-Aid and a potent mix of vodka, tequila, and Bacardi 151. Their lackadaisical attitudes evaporated when Claire revealed the last ingredient she meant to add to her witch's brew.

"I've been saving these for a special occasion," Claire announced. "It's not much, I know, but maybe it'll give the party a little extra kick."

Before anyone could react, she crumbled a scant few lotus flowers into the whoop juice – enough to tease but not nearly enough to satisfy. They desired the lotus far more than the alcohol but the only way to get at the lotus dissolved in her concoction was to drink. Her friends drank themselves into stupors.

After they passed out, Claire moved on to the next step of her grand plan.

Strong liquor, as it turns out, is quite flammable, especially when exposed to the open flame of a burning candle. Ideally, her friends would simply never wake up and would die a painless death by smoke inhalation. The same went for the boy who was asleep in his room. Claire did the best she could to make it appear as if the fire were accidental, though, if the rest of her plan panned out, it really wouldn't matter how it looked.

It was regrettable that the boy got caught up in all of this but he knew all about the lotus – what it was and, more than anyone else, where to find it. She would have liked more time to persuade the boy to tell her where he found the curious purple lotus fruit that he left under her pillow, but maybe it didn't matter anyway. Though she would be extremely interested in examining the lotus plant that bore that novel fruit, all Claire really wanted was to reproduce the feeling derived from the lotus blooms, and the fruit did nothing of the sort. She knew because, not knowing what else to do with the lotus fruit, she had eaten it and afterwards felt nothing like the euphoria that was the trademark effect of the lotus blooms.

Claire stood guard outside the only exterior door and watched the fire quickly spread throughout the commune. For the eighteenth time she ran her hand over the Saturday-night-special inside her coat pocket and imagined how she would draw the weapon and shoot if anyone came out. Everything went as planned, save one tense moment when she heard the sound of glass breaking. Claire charged around to the back side of the house to find the window in the boy's room broken out, presumably exploded by the fire's heat. She stood for several minutes peering inside but could make nothing out other than the flames and smoke that filled his room. No one inside that room could still be alive. By the time she circled back around to the front of the commune, the flames had broken through the roof.

Satisfied that no one had survived the inferno, Claire slipped away into the night. With any luck, it would be days, or even weeks before anyone became aware of the burning. When it was discovered, she knew she could count on the medical examiner – good ole Zach – to execute his part of the plan.

CHAPTER *47*

Sunday, December 21

A S Jeremy slogged through Reefers Woods, he tried to process what went down last night. He questioned his choices, starting with his decision to run from the police. Had he not been so hyped up from the ceremony and so hopped up on the Unreal, he might have chosen a different course. However, much of the blame for his ever-increasing troubles he laid at Monika's feet. He envisioned again the look that flashed across her face when he hesitated at the altar. She let something slip out, something that had been there all along but hidden from sight. Jeremy had often wondered what hid behind that faraway, unfathomable expression common to her eyes. He imagined it to be something beautiful and strange but he was wrong. What Monika had been hiding was not beautiful; strange, yes, but wicked-strange.

And then there was Jinni. In losing her over Monika, he traded his soul mate for a shyster, his bride for a whore. Jeremy now realized that Jinni had been right to postpone sex until they were married. All along Jeremy believed it was he who was waiting on Jinni, but he was wrong. It was Jinni who stood patiently by, waiting on *him* to commit to her, to love and, ultimately, to marry her.

Something Grady once said came to mind: *The harlot always sets herself up in opposition to the bride. Cling to the bride like life itself.*

At the time, Grady made it clear that *the bride* to whom he referred was Jinni. Grady whispered those words in Jeremy's ear on the afternoon of October 31. He and Jinni were sitting on the front steps of the Facility, waiting on Tavalin. It had been later that night, at the Singe show, when Jeremy first met Monika. That made the timing of that particular installment of *Grady-speak* especially noteworthy.

If Jinni were the bride, it seemed obvious that Monika played the role of the harlot. Was it possible that Grady's words were meant as a warning? Did Grady know beforehand that this was the night Jeremy would encounter Monika and that she was the antithesis to Jinni's goodness? His words certainly seemed to apply.

Jeremy dredged up other instances where Grady foresaw or forewarned. He could still see the cryptic smile on Grady's face when he asked, "Do you ever dream dreams?" Grady had followed up the question with the comment, "Pay attention, your dreams might be trying to tell you something."

If ever Jeremy had a dream that *told him something*, it was his so-called wedding dream. The similarities between the wedding dream and Monika's ceremony in the church were irrefutable, starting with the shared setting of a dilapidated church. In both, Jeremy was asked to recite a vow to Monika. In both, Monika uttered the words, "Listen to the music; it helps you to become." In the dream Jeremy came to understand that this *becoming* was not something to be desired but something to dread. The wedding dream began bright and happy, only to *become* forlorn and foreboding. Jeremy interpreted the dream as a metaphor for what he would have become had he not bailed from Monika's ceremony when he did.

While Grady may have saved Jeremy from Monika, he could not save himself. Ironically, Grady lost his life in Reefers Woods after warning Jeremy to steer clear of the area. Now Grady's name could be added to the list of the others – the hippies at the commune, Maurice the biologist, and the medical examiner – who met their demise within its borders. As Jeremy trudged deeper into the heart of Reefers Woods, he wondered if he too might be marked down as dead.

By midmorning Jeremy should have been reassured by the buffer zone provided by two hours of relentless walking, but the repetitive motion, redundant scenery and persistent atmosphere of fog and rain replicated the sensation of walking on a treadmill. He felt as if he were going nowhere, running to stand still. When he paused to cock his ear for any intruding sound, Jeremy heard nothing of the sort – no bloodhounds baying and no helicopter blades thumping the air. Perhaps, he thought, the rainy weather precluded the use of either tracking method, or, better yet, the police were so thrown off his trail that they had no idea where to begin to search.

Exhausted, Jeremy wanted to stop but he pressed on. Sixty tortuous minutes later he came upon a towering magnolia tree that he could not pass up. Its low-hanging limbs and evergreen foliage should offer cover from an aerial search, if the police were so inclined.

Here, he thought, *I can sleep.*

As Jeremy swept back the heavy layer of seed pods that had accumulated under the tree, he noticed that each of the cone-like pods were of the same size and shape as hand grenades. One by one, he pulled the stems from the make-believe grenades and heaved them like some desperate GI from the cover of a muddy war trench. He wasn't so delusional that he thought them real pull-pins and real grenades, but the exploding sound effects and cackling laughter he provided after each toss revealed his fragile state of mind.

Finally, ammo discharged and enemies repelled, Jeremy pulled the pin on his pop-up tent, threw his backpack inside, took off his boots at the door, crawled inside, spread out his pad and sleeping bag and lay down. Never before had camping quarters felt so luxurious and comfortable as it did that dreary midmorning day in Reefers Woods.

***

When Jeremy awoke, night had fallen. His rattling stomach and dry mouth reminded him of the time expired since he last ate or drank. Checking his backpack, he found nothing to eat, and the canteen attached to his backpack was bone dry. A small quantity of rainwater had collected in the fold of the poncho lying on the ground by the tent door. Jeremy bent down and managed to slurp one swallow of the life-giving liquid, but that only enflamed his desire for more. He quickly packed up and resumed his westward jaunt toward the river.

The rain had ceased and the skies were clear but moonless. Wanting to conserve battery juice, Jeremy switched off the flashlight, but, after a vicious poke-in-the-eye from an unseen limb, thought better of it. To his dismay, the flashlight offered little help; its fading beam could scarcely pierce the disorienting darkness. His watering left eye further hampered his ability to navigate. His runner's remorse revived.

What are you doing out here, Jeremy? he asked himself.

Although the area offered a perfect place in which to hide from the police, he could not stay here indefinitely. He had no food, and, lacking a gun, he would be hard-pressed to harvest any game. A sardonic smile invaded his lips when he pictured how he might attempt to stalk and kill anything – a squirrel, a deer or a fish in the river – using only his buck knife and his wits.

Too often, he fought back the sensation that he was not alone, that someone or something was watching from a nearby knoll or lurking behind a tree trunk. Whenever that happened, Jeremy hustled on past and tried, as best he could, to shove the unsettling thought from his mind.

After over six hours of his self-imposed hell-hike, Jeremy broke into the clear. The water before him loomed larger than the river and the slender ribbon of sand rang familiar. In an instant, he knew why it took longer than expected to get here. Because of the darkness and the difficult walking conditions, his route deviated significantly to the south of west. Jeremy knew this because he recognized the water before him as that of Sticks River Lake and the sand beneath his boots as that of Monika's secret beach.

As he took in his new surroundings, Jeremy realized he was not alone. Approximately 300 yards offshore were the subdued lights of a boat sitting still in the water. Jeremy first thought the vessel might belong to some branch of law enforcement, stationed here for his express benefit. However, by way of the small field glasses retrieved from his backpack, he decided it better fit the profile of a civilian craft. It looked like a houseboat.

Keeping a wary eye on the boat, Jeremy made for the water's edge, filled his canteen and drank gustily. He wondered to whom the boat belonged and if he had reason to fear its presence, especially in light of what he had already decided to do next.

Jeremy followed the shoreline of the lake toward the landing, retracing the path he and Tavalin had taken from the car to the beach on the night of Monika's bonfire. He made sure there were no police cruisers stationed in the parking area of Sticks River Landing before emerging from the cover of the woods.

This would be the third time he had made use of the racked canoe. The first was the river trip with Jinni. The other time had been the day of the lotus swamp quest. After the last outing, he had jammed the paddle into the space between the canoe and the rack. When he checked, fortunately, it was still there. Jeremy hoped the canoe would be his ticket out of here. With any luck, he could paddle across the lake to escape the area, but the plan hinged on being able to do so undetected. As it was already almost five a.m., he only had a couple of hours of darkness left. He could not risk being exposed in the openness of the lake after sunrise; he would have to hunker down until night fell again.

As Jeremy paddled north along the shoreline, toward the secret beach, he wondered about that houseboat. He thought it plenty curious that it was anchored in this desolate place. His curiosity and the lack of activity on the boat emboldened Jeremy to swing in for a closer look. The canoe would provide a noiseless approach and he could count on the darkness for cover should anyone unexpectedly appear on deck. As for what he hoped to accomplish, he was not sure. At the very least, he might spot something of use on deck. An ice chest full of leftover grilled meat of any kind and some cold beverages would certainly be a godsend.

Closer he approached, until he was near enough to see inside. The curtains on the large window of the single-room cabin were partially open. A nightlight of some sort illuminated the interior enough for him to see that the room was unoccupied. The bed was neatly made but empty. In a bold move, fueled more by his ravenous hunger than anything else, he tied up and climbed onto the back deck. The sliding glass door that led inside was unlocked. Jeremy slipped inside.

First he tiptoed to the front section of the cabin where the captain's chair and the boat controls were located. Vacant was the ignition slot, and a slipshod search of the immediate vicinity revealed no key but Jeremy minded little. Driving a stolen houseboat across the open, soon-to-be-illuminated waters of the lake would likely get him caught anyway. What really tweaked his interest was the small kitchenette, or, more specifically, the little refrigerator it housed. Jeremy was more than thrilled to find the package of hotdogs inside. It didn't matter that the boat's owner would notice his food missing. Those hotdogs were coming with him.

Like a quarterback too-long in the pocket, Jeremy felt the clock ticking and would have immediately left, food-in-hand, had he not noticed the table. Strewn across its surface were several maps or, more precisely, aerial photos of Reefers Woods. Jeremy recognized them right off because there were, lying around his apartment, some of the same representations. His, he had printed from a specific online site for the purpose of locating the lotus swamps. The logo on these maps matched his, and the web address printed along the bottom of each page verified their common origin.

Could the fact that these maps were printed from the same web site be a coincidence? This, he doubted. Besides Jinni, only Monika had been privy to his maps. He plainly remembered telling Monika, at her insistence, how he used the maps to find the lotus swamps and where he obtained the maps. Might the houseboat, anchored off the southern shoreline of Reefers Woods, belong to Monika? It made sense, in light of the maps and her well-documented connections to the area.

A soft sound – a *clunk* – of unknown origin prompted Jeremy to look nervously about. Was someone there? The ease with which he found, boarded, and gained entry to the houseboat made him very uneasy. He felt as if this were a ship found deserted in the Bermuda Triangle and that he was being baited. Would the ghosts of the dead crew – or Monika – suddenly materialize and steal away his immortal soul?

Get a grip, Jeremy told himself. *No one is here.*

He turned his attention to one map in particular that had been marked over with red ink. Interestingly, a heavy, X-marks-the-spot annotation had been scratched next to the meandering ribbon of Sticks River at a place where the river split. Jeremy knew of only one such bifurcation of the channel, that of The Devil's Crotch. For whatever reason, Monika had circled that sheer-walled mini-mountain that bordered the rapids. Further emphasizing the spot on the map was a label she printed, also in red ink: *The King's Pinnacle*, it read.

As Jeremy wondered what all this might mean, he heard the hum of something – an engine of some sort. Someone was coming. He stuffed the map into his back pocket and scrambled out of the cabin. There, approaching from the north, were two headlights aimed directly at the boat and closing fast. Jeremy did not wish to bump into either of the two possible parties – Monika *or* the police – that might be tooling around the lake in the predawn gloom.

Jeremy lunged up the steps and through the open sliding-glass door and paddled quickly away in a heading that kept the houseboat between him and the encroaching lights. Had the two jet-skis bypassed the boat, he would certainly have been caught, revealed by their headlights. As it was, he was able to slip away undetected. As he made for the relative cover of the shoreline, he watched two vague shadows clamber aboard the houseboat and disappear within the cabin. It was impossible to positively identify them but he had to assume that one of the dark shapes belonged to Monika. Jeremy had no clue as to the possible identity of the other person.

As thrilled Jeremy was to escape, he realized that in his frenzy to leave he had forgotten one very important item. He wondered what the two individuals just come to the boat would infer from the package of hotdogs left behind in plain view, fresh from the fridge, sitting like a beacon among the maps on the table. He wondered also how quickly they would recognize that one of their maps had gone missing.

CHAPTER *48*

Monday, December 22

W*HILE* he paddled, Jeremy pondered the significance of the maps he found on the boat. At first he theorized that Monika might be using them to search for additional lotus habitat, but something made him wonder if she might be looking for something else.

Ever since Jeremy had arrived in the woods, Grady's words had flooded his mind. This time, Jeremy recalled something Grady said the day they met, that "Reefers Woods holds the source of certain objects of desire, both good and evil."

Reefers Woods holds the source...

Could it be that Grady's source and the Source from Monika's ceremony were one and the same? Could it be that the Source was one of the so-called evil *objects of desire* referred to by Grady? Somehow, it made sense in Jeremy's mind. Had Monika used the maps to find the Source in the same way Jeremy had used them to find the lotus swamps? It pained him to think that he might have done the very thing that Grady had warned him not to do from the beginning: loosed this evil object of desire, via Monika, onto the world.

By the time Jeremy reached the place where Sticks River emptied into the lake, the earliest twinges of dawn had materialized above the tree line to the east. He could not risk staying exposed on the open water for much longer. As the river's current was negligible this close to the lake, Jeremy continued upstream a ways before stopping. He dragged the canoe farther than necessary into the woods on the east side of the river and paced about as he tried to determine what his next move should be. One option, based solely on the concept of self-preservation, would be to camp here until nightfall and then to paddle to the other side of the lake under cover of darkness. Making it to the other side undetected would greatly enhance his chances of eluding the police, at least in the short term.

The other option had nothing to do with getting away but everything to do with what Grady would have him do. Grady had said, "With knowledge comes responsibility. By knowing more you must do more."

Jeremy definitely knew more – he knew the location of the Source – and he could not deny that he knew what he was supposed to do next. Grady – or rather Dream-Grady – had made that abundantly clear. Under normal circumstances, Jeremy would have thought it laughable that anyone, especially him, would undertake what could be an ill-advised, even dangerous, course based on a dream. Wasn't he supposed to be the scientist, the logical one? He was, but the more Jeremy reflected on the wedding dream, the more he understood that it was less like a dream and more like – for lack of a better word – a vision. Had it not been for it – that vision – he likely would have gone through with the ceremony. Grady's role in the vision, besides his obvious objections to Jeremy taking the vow, was defined by the words he uttered:

The task falls to you. You must destroy the Source.

Did Grady mean for him to rip the challis from Monika's clutch and spill it, like a blood sacrifice, onto the altar in the abandoned church? Perhaps, but more likely he meant for Jeremy to find where she got it, that is, the source of the Source, and destroy it. But what of the police? Jeremy could worry about the cops all he wanted but, somehow, he sensed that this business of Grady, Monika and the Source trumped his legal troubles.

Though Jeremy still did not know *what* the Source was, other than the mysterious elixir from Monika's ceremony, he now had a notion *where* it could be found. That he learned from the aerial pictures and Monika's big red *X* at the place she called the King's Pinnacle. Jeremy had not known it as such, but he was familiar with that 100-foot-high chunk of rock that bordered the rapids of The Devil's Crotch, as he and Jinni had, once upon a time, walked its perimeter looking for a way to the top.

When Jeremy pulled out the map stolen from the houseboat, he noticed – and subsequently remembered – the stream that ran underground on the back side of the King's Pinnacle. Interestingly, he thought he could just make out its re-emergence on the other side of the sheer rock wall. But, since water does not run uphill, that could only mean that what he had assumed to be a solid block of rock was actually hollowed out on the inside. This Jeremy had not expected. This new information, interesting as it might be, did nothing to help him comprehend what the Source might be or how the maps helped Monika find it. Perhaps the copious red ink obscured it. With a clean copy, he might better be able to discern what was hiding inside but the most expedient course of action would be to hike the five miles to the King's Pinnacle. If he could find a way inside, he could then see the Source for himself and decide if he should or should not heed Grady's decree and destroy it.

His decision settled, Jeremy flipped the canoe and threw enough leaves and branches on top to break up its shape. He struck out in a northerly direction, following the river channel toward The Devil's Crotch and the King's Pinnacle; toward the Source. As he walked, he realized that, even after the 12 hours of nonstop walking and canoeing, his body was not yet weary. He had not trained at all during the past few weeks, and, absent that measuring stick, Jeremy wondered if perhaps the increased endurance that allowed him to finish first at the triathlon had faded. The way he now felt, strong and fresh, reassured him that the strengthening effect remained with him. After all the time he and June spent studying the effect, and after June was likely murdered by Dr. Cain on account of it, he was at least happy to know that he had not lost it.

***

It took two more hours of walking, but the unmistakable sound of water churning informed him that his destination was near. Jeremy stopped when he came upon the place where he and Jinni had camped before, near where they crawled from the river after being spit out the tail end of The Devil's Crotch. For no better reason than for old time's sake, he would sleep the day away here.

As he lay in the tent, he recalled that Sunday in September and how wonderful it felt lying next to Jinni, but something else of significance occurred that night, something that played a crucial role in his escape from Monika's ceremony in the abandoned church.

The wedding dream, the animated Christ, the specter of what the ceremony might cause him *to become*, the vow, and Monika's malevolent expression – all these things had been plenty to get him moving away from the altar. But, halfway up the aisle, when Monika cued the music of Singe, he faltered. The music had a hold over him and hearing it overrode his good sense. At that moment he had been a hair's breadth away from turning back to Monika – to drink her elixir and take her vow – and he might have, had it not been for the epiphany that swept over him. At that moment, as he teetered, halfway between staying and leaving, halfway between the altar and the tree of his eventual escape, Jeremy remembered where he first heard the song he loved. It was not at the Singe show or that first night with Monika in his car at the break in the road. No, he heard it for the first time right here in the heart of Reefers Woods, back in September, before the Singe show and before he met Monika.

How he could have forgotten, he did not know, but it wasn't until that pivotal moment in the church that this other dream, his *vision of the real* – in all its majesty – came back to him. It was inside that vision where he first heard the song, and the Singe version – as captivating as it was – could not hold a candle to the dream version. The Singe version consisted of four parts, played by four members of an earthly band. In the vision Jeremy was somehow able to discern each of a *million* marvelously intertwined parts, generated by the legion of dream-beings.

And, just as the song Jeremy loved echoed, but did not reproduce the grand music of the vision, the Unreal delivered but a fleeting moment of ecstasy that could not compare to the transcending euphoria of the vision. Every time Jeremy listened to the song he loved, he should have been reminded of that vision and all that it represented; instead he thought of that first night out with Monika. The Unreal had not opened up his mind like she said it would. Rather, it had closed his mind to the hidden realms revealed in his vision. Singe's version of the music and the Unreal's version of the euphoria were but cheap imitations; that which he experienced in the vision were of *the real*.

This did not mean that the Unreal did not have the capacity to change a person. Monika indicated as much when she said that the Unreal opens up a person's mind, implying the effect of setting one free. However, Jeremy's sense of the change that had begun to occur in him was more like a binding up. The Unreal burrowed a hole on the inside, an insatiable longing that could only be filled with more of the thing that dug the hole in the first place. Likewise, Monika's presence was of an addicting nature. The more he took of her, the less satisfied he was and the more he wanted.

Claire's Way, touted by Monika, focused on this world and this life to the exclusion of anything else that might be out there. The memory of that first night out with Monika and the Unreal covered over the glorious feeling he experienced in his vision like cheap wallpaper over the ceiling of the Sistine Chapel. On more than one occasion, she referred to the circumstances of this or that Unreal-fueled moment as *just like heaven*. But be that as it may, *just like heaven* may be like heaven, but it is not heaven; it is an imposter, just as he now knew Monika also to be.

But how was it that the songs of Singe reproduced, more or less, the same music Jeremy first heard in a dream? The music of Singe was unreleased and, prior to their Halloween show, had never been played in public. How, then, did the music come to be composed and played by Singe? What if the music of Singe also flowed to them from elsewhere, that they essentially plagiarized it from the same *vision of the real* Jeremy experienced on the night he and Jinni camped here in the shadow of the King's Pinnacle? Might one of the band members of Singe have shared the same vision?

It wouldn't be the first time Jeremy had shared something akin to a vision. He and Monika had both seen the mysterious children of Reefers Woods in what Jeremy initially characterized as a shared hallucination and, later, as a waking dream. Dreams, hallucinations, visions – they all seemed interconnected, especially in the context of Reefers Woods.

He and Monika were the only two souls – with the possible exception of Claire – who perceived the strange children of Reefers Woods. Therefore, it seemed likely that if anyone else was privy to the *vision of the real* and the music integral to it, it was Monika. Tellingly, Monika's connections to the band were evident. She attended the Singe show and provided him with a compact disc with their songs before anybody else in the world had a copy, and Jeremy recognized at least two members of the band at the transformation ceremony. Putting it all together, it seemed reasonable, even likely, that Monika was the one who brought to earth, or manifested, so to speak, the music of the vision. Singe might even be a creation entirely of Monika's own making. That the title of the band – Singe – alluded to fire also seemed especially significant considering Monika's association of fire with the Unreal.

Do you know what it is to burn? Burn, baby, burn.

But why? What motivation might Monika have to assemble the band to play music she first heard in a vision? Jeremy thought he knew the answer. Monika used the music, the Unreal, and her charisma to suck people in, to acquire followers of what she referred to as Claire's Way, and it worked. Jeremy had experienced the allure first-hand and he had seen it at work with the members of Monika's group, who seemed perfectly willing to give themselves away, without even knowing for certain what they were committing to. In that sense, Claire's Way could be likened to a cult with Monika as its charismatic leader.

Before crossing over into the realm of sleep, Jeremy's rambling mind touched on – but could not answer – one final question: What enabled Monika and him to share in these visions and hallucinations that others seemed unable to perceive? What was it that he and Monika had in common?

***

At dusk Jeremy awoke, ready to proceed with his plan to identify and destroy the Source. Unfortunately, it hinged on finding a way to the inside of the King's Pinnacle. This evening was the second time Jeremy had walked its perimeter; however, the conclusions reached were the same as before. The only obvious way past the sheer rock walls was up and over, but one would have to have specialized climbing equipment and knowhow to accomplish that feat.

Stumped, he re-examined the map he took from the houseboat. Jeremy noticed for the first time another map printed on the flip side of the first. It took him a little while to figure out that this other map was a small-scale version of the same area, stretching from the river all the way to Sticks River Road and as far as the lake five miles to the south. Using his ailing flashlight, he picked out a solitary structure just inside the northeast border of the map, next to Sticks River Road. It was Grady's house and it beckoned to Jeremy. He could not stay out here forever. It had been 48 hours since he last ate, and though he knew he could probably hold out a couple more days, he would eventually need nourishment. Grady's house, if it were unoccupied, might be the perfect place to score some food. Jeremy certainly could not see himself be-bopping into any fast-food restaurant or grocery store anytime soon.

One last feature Jeremy noticed on the map was the tiny squiggly line that connected the King's Pinnacle and Grady's house. It was the stream, and, conveniently, it cut across the intervening five miles of forest, leading directly to Grady's house. Even if he deemed it too dangerous to go all the way to Grady's house, Jeremy could conceivably follow the stream until he was close enough to civilization to get reception on his phone. Once in range, he could call Tavalin. If Tavalin had done his part and informed the police of Dr. Cain's apparent culpability in June's murder, Jeremy might already be in the clear. Perhaps, for once, Tavalin would be the bearer of good news.

As he headed out, Jeremy dreamed of the comforts of a home – things like a hot shower, a comfortable couch on which to lie, maybe even the smell of a frozen pizza cooking in Grady's oven – though he realized that was asking a little much. The best he could hope for was some information from Tavalin and a few cans of food and not to get caught.

Using the stream as a path, Jeremy made good time. The water in the stream was generally only a couple of inches deep and the white-sand bottom lent itself well to walking. Periodically, he stopped and switched on his phone to check for coverage. Once in range, Jeremy tried Tavalin's cell phone. Much to his chagrin, he got no answer.

"Well isn't that just ducky?" Jeremy remarked to himself. At the beep, he said, "Call me ASAP."

Needing information but loath to wait on Tavalin to call back, Jeremy debated calling Jinni. Even if she knew nothing of the specifics of the investigation, he could at least find out what they were saying on the news. It would also give him the opportunity to apologize to her. Maybe she would even find it in her heart to forgive him, though he knew that was not likely. Of course, his plan presumed that Jinni was no longer ignoring his calls.

She answered on the second ring.

"Jinni, this is Jeremy. Is it safe to talk on this line?"

"As far as I know," she replied.

"You know what's going on with me and the cops, right?"

"Yes, to a certain extent." Jinni's tone was flat; unreadable.

"What are they saying on the news?" asked Jeremy.

"Nothing on the news but Tavalin told me what he knew."

"There's nothing on the news? Are you sure?"

"I'm sure."

"That's odd," remarked Jeremy. "What did Tavalin tell you?"

"He said that you were a suspect again."

"Did he happen to mention my belief that Dr. Cain killed June, framed Grady, and now is trying to frame me?"

"Tavalin said the police found June's earring in your apartment and that it didn't look good for you. I don't think he mentioned Dr. Cain."

Jeremy wondered if Tavalin was, for once, trying to use some discretion.

"Do you really think Dr. Cain did it?" asked Jinni.

"He's the only one, besides me, who had access to the cold room."

"But why would he do it?" asked Jinni doubtfully.

"You don't think I had anything to do with it, do you?" asked Jeremy.

"I would say no, but after the way you lied straight to my face, I'm not sure why I should believe anything you say."

"Listen, Jinni, about all of that – you never let me fully explain my side of it."

"I don't want to hear it, Jeremy."

"I can't blame you for that, but I wanted to explain-"

Jinni cut him off. "I was too angry to listen."

"And now?" asked Jeremy hesitantly. "What are you now?"

"Now I'm-" Jinni cut herself off and started over. "Now I'm just concerned for your wellbeing."

Reading between the lines, Jeremy feared that *concern* might be the most Jinni would ever feel for him, and though he doubted he could change the way she felt, he had to try.

"Listen to me, Jinni," he began, "I want to apologize to you. I don't know what got into me. I was a jerk and I am sick over what I did to us. I'm sorry." Before Jinni could respond, he added, "And, FYI, Monika and I are finished – for good."

"What happened?"

"She's not what I thought she was. Monika is – how can I put this? She's evil."

"Evil?"

Jeremy tried to explain. "There was this ceremony she put on at a spooky old church and a vow that was supposed to change everyone there into something else – and I had this dream about it beforehand…" Realizing how crazy he must sound, Jeremy stopped himself. "It's a long story but I'm pretty sure she's after me too."

Jinni actually laughed. It was not the response he was seeking.

"See what happens when you do me wrong?" she asked.

"Anyway," added Jeremy, "I hope that some day you can find it in your heart to forgive me."

The silent pause from Jinni's end of the line did little to instill confidence in Jeremy's hope for redemption.

"Are you still there?" he asked.

Finally Jinni responded. "If you are really done with that witch, I've got something important to give to you."

"What is it?" he asked.

"I can't say over the phone but you really should see it, like right now."

Jeremy did not expect this. "I can't come to town, for obvious reasons."

"Tell me where you are and I'll come to you."

"I don't think that's such a good idea."

"I realize you don't understand," said Jinni, "but it's imperative that I see you – in person. Where are you?"

"You know if we did meet up, you could be committing a crime – what do they call it – aiding and abetting? I don't want to drag you into the middle of all this."

Stubbornly, it seemed, she repeated the question. "Where are you, Jeremy?"

"I've been hiding out in Reefers Woods for the last two days."

"If I drive out that way, will you meet me? Are you near the road?"

"I could be," replied Jeremy. "But what about the police? I'm sure they must still be patrolling the area. I just don't know to what extent."

"If I see any sign of the police, I won't stop," she remarked in a flippant tone. "If the coast is clear, I will. I just need some place to hide my car."

Going along, Jeremy added, "You also need an excuse for being out this way. Maybe you should wear your running gear. That way, if someone asked, you could say you came out here to go for a run."

"That's a good idea, but where should I park?"

"You might park at the TVA microwave tower and jog the rest of the way. I'd guess it's about three miles from there to Grady's house."

"Grady's house?" she asked. "Is that where you are now?"

"Not yet but I'm pretty close," he replied. "But I still don't understand why you are taking this risk."

"The time has come, that's all."

"Interesting choice of words," muttered Jeremy.

"What?" asked Jinni.

"Never mind. Just meet me behind Grady's house. Also, could you bring me something to eat?"

"What do you want?"

"I would like a very large sack of fast food, but I don't know too many people who pack their pockets with Big Macs while exercising."

Just like old times, Jinni laughed at his marginal joke. "I have some granola bars I could bring."

"I guess that will have to do."

After Jeremy hung up the phone, he wondered about Jinni's little visit. What was so important that she would risk trouble with the police to see him? Two weeks ago, she wouldn't take his calls or even answer the door when he came knocking. Why this sudden change of heart? After all that had happened between them, he could not be sure of her intentions. Would she show up with the police in tow? Could he still trust her?

If you can't trust Jinni, he asked himself, *who can you trust?*

Jeremy resumed his walk along the stream, toward Grady's house and, presumably, toward answers.

***

From the outside it appeared that Grady's house might still be occupied. A faint but definite light emanated from the side bay window, and Grady's truck was parked in the driveway. Jeremy staked out a spot in the edge of the woods where he had a clear view of both the house and the road. It did not take long before a police car came creeping by in the direction of the lake. Jeremy was safely hidden but he feared for Jinni, who would be exposed as she jogged out Sticks River Road. If they saw her, the police would surely stop and question her. It wouldn't take much for them to figure out that her presence out here was more than happenstance. Perhaps it had been foolish of him to call her – and Tavalin – from his phone. Sooner or later, the police would check the phone records.

Finally, he sensed a tentative movement along the side of the house and, as he watched, a silhouette slipped by the bay window. Jeremy waited another full minute before he stepped from the shadows.

"There you are," Jinni said with a relieved tone. "I was afraid you might not show."

Jeremy knew full well that he missed Jinni but he was surprised at the depth of his feelings invoked by her presence. It was as if he had somehow forgotten her palpable sweetness, that aura of love that surrounded Jinni Malone. Jeremy fought back the urge to hug her because he did not know what her reaction might be.

"Did you see that police car?" he asked.

"I did," she replied.

"And?"

"And I hid in the ditch until he passed."

"Good girl."

Jeremy breathed a little easier. Whatever Jinni's purpose in coming out here, apparently it wasn't to have him arrested.

"Here," Jinni said. "I brought you these."

Jeremy devoured the three high-energy granola bars Jinni provided on the spot.

"Thanks," he said. "I needed that in the worst way."

"And this is the other thing…"

Very slowly, and ominously, Jinni unzipped her front jacket pocket.

"This is why I had to meet you in person," she said.

Jeremy envisioned Jinni's next move in his mind's eye. Her jacket pocket held a gun and she meant to kill him for his indiscretions. He had walked right into an ambush, predicated on an ex-girlfriend's festering jealousy and rage.

Jeremy let loose a big sigh of relief when Jinni instead handed him a round plastic case of some sort. He held it gingerly, like one might handle some explosive device.

"What is it?" he asked.

"It's an old reel-to-reel movie. Grady told me it was vital that I give this to you, but only if you broke free of Monika."

"When did you talk to Grady?"

"I had just walked out of church on Sunday, two weeks back, and there he was. He said he needed to talk to me and suggested I follow him home."

"You came here? Alone?"

"Yes," she replied. "I trusted him."

"And that's when he gave you the reel-to-reel?"

"Yes. He said that I should wait and watch it with you, but only if you escaped Monika's influence." In a wary gesture, Jinni raised one eyebrow but not the other and asked, "You *are* done with her, aren't you?"

"Yes," replied Jeremy, nodding his head. "I really am."

Jeremy pulled the tape from its case. "Any idea *how* we are supposed to watch this?" he asked.

"I know Grady has a projector, but it's inside."

"Did he happen to give you a key?"

"Nope."

"We don't need a key."

Jeremy used the butt of his buck knife to break the glass of the back door window. He reached in and disengaged the latch from the inside. The broken glass crunched under their feet as they stepped into a small utility room that held a washer and dryer, a counter and a large sink. Beyond that was a room of modest proportions and equally modest furnishings, illuminated by a small, dim lamp.

Jinni pointed to the closet in the back corner. "The projector is in there," she said.

From the high closet shelf, Jeremy retrieved the encasement, a metal box with a green exterior and black plastic handle.

"Now let's see if this thing still works."

Nestled inside the case on top of the projector was a ziplock bag. Jeremy opened it, assuming it to be the operating instructions, but instead found a small notebook filled with penned words, which Jeremy had neither the time nor the inclination to read.

With no directions for use, it took a while to figure out how to operate the old projector. After some trial and error they finally succeeded in threading the 8mm tape and focusing the moving pictures on the wall. The images were in color, though dull, and the only audio was the loud clicking sound produced by the projector itself. With great anticipation, they settled in to watch Grady's movie, with Jinni occupying one end of the couch and Jeremy manning the other.

Grady's reel-to-reel film opened with an image of a ramshackle cabin built from a hodgepodge of various boards, small logs, rocks and sheets of tin. A stove pipe pierced one side wall. As they watched, the screen door opened and out shot a child. He raced toward the camera and then past it. An arm appeared – that of the camera operator – and motioned in the direction of the cabin. The child reappeared and trudged back toward the front door stoop. Like a soldier he pivoted an about-face and stood dutifully at attention. He looked to be no more than 10 or 11 years old. Overalls hung from his scrawny shoulders and a camera-conscious smile adorned his face. Like blue jewels, his eyes sparkled against the rich brown complexion of his face.

"That's Grady!" The words erupted spontaneously from Jeremy's lips. "As a child," he added.

Abruptly the scene cut to a garden. Three persons of the Caucasian persuasion worked, one hoeing a row of puny plants, while the other two pulled weeds. When they became aware of the camera, the one dropped his hoe and the three stood arm-in-arm and smiled and waved and mouthed words to the camera. They appeared to be college-aged and were dressed in soiled shorts, sweaty tee shirts and sandals. All three had hair down to their shoulders and the two males sported scraggly beards.

"What is this?" asked Jinni.

"I'm not sure," Jeremy didn't know what he had expected to see on Grady's tape but this certainly was not it.

Without warning, the scene switched to a river bank. A girl sat on a large flat rock, facing the river, her back to the camera, her legs spread out before her, her bare back arched, her face skyward. It was a classic sunbather's pose. A tumultuous mane of dark hair flowed down to the small of her back. She did a half-turn and shot a surprised expression toward the camera. In a quick motion she crossed her arms over her breasts. Jeremy whistled appreciatively, hoping to get a rise out of Jinni. In the past she would typically have responded with a good-natured jab to his upper arm, but tonight his needling garnered no reaction from her whatsoever.

The camera view zoomed in, losing focus as it did so. The blurriness lent a short-lived impressionistic quality to the shot before it degraded into an indiscrete smudge on the wall. Slowly the ambiguity cleared to reveal a close-up view of the sunbather. She was young, brunette, petite yet nicely proportioned, beautiful and strange, with eyes as black as night.

Jeremy almost fell off the couch. "That girl-" he exclaimed. "She looks just like Monika!" As quickly as his scrambling thoughts would allow, he added, "But obviously it's not her. This tape is from a long time ago."

Jeremy felt acutely uncomfortable, not due to the sexy, half-dressed girl but because the sexy, half-dressed girl looked exactly like Monika. It felt as if he were reliving his unfaithfulness with Monika, only this time with Jinni watching the whole spectacle.

"She *is* beautiful." The words spilled from Jinni's mouth like an admission.

It occurred to Jeremy that Jinni must wonder what Monika looks like. More pertinently, Jinni would want to know what it was about Monika that had so ensnared him. She had seen Monika that one time, driving her car, but it had been dark and Jinni could not have gotten a good look.

Jinni's eyes were riveted to the images on the wall. As Jeremy studied her pained expression, he recognized that, in spite of his desire to the contrary, Jinni still wore the wound inflicted by his infidelity and that the injury was still raw and prone to bleed.

The urgency of the moment forced his attention back to the silent movie. He had to figure out what Grady meant for them to glean from it. The scene had shifted again, away from the river. The Monika look-a-like swept one slender arm through the air, like a model presenting merchandise on a daytime game show. The camera operator panned slowly through 180 degrees, revealing a swampy landscape of black water dotted with the knees of cypress trees and lily pads. Jeremy recognized it as the lotus swamp, the very same lowlands that he had first spotted on the aerial photos and in the general vicinity of where he later found the single purple blossom.

The bright square of light on the wall and the flapping of the loose tape pronounced the end of the home movie. Without comment Jinni disappeared into the bathroom and shut the door. Jeremy flipped the switch on the lamp and after some fumbling, was able to adjust the arm of the old projector to the rewind configuration and connect the tape's end to the empty reel.

As the spools whirled, Jeremy tried to wrap his mind around this new perspective. If this were indeed the lotus swamps of Reefers Woods, then the shack must be the old hippie commune and the people on the tape were the ones who lived there before it burned. But who was the sunbather and why did she look so much like Monika? Were Monika and the hippie queen related? Could Claire be Monika's mother?

Jeremy flipped the arm that held the tape back down to the playing position, threaded the tape through the play path, connected the end of the tape to the far reel and slid the play switch forward. Old technology could certainly be labor intensive.

By the time Jinni returned from the bathroom, the movie had begun again and the child was once again standing in the doorway of the ramshackle house. Jeremy noticed for the first time the sign nailed above the door.

"Can you read what it says, there above the door?" Jeremy asked.

The letters, written in bright yellow paint were blurred and difficult to discern. When Jeremy finally deciphered the letters, he knew without a doubt that this must be Claire's commune.

"*LotosLand*," he said with a smile. "Claire named her commune after the purple lotus that she discovered, and I'm pretty sure it was because of the effects of the lotus blooms – the Unreal – that she and her friends moved to Reefers Woods in the first place." Jeremy rambled on. "The shack is the old hippie commune and the boy with the blue eyes must be Grady."

When the garden scene began, Jinni asked, "So everyone in the movie died in the fire?"

"I'm pretty sure," replied Jeremy, "everyone except for Grady."

"And the girl by the river, the one that looks so much like your little girl friend? Who do you think she is?"

Jeremy ignored the *little girl friend* jab. "I'm assuming she's Claire – the hippie queen – and since she looks so much like Monika, they must be related. Maybe Claire is Monika's mother. If so, that would explain how Monika knows so much about the lotus and its effects. Also, Monika has been able to fool some very smart people with her paintings. As Claire's daughter, Monika would be in the best position to learn and mimic Claire's painting style and techniques."

"But Claire died in the fire 40 years ago. Monika is too young to be Claire's daughter."

"You're right," replied Jeremy. "Maybe Claire is Monika's grandmother or some other relative. I really don't know how it all fits together, but I've got to believe that Claire and Monika are related and that this is how Monika knows so much about Claire and her lotus. At least we understand a little more about Grady's involvement in all of this."

"I must be missing something," Jinni complained. "Can you please back up a bit and explain to me the significance of this LotosLand sign and the purple lotus?"

As quickly as he could, Jeremy brought Jinni up to speed on Claire's lotus, the Unreal and the ceremony at the old abandoned church. He related more details about the Source and did his best to explain why he believed his dreams to be more than just dreams. He also told Jinni about the houseboat anchored in the lake and how Monika might have located the Source using the maps and methods he unwittingly provided.

***

Jeremy jumped when his cell phone rang. He had meant to turn it off. Against his better judgment, he answered the call.

"Hello?"

"Is this Jeremy Spires?" asked a female voice with the flattest of inflections.

"It might be. Who is this?"

"Please hold," she instructed.

Curious, Jeremy complied.

Without delay, a gruff voice intruded onto the line. "Who in the hell do you think you are?" demanded Lieutenant Sykes, skipping the pleasantries. "When we catch you – and we will catch you – I'm personally gonna jack you up!"

"Nice to talk to you, too, boss," muttered Jeremy. "What do you want?"

"We need to talk. Tell me where you are and I'll have someone pick you up."

"And let you *jack me up*?" retorted Jeremy. "I don't know exactly what that entails but I think I'll pass."

"Tell the truth, Jeremy. Did you kill June Song?"

"No, sir."

"Then how do you explain the earring we found in your apartment?"

"I found it in my lab, in the cold room drain." In retrospect, Jeremy wished he had made that simple declaration when he first discovered it 10 days ago.

"Are you aware it belonged to the deceased and that she lost it the night she was killed?"

"I suspected as much."

"It this is true, why didn't you tell me what you found?"

"I wish I had, but at that time, I believed it to be in my best interest to investigate on my own."

"And did you discover anything?" asked Lieutenant Sykes.

"I found out that Grady did not have a key to the cold room and so could not have killed June. Dr. Cain was the only one with access to the cold room; therefore, he must be the killer."

Lieutenant Sykes corrected him. "Two people had access to the cold room, Dr. Cain and *you*."

"This," said Jeremy, "is exactly why I waited to tell you about the earring."

"You didn't tell me anything, Jeremy. I had to get a warrant and find it myself, and, on top of everything, you ran from us. What am I supposed to think?"

"Can't you see?" asked Jeremy. "Whoever killed June must have framed Grady and now they are trying to do the same to me." In a flash Jeremy realized the point he needed to make. "By any chance, was it Dr. Cain who provided the impetus for you to search my apartment?"

"I can't say who tipped us off."

"Why not?"

"Because I don't know," replied Sykes. "The call came in on our anonymous crime tips line."

"Well, isn't that convenient for the real killer," retorted Jeremy. "Tell me this – how did this person convince you to search my apartment in the first place?"

"The tipster told us we would find evidence linking you to the murder."

"What else did you find?" Jeremy hated to ask, knowing that Dr. Cain had used actual body parts to frame Grady.

"Nothing," replied the Lieutenant. "What did we miss? Is there something else you're not telling us?"

"No, no, that's not it at all."

Jeremy was confused. Since Dr. Cain could not have known about the earring, Jeremy had assumed that Dr. Cain provided some other evidence by which to frame him and that the discovery of the earring in Jeremy's condo was incidental.

"The important thing to remember," added Jeremy, trying to regroup, "is that the killer had access to the cold room and Dr. Cain had access to the cold room key. Based on that alone, you have to check him out."

Jeremy covered the mouthpiece to his phone and, to Jinni, whispered, "We've got to get out of here."

Jeremy did not know how easily the police could track his phone signal, but prudence dictated they exit the premises. Jeremy removed the reel-to-reel tape and stuck it in his backpack. As an afterthought, he snatched up Grady's notebook, still held within the ziplock bag, folded it in half and stuck it into the inside pocket of his coat.

Lieutenant Sykes was saying something that Jeremy missed.

"What was that, boss?"

"I said, we do not consider Cecil Cain to be a suspect at this time."

"Why not?" demanded Jeremy. "Does he hold such a prestigious position that he is above reproach?"

"No one is above reproach," insisted the lieutenant. "His alibi is ironclad."

"If Dr. Sloan is his alibi, then it's anything but ironclad," countered Jeremy. "My guess is that Cain and Sloan are in it together."

"Dr. Sloan is not an essential part of Dr. Cain's alibi."

"How so?" prodded Jeremy. By now, he and Jinni had vacated the house and, at Jeremy's direction, headed for the small storage shed out back.

"When you saw the two of them leaving the back parking lot of the Facility that night, they were en route to a certain – how shall I say – all-night get-together with a group of male friends."

At first Jeremy did not catch the meaning of the lieutenant's innuendo. When it finally dawned on him, he exclaimed, "I knew it! They're gay, aren't they?"

"I never said that," Lieutenant Sykes replied quickly. "Multiple partners, er – I mean witnesses – verified their whereabouts. Because of the time required to mutilate the body, it's simply not possible that either man had a hand in June Song's death."

"But what of my alibi?" asked Jeremy. "I have people vouching for me too."

"But not for the entire night."

"You're wrong," objected Jeremy. "My friend Tavalin was right there with me, all night. He knows I didn't leave my apartment."

"He was there, but he was asleep for several hours, long enough for you to kill June and perform the mutilation."

The cop's declaration caught Jeremy off guard. Tavalin had slept some but they never mentioned that tidbit to the cops.

"That's not right," insisted Jeremy. "You need to go back and check your notes."

"I know that was the original statement," replied Lieutenant Sykes, "but that statement has since been amended."

"Amended? By whom?"

"By your good friend Tavalin, who else?"

"I don't believe you."

"Why would I lie?" asked Lieutenant Sykes.

"Because that's the game you cops always play. You bluff and lie just to see if you can trick suspects into an admission."

"Sometimes we do that," admitted Lieutenant Sykes, "but not this time."

Jeremy did not know what to believe, but his gut feeling informed him that the lieutenant spoke the truth.

"I don't understand," said Jeremy, deflated. "Why would Tavalin change his story now?"

Sensing victory, Sykes said, "Give up, Jeremy. Come on in and we'll talk, man to man."

"I did not kill June. You've got to believe me."

Jeremy flipped closed his phone, killing the connection.

"That was the police?" asked Jinni.

"Yes."

"What did they say?"

"Basically, that Dr. Cain could not have killed June."

"If he didn't do it, who did?"

"I don't know," replied Jeremy," but if we don't figure it out soon, they'll have my head on a platter."

Jeremy yanked the string to switch on the light inside the storage shed.

"Shut the door," he instructed, "so the police won't see the light."

"What are you looking for?" Jinni asked.

Jeremy scanned the contents of Grady's shed, looking for something – anything – that might aid him in his mission to first reach and then destroy the Source. There were gardening tools, carpentry tools, a small push mower and a hand-held leaf blower and, on the shelves, various pesticides and herbicides, plus all the miscellaneous items that end up in spaces like this. From that latter category, Jeremy scavenged several interesting items.

The first was one hundred feet of ski-rope, still in its package. The second was, of all things, a machete, scabbard and all.

"What are you going to do with that?" asked Jinni incredulously.

"What *can't* a man do with a machete strapped to his side?" joked Jeremy.

The last item that caught Jeremy's eye was a pint jar that at first glance looked a little like a pickle in a jar of vinegar. The label, however, told a different story.

"What is *that*?" asked Jinni.

Jeremy held the thick-walled jar so Jinni could take her turn reading the label.

100 Gms RUBIDIUM METAL (Rb) under kerosene

DANGER! FLAMMABLE SOLID. CORROSIVE. EXPLODES ON EXPOSURE
TO WATER OR MOISTURE. HARMFUL OR FATAL IF SWALLOWED.
HARMFUL IF INHALED OR ABSORBED THROUGH SKIN.
CONTACT MAY CAUSE BURNS TO ALL BODY TISSUE.

"That sounds dangerous. Why in the world would Grady have that?"

"I have no idea," replied Jeremy. "This is not something one can purchase down at the County Co-op. My guess is he ripped it off from the Facility."

"What are you doing?"

Jinni watched with disbelief as Jeremy proceeded to wrap the jar in an old towel and gingerly placed it in his backpack.

"I think you should leave that stuff right here," she added.

"You're probably right, but since my assignment is to destroy the Source and rubidium is highly explosive…"

"And if the glass gets broken accidentally?"

"Hopefully that won't happen," Jeremy replied, "but if it did, God forbid, I suppose I'd run like hell, especially if it is anywhere near water. It may spontaneously ignite in air but it will explode in water."

Back outside the shed, Jeremy remarked, "It's warmer tonight than it's been."

"Not for long," said Jinni. "A cold front is dropping down later on tonight, along with some rain. Will that be a problem with the bomb in the backpack?"

"Not as long as it stays sealed in its jar of kerosene."

Jinni smiled. "Don't expect me to walk too close to you on the way in."

"You're not coming." Jeremy was adamant. "It's too dangerous."

"But I want to come." After a thoughtful pause, Jinni added, "I think Grady meant for us to do this together."

The rubidium was dangerous, but there was another reason why Jeremy did not want Jinni to come. Though only an inkling, it had less to do with her safety and more to do with his own.

"You've helped enough, Jinni. Go home before the police figure out that you've been aiding and abetting a fugitive."

Jinni objected, but, at Jeremy's continued urging, she gave in. She surprised him with a quick hug before she jogged off down the driveway.

***

As Jeremy began the long trek back to the King's Pinnacle, he contemplated the barrier of the sheer rock walls. He had looked for a way over on two prior trips, all for naught. What, he wondered, was different this time? He considered the three items – the machete, the rope, and the rubidium – which he confiscated from Grady's shed. Could the ski rope be the key? Was there some way to secure one end of the rope to the top of the wall and climb up that way? What if, like before, he simply could not get up and over those walls? If he could not get to the Source, he couldn't very well follow through on Grady's directive to destroy it. And, with the police waiting in the wings, Jeremy knew he could not be guaranteed another opportunity to try. Jeremy had the distinct feeling that it was now or never – tonight was it. After tonight's digression, he would have to refocus on the problem that refused to go away, that of June's death and the investigation.

His phone rang, again.

"Unbelievable," he muttered to himself as he wondered why he had suddenly become so popular. Jeremy half-expected it to be the police calling again, but it was not.

"Good evening, Jeremy." It was Tavalin. "Are you in jail yet?"

"Not yet, but funny you should ask. I just spoke to the police. They told me what you told them, and now I would very much like for you to tell me why you said what you did."

Tavalin's tone turned defensive. "I did what you asked me to do, Jeremy. I told the police where you found the earring and how they should check Dr. Cain's alibi again."

"That's great, Tavalin." Jeremy's tone dripped with sarcasm. "Now, what about the other part?"

"What other part?"

"The part where you bailed on *my* alibi," snapped Jeremy. "Tell me about that."

With some snappiness of his own, Tavalin replied, "It's your own fault, Jeremy. You should not have run, and you should have listened to me when I told you to get rid of June's earring. You brought this on yourself."

"What exactly did you tell them?" demanded Jeremy.

"All I did was tell the truth. You can't fault me for falling asleep on the couch and you can't expect me to lie to the police."

"All you had to say was that you stayed awake to watch those two movies and that I could not have left the apartment," retorted Jeremy. "Would it have been so hard to do that? You know I didn't kill June."

"Look at it from my side," pleaded Tavalin. "If I lie about your alibi and the police end up pinning the murder on you, they'll take me down too. I'm sorry, but all I'm really guilty of is falling asleep on your couch and telling the police the truth."

Jeremy's phone beeped. "My battery is almost gone," he said. "We can talk about all this later."

"Where are you now?" asked Tavalin.

Mostly for dramatic effect, Jeremy replied, "I'm on my way to The Devil's Crotch."

"Why in God's name are you going there?"

"You wouldn't believe me if I told you," replied Jeremy, "and it's a very long story."

"I feel terrible about the police thing," said Tavalin. "Wait for me and I'll help you do whatever it is you need to do. For once I will volunteer for one of your wild goose chases."

Jeremy considered the notion a moment before answering. "Thanks," he finally said, "but I think I better handle this one alone."

Jeremy's phone beeped again. "I've got to go now."

"I'm sorry, Jeremy, I really am." Tavalin sounded pitiful. "If ever I had a real friend, it's you."

"It's okay, Tavalin, really..." At this point, it was easier to excuse Tavalin than to suffer his sniveling. "I forgive you."

"Thanks, Jeremy. That means a lot to me."

"I gotta go…"

As Jeremy forged deeper into Reefers Woods, his thoughts returned to the overriding question of the moment: Who killed June? That the police had ruled out Dr. Cain as a suspect forced Jeremy to consider the notion that someone, somehow, might have used *his* key to access the cold room.

But who?

Jeremy could think of only two persons who had the opportunity to borrow his lab keys without his knowledge – one of two persons who might have killed June. Both of them, he trusted. Both were also aware of the earring he found in the cold room; either of them could have made the anonymous call to the police.

The first was his best friend. On the night of the murder, Tavalin arrived at Jeremy's condo around one a.m. He, therefore, had access to Jeremy's lab keys, which were in their usual place, hanging from the hook in the hallway. While Jeremy could not picture Tavalin as a cold, calculating killer, he could envision circumstances whereby he might let his emotions get the best of him. June had rejected Tavalin and this no doubt made him angry – but angry enough to kill?

One major problem with this theory was that whoever killed June required a large block of time – two hours at the minimum, according to the police – to dissect the body and to carve the intricate symbol into her forehead. It was that very specific time requirement that helped Tavalin's case the most. Besides the issue of Tavalin's clothes being in the washing machine all night, Jeremy had been awake enough to remember how the second movie of the pay-per-view double-feature ended. The second movie did not end until after five a.m. and, while Jeremy certainly dozed some, there was no two-hour window available during which Tavalin could have sneaked past Jeremy, borrowed clothes from the bedroom, exited through the squeaky door of the condo, stayed gone long enough to do the mutilation, returned through that same cantankerous door, undressed and returned to the couch unbeknown to Jeremy. Other than the time Tavalin spent downstairs in his underwear waiting for the pizza, he had not strayed from Jeremy's sight the entire night.

Besides Tavalin, only one other person visited Jeremy's condo the night of the murder. As unlikely as it seemed, the circumstantial evidence forced Jeremy to consider that Jinni might be the one who lifted his lab keys, returned to the Facility, killed and mutilated June, and returned the keys the following day when she dropped by. Indeed, thinking as a detective might, jealousy or suspicion of infidelity ranked high up the list as a plausible motive for murder. And, most importantly, Jinni had the time. Unlike Tavalin, she would have had plenty of time after she left Jeremy's condo to return to the Facility and perform all aspects of the dirty deed. Also, whoever killed June must also have killed Grady. Jinni admitted visiting Grady's house on that Sunday two weeks back, which was, coincidentally, one day before Grady's body was discovered behind his house on the edge of Reefers Woods.

But could he really accept the idea that his Jinni could be jealous enough to kill June in the first place? Jeremy simply could not imagine her playing the murderer's role but neither could he discount the facts. Jinni had motive and she was the only one who had access to his key *and* the time to perform the mutilation. And what of the mutilation itself? Why would either of them, Jinni or Tavalin, go to the trouble and the risk of carving the insignia of the band Cocytus into the body? Of the two, Tavalin was the more knowledgeable of the band and its genre of music known as *deathcore*. Jinni hated the band. Jinni would never choose to inscribe that particular symbol, would she?

Unless, reckoned Jeremy, the representation was put there as a diversion, to throw off the would-be investigators.

***

About two hours later, Jeremy arrived back at the King's Pinnacle. He stopped at the point where the stream ran underground.

"Okay, Grady. I followed the stream, just like you said. Now what am I supposed to do?"

Jeremy asked the question aloud but never expected an answer.

"Maybe you should *keep* following it," suggested a voice from the darkness.

Jeremy's head snapped violently around. "Who's there?" he demanded. His hand found the handle of the machete hanging from his belt.

Low and behold, Jinni stepped out.

Jeremy managed only one flabbergasted word as he watched her deliberate approach. "You?"

"Yes," she replied. "It's me."

Jeremy tried not to take Jinni's choice of words as a verification of his new suspicions of her but he wasn't about to let loose his grip on the machete handle.

"What are you doing here?" he asked.

"Grady meant for me to come," she replied. "I'm *supposed* to help."

"I gotta say, Jinni, your showing up way out here is freaking me out a little." Jeremy didn't mention the reason behind his skittishness.

"I know how to get inside," she announced, "but we are going to have put on our spelunker hats."

"Our what?" asked Jeremy.

"I'm pretty sure we need to go underground." She indicated the place where the stream disappeared into the fissure in the rock.

Keeping one, still-suspicious eye on Jinni, Jeremy got down on his hands and knees and shined his flashlight beam into the dark space within. He could not see much except that the water ran into the ground at a steep angle. "It looks a bit like a water slide," he said, "except skinnier."

"You're pretty skinny," remarked Jinni.

"Yeah, but I would really, really hate to get lodged inside."

"We can use the rope you brought. If it gets too tight, I'll just pull you out," said Jinni. "No worries."

"Easy for you to say," muttered Jeremy.

Jeremy stood at the crossroads. He wanted to do right by Grady – God rest his soul – and destroy the Source and he couldn't do that without getting inside. The map he lifted from Monika's boat seemed to show that the stream traversed the wall but that did not necessarily mean that a person could also enter that way. And what about Jinni? She seemed nothing but friendly and helpful but what if that were all an act? If he did get wedged in the hole, did he fully trust her to assist him? If she murdered June, wouldn't it be in her best interest to walk away? He was the only one who had a vested interest in discovering the true identity of June's murderer. Stuck, he would be unable to lobby his case and the real killer – Jinni in the present scenario – would go free and he would be doomed to die a slow, miserable death in the hole.

"Well?" asked Jinni. "Are you going to try or not?"

"Why are you so eager?" he asked. "Are you trying to get rid of me?"

"Jeremy," she stated plainly. "Why would you say such a thing?"

He shrugged.

Jinni pressed her position. "Grady didn't say to follow the stream and stop at the point where it goes underground. He said to follow it – simple as that. The stream leads underground."

"If you're so sure, maybe you should go first," suggested Jeremy.

"That might not be a bad idea. I am smaller than you." Jinni answered quickly, so much so that Jeremy dropped his guard.

"No, no," he protested. "I'll do it. I can't stand here and watch my girlfriend crawl down a dark hole." Realizing his errant choice of words, Jeremy added, "Sorry. For a second I forgot that you aren't my, you know…"

As his words tapered to silence, Jeremy felt, but could not banish the self-conscious expression stamped on his face. Jinni seemed confidently amused at his discomfort.

"Alright," Jeremy finally said. "Let's get this over with."

When it occurred to Jeremy that he would have to leave behind not only his machete but also his backpack, he almost backed out. Jinni would have at her disposal not one, but two, murder weapons. If she were so inclined, she could render death by the machete shish-ka-bob method or, if she were in the mood for fireworks, the hole would be especially conducive to a water-triggered rubidium explosion.

In the end he went forward with the original plan, convincing himself, as best he could, that Jinni was not the enemy. He eased his bottom into the icy stream and slid in feet first, holding his arms above his head like a teenager on a roller coaster ride. The last image his uplifted gaze recorded was Jinni's stoic face. She kept the rope taunt at first, but suddenly the rope went slack and he slid uncontrollably down into the hole. Had Jinni dropped him on purpose? Jeremy had little time to ponder the possibility as, perhaps a dozen feet down, his boots impacted a hard flat surface and his body crumpled into a heap on the rock floor of the cave.

"Jeremy!" cried the voice from above. "Are you okay?" At least Jinni sounded distraught.

"I think so." Jeremy felt for his coat pocket, unzipped it and pulled out the flashlight.

"What happened?" he asked.

"I'm sorry," she replied. "I lost my grip. Are you stuck?"

"No," he replied. "It's actually fairly roomy down here. Hang on while I look around."

The cave was tall enough to stand up in and deep enough that Jeremy could not tell if it was a dead end or if it continued farther into the rock. He followed the stream to the point where it gurgled down another hole that no human could squeeze through. The cave was a dead end.

As Jeremy continued his visual exploration of the space, the flashlight beam swept past a face in the darkness. Jeremy jumped back even as he realized that the uplifted eyes belonged, not to a living person, but to a different kind of creature. With a broad sweeping motion of the flashlight, Jeremy revealed the scope of an elaborate scene painted on the cave wall. Backed by a sky of deep blue and over-hanging limbs were two angelic beings of intricate detail. In the very center of the depiction, between the angels, was a sword, erect and wrapped in believable flames. Jeremy wondered if Grady could have painted something as magnificent as this.

Just beneath the hilt of the sword Jeremy noticed the indentation, black and round, from which the fire seemed to emerge. The indentation, as it turned out, was actually a circular opening, about thigh-high and big enough to accommodate a full-sized man. Jeremy crawled inside and followed the upward-tilted shaft. After 20 feet or so, it opened up enough so that Jeremy could stand, albeit in a stooped posture. About 50 feet in, he paused. The rope, still tied around his wrist, had run out of slack. Realizing that the cord was probably unnecessary at this point, he untied it and as he did, he became aware of the draft. A shot of cool air moved past in the direction he had been traveling. That, Jeremy deduced, could mean only one thing: There must be an outlet up ahead. How far ahead he did not know, but knowing that the tunnel did indeed lead somewhere, he turned back. Jinni still had his backpack and if he really were going to blow up something, Jeremy would need the rubidium it held.

***

As Jeremy neared the entrance to the outside, he heard Jinni's voice.

"Jeremy?" she was saying. "Are you there? Answer me if you can hear me."

He listened for a bit before he answered. His distrustful mind pictured Jinni standing above the hole, waiting for him to answer, waiting to throw the jar of rubidium down the hole to detonate it and him. When he finally answered, "I'm here," no such explosion occurred.

"Thank God," she said. "It took you long enough."

"You were right," he said. "I'm pretty sure I can get in this way."

Jinni corrected him. "You mean *we* can get in this way," she said. "I'm coming too."

Each time Jinni passed up a chance to take him out, Jeremy's suspicions lessened a bit. "Can you pass my stuff down?" he asked.

"Is it okay that the backpack gets wet?" she asked.

"As long as the jar doesn't break, it should be fine."

Carefully, using the rope, Jinni lowered the backpack down to him, then the machete. "Me next," she warned.

Jeremy arrested Jinni's slide as best he could. Once safely at the bottom, they made their way to the hole in the rock wall and crawled inside.

"What do you think it is?" asked Jinni. "What is the Source?"

"I don't know," replied Jeremy, "but I can't wait to find out."

With Jeremy leading the way, they crawled or, more accurately, climbed toward their goal. Besides the tunnel's decidedly upward tilt, its girth shrank as they moved along, so much so that Jeremy worried that they might not be able to squeeze through. At last, he caught sight of a small opening above him.

"Up there," he whispered excitedly. "I see it."

A certain, indescribable feeling came over him as he moved closer to the threshold of the inner courts of the King's Pinnacle. It was as if each step was measured, not in inches and feet, but rather in millions of light years, and the narrow passage was a wormhole that linked two worlds a universe apart.

They emerged in a small boulder field on the edge of what could best be described as a small valley, or a gorge, encompassing an area of perhaps two acres with walls rising to a height of about fifty feet. A subtle, whitish glow seemed to emanate not from the overcast sky but, inexplicitly, from within the gorge itself. The magnificence of the landscape glossed over Jeremy's worries, suspicions and regrets. For a moment he even forgot that he and Jinni were no longer an item. His hand found hers and they walked, hand-in-hand, beneath towering evergreen firs and Ginkgo trees that split their bounty of golden-yellow leaves between their limbs and the ground. The ground-level growth included a multitude of ferns and unfamiliar flowering plants and a carpet of green, spongy moss. The whole of the place reminded Jeremy of a plush rain forest or, more aptly, a hidden garden.

As they approached the geometric center of the gorge, the atmosphere became thicker and damp; foggier. It was there that they came upon the steaming pool of water, no more than ten feet in diameter. From the pool flowed a stream of crystal-clear water that ran step-wise down the slope through a series of several smaller pools before vanishing into the ground. When Jeremy knelt down to caress the surface of the pool, he found that the water was exceptionally warm, bordering on hot.

Smiling, he looked up at Jinni who, like himself, appeared awestruck by the whole experience.

"Feel it," he said. "It's a hot spring."

From the steaming waters grew a tree. It stood about 30 feet high. Its trunk, eight or ten inches in diameter, emerged from the pool next to the bank and possessed an odd lumpy quality. Closer inspection revealed it to be a braid of three separate plants that over time had fused together as one. Vine-like streamers like those of a weeping willow hung from the limbs, low enough to touch the ground and the waters of the pool. Those that drooped into the pool had grown thicker, more like saplings than vines. Jeremy tugged at one of these and found the base to be sturdy, presumably rooted to the bottom of the pool. Scads of purple flowers and purple fruit adorned the limbs like decorations on a Christmas tree.

As implausible as it seemed, the blooms on this tree were identical to those of the lotus plants that grew perennially in the swamps outside, the same lotus discovered by Claire and from which the Unreal originated. So, too, were the leaves similar, except these were folded in half in the shape of a half-moon. The most noticeable difference between this plant and the common purple lotus plants on the outside was its size. Though its roots and base originated from the hot spring pool, its woody trunk enabled it to grow like a tree, while its smaller cousins on the outside did not have the capacity to grow above the surface of the water.

Jinni was the first to voice their shared sentiments. "It's beautiful," she said. "Is this the Source?"

"It must be."

Another major difference between this specimen and the others was the fruit. This, the giant purple lotus of the King's Pinnacle, bore fruit that was large and meaty, completely dissimilar to the cone-shaped seed pods common to Claire's regular purple lotus plants. Here, the fruit came in a full range of sizes, from pea-sized all the way up to the mature fruit, which were about the same size as a large orange but of a more oval shape. Though most other plants only produced flowers and fruit during the spring and summer, this tree possessed flowers and fruit at every stage of development, even now at the tail end of December. Jeremy wondered if it were possible that the tree bore fruit year-round. He was no expert in the fruiting cycles of plants but he did not know of any other plant that produced fruit in perpetuity.

Jeremy picked one and cut into it with his knife. The consistency of the meat was similar to that of a plum, while the liquid that ran out was of a deep purple hue, like concentrated grape juice. Jeremy thought of the very *purple* stain that he wore on his shirt like a coat of arms, remnants of the spilt Source from the challis at Monika's ceremony.

"What do you think made this one grow differently from the rest?" asked Jinni.

"I suspect this is the product of the very specific conditions of this hot-spring-fed pool," replied Jeremy. "A specimen like this would take years to get this big. The lotus plants on the outside get killed off every year at the first hard freeze whereas the steam and hot water protect this one." Jeremy thought for a moment before adding, "Also, it might be that the percolating action of the springs brings up dissolved nutrients and minerals that act as a kind of supercharged fertilizer.

And," he continued, "it boggles the mind, but this might very well be the only one in existence."

"How do you figure?" asked Jinni.

"Presumably, these conditions – the heat and the fertilizer – are unique to this hot spring, and since Claire's lotus only grows in Reefers Woods, it stands to reason that this plant is one-of-a-kind."

"And if it is unique and its fruit – the Source – conveys some great benefit as Monika contends…?" Jinni's question was open-ended.

Jeremy filled in the blank: "Then, by destroying it, the world might forever be without that benefit, whatever it may be."

"Can you really go though with it?" she asked.

"Seeing how it's probably my fault Monika found the Source in the first place, I don't really have a choice. I don't want to, but I believe it is the right thing to do. I went against Grady too many times; I won't do it again."

CHAPTER 49

Tuesday, December 23

A T Jeremy's bidding, Jinni moved a safe distance away while he readied the explosive rubidium. He planned to remove the lid and set the jar afloat in the pool or, if that did not work, prop the open jar up beside the water. The jar could then be submerged or knocked into the pool by throwing something – a rock or a stick, say – to cause the water to come into contact with the rubidium, thus setting off the explosion. At least that was the plan.

Jeremy removed the jar's lid and, ever so carefully, eased the jar into the water.

"Good evening, Jeremy."

So utterly unexpected was the greeting that Jeremy fumbled the jar at the most crucial of moments. The jar, minus its lid, got away from him and bobbed on the surface of the pool, so low in the water that Jeremy thought the water would certainly cascade over the lip, causing an instantaneous and substantial detonation. Fearing for his life, Jeremy vaulted up and away from the pool, startling Tavalin in the process.

"Watch out!" exclaimed Tavalin. "Stay where you are!"

Jeremy kept his eyes peeled on the pool, but all remained quiet and still. It was only after the rubidium did not explode that Jeremy attempted to process Tavalin's presence and his strange choice of words.

"Stay where I am?" asked Jeremy. "What is that supposed to mean?"

"You scared me, that's all," replied Tavalin. "What were you doing down there anyway?"

Jeremy ignored his friend's question. "How did you get in here?" asked Jeremy.

"The same way you did," Tavalin replied. "I thought you might need my help so I followed you in."

Jeremy studied his friend's anxious body language and said, disingenuously, "Oh, okay. That explains everything."

First Jinni, and now Tavalin, claimed to have followed Jeremy here to *help*.

One of them was most certainly lying, coinciding with the one who killed June. But which one? More and more, the signs pointed to Tavalin.

"Why are you lying to me, Tavalin?"

"I'm not."

"Then why is your butt not wet."

"Huh?"

Tavalin's dry pants indicated he did not enter the gulch by way of the underground stream.

Jeremy scanned the vicinity on the far side of the pool for any sign of Jinni. Apparently, she was just as suspicious of Tavalin as was he. He hoped she meant to stay concealed, at least until Tavalin's motives could be unmasked.

Jeremy repeated his question from before. "How did you get in here?"

Tavalin evaded the question. "That's for me to know and for you to find out."

It seemed obvious that Tavalin had a secret, barely concealed. Building on his suspicions from before, Jeremy turned the subject to June's murder. One way or another, Jeremy meant to find out which of his trusted companions killed June.

Jeremy forced the issue with Tavalin with the question, "Why did you wash your clothes at my place the night of the murder?"

A sly look came and, just as quickly, left Tavalin's face. "If you've got something to say, Jeremy, just say it."

"Could it be you were washing blood – not vomit – out of your clothes that night?" Jeremy's gaze was unflinching though he had no hard evidence to back up the accusation. "Tell me now, Tavalin – did you kill June?"

"You know what the police said – the mutilation took a long time and I was right there at your condo." Tavalin turned uncharacteristically cool and collected. "You know as well as I do, I could not have mutilated the body. *You* are my alibi."

"Yes, but…"

Jeremy's words trailed off as he tried to assimilate the clues. Everything Tavalin said was true but, tellingly, he failed to deny killing June. Tavalin had sufficient time to kill June before he came over to Jeremy's condo; he just didn't have the time or the opportunity to conduct a two-hour mutilation session. Putting it together, Jeremy hit upon a novel idea: *What if Tavalin killed June and an accomplice did the rest?* Tavalin could have passed Jeremy's lab key to his collaborator while he waited downstairs in the foyer for the pizza to arrive. The new theory made decent sense, but who was so loyal to Tavalin that they would assist him in the commission of a murder? As far as Jeremy knew, Tavalin had no other friends. Jeremy could think of no one with whom Tavalin had recurring contact, with one exception – his mom. Jeremy had never met the woman, but Tavalin spoke to her on a regular basis on the phone. Could his mother be the accomplice? Though this did not seem likely, Jeremy supposed it was possible.

Whoever the accomplice might be, Jeremy felt confident with his new insight. The time had come for everyone present to acknowledge that Tavalin killed June. Like some swash-buckling pirate, Jeremy went to draw his machete, but Tavalin brandished a weapon of his own. Tavalin held the gun sideways, gangsta' style, and, just as rock beats scissors, firearm beats blade and, apparently, gangsta' beats pirate.

"Take that thing off and throw it to me," snarled Tavalin.

"You don't have the guts to shoot me." Jeremy spoke louder than he had to so Jinni might hear and understand that Tavalin had a gun.

As it turned out, it didn't matter if Jinni heard his words or not, for she certainly heard the gun's retort. The bullet tore into the soft ground directly in front of Jeremy's feet. Dirt showered his front side, including one small clod that landed in his open mouth.

"I'm not kidding, Jeremy. Lose the sword or, I swear, I'll shoot you."

"It's a machete, you idiot," muttered Jeremy, even as Tavalin's choice of words jarred his memory of the painting on the cave wall and how it happened to include a sword – a *flaming* sword.

Jeremy spat out the last of the gritty mud, removed the holster and tossed it at Tavalin's feet.

"So tell me," Jeremy asked, "who did you give my lab key to? Who helped you?"

Tavalin picked up the machete. "Walk," he said, and with the gun motioned in the direction of the river.

Jeremy could only hope that Jinni could somehow rectify the situation. He thought that her best option might be to set off the explosion. A well-placed rock toss could sink the jar in the pool and trigger the blast and, hopefully, divert Tavalin's attention long enough for Jeremy to make a move for the gun.

Per Tavalin's directions, they ascended a rocky path that terminated on a flat shelf high up on the lip of the gorge. When Jeremy peered cautiously over the other side, it was the rapids of the Devil's Crotch he saw swirling far below. The three ropes that hung down the cliff face and the miscellaneous climbing equipment on the ground answered one of Jeremy's many questions.

"This is how you got in?"

Tavalin ignored Jeremy's question. "Sit down," he said.

That Tavalin did not follow them in by way of the underground stream meant he must have had prior knowledge of this place. But how was that possible? Besides Grady, Jeremy was aware of only one other person who knew of the King's Pinnacle and the Source it hid.

That person was Monika.

Although Jeremy would have hoped that Tavalin would be loyal to him, why else would he be here now except on her behalf? No doubt Monika meant to find Jeremy and exact her revenge after he reneged on her at the ceremony. What better way for Monika to track him down than through Tavalin? But was Tavalin so fickle that she corrupted him during the two days that had passed since the ceremony? It actually didn't seem such a stretch, considering Monika's charisma and power of persuasion. Jeremy, too, had been victim to her cunning ways, beginning with the serendipitous meeting and impromptu kiss at the Singe show.

But, Jeremy wondered, were the circumstances of their meeting really as they seemed? Considering that Monika always seemed to be working toward some enigmatic end, could it be that their meeting was connived? Jeremy thought back to how Monika approached him at the Singe show and how she so boldly snared him with a kiss. She had also passed him the five dollar bill with the repeated words, *burn baby burn baby burn...*, around all four edges, front and back, a message she later claimed was a secret message for him. But if that were true, when did she transcribe the words onto the bill? She certainly did not do it while she was waiting for him to buy her drink, which meant their meeting was anything but happenstance. Someone must have informed Monika ahead of time that Jeremy would be in attendance.

Besides Jinni, only Tavalin had prior knowledge of Jeremy's plans to attend the Singe show. Tavalin could have, therefore, helped set up the meeting, which led rather quickly to Jeremy's intimate involvement with Monika. Had Tavalin and Monika been in cahoots from the beginning?

The next stop on Jeremy's train of thought was this: What if Monika was the accomplice? What if Tavalin killed June and Monika did the rest? All along, Jeremy assumed Monika was unconnected to the Biotech Facility and June's death when, in fact, she must be the crucial missing link, the center piece on this table of deception and evil deeds. Tavalin alone could not have killed June and dissected her body and Monika working alone did not have access to Jeremy's lab. How could he have been so blind? They worked together, a tag-team of dishonesty and trickery, with Tavalin as the traitor-murderer and Monika as the seductress-mutilator.

Laying his cards on the table, Jeremy asked, "How long have you and Monika been allies?"

Tavalin replied nonchalantly, "We go back a good little ways." Looking over Jeremy's shoulder, he added, "Speak of the devil."

The full expanse of the gulch, including the still-standing lotus tree, was plainly visible from their perch. Dark shapes, two of them, crept across the midst of the valley floor.

Tavalin called out, "Is everything under control down there?"

Jeremy's spirits sagged as the seductress-mutilator's voice rang up from below. "Relax," replied Monika. "I've got her."

***

Tavalin squirted a copious amount of lighter fluid on the pile of sticks previously gathered and stacked on the lip of the gorge. Without taking his eyes or the gun off Jeremy, he bent down and lit the fire with a Bic lighter. The fire took hold quickly and bathed the perch with heat and light.

A subdued Jinni appeared first on the rock shelf. Monika, gun drawn and hammer cocked, followed closely behind.

As Jinni shuffled by, she mouthed the words, "I'm sorry."

"Sit down," instructed Monika.

Dutifully, Jinni sat next to Jeremy on one side of the fire while Monika and Tavalin stood on the other side, keeping a close watch on their prisoners.

"Do either of you lovebirds care to tell me what you were doing down there?"

Jeremy wasn't about to confess their plans to blow up the tree. "We came here looking for the Source," he replied.

"How did you get in?" asked Monika.

"We climbed up, the same as you." Jeremy lied in the hope that he and Jinni might yet manage to somehow escape through the tunnel.

"That's not what he said a minute ago," tattled Tavalin. "I'm pretty sure they came in some other way."

"Tell the truth," demanded Monika. "How'd you get in?"

"You first," countered Jeremy. "Why did you and Tavalin have to kill June?"

"Ask him." Monika pointed to Tavalin. "It was all his idea."

"Why would you do such a thing?" Jeremy glared at Tavalin through the smoke.

"June caught me snooping in her lab," replied Tavalin. "I guess I just panicked, but it didn't matter. We would have had to get rid of her eventually anyway."

"Why?" begged Jeremy.

"Because she knew the structure of the Unreal. We couldn't let that information get out."

"So why didn't you kill me?" asked Jeremy. "I also knew the structure."

"Because that's just his excuse." Monika jumped into the fray. "Tavalin didn't kill June to keep the structure of the Unreal secret. He did it because she accomplished in short order what he couldn't do in two years – *and* she rebuffed his advances. He killed June because her existence highlighted his impotence."

"You're the one who beat it into my head how important it is that we keep the structure of the Unreal a secret," argued Tavalin. "We had to kill her."

"Even if it eventually came to that," Monika said, "we could have done it inconspicuously. We were supposed to keep everything on the down low, but your temper tantrum put the spotlight of the world on us. But then again, you always screw everything up."

Much to Jeremy's satisfaction, Monika was now waving her gun at Tavalin. Perhaps they would shoot each other.

"Must you dog me all the time?" Tavalin was distraught. "I do the best I can."

Jeremy listened intently to the exchange. He was not surprised that Tavalin killed June but he would never have guessed the role played by the Unreal. By asking for June's assistance in the analysis, Jeremy had, essentially, placed June in the cross hairs.

As if reading his mind, Monika turned to Jeremy and said, "You know, June's death was really your fault. You're the one who involved her."

"And you're the one who involved me," said Jeremy, miserable in his newly discovered culpability. "What I don't understand is why you targeted me in the first place. Did you really want me in your group so badly or was there some other reason?"

"Once again, it was your good friend Tavalin's idea," replied Monika. "You know, he didn't even tell me at first that he had been bringing you out here to Reefers Woods."

"Oh, he showed me more than you can even imagine," said Jeremy, hoping to refocus Monika's wrath on Tavalin. "Tavalin helped me find the hippie queen's grave and he even insisted we eavesdrop on you at the secret beach that night."

"Liar!" Tavalin exclaimed. "That's not true at all! I did everything I could to get him to go home."

Monika glared at Tavalin before addressing Jeremy again. "Tavalin wasn't supposed to bring you or anybody else out here, but you befriended him when no one else ever would. He wanted to return the favor. He asked me if I'd let you join my circle of friends and be a part of Claire's Way. Against my better judgment, I agreed to give you a chance. And, thorn in my side that you have been, I must say you helped our cause more than I ever could have imagined. If it weren't for you and June, we still wouldn't know the structure of the Unreal. And, after looking for years and years for this place – for the Source – it was through you that I finally found it."

"Glad to have helped your cause," muttered Jeremy sarcastically, "whatever it is."

Monika laughed cynically. "Isn't it tragic how close you came, yet you were never quite able to really figure anything out?"

"I know more than you think." Jeremy didn't know why he even bothered jousting with Monika, but he couldn't help it.

"Like what?"

"Like Grady." Jeremy had long suspected that whoever killed June also killed Grady. "Grady didn't kill himself. One of you did it, am I right?"

"I did it," admitted Monika, "but do you know why?"

"Probably because your original plan failed." Jeremy articulated his thoughts as they streamed to him. "Wasn't the whole purpose of the symbol carved into June's forehead to throw off the police, to make them believe she was murdered by some random Cocytus fan?"

"Go on."

"But when the cops found June's hair caught in the lab window, they knew the murderer had keys to the building and to my lab, proving the murder was an inside job. Grady had keys to my lab so you chose to frame – and kill – him."

"That's fairly accurate. I had originally hoped that the police would believe that the murder occurred outside of the Facility, but I also needed some way to exonerate Tavalin," explained Monika. "If not for the time requirement of the mutilation, Tavalin had no alibi."

"That's what threw me off for so long." Jeremy couldn't help noticing that his comment seemed vaguely complimentary. He had not meant to defer to Monika's deviousness.

"You also seem ignorant of the essential role *you* played in Grady's death," Monika added.

"Which was?" asked Jeremy, dreading the answer.

"Please," chimed in Tavalin, "let me. Remember, Jeremy, our conversation at the Chevron, after we chugged all that beer at Cooter's?"

Jeremy shrugged.

"Two words-" said Tavalin. "Blue eyes. I called my partner here as soon as I thought you were gone – only you came back and caught me, remember?"

"I remember you said you were talking to your mom," interjected Jeremy.

"And do you remember when Grady died?" asked Tavalin.

Jeremy shook his head.

Tavalin was happy to oblige the information. "He died three days later. Your loose tongue gave him away."

"And," added Monika, "like you said, it wasn't suicide. I killed him and placed the heart I cut out of your friend's chest right in Grady's hand. How's that for a dramatic pose?"

Jeremy had thought he wanted answers, but not these. Grady had warned Jeremy not to betray his unusual blue eyes but he told Tavalin anyway. Not only had Jeremy placed June directly in the line of fire, his indiscretions had apparently led to Grady's death as well. But there were a couple of things he still did not understand.

"How did my mention of Grady's blue eyes give him away?" asked Jeremy.

"A person never forgets eyes like his," replied Monika. "When Tavalin relayed the information to me, I knew exactly who he was."

"You had prior dealings with Grady?" asked Jeremy.

"Do you still not get it? Can't you figure it out?" Monika was taunting him now. "Come on Jeremy, this is the big kahuna."

"Just tell me, why don't you?"

"Grady's the one who turned me on to the Source to begin with."

"What do you mean, *Grady turned you on to the Source*?" asked Jeremy. "I don't understand."

Monika did not address Jeremy's question but chose instead to revisit an earlier query.

"You asked me why we targeted you," she began, "and I told you it was because of Tavalin's recommendation. What I didn't tell you was that you stirred up something in me that I haven't felt in years. I wasn't kidding when I offered to be your girlfriend. I liked you, Jeremy – I really did."

Jeremy could not believe what he was hearing. He had assumed that every aspect of his relationship with Monika had been a deception.

"And," continued Monika, "if you really want to hear something funny, I still do. Come with us, Jeremy. Take the vow, drink of the Source and all the world will be yours. It's not too late for us to be together."

Besides being floored by Monika's proclamation, Jeremy saw this as a golden opportunity. "What about Jinni?" he asked.

"What about her?" Monika's tone was cold. "I'm sure she would never be a party to Claire's Way."

"You've got that right!" exclaimed Jinni. "I won't and Jeremy won't either!"

Until now, Jinni had let Jeremy do all the talking.

"He's made his choice," added Jinni.

"It's not over till the fat lady sings," remarked Monika. Turning to Tavalin, she said, "Can't you shut her up?"

"Don't listen to her, Jeremy," pleaded Jinni. "You said it yourself – she's evil."

Tavalin tied Jinni's hands behind her back and taped her mouth shut with a patch of duct tape, but not before she managed to spit on him.

"Now maybe we can talk in peace," Monika said. "Would you consider joining us, Jeremy?"

"Why would I want to come with you?" he asked.

"If you knew the details of Claire's Way, you would want to come."

A certain look passed between Tavalin and Monika.

Tavalin asked, "Are you going to tell him?"

"Tell me what?" asked Jeremy.

"As much as I want to, I can't break my own rule," replied Monika. "Everybody else had to commit before understanding the full extent of the rewards. But Jeremy, believe what I say: You want what the Source provides, but to get it, you first have to take the vow. That's the deal."

Incredibly, Jeremy recognized that a wretched side of him still longed for

Monika, even after all that she had done. This defect in him actually thought this the ideal situation: What if the only way to save Jinni was to take the vow and drink of the Source and become whatever it was that Monika wanted him to become? Could a cause as noble as saving Jinni's life justify a deal with the devil?

Meaning to milk this for all it was worth, Jeremy asked Tavalin, "If you were me, what would you do?"

The wind gusted and a few stray sprinkles of rain landed on Jeremy's face.

"The answer, my friend, is blowin' in the wind," replied Tavalin, stealing a line from a Dylan song. "It's really quite simple. Join us and live. Don't, and die."

"I'll do it," Jeremy said, "but only if you let Jinni go."

"No can do." Monika did not waver. "Either way, Jinni's toast, and we won't be able to move forward with any of this until she is out of the way."

"And if I refuse?" asked Jeremy.

"If you refuse, we kill the both of you."

There was no reason to doubt Monika's ultimatum. She had killed before and Jeremy knew she would not hesitate to skip along the same murderous path with Jinni and him.

"If you won't let Jinni go, then I'm not interested in anything you or Claire's Way has to offer," Jeremy declared.

"Alright, then." Monika's tone was cold. To Tavalin, she added, "Tie them up – to each other."

Monika held both guns while Tavalin tied Jeremy's ankles together and his wrists behind his back. He repeated the process for Jinni.

Jeremy pleaded, "Can't we settle this in some civilized fashion, Monika? It doesn't have to end like this."

"You made your bed and now you will damn well sleep in it." Monika was livid. "I offered you the world and you turned me down – twice. And for what? This? Your precious little Jinnigirl?"

Monika's face filled with contempt as she gave Jinni the once-over. "Now, I'm going to need for both of you to stand up." Monika's tone had a disturbing finality about it.

Finally, Jeremy's anger erupted. "Grady was a good man and June was a friend of mine and you – you, Monika, are nothing but a despicable beast! Hell would be too fine a fate for you."

"If hell is my destiny then I say bring it on!" With a brazen grin she added, "Burn, baby, burn."

In the distance, thunder rumbled.

Jeremy and Jinni stood back to back while Tavalin bound their wrists and ankles together in pairs, leaving just enough slack so they could stand. When he was done, Tavalin stepped back to admire his handiwork.

"That ought to hold them," he bragged. "Now what?"

"Come here, Tavalin," replied Monika, "so we can talk privately."

While Tavalin and Monika whispered their dark plans on the far side of the fire, Jeremy lent a voice to his regrets. More than anything, he wished to erase all the bad decisions that led him to this point in time. If he were granted a do-over, he would certainly choose to stay away from Monika and Reefers Woods, just as Grady had advised. Had he stayed true to Jinni and listened to Grady, Grady and June would not have died and he and Jinni would not be standing here, tied back to back with each other and standing face to face with death.

Considering that this might be the bitter end, Jeremy felt fear and sorrow and regret for himself, but all paled in comparison to the despair he felt for Jinni's sake. She was the innocent one, yet fate had rendered this to be her final hour, bound and gagged atop this God-forsaken rock. But could he really expect fate to step in and take the blame for this? It sickened Jeremy, but he knew it was he who bore full responsibility for plunging Jinni, the light of his life, under the mantle of Monika's dark dominion.

***

Jeremy had been raised in the church and had been taught that the human soul survives death. But now, as he faced the stone-cold reality of his own demise, he found he had no idea what he believed in his heart. Before tonight, death had been this monster in the closet that he knew one day he would have to face, but the closet door had been locked up tight and the dreaded confrontation a problem for the distant future, abstract and unfathomable. Now, suddenly and unexpectedly, the monster had been released to whisper its oft-repeated elegy of the ages.

The bell tolls for thee.

Every experience, every problem and every thought became totally insignificant and irrelevant in the context of this single climactic moment. If only he had spent less time worrying about the trivialities of day-to-day living and had instead searched for those things that make a man's life worthwhile, whatever they might be.

How ironic, he thought, *that one sees life best through the perspective of dying eyes.*

Of all that Jeremy feared, the worst was that he might be held accountable for all he did wrong. Because of his lust for Monika and the Unreal, and because of his disregard for Grady's warnings, Jeremy was responsible for June's and Grady's deaths. It seemed likely that Jinni's name would soon be added to the list.

What if, Jeremy wondered, *all those Bible stories are true and there really is a price to pay for my transgressions?*

What if God is real?

As disquieting as was the idea of a personal judgment day, the alternative lent Jeremy little consolation.

What if the evolutionists are correct in their belief that life arose spontaneously from some primeval broth, unassisted by any benevolent creator, and death is the end of all ends?

Jeremy didn't know which would be worse – life after death with judgment rendered or the equally disturbing notion of oblivion after death.

In consideration of that latter concept, Jeremy wondered, *how will it feel to be deprived of the sensations of living in this world? Will this bitterness coating my mouth and heart never turn sweet again? Will this smell of wood smoke and rain be the last to register in my nostrils? Are these rumblings of thunder the last sounds to vibrate upon the drums of my ears? When I'm gone, who will recall the foolish days, the wasted days and the rarer days when wisdom reigned? What of my mom, my dad, my sister, and all the friends who came and went?*

The predestined rain finally arrived at the King's Pinnacle, prompting Tavalin to grab raincoats from a nearby bag for Monika and him. Jeremy and Jinni had no provision to repel the cold water. The raindrops sizzled as they hit the fire but did not immediately diminish the flames. Rather, it was the wind that seized control, whipping the flames violently about with an intriguingly familiar sound.

And what of Jinni? Will I ever again look upon her face or will her dwindling body heat against my back be the last sensation that will pass between us? What of the intimate connection shared by two souls who knew one another so well that a secret smile passed between them spoke a thousand words? Must all great loves one day part? Will death —as the atheists proclaim – erase everyone and everything, including the love I share with Jinni?

More than anything, Jeremy wanted the true answer to all of his questions. Yet, it was the distinct fluttering sound produced by the wind in the fire that his mind insisted he dwell upon.

Where have I heard that sound before?

Finally, it hit him. He had been standing right here in his dream, in his *vision of the real*, and in it he heard that same fluttery-flapping sound. In the vision, it originated from the wings of the angel-being as she took flight.

With a thunderous retort, the rain shower became a deluge. Before Jeremy could guess what might happen next, an ear-splitting concussion shook the foundations of his world. What he initially thought was a brilliant lightning flash and concurrent thunder was something altogether different. Below, there appeared a huge sphere of white light, as large as the gorge itself, rising up and away from the valley floor. More beautiful than any earthly fireworks display, its appearance was exactly as it had been in Jeremy's vision, with beams of ethereal light shooting off in every direction like from an enormous disco ball. Gleefully, Jeremy read the dumb amazement, confusion and fear in the silhouettes of their captors, and though Monika and Tavalin did not understand, Jeremy did: The rain caused the jar left floating in the pool to sink, and, as advertised, rubidium does indeed detonate upon contact with water. As for the very strange and beautiful way in which the fireball of white light dispersed, Jeremy attributed to the rain-soaked atmosphere. Residual rubidium, pulverized but not consumed by the initial blast, was thrust heavenward into the saturating rain to transmit the white light of the reaction ubiquitously through the atmosphere like an electric current.

As quickly as it came, the white light of the rubidium explosion faded, though its image remained entrenched on Jeremy's retinas. Doused by the same rain that triggered the blast, Tavalin's fire fizzled and its bubble of warm light contracted until all that remained were some glowing embers and a few curly streamers of white smoke.

Monika marched over to Jeremy and, like an angry drill sergeant at close range, screamed, "What the hell was that? What did you do to my tree?"

"I have no idea," Jeremy replied. "But whatever it was, it was beautiful, don't you think?"

Monika slapped Jeremy hard across his left cheek and glared at him with eyes ruthless and wild. "The time has come to say goodbye," she said as she pressed the barrel of the cocked gun hard against his temple. Without removing the gun from Jeremy's head, she rotated around to Jinni and cruelly ripped the duct tape from her lips. "Tell me what just happened or your boyfriend dies."

"I don't know," Jinni stammered. "We didn't do anything. Maybe it was a lightening strike or something."

Monika's countenance softened ever so slightly. "You better hope that's all it was," she said and abruptly turned and picked her way down the slope that led to the floor of the gorge. "Watch them, Tavalin, while I investigate."

As soon as Monika was gone, Jinni whispered, "She's going to kill us when she finds out what we did, isn't she?"

"Yes," Jeremy replied somberly. "I'm afraid so."

"Then we have to jump."

Jeremy considered Jinni's proposal. "I'm pretty sure the fall would kill us both," he finally said.

"After Monika shoots us, she'll probably throw us over the edge anyway."

Jeremy almost laughed. "I guess you've got a point."

Tavalin, whose attention had been directed toward the floor of the gulch, glared across at them. "Shut up," he said, "or *I* get to shoot you."

As Jeremy envisioned the jump, a queasy sensation swept through his stomach and down into his legs, as if he were already falling. His leap from the church belfry had been tough enough and then he had only to transverse a few feet of space between the rail and the tree. Jinni's plan, if one could even call it that, was infinitely more terrifying and the chances of escape – indeed, their chances of survival – were infinitesimally small.

Jeremy waited until Tavalin once again turned his attention toward the floor of the gulch before whispering, "Let's just wait a bit and see what happens."

"We have to decide now," Jinni implored, "before she comes back."

After a long pause, Jeremy finally replied, "I'll do it but only if there's no other way."

"How will I know when you're ready?"

"If it comes to that, I'll squeeze your hand three times." Jeremy hoped it wouldn't come to that. "If you still want to jump, just squeeze back."

"And then?"

"And then we just hop off."

Jeremy looked over his shoulder, beyond the frightened profile of Jinni's face and over the cliff's edge to where the dying firelight gave way to the hovering darkness. He could hear the sound of the river as it boiled below, and he cringed at the thought of every aspect of their meager plan. Even if they survived the fall, they must still contend with The Devil's Crotch – all while bound together. As much as the thought of the fall scared him, the proposition of death by drowning was worse.

While he had the chance, Jeremy wanted to say something that would convey his feelings toward Jinni. But what? If this was the end, he didn't want his last words to consist of trite clichés.

With a jolt he remembered that he never did tell Jinni about the engagement ring he bought for her. "You know, Jinni, I picked up something a while back," he said, "but I never got the chance to give it to you."

"Oh yeah? What is it?"

"A ring."

"A ring? What kind of ring?"

"I was wondering-," he began haltingly, "if we get out of this alive – if you would, you know, consider marrying me?"

Jinni did not reply, but Jeremy could feel the undulations of her body against his back and even Tavalin, distracted as he was peering into the gorge after Monika, took note of Jinni's heaving sobs.

"I've been waiting for this moment," Jinni finally managed to say. "But I must say, your timing sucks. Why did you wait so long?"

"I'm sorry. I know now what a fool I've been."

By the time Monika returned, Tavalin's fire was extinguished and darkness had engulfed the rock shelf.

Eagerly, Tavalin asked, "Well? What did you see down there?"

"It's gone," Monika replied morosely. "The tree is completely destroyed. And lightning," she added as she turned to glare at Jeremy, "had nothing to do with it."

Even in the intermittent illumination afforded by Tavalin's flashlight, Jeremy recognized the look on Monika's face as that same expression of pure, unadulterated evil she had let show at the ceremony when he refused the vow. He knew, without a doubt, they had no recourse. Jeremy gathered his resolve and thrice squeezed Jinni's hand. She responded in kind and thus initiated their plan of last resort. Like some lame version of a three-legged race, they hopped to the edge of the precipice. As they toppled over the edge, Jeremy thought he heard the crack of a gun, but could not be sure.

As they dropped into the void, their bodies rotated slowly on a horizontal axis, head over heels. Jeremy felt as if he were floating. Would they ever hit bottom? When they did, might some version of salvation be waiting for them there, or was it a destiny of a more sinister nature that lurked below in the swirling waters of the River Sticks?

***

So severe was the impact that Jeremy assumed they had missed the water and landed on the rocks. The next thing he knew, someone had a stranglehold around his neck. He struggled to break free but his assailant's grip squeezed all the tighter.

"Stop! Stop it!" urged a familiar voice. "You'll drown the both of us."

As more of his facilities returned, he realized they were on the downriver side of the rapids and he was being dragged across the surface of the frigid water.

"You saved me?" asked Jeremy.

Somehow Jinni had managed to keep the both of them afloat and alive, even though he had been rendered temporarily unconscious by the impact with the water's surface.

Through chattering teeth, Jinni replied, "I guess all those summers working as a lifeguard finally paid off. "But without this," she added, "I would have lost hold of you for sure."

Jinni lifted a leg from the water to reveal the rope still tied to her ankle. Tavalin's tie job had unwound so that she and Jeremy were still tethered together, but with two or three feet of slack in between. The ropes that had bound their wrists together were nowhere to be found.

"Where are they now?" Jeremy asked, as he worked to untie the rope from their ankles.

Before Jinni could answer, gunfire erupted.

"We've got to hide!" exclaimed Jeremy.

"No we don't – look!"

Jinni's trembling forefinger pointed toward the shore. Right there, at the river's edge were two jet-skis – Monika's and Tavalin's rides.

Jinni waded over and quickly announced the good news. "They left the keys."

"Get on," urged Jeremy.

As Jeremy climbed aboard the other jet-ski, a bullet tore into the water mere inches away. Their foes had a solid fix on their positions. He ran his hands over the handlebars, feeling frantically for an ignition switch or a key.

"How do you crank this thing?" he cried.

Jinni grabbed his hand and directed it to the switch.

"Go, go!" he yelled.

Jinni took off. As Jeremy maneuvered his craft away from the bank, the last thing he heard was Monika's voice, screaming and cursing. Finally, Jeremy got his jet ski pointed in the right direction and lurched away, following in Jinni's wake.

Scant minutes later, barely out of gunshot range, Jinni's craft slowed dramatically. Jeremy feared the worst.

Pulling alongside, he asked, "What's wrong? Are you hit?"

"Not that," she replied ominously. "I'm freezing."

The only protection Jinni had from the elements was a paper-thin windbreaker worn over her sopping-wet sweat suit. Plowing through the wind, as they were, only accelerated what the rain and the dip in the ice-cold water had set into motion. Jeremy could now see that Jinni was shaking violently and he knew, under these conditions, hypothermia was inevitable.

"Here, take this."

Jeremy doubted his wet coat could hold in much heat, but he helped put it on Jinni anyway. No matter, she could not stand to stay exposed for much longer and neither could he. Sunrise was still two hours removed and the temperature was dropping fast. They needed shelter or, better yet, a fire. The heaviest part of the rain had let up for now, but Jeremy knew it would be next to impossible to get a fire going under these wet conditions. He wasn't even sure he had the means to start a fire, as he had left his backpack and everything in it behind at the gulch.

"What are we going to do?" asked Jinni.

Jeremy's heart ached at the slurring of her words and her glazed eyes, sure proof that her bodily systems were already slowing down. Jinni was freezing before his eyes. After all they had withstood, would they now succumb to the dropping temperature?

"First off," Jeremy replied, "you'll be warmer riding behind me."

Jinni climbed aboard, leaving her jet-ski bobbing in the river. Jeremy goosed the throttle. After putting two or three miles between them and their would-be attackers, Jeremy slowed. He didn't know what else to do but to pull over and to take shelter in the woods. At least there they could gain some protection from the brutal wind. As he zeroed in on a sand bar where they could stop, a better idea came to him. Taking advantage of their slower speed, Jeremy twisted around to look at his hunkered-down passenger.

"Jinni, honey," he said, "if you can just hang on for a little while longer, I think I know a place we can go."

Jinni garnered a tepid smile. "I'm right behind you," she said in a weak voice.

Jeremy accelerated past the sand bar with a broad, sweeping turn and continued toward the lake. Feeling more optimistic in anticipation of warmer quarters, his thoughts meandered back to Monika's curious edict on the cliff, a few minutes before:

The man whom you knew as Grady turned me on to the Source...

Years ago, she had added with a certain gleam in her eye. Monika loved to tease and this was yet another carrot she dangled before Jeremy, presumably a clue to help him unravel her secrets. But when and under what circumstances could Monika have known Grady? It was obvious that she had since lost touch with him because it wasn't until Jeremy mentioned Grady's blue eyes that she had tracked Grady down. Interestingly, while Grady might have *turned Monika on* to the Source *years ago,* he apparently never spelled out to her *where* he found it.

Also sticking in Jeremy's craw was something Monika uttered back at the ceremony. After she gave Trey his drink of the Source, she asked a curious request of him: *Call me Claire,* she said. What thought processes did Monika entertain that could trigger such a statement? It wasn't the first time she had expressed similar sentiments. Jeremy remembered when he first informed her of the out-of-place, or rather the *out-of-time* wingtips in Claire's painting, *The Ends,* how Monika, after admitting authorship, had joked that Claire's spirit might be living within her, or something to that effect. While Jeremy wasn't quite ready to accept this indwelling of spirits, Monika was, undoubtedly, the resident expert in all things related to Claire. She knew about the lotus, what it did, where it could be found; she knew Claire's painting technique, including how to prepare the same unique paints that Claire used. Monika even subscribed to a philosophy she referred to as Claire's Way.

Had Monika so wrapped herself in Claire's lotus and Claire's paintings and Claire's Way that she believed she was Claire?

Had Jeremy's powers of reasoning not been hampered by his dropping core temperature, he would likely have cut the thread right there, for though he reached the ensuing conclusion via logical steps, the conclusion was anything but logical. This evening Jeremy had seen Claire for the first time on Grady's home movie. His assumption had been that Monika and Claire were related, but what if the eerie resemblance was due not to them being of the same blood-line but of the same exact blood? Could it be possible that Monika and Claire were, in fact, one and the same person?

Everything pointed toward that end; everything, that is, save Monika's apparent agelessness. If Monika and Claire were the same person, how, after so many trips around the sun, had she managed to preserve her vitality and youthful appearance? Plastic surgery and makeup? Jeremy knew this could not be the case.

Jeremy remembered Monika's riddle – *when the time comes, you will become and time will come.* Monika touted some grand effect of the Source, a certain change, or *becoming*, that she claimed would befall anyone who drank of it. The mystery had been what this purported change might be. The last line of the riddle – *and time will come* – held the answer. If Claire and Monika really were the same person, then she had most certainly been granted extra time. Might her insinuated claim be that the Source arrested the aging process and that she was the living proof? Had Grady, as a child – all those *years ago* – discovered the lotus tree and given Claire a taste of its fruit? Was this fruit, known also as the Source, responsible for Claire's youthful longevity?

Jeremy's mind reeled. If all this were true, as Monika's clues seemed to indicate, the tree of the King's Pinnacle represented perhaps the most sought-after, most fabulously amazing discovery mankind had ever known. Jeremy felt a large measure of dismay as he corrected himself: The Source *would have been* the most amazing discovery, had he not just succeeded in blowing it to smithereens.

***

Once in the lake, Jeremy guided the jet-ski south along the shoreline until they drew even with the secret beach. The warm place he promised Jinni was exactly where it was supposed to be, anchored 300 yards to the west.

Jeremy could scarcely feel his body as they climbed on board the houseboat. Jinni had ceased her violent shivering, but acted more like a zombie than a functioning human being. Inside, Jeremy stripped away her wet clothes and replaced them with several layers of dry clothes retrieved from a drawer. Finally he switched his clothes out and crawled into bed with Jinni. They snuggled for a good while, until he felt warmer and she at last began to show signs of recovery.

"This is Monika's boat?"

Jeremy interpreted Jinni's revived shivering as a good sign. It meant her body was once again doing its part to reheat itself.

"Yes," he replied.

"And these are her clothes I'm wearing?" she asked disdainfully.

"It's better than freezing."

"I suppose." After a thoughtful pause, she added, "What was that you said back there on the cliff – something about a ring?"

Jeremy laughed. "It's right over there in my coat pocket, if I didn't lose it in during all the excitement. Let me show you-"

"Don't get up," insisted Jinni. "You know I don't care diddly-squat about the ring, except to know that you made real plans for us – permanent plans."

"So the answer you gave me on the cliff still stands?" he asked.

"Yes, you idiot. You could have asked me a year ago and I would have said the same thing. The day we met, I knew."

"I did too, Jinni."

She elbowed him in his ribs. "Then *why* are you just now asking?"

With a sly smile, he replied, "I guess I was waiting for the perfect moment."

"What, a near-death experience?"

When they kissed, Jinni's lips were warm. At least he could be confident that her thought processes were no longer muddled by the hypothermia. She meant what she said.

As they cuddled – in Monika's bed of all places – Jeremy attempted to get Jinni up to speed with respect to the Source and Monika. As quickly as he could manage, he told her how Monika's clues and insinuations led him to believe that she and Claire were the same person.

Jinni reacted skeptically. She asked, "Which do you think is more likely, that Monika and Claire are the same person or that Monika is making all of this up in order to gain control over the people in her group. I can see how a lot of people would want to follow her if she made them believe she had something that would keep them young."

"You make a good point," conceded Jeremy. "I know Monika used the Unreal in that same fashion to wield influence over her group and over me. Now that I think about it, how brilliant would it be for her to fabricate this lie about her being Claire and having sole access to some magical potion that staves off aging? It would take years for all those twenty-year-olds to realize that the Source was nothing more than a modern-day snake oil being peddled by a hustler. Then again," added Jeremy, "if that is true, why did we have to go through all that we did to destroy it?"

"We did it because Grady asked us to," replied Jinni.

Despite Jeremy's feeling that there was more information to mine from the subject, they needed to get moving. They had survived the jump, the rapids, the gunfire and the cold, but they still had worries. In all likelihood, the police were still in the vicinity searching for Jeremy and that made the fast-approaching daylight their enemy.

Begrudgingly, Jeremy crawled from the cozy bed. "We need to get to the other side."

"Then where?" Jinni asked. "Won't we need transportation once we get there?"

Jeremy thought for a moment before he walked to the front of the boat. He found the decal in the upper right corner of the windshield:

Sid's Marina
Slip A-17

"So far, so good," he said as he passed Jinni on the way out the back sliding door of the cabin. He examined the two extra keys on the key chain hanging from the jet-ski's ignition. The butt of the each key sported the insignia of a galloping horse and, in cursive script below it, the word *Mustang*. These were the keys to Monika's car.

"You wouldn't happen to know how to get to Sid's Marina from here, would you?" he asked.

"Not hardly."

Jeremy scurried back toward the bow. He found what he was looking for in the small drawer next to the steering wheel. He powered up the handheld GPS and scrolled down until he found an entry entitled *Sid's*. According to the digital display, the marina was nine miles from their present position.

"Got it," he announced exuberantly. "With any luck, we'll find Monika's car parked at Sid's Marina. We just have to get there before first light."

"What do you think Monika and Tavalin are doing right now?" asked Jinni.

"You know they're doing all they can to figure out a way to track us down and kill us." For the first time, Jeremy thought about what they left behind in the river. "Did we leave the keys in the other jet-ski?"

"I don't remember taking them out," replied Jinni.

"Wouldn't that be something…?"

***

The jet-ski's hull sliced the water with a sound like a hard falling rain as Jinni and Jeremy rode west across the lake toward Sid's Marina. There was no sign of the police or of Monika and Tavalin, though the Spanish Armada could have been alongside and they would not have known it on account of the fog. Jeremy drove slower than he would have liked as he scanned for unseen obstacles while Jinni monitored the GPS and kept them on the right heading.

As the jet-ski's headlights poked and prodded at the impenetrable fog, Jeremy took another stab at the unresolved riddles surrounding Monika, Claire, and the Source. Ever since Jeremy heard Monika's spiel at the secret beach bonfire, he had hoped that it was like she said, that he could *dare to believe in the supernatural* and know that *something big is coming down*. It was obvious now that Monika was speaking of the Source. And her riddle for him, *when the time comes, you will become, and time will come*, in retrospect, was a perfect allusion to the ceremony, where she planned to administer the Source to him and to her other disciples.

But was it really as Jinni suggested? Had it instead all been a clever campaign of deceit, hatched and ingeniously implemented by Monika so she could gain the allegiance of her group? It was certainly possible, but there were still some nagging details to address. When he and Jinni cut into the fruit from the tree in the gorge, Jeremy recognized the smell, and not just from Monika's ceremonial challis at the abandoned church. His intuition insisted on another connection; an *earlier* link. The inkling grew until Jeremy traced the smell of the Source back to the most unlikely of places: Grady's kitchen. On the day they met, Grady made eggs, sausage, biscuits and, to drink, the fruit juice with the odd aftertaste. Hadn't the purple lotus fruit and the liquid contained in the challis emitted the same fermented-sweet aroma as had Grady's homemade juice?

Jeremy really couldn't trust his memory enough to say for sure, but the possibility took him back around to the questions raised by the secret research project. After his stellar performance at the Fryin' Bacon Triathlon, he and June had found his mitochondria to be different; *intelligently redesigned*, to quote June. This explained well his increased endurance but did not address how his mitochondria got changed in the first place. Could the change be a result of his unwitting drinking of the Source?

Considering the timing of his visit to Grady's house, which preceded the race, and in light of his and June's findings, Jeremy had an idea as to how the Source might suspend aging. Molecular biologists have long theorized a link between aging and the release of free radicals by one's mitochondria. Their reasoning went something like this: As people get older, their mitochondria accumulate errors due to imperfect replication, which results in an increase in the release of free radicals, a byproduct of energy production. Like molecular bullets, these highly-reactive molecules punch holes into everything they come into contact with, including cellular DNA. The damage accumulates over time until the DNA, which serves as the blueprint for the body, produces imperfect proteins and enzymes that do not work as they were originally designed. The outward effect is a slow, broad-based decline of bodily functions, which sounds a lot like a description of the aging process. The Source might work by mitigating the changes in the mitochondria over time so that they function just as well in an older individual as they do in the young. There is no increase in free radical production and the integrity of the DNA is thusly maintained.

And though Jeremy could not explain many of the things that had occurred of late in and around Reefers Woods – especially the prophetic visions and dreams – he was ready to accept that which Monika and Grady believed and the science supported. The effect was real, but what did it mean in exact terms for him personally? Supposing he could avoid death by trauma, which no change at the cellular level could protect against, could he dare entertain the unimaginable, incredibly marvelous notion that he might not only stay young but also *live* indefinitely?

Without warning, legions of glorious snowflakes burst forth from above, inundating the bubble of light that encompassed the jet-ski like a snow globe hard shaken. As rare as snow events were in this part of the country, Jeremy would not have been surprised to learn that the snow fell on them alone, a sign of joy and hope and deliverance from all who would do them harm.

Not only had Grady known where to find the Source, he had arranged for Jeremy to drink of it long before Monika offered him a swig of the same. Jeremy wanted to stop the jet-ski and tell Jinni the splendid news, but he didn't right away. He began to worry that while Jinni would certainly be happy for him, she might not be happy for *them*. If all this was really true, how would Jinni feel, knowing that for every year that passed, she would age and he would not? And how excruciating would it be for him to watch her fight her losing battle against Old Man Time while he maintained the vitality of youth?

And if this change were such a wonderful thing, why had all the signs, and indeed, every instinct in his body steered him away from the ceremony and the vow at the altar? If he had already *become*, didn't that mean that all his objections were for naught or would another shot of the Source have been harmful in some way?

Finally Jeremy hit upon the notion that it was the other part of the ceremony, the part that comprised Claire's Way that was inherently wrong. The vow, or more precisely, the *disavow*, made it wrong. All this made sense in the context of Grady's admonition when he said that *Reefers Woods holds the source of things... both good and evil.* Jeremy had assumed that these *things* were separate. However, what Grady really meant was that the Source, *by itself*, could be used in one of two ways. Presumably, the way that Jeremy had received it, as a free gift from Grady was of the good variety, whereas Monika's way changed that which was meant for good to evil.

***

The pitched roof of the easterly dock house rose to meet them like a phoenix from the fog and snow. They puttered by the deserted waterfront of Sid's Marina, pulling behind them a symmetrical wake.

"Home sweet home," crooned Jeremy as he maneuvered into covered slip #A-17.

Jinni stood by, her arms wrapped around her, while Jeremy worked to secure the jet-ski.

The long row of docked boats bumped and swayed under the dying influence of the jet-ski's wake, reminding Jeremy how everything in and on the lake was connected to every other thing in the water by the water itself. Though the jet-ski was still now, the repercussions of its passage through the water carried on. Jeremy saw this as an analogy to his travels and travails in and around Reefers Woods. When Tavalin first took Jeremy past the *Keep Out* sign on Sticks River

Road, a chain of events was set into motion that propagated throughout every aspect of Jeremy's life. Lives were changed and lives were lost, all because Jeremy ventured into that place known as Reefers Woods. Everything that happened from that point forward seemed beyond his control, almost preordained.

"There," he said as he finished tying off the ropes. "All secure, right where it's supposed to be."

Turning his attention to Jinni, he asked, "Are you cold?"

"Just a little chilly, that's all."

Jeremy put his arm around Jinni and they walked together down the aisle of the pier. He smiled to himself. Somehow, he had emerged from it all with the real girl of his dreams at his hip. As they passed by, the long row of boats bobbed in the water as if nodding their approval.

They emerged from the covered pier into a world made white by the snow.

"What do you think?" Jeremy swept his free arm in a grand arc.

"It's beautiful," replied Jinni. "The forecast didn't say anything about a snow storm."

"My own forecast didn't give us a chance in hell either," said Jeremy, "but look at us now."

Of the three snow-covered cars in the parking lot, one was Monika's '69 Mustang.

"There's our ride," said Jeremy triumphantly.

He escorted Jinni to the passenger side and unlocked the door.

"Wanna go for a ride?" he asked.

"Let's get out of here," she said, stepping in.

As they drove off into the snow-muted dawn, they were tired but warm and their mood was ecstatic.

"Where do we go from here?" asked Jinni.

"That is an incredibly good question." Jeremy was thinking of the huge ramifications of his *becoming* as much as any transient destination.

Jeremy knew he was right about the Source, right about Monika being Claire, and right about her protracted youthfulness – and his own. But what would he tell Jinni about the change? Should he even mention it at all? He had promised to marry Jinni and to walk with her through all the days of their lives. But now, the path of his life must necessarily deviate from hers. She would grow old while he, in all likelihood, would not.

Jinni interrupted the deliberations. "What are you thinking about?" she asked.

"You," he replied, "and all the time we have ahead of us."

After a contemplative silence, Jeremy asked, "What if it's true?" He waded in, not knowing how deeply he might delve into the subject. "What if Monika really is Claire and the Source is keeping her young?"

"Oh brother," sighed Jinni. "Are you saying you believe it now?"

"Maybe. I thought of a couple more things on the ride in."

"Why am I not surprised?" she asked rhetorically. "What do you *think* you've figured out?"

"For starters," Jeremy began, "Monika went to a lot of trouble to track down that particular tree, and Grady gave up his life rather than reveal its location to her. Their actions, I think, prove they weren't lying."

"Even if they believed it themselves, it doesn't necessarily mean it's true," said Jinni. "I don't pretend to understand why Monika does what she does and why Grady did what he did, but I would need more definite proof, something that doesn't depend on the actions of those two."

"What about Grady's home movie?" he asked. "You have to admit Monika and Claire do look alike."

"They could be related. You said so yourself."

"But what if it were true?" Jeremy asked, belaboring the point. "Can you imagine how awesome a thing it would be to stay young?"

"It would be nice," agreed Jinni, "but even if the Source could do all that, it's gone now. It has no bearing on us at all."

"Yeah, maybe you're right," he said.

Without informing Jinni of the mitochondria connection, she would never accept what he suggested and he respected her for not giving in. Jeremy wasn't even sure why he tried to convince Jinni if he didn't intend on telling her everything, including how the changes in his mitochondria were the proof in the pudding.

Appropriate or not, in this moment, Jeremy no longer worried about Monika, or the police, or, for that matter, anything at all. It was the first time in a long time he actually felt optimistic about the future. Jeremy opened his mouth to comment again on the sheer beauty of the snow and of their vastly improved state of affairs, but hushed up when he saw that Jinni had found her own measure of serenity. Her eyes were closed.

***

"I never really had a chance to tell you but, I had this dream…"

Jinni spoke without raising her head or opening her eyes, as if talking in her sleep.

"Dream?" prodded Jeremy. "What dream?"

"The gulch, the river, the white ball of light and the thunder snow," Jinni replied. "I dreamed the whole thing."

Jeremy's heart quickened. "What else can you tell me about it?"

"There was this creepy old woman crouching like an animal on a rock, and there were angels playing your music."

"My music?"

"It sounded a little like that band you like – Singe, right? – only a whole lot better."

When it seemed that Jinni might be drifting off again, Jeremy asked, "In this dream – did anyone speak to you?"

"Yeah, there was this one angel up on top of the cliff. She said-"

"Hold that thought." Jeremy cut Jinni off before she could finish her sentence.

Jeremy found a pen in the console. He was just able to squeeze the seven words onto the palm of his left hand.

"Now tell me. What did the angel say?"

"Open your mind and experience the real," Jinni replied, reciting from heart. Jeremy held out his hand.

Jinni had to strain to read the words in the pale glow of the dashboard lights.

"Word for word!" she exclaimed with as much muster as her exhausted state would allow. "How did you know?"

"I knew," Jeremy replied, "because I had the exact same dream."

"What does it mean?"

"Something, but I'm not exactly sure what," he replied. "I guess it means I don't have a monopoly on prophetic dreams."

"Well," she said with a gaping yawn, "when you get it figured out, you can tell me all about it. I just can't stay awake any longer. Do you mind?"

"No, be my guest," replied Jeremy. "Sweet dreams."

For the next hour or so, Jinni scarcely moved a muscle. Jeremy, driving on autopilot, tried to consolidate all he knew about the shared visions, starting with the mysterious reappearing children. He had been initially introduced to them in his *vision of the real*, which began with children's voices chanting – *Red rover, red rover, send Jeremy right over* – and then, most recently, there were the children he perceived in the road at the tail end of the police chase, reciting the same childhood rhyme. Their presence proved their good intentions, as he otherwise would never have slowed in time to turn at the three-pronged tree. Had they not shown up when they did, he would likely have been caught by the police.

Monika herself had provided another indication of the good nature of a certain child she saw in Reefers Woods. Monika (a.k.a. Claire) chose to include the girl-child of her visions in her paintings. Monika had even explained to Jeremy how the melancholy child represented "Claire's" prior state of innocence and pureness of heart that she let get away – her lost childhood.

More children made appearances around the bonfire at the secret beach, each child, it seemed, associated with a different member of Monika's group. Interestingly, Monika's late-arriving companion there had not been a child but rather an old woman, the craggy character who also appeared in his wedding dream in the preacher's role and in the *vision of the real* as a bystander on the cliff. In the wedding dream, Monika and the old woman had recited the final proclamation of the ceremony in unison: *With this ring I thee wed*, a clear indication of their shared identity.

That she appeared as an elderly woman also made sense because Monika, despite her youthful façade, was old – at least 60 years old by Jeremy's calculations. More importantly, if the children represented innocence and blamelessness, the appearance of the old woman laid bare Monika's opposite condition: she was unclean and her heart was dark and sinister. That explained why it was the old woman who joined Monika around the bonfire while the other group members were attended by children. The innocence of the other group members had not yet been irreconcilably lost; it wasn't until the recitation of Monika's vow that that point in time – the point of no return – came and went.

Based on all of this, Jeremy thought that maybe the children's job was to plead for their grown counterparts to resist the dark side. The chant – *red rover, red rover, send Jeremy right over* – was an appeal by the children for Jeremy to resist Claire's evil ways and to run to them where they might capture him on the side of purity and righteousness.

Having satisfactorily resolved the meaning of the children's presence in the dreams and visions, Jeremy tackled the question of why it was that he, Jinni, and Monika all shared the same *vision of the real*. For Monika and him, it did not seem a complete surprise. Early on, Jeremy noticed the similarities between his dreams and the hallucinations he experienced in Reefers Woods, even going so far as to refer to the hallucinations as waking dreams. After Monika convinced him that she also saw the children and the old woman around the bonfire, it seemed fitting to learn that she also experienced the *vision of the real*.

But what triggered the vision in the first place? What did he have in common with Monika? After learning that Jinni experienced the same vision, the more intriguing question was what could the three of them – Monika, Jeremy and Jinni – possibly have in common?

***

For every thing that Jeremy thought he had figured out, a dozen questions remained. How, for instance, had Tavalin come to join forces with Monika? He didn't seem to be part of her group, or if he was, Monika never invited him to the meetings. Jeremy's first guess had been that she recruited Tavalin late in the game to take advantage of Tavalin's association with him. However, since Tavalin apparently orchestrated that first meeting of Jeremy and Monika at the Halloween Singe show, his links to her must have preceded that time. After observing how they interacted, Jeremy's strong feeling was that Monika and Tavalin had known one another for a long time.

Another cloudy subject was what Monika meant to do next. It seemed obvious that she had nefarious plans for the future and that those plans were directly related to what she referred to as Claire's Way. While she never really said what it was, one thing Jeremy did know: Claire's Way led away from the grander realms alluded to in his *vision of the real*, and though he did not yet know the ultimate end of her wayward path, he knew that sooner or later their paths would cross. Despite having lost the Source, Jeremy knew that Monika would continue to implement her ruse of fools. He also realized that she would never stop looking for him, knowing what he knew. Likewise, because of his unique position of knowledge, the task to foil her plans – whatever they might be – fell to him. That was what Grady had meant when he said that, by knowing more, one had a responsibility to do more, and Jeremy – by his own choice – knew plenty.

But, alas, that was tomorrow's worry. For now, Jeremy would be satisfied to be alive and unhindered in this moment, riding along in Monika's car in a freakishly beautiful snowstorm with Jinni sleeping at his side.

Jinni, who had been stirring around for the last couple of minutes, sat up and raised her seat to a more upright position.

"You'll never guess what I was dreaming about just now," she said.

"Let's see. Was it angels, white light and the sort?"

"Nope, something else," Jinni replied with a smile. "Where's your jacket?"

"I threw it in the back seat but I'm sure it's still wet," he replied, thinking she meant to use it as a blanket.

"Which pocket?" she asked with gleaming eyes.

"I should have known. Check the right side."

Jinni produced a small black box from within his coat pocket. She flipped open the lid and peered intently inside. "Will you do the honors?" she asked as she pressed the ring passionately into the palm of his hand.

As Jeremy looked down to slip the ring onto Jinni's outstretched finger, the car drifted over the center line, directly into the path of an oncoming pickup truck. Alerted to his blunder by a blaring horn, Jeremy jerked the steering wheel to the right, too abruptly for the slick conditions. The rear end fishtailed, first to the left and then back again as he struggled to keep the car in the right lane. It wasn't until after the pickup truck had passed that Jeremy regained full control of the Mustang. He exhaled and glanced over at Jinni.

Without acknowledging their close call, Jinni whispered, "I love it. It's beautiful."

Jinni was about to toss Jeremy's jacket into the back when she paused. "What's this?" she asked as she poked at a lump concealed in the coat.

"Oh yeah," replied Jeremy. "I forgot all about that."

Jinni removed the ziplock bag from the large inner breast pocket of the coat and flipped on the overhead light.

"I found that in the closet at Grady's house but I never got a chance to look at it," explained Jeremy.

Jinni peeled apart the bag and pulled out the small notebook.

Jeremy asked, "Is it wet?"

Jinni held it up in the light. "No, it's bone dry," she replied, "in spite the rain and our plunge into the river. How do you think Grady happened to put this into a waterproof bag?"

"Grady seemed to know about a lot of things before they happened."

Jinni flipped through the first few pages. "It seems to be a journal, or a diary of sorts. Listen to what Grady wrote on the first page," she said. "*To the Elect, strangers in the world, who have been chosen according to the foreknowledge... I will open my mouth in parables. I will utter hidden things, things from of old.*"

"More *Grady-speak*," remarked Jeremy with a smile. "Just what we need."

Jinni said, "It goes on to say: *Your sons and daughters will prophesy, your old men will dream dreams, your young men will see visions.*"

"Dreams and visions?" asked Jeremy. "That sounds familiar."

She continued, "And finally: *Behold, I make all things new.*"

Jeremy thought how his body, in a sense, had been *made new*, thanks to Grady's special grape juice derived from the Source. On a grander scale, his outlook on life and his commitment to a more righteous and upstanding way of living had also been made new.

"That last one sounds like a quote from the Bible," he noted.

"They all are," replied Jinni.

Jeremy hadn't seen that one coming. "Did you realize Grady was a believer?" he asked.

"I had a feeling, and I did run into him at church, you know."

Jeremy looked blankly at his copilot.

"I told you, remember? I saw Grady outside my church on the Sunday before he died," recounted Jinni. "He invited me to his house for brunch and, while I was there, he gave me the home movie to give to you."

"I don't recall your saying anything about brunch," mumbled Jeremy.

A euphoric surge, better than ten hits of the Unreal, ripped into Jeremy as the words to his next question made the long journey from his mind to his mouth.

"Jinni, when you ate brunch with Grady, what did he give you to drink?"

All around them the snow fell, obscuring the car's passage with torrents of white.

Jinni returned a curious look. "Grape juice," she replied, "only it didn't really taste like grape juice. Grady said he made it himself."

Epilogue

Wanderings of Claire, The Hippie Queen
1969-2009

Claire and Zach

CLAIRE had been the one to seek out and initiate the affair. It worked out nicely that Zach, the medical examiner, was married and was terrified that his wife, or someone else in town, would find out. That made him the perfect accomplice.

Zach told her he loved her but Claire had no feelings for him, one way or the other – at least not in the beginning. Upon learning that it was he who paid for and placed the sculpture at the grave, her nonchalance turned into vitriol. The medical examiner, in his guilt, placed it as a memorial to the one whose body took the place of Claire's. The last thing Claire needed was for any extra attention to be directed toward any of this. She meant for the fire and everything associated with it to die down, but the buzz generated by the mysterious appearance of such an exquisite sculpture at a pauper's grave kept the fire stoked.

Claire had coerced the medical examiner into declaring that hers was one of the burnt bodies recovered from the commune ruins and, while he had been true to his vow of silence, Zach knew too much. She had promised to return to him when the smoke cleared to revive their affair. She arranged to meet him at Sticks River Landing, one year to the day after the burning.

When he arrived at Sticks River Landing on the eve of December 22, 1970, Claire wasted no time. She got in his car, kissed him and shot him in the head. With the medical examiner out of the picture, she felt a lot better. She had gotten away with the murder of Zach, the medical examiner (made to look like a suicide), her hippie friends (made to look like an accident), and also her fellow graduate student, Maurice (presumed lost and given up for dead). Maurice, for his part, paid the ultimate price when he ventured too close to her beloved lotus swamps.

Claire drove away in her new Mustang, humming that melody she so loved, the one she first heard in a dream.

341

Claire and Nick

With her looks and savvy Claire knew she could land just about any man she met. She trolled the New York City night clubs until she met an acceptable match. Nick was good-looking, he liked to party and he was smitten with her. Most importantly, Nick had a lot of money.

After the fire, Claire dropped her old identity and created a new one. She provided the state of New York a forged birth certificate when she married Nick in the spring of 1979. Claire Wales, known now as Monika Cassel, was 32 years old. Nick's friends became her friends as she settled into her upper-middle class, suburban-wife life. At 36, she quit taking her birth control pills and became pregnant. At 37, Monika gave birth to a baby boy.

With each passing year, the difference between Monika and her peers became more pronounced. Where her friends developed fine wrinkles and crow's feet and permanently creased foreheads, Monika's skin remained supple and smooth. She never went to the gym yet somehow avoided the inevitable flabby bellies, sagging boobs, and legs dimpled by cellulite exhibited by her fellow middle-agers. Despite her devil-may-care attitude, she maintained the youthful body, hair, and overall glow typical of a woman in her twenties. Her friends could only assume that she had work done, thinking that no one her age could look that good without the lifts, implants, tucks and/or liposuction increasingly marketed by the cosmetic surgeons.

At first Monika laughed off their questions and innuendoes. "I guess I've just got good genes," she would say, but her sneaking suspicions insisted there was more to it than that.

By the time she turned 48, there could be no denying the obvious. It didn't matter what the calendar indicated; her body was still young and she began to entertain grand thoughts. Monika wondered if she might stay young indefinitely.

She now viewed Nick as a problem. Monika had a higher calling and he was not a party to it. She couldn't stay with him.

***

"Baby, I've got some bad news."

Every year, during the brunt of the late summer heat, Monika made a pilgrimage to the swamps of Reefers Woods to harvest the lotus blooms. The year was 1999, and she had just returned home to New York.

"There has been a drought in Destiny," she declared solemnly. "The swamps dried up and all the lotus plants have died."

Nick made no effort to hide his distress. "What in God's name are we going to do?"

"We'll just have to learn to live without it," she replied.

The truth was that this would be Nick's cross to bear. The lotus crop had come in this year, just as it had every summer, once the plants recovered from the commune fiasco of '69. Most years, Monika harvested far more than she and her husband could possibly use. As a result, she had amassed a substantial stockpile of the dried lotus blooms. Of this, Nick was completely unaware, but she had hers. Monika burned when she had time away from Nick or at doses too low for him to notice. As his mental state deteriorated, her lies and deceptions became easier to slip past him. In the end, he became so completely lost to himself and so totally dependent on her that she could have convinced him to do anything, even to kill himself.

And that was exactly what Monika had done.

Nick had been more than willing to end his misery and had wrapped his car around a tree on a lonely stretch of road in upstate New York. The highway patrol officer who wrote the report observed that *the severity of the crash split the vehicle in two and attested to the high rate of speed at which the vehicle was traveling.*

Her late husband's life insurance policy, however, was intact. With great anticipation, Monika liquidated his assets and set out to begin the next phase of her existence. A larger life beckoned. She left Gotham City, driving the same 1969 vintage Mustang she drove into the city thirty years prior. This time, however, Monika was not alone. Tavalin, her son, now 16, accompanied her as they headed south, toward the small town called Destiny.

Claire and Tavalin

Tavalin was halfway through college by the time Monika figured out how to isolate and concentrate the active ingredient from the lotus blooms. This advancement made for much easier storage and transport of her burgeoning stash, but more importantly, it changed the nature of the experience. Before, she prepared a tea of sorts by soaking the blooms in wine or some other alcoholic beverage. This made for a pleasant trip but it did not compare to the intensity of the experience using the new extraction method. In the process Monika learned a thing or two about chemistry. She realized that it might be possible to synthesize the active ingredient from scratch, thus bypassing the laborious trips to Reefers Woods entirely.

At his mother's bidding, Tavalin finished out his undergraduate years as a chemistry major. Afterwards, he enrolled in graduate school at the University in Destiny, where his mandate was to amass a deeper knowledge of chemistry, specifically of the chemical synthetic techniques that would be required to synthesize the Unreal.

After two years at the Facility, Tavalin had been unsuccessful in his bid to determine the exact chemical structure of the Unreal, the prerequisite step for the synthesis. Monika grew impatient with him and constantly reminded him of his ineptitude. In the end, Tavalin obtained the structure, not from his own research, but from June's research notebook.

The string of events that led to Tavalin's fortuitous discovery began after he grew suspicious of Jeremy and all the late hours Jeremy spent working in June's lab. Whenever Tavalin dropped in on them, they always stopped in the middle of whatever they were working on and seemed overly protective of whichever notes or papers that might be lying about. Whenever he asked Jeremy what he and June were working on, Jeremy turned evasive. On the night of the RockFest, Tavalin entered June's unoccupied lab and found her research notebook hidden inside her desk. He was unable to decipher much of what was written inside until he came to the page where she had sketched out a certain three-ringed molecule. Tavalin had made just enough progress on his own to recognize that this was what he had been trying to figure out for the past two years. This was it – the detailed structure of the Unreal.

At that precise moment, June walked in and caught Tavalin red-handed. For a long time, he had resented June for refusing to go out with him. He believed she thought herself too good for him. Tavalin imagined the denigrating words that would spew from Monika's mouth when she found out how easily and quickly June had figured out what he hadn't been able to do in two years. Fueled by his anger and embarrassment, as well as by all the beer he had drunk, Tavalin attacked June. He stabbed her with the scissors from her desk and, in the end, choked her until her body went limp.

"You did what?" exclaimed Monika when she answered Tavalin's frantic call. "What do you propose we do now, you idiot?"

Tavalin had no clue.

"Just leave."

Monika told him to find June's keys, lock the door, and to call her after he got to Jeremy's condo. When Tavalin arrived at Jeremy's condominium, he immediately stripped down to his underwear and put his blood-tainted clothes in the washing machine. He told Jeremy that he had thrown up on his clothes and that was why they needed to be washed.

Tavalin volunteered to order and pay for a pizza so he would have an excuse to wait downstairs in the foyer, ostensibly to watch for the delivery person. Monika swung by on her way to the Facility to pick up the keys to June's lab. She also obtained Jeremy's key chain, which Tavalin swiped from the hook in the hallway. This gave Monika access to Jeremy's lab and the cold room. She dragged the body from June's lab to Jeremy's lab and into the cold room, an area specifically designed for tissue dissection. She painstakingly carved up the body on the stainless steel counter, making sure these operations took much longer than the time available to Tavalin. That way, Jeremy could vouch for Tavalin's whereabouts and lead the police to believe that Tavalin could not have been involved in the murder. Afterwards, Monika used the overhead water sprayer and chemical cleaners to wash away all vestiges of her actions. She did not hear June's loose earring as it tinkled down the sink drain, the same earring Jeremy would later discover.

Monika tossed the body out the window into the dumpster to make it appear as if the crime were perpetrated by some random deathcore rocker who got a little too excited at the RockFest. That was also her reasoning for choosing to inscribe the symbol ascribed to one of the bands – Cocytus – that had performed earlier that night. It was an ingenious plan, especially considering Monika made it all up on the fly, and it might have worked, were it not for the lost earring and the clump of June's hair that got caught on the window frame.

Even then, Monika reserved a back-up plan. She wrapped June's excised heart in a plastic bag and took it with her, knowing it could serve as a most convincing means of framing someone else, if need be. As it turned out, Grady became the perfect fall guy. She would have killed him anyway when he refused to tell her where he got the youth-preserving fruit but to be able to get rid of Grady and, in the process, frame him for the murder worked out better than she could ever have imagined.

The Fruit of the Lotus Tree

Youth is wasted on the young.

Only someone who had seen their youth come and go would likely agree with the adage. Monika, however, represented the ultimate exception. She was a beautiful and sexy young girl who knew precisely the clout of a beautiful and sexy young girl. She possessed 60 years of experience in this world and knew all the tricks of life's trade. Hers was a considerable arsenal and she meant to make the most of it.

Ever since she first discovered the effects of the lotus blooms that grew in the swamps of Reefers Woods, Monika had entertained ideas about a new utopian society, what she coined as Claire's Alternative Way. If she could find and harness the source of her enduring youthfulness, she would be an unstoppable force. What would anyone, even world leaders, give in exchange for extended, if not unlimited, days on this earth?

But what in the world was the root of this wonderful gift? Monika wondered if the lotus bloom extract, of which she was so fond, might have something to do with her youthful appearance. It seemed a reasonable hypothesis, were it not for her husband. Nick had also partaken of the lotus flowers over the last two decades and his youthfulness had faded in a manner typical for a man his age.

He had not, however, been a party to the *fruit* of the purple lotus.

That a single fruit might exert such an effect was an intriguing notion. Every summer, Monika searched a different part of Reefer's Woods but she never came across any fruiting lotus. She even set aside a small plot of the lotus plants whose flowers she never harvested but none ever developed anything other than the seed pods typically produced by the plants. Except for the single fruit presented to her by the boy so many years ago, she had absolutely no evidence of its existence, even though she had visited the lotus fields every summer for the past 39 years.

Finally, with Jeremy's assistance, Monika had found it. She smiled at Jeremy's crucial role in her grand plans. Through him – and June – she obtained the structure of the Unreal, paving the way for its synthesis. Jeremy had also helped her find the Source, and even though he had also managed to blow it up, it was not before she bestowed its benefits upon Tavalin and the 11 members of her group. When she found Jeremy – and she would find him – she would have to remember to thank him before she killed him.

Begin Again

It was still wintertime when Monika and Tavalin returned to the King's Pinnacle for the first time since that night in late December.

"This place brings back bad memories," said Monika. "I still can't believe those two got away from us."

"I can't believe they survived that jump into the river," added Tavalin. "Someone must have been looking out for them."

"No, they were just lucky." Monika caught herself clinching her jaw. Thinking of that night still made her furious. "They won't be so lucky the next time I get hold of them."

When they reached the pool, it was impossible to see much other than the steam that wafted heavenward. Tavalin used his arms as fans to disperse the cloud.

"You were right!" he exclaimed excitedly. "There's definitely something here."

Together, mother and son knelt at the edge of the hot-spring pool as they examined the jagged stump and the tender shoots sprouting from it.

"How long do you think it will take to grow back all the way?" asked Tavalin.

"Does it really matter?" Elation beamed from Monika's face like from a fire burning within. "We've got all the time in the world."

Visit James Cole's website for all things related to THE REAL, including a forum where readers and the author discuss the layers of hidden meanings and symbolism that help make THE REAL the unique reading experience that it is.

www.secretrealms.com

Open your mind and experience the real…